Eddie Pittman

Red's Planet

FRIENDS AND FOES

AMULET BOOKS
NEW YORK

Cataloging-in-Publication Data has been applied for and may be obtained from the Library of Congress.

ISBN 978-1-4197-2314-8 (hardback)
ISBN 978-1-4197-2315-5 (paperback)

Copyright © 2017 Eddie Pittman
Book design by Eddie Pittman and Chad W. Beckerman

Printed and bound in China
10 9 8 7 6 5 4 3 2 1

Amulet Books are available at special discounts when purchased in quantity for premiums and promotions as well as fundraising or educational use. Special editions can also be created to specification. For details, contact specialsales@abramsbooks.com or the address below

ABRAMS The Art of Books
115 West 18th Street, New York, NY 10011
abramsbooks.com

To Ginny and Teagan—
my first and most important audience

Thanks to:

Beth Pittman, for her support, encouragement, and help along the journey.

Ginny Pittman, Jose Mari Flores, Rachel Polk, John Steventon, and Scott Ball for their production assistance.

Charlie Kochman, Andrew Smith, Jody Mosley, Amy Vreeland, Chad W. Beckerman, Maya Bradford, Trish McNamara, and the whole amazing team at Abrams for their continued support.

My wonderful agent, Judy Hansen.

And all the librarians, booksellers, and Red's Planet fans whom I've had the chance to meet over the past year; your enthusiasm keeps me going.

Made on a Wacom Cintiq.

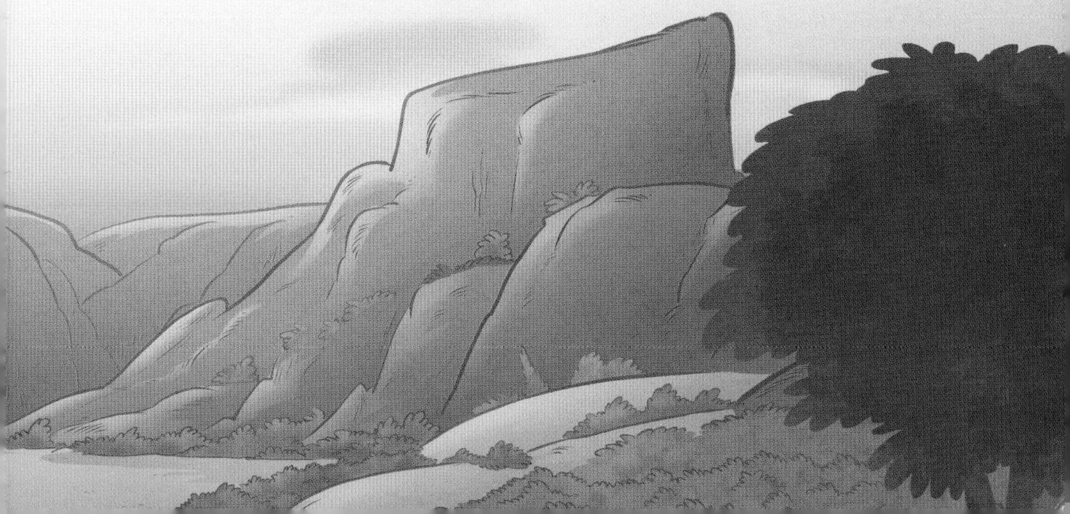

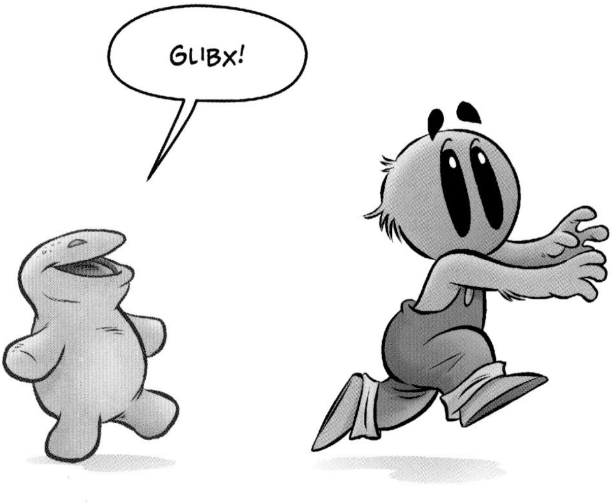
GLIBX!

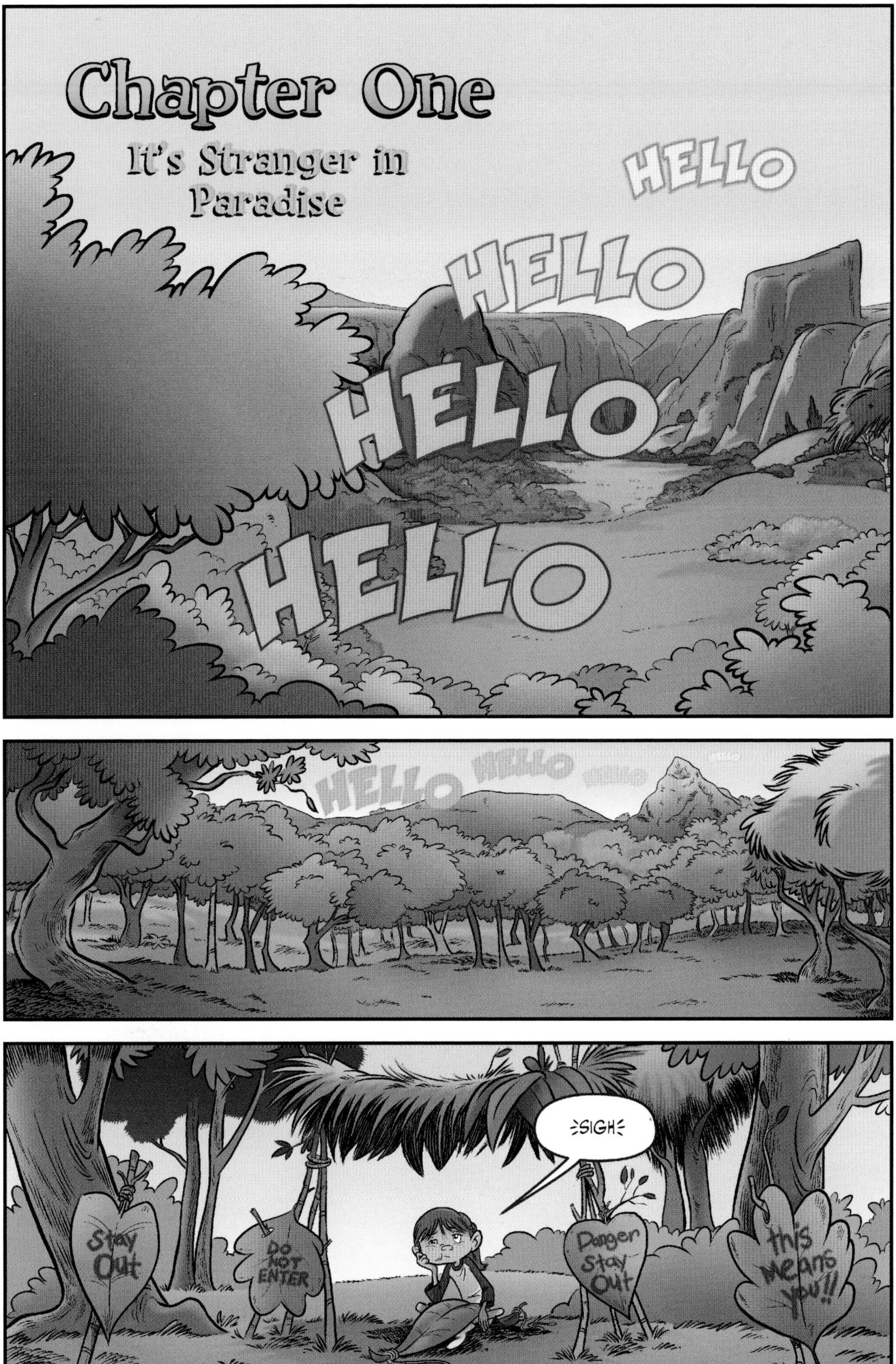
Chapter One
It's Stranger in Paradise
HELLO
HELLO
HELLO
HELLO
HELLO HELLO HELLO
SIGH
Stay Out
DO NOT ENTER
Danger Stay Out
this means you!!

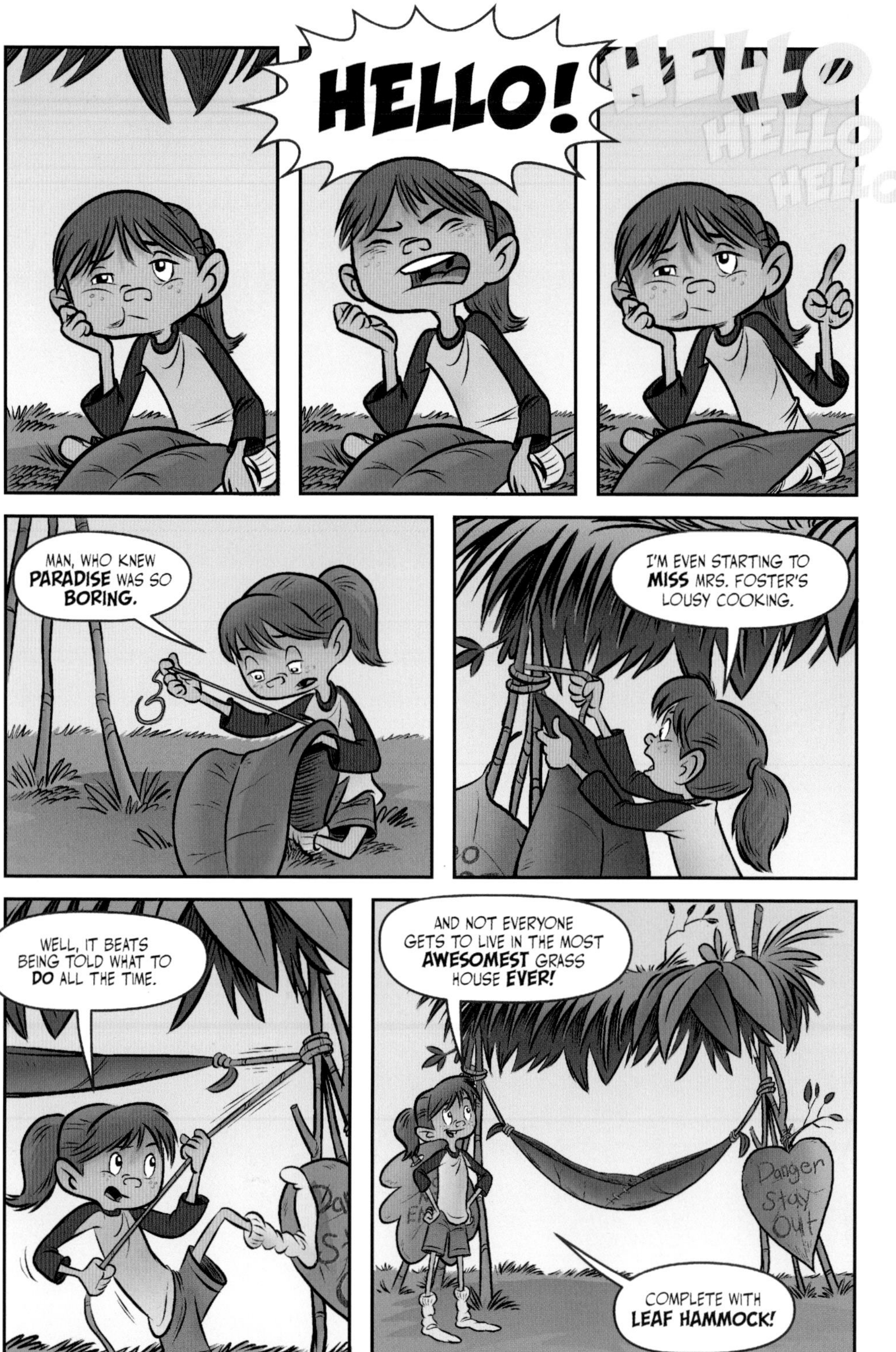
HELLO!
HELLO
HELLO
HELLO
MAN, WHO KNEW PARADISE WAS SO BORING.
I'M EVEN STARTING TO MISS MRS. FOSTER'S LOUSY COOKING.
WELL, IT BEATS BEING TOLD WHAT TO DO ALL THE TIME.
AND NOT EVERYONE GETS TO LIVE IN THE MOST AWESOMEST GRASS HOUSE EVER!
Danger Stay Out
COMPLETE WITH LEAF HAMMOCK!

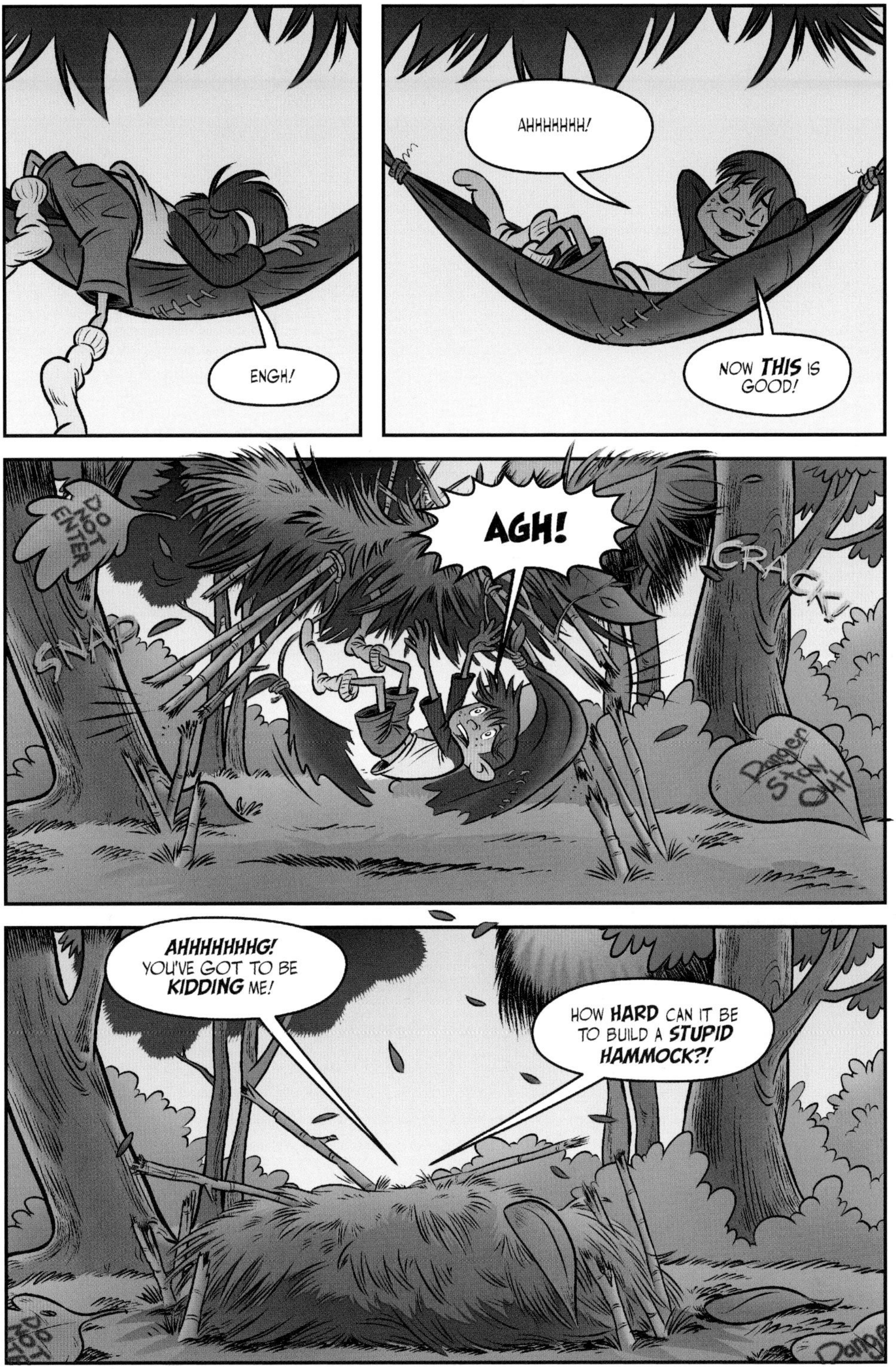
ENGH!
AHHHHHHH!
NOW **THIS** IS GOOD!
DO NOT ENTER
AGH!
SNAP
CRACK
Danger Stay Out
AHHHHHHHG! YOU'VE GOT TO BE **KIDDING** ME!
HOW **HARD** CAN IT BE TO BUILD A **STUPID HAMMOCK?!**

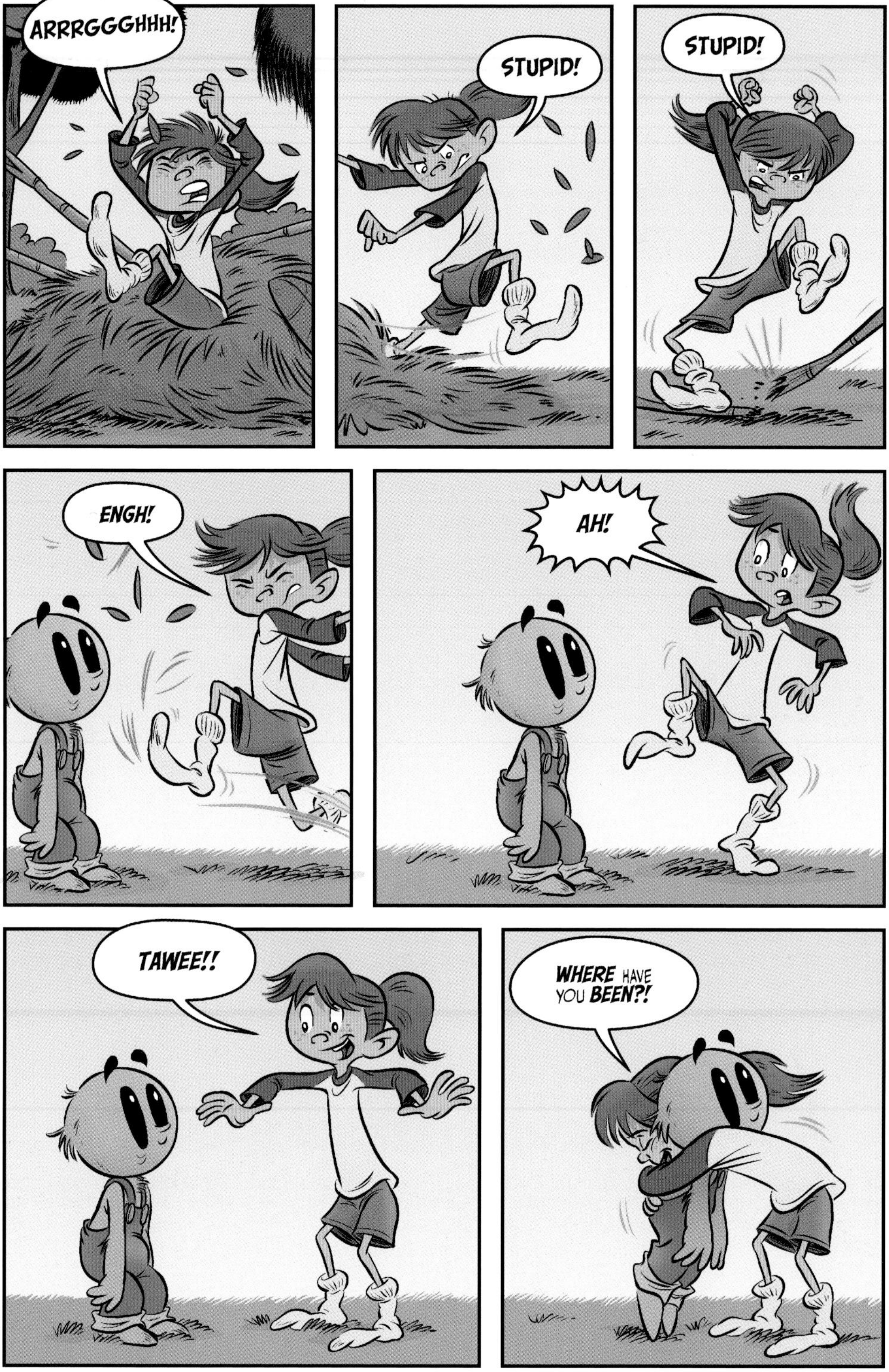
ARRRGGGHHH!
STUPID!
STUPID!
ENGH!
AH!
TAWEE!!
WHERE HAVE YOU BEEN?!

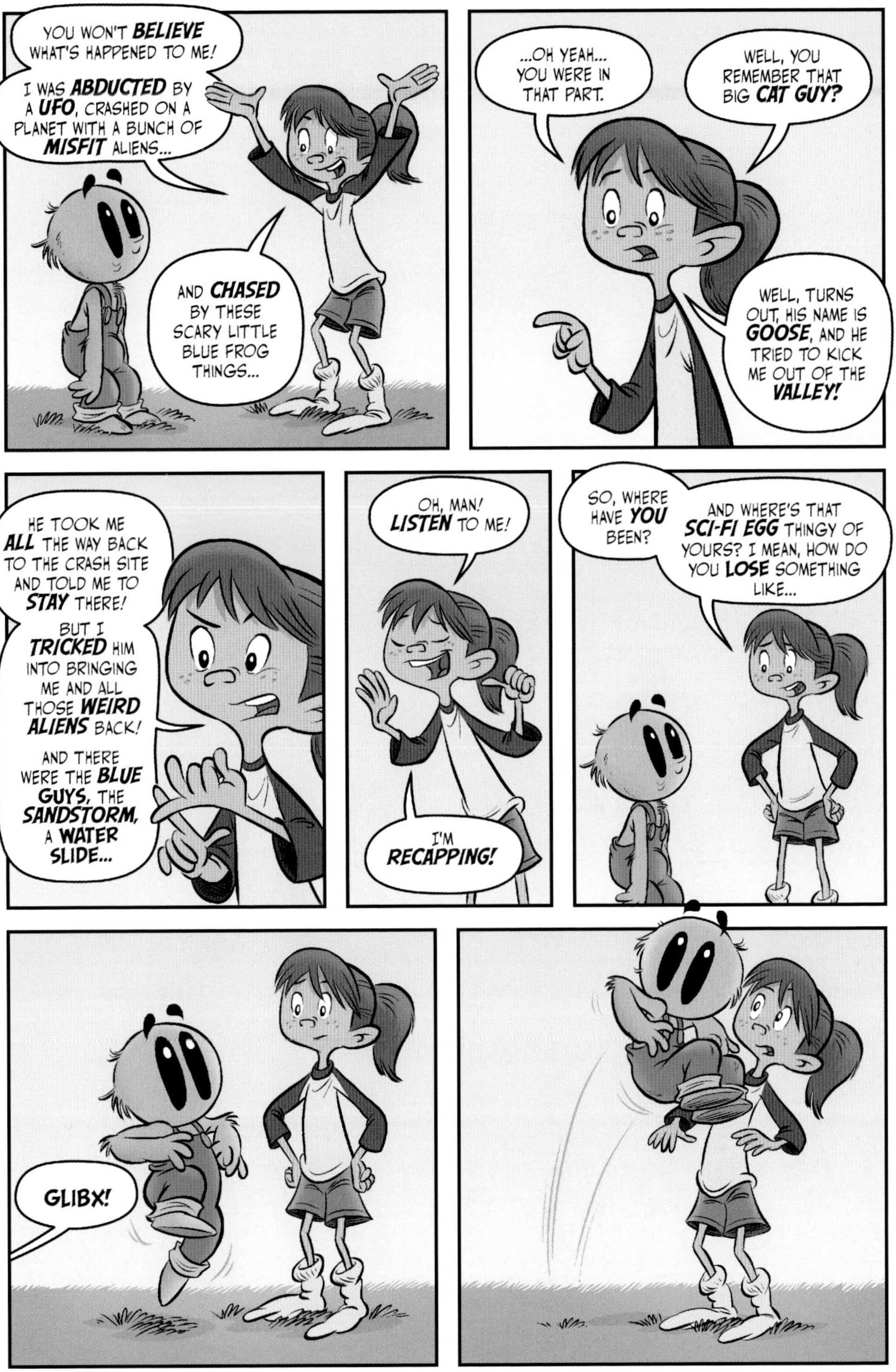
YOU WON'T BELIEVE WHAT'S HAPPENED TO ME!
I WAS ABDUCTED BY A UFO, CRASHED ON A PLANET WITH A BUNCH OF MISFIT ALIENS...
AND CHASED BY THESE SCARY LITTLE BLUE FROG THINGS...
...OH YEAH... YOU WERE IN THAT PART.
WELL, YOU REMEMBER THAT BIG CAT GUY?
WELL, TURNS OUT, HIS NAME IS GOOSE, AND HE TRIED TO KICK ME OUT OF THE VALLEY!
HE TOOK ME ALL THE WAY BACK TO THE CRASH SITE AND TOLD ME TO STAY THERE!
BUT I TRICKED HIM INTO BRINGING ME AND ALL THOSE WEIRD ALIENS BACK!
AND THERE WERE THE BLUE GUYS, THE SANDSTORM, A WATER SLIDE...
OH, MAN! LISTEN TO ME!
I'M RECAPPING!
SO, WHERE HAVE YOU BEEN?
AND WHERE'S THAT SCI-FI EGG THINGY OF YOURS? I MEAN, HOW DO YOU LOSE SOMETHING LIKE...
GLIBX!

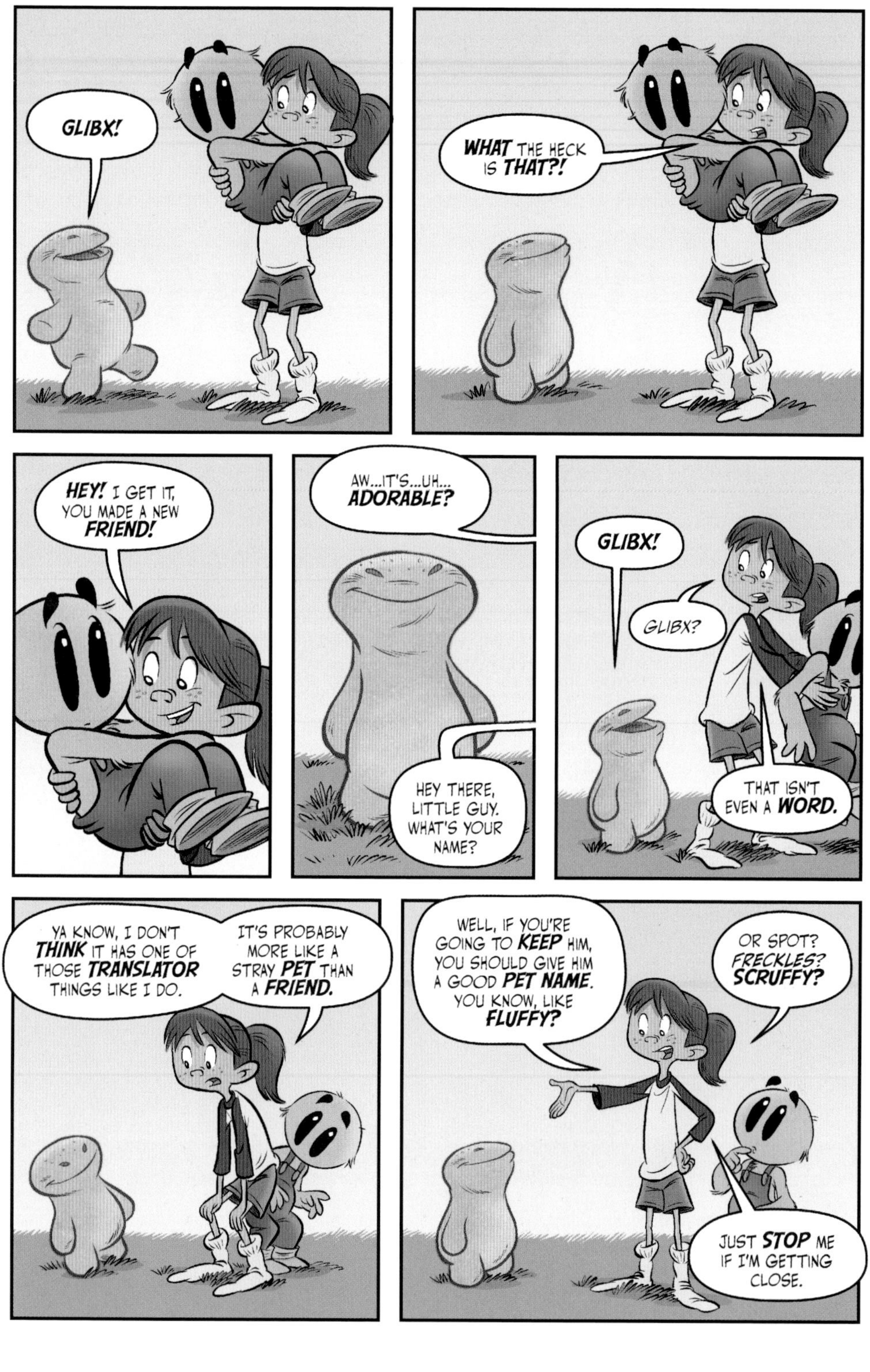
GLIBX!
WHAT THE HECK IS THAT?!
HEY! I GET IT, YOU MADE A NEW FRIEND!
AW...IT'S...UH... ADORABLE?
HEY THERE, LITTLE GUY. WHAT'S YOUR NAME?
GLIBX!
GLIBX?
THAT ISN'T EVEN A WORD.
YA KNOW, I DON'T THINK IT HAS ONE OF THOSE TRANSLATOR THINGS LIKE I DO.
IT'S PROBABLY MORE LIKE A STRAY PET THAN A FRIEND.
WELL, IF YOU'RE GOING TO KEEP HIM, YOU SHOULD GIVE HIM A GOOD PET NAME. YOU KNOW, LIKE FLUFFY?
OR SPOT? FRECKLES? SCRUFFY?
JUST STOP ME IF I'M GETTING CLOSE.

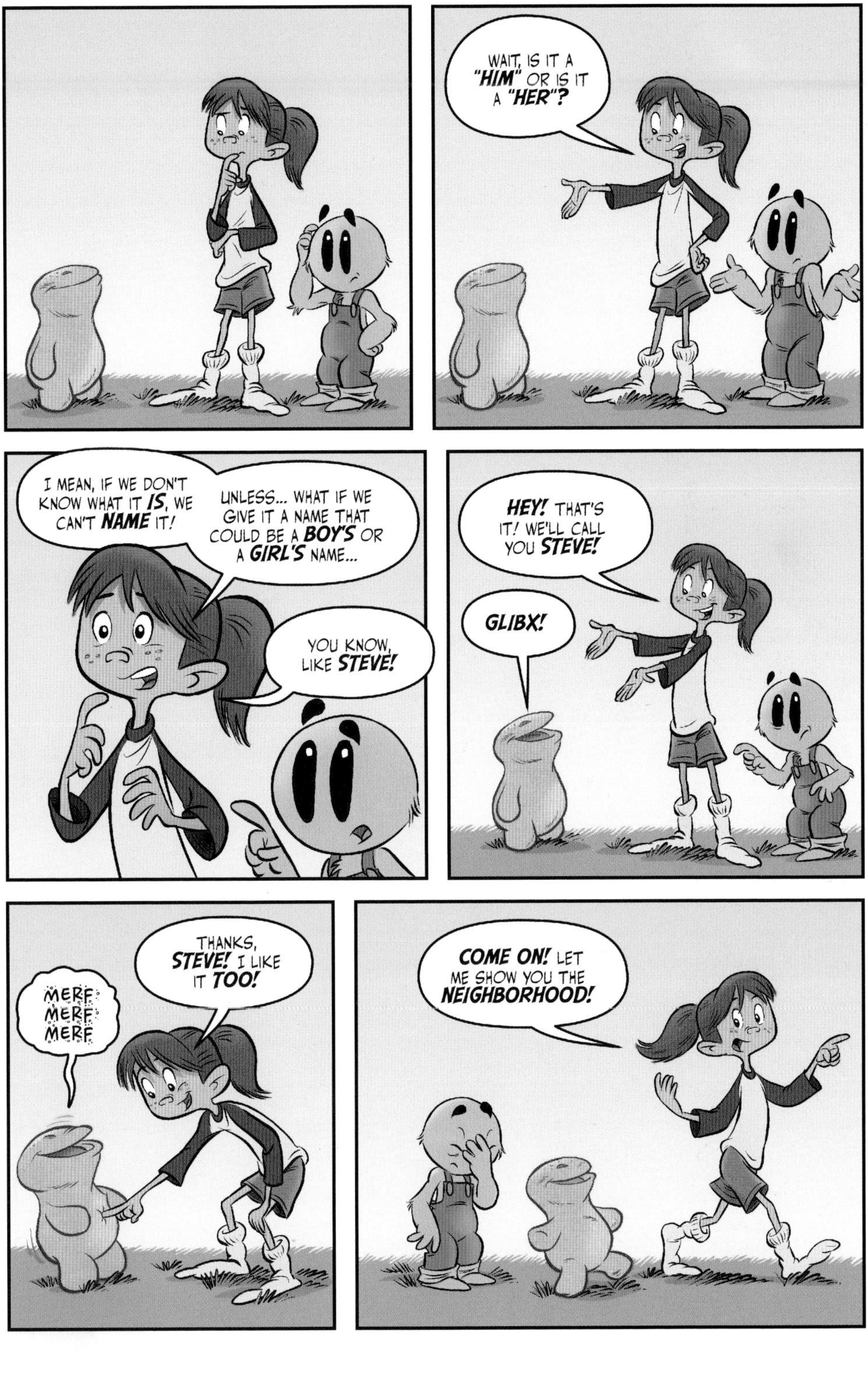
WAIT, IS IT A "HIM" OR IS IT A "HER"?
I MEAN, IF WE DON'T KNOW WHAT IT IS, WE CAN'T NAME IT!
UNLESS... WHAT IF WE GIVE IT A NAME THAT COULD BE A BOY'S OR A GIRL'S NAME...
YOU KNOW, LIKE STEVE!
HEY! THAT'S IT! WE'LL CALL YOU STEVE!
GLIBX!
MERF MERF MERF
THANKS, STEVE! I LIKE IT TOO!
COME ON! LET ME SHOW YOU THE NEIGHBORHOOD!

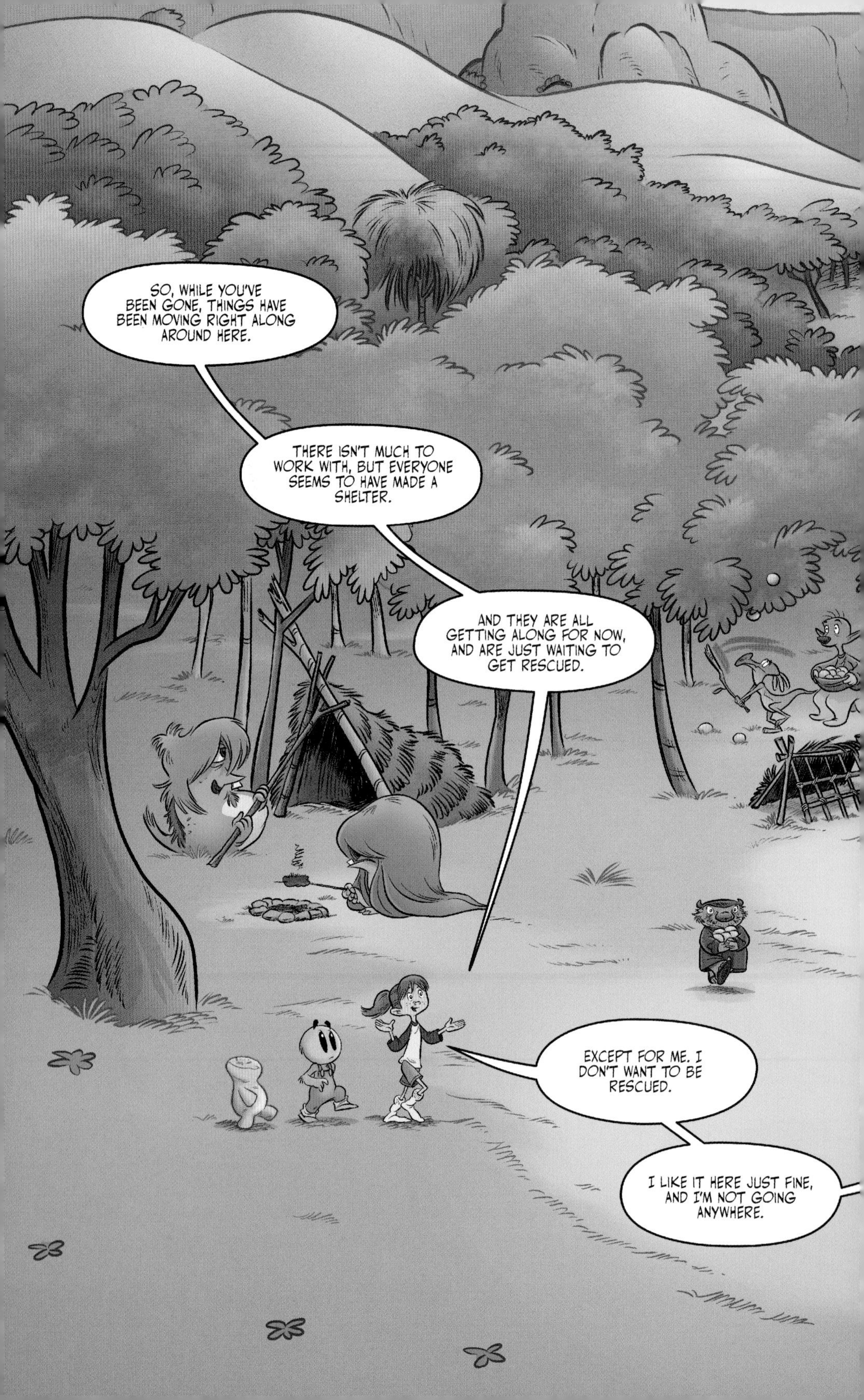
SO, WHILE YOU'VE BEEN GONE, THINGS HAVE BEEN MOVING RIGHT ALONG AROUND HERE.
THERE ISN'T MUCH TO WORK WITH, BUT EVERYONE SEEMS TO HAVE MADE A SHELTER.
AND THEY ARE ALL GETTING ALONG FOR NOW, AND ARE JUST WAITING TO GET RESCUED.
EXCEPT FOR ME. I DON'T WANT TO BE RESCUED.
I LIKE IT HERE JUST FINE, AND I'M NOT GOING ANYWHERE.

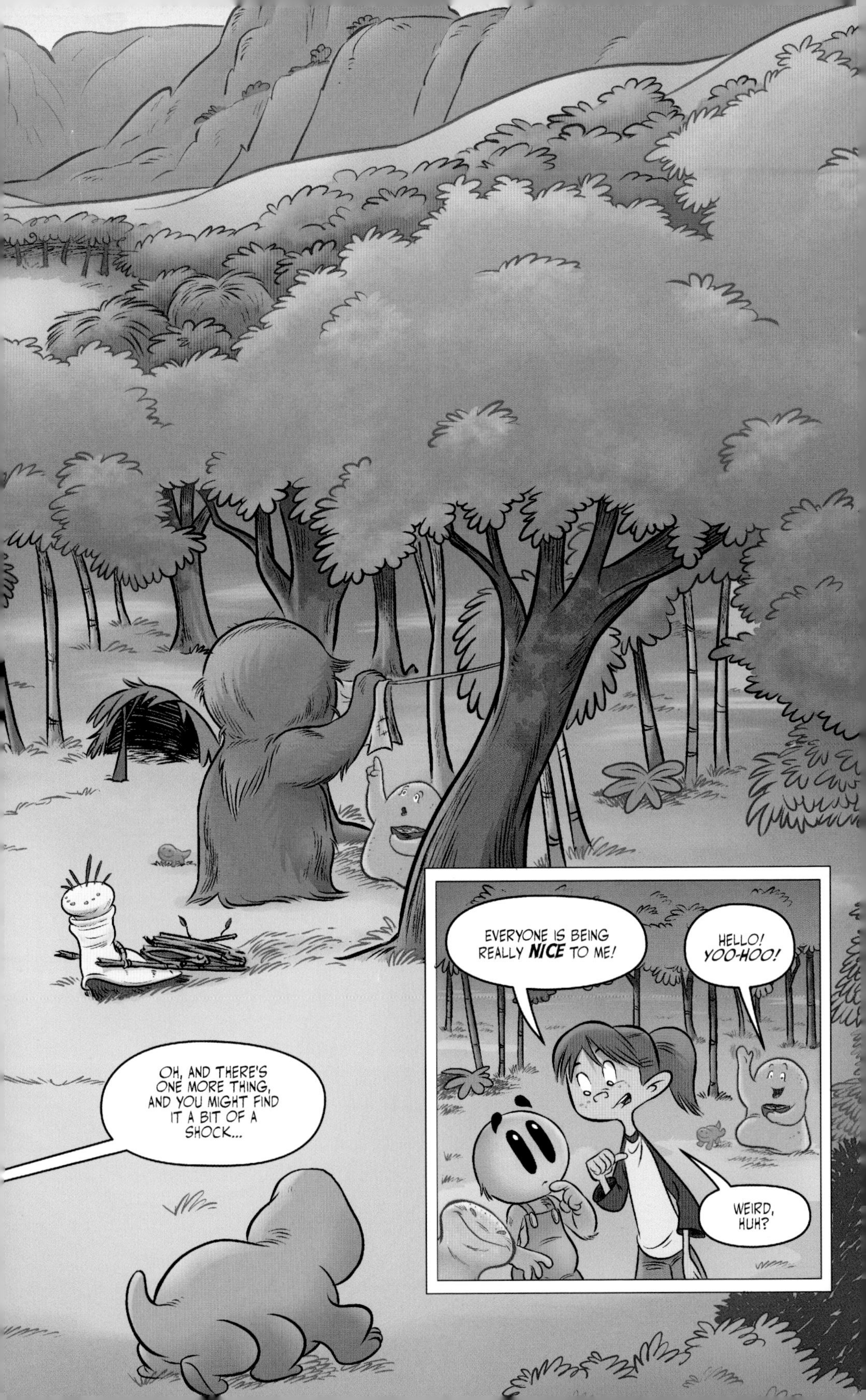
OH, AND THERE'S ONE MORE THING, AND YOU MIGHT FIND IT A BIT OF A SHOCK...
EVERYONE IS BEING REALLY NICE TO ME!
HELLO! YOO-HOO!
WEIRD, HUH?

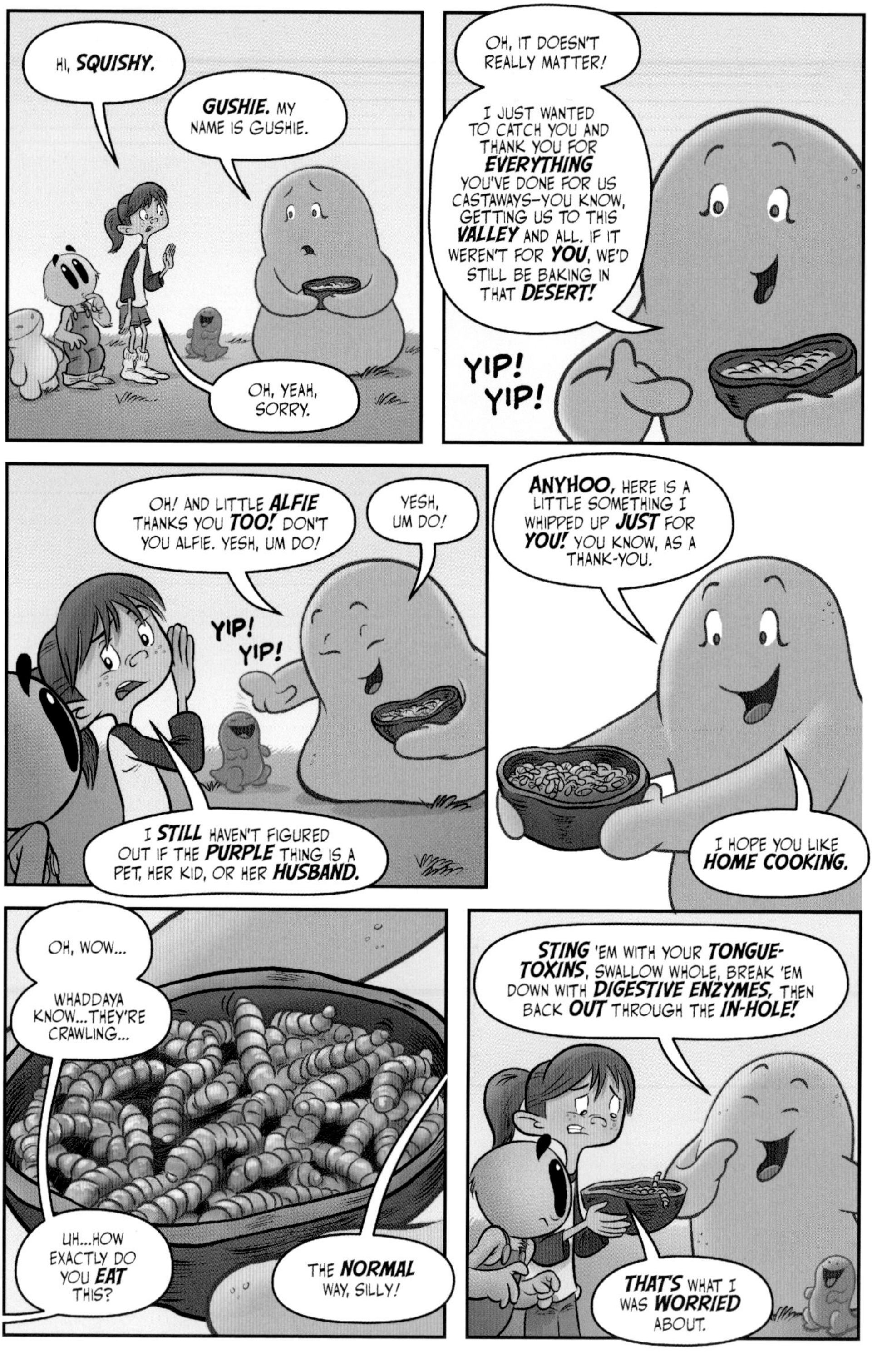

HI, SQUISHY.
GUSHIE. MY NAME IS GUSHIE.
OH, YEAH, SORRY.
OH, IT DOESN'T REALLY MATTER!
I JUST WANTED TO CATCH YOU AND THANK YOU FOR EVERYTHING YOU'VE DONE FOR US CASTAWAYS—YOU KNOW, GETTING US TO THIS VALLEY AND ALL. IF IT WEREN'T FOR YOU, WE'D STILL BE BAKING IN THAT DESERT!
YIP! YIP!
OH! AND LITTLE ALFIE THANKS YOU TOO! DON'T YOU ALFIE. YESH, UM DO!
YESH, UM DO!
YIP! YIP!
I STILL HAVEN'T FIGURED OUT IF THE PURPLE THING IS A PET, HER KID, OR HER HUSBAND.
ANYHOO, HERE IS A LITTLE SOMETHING I WHIPPED UP JUST FOR YOU! YOU KNOW, AS A THANK-YOU.
I HOPE YOU LIKE HOME COOKING.
OH, WOW...
WHADDAYA KNOW...THEY'RE CRAWLING...
UH...HOW EXACTLY DO YOU EAT THIS?
THE NORMAL WAY, SILLY!
STING 'EM WITH YOUR TONGUE-TOXINS, SWALLOW WHOLE, BREAK 'EM DOWN WITH DIGESTIVE ENZYMES, THEN BACK OUT THROUGH THE IN-HOLE!
THAT'S WHAT I WAS WORRIED ABOUT.

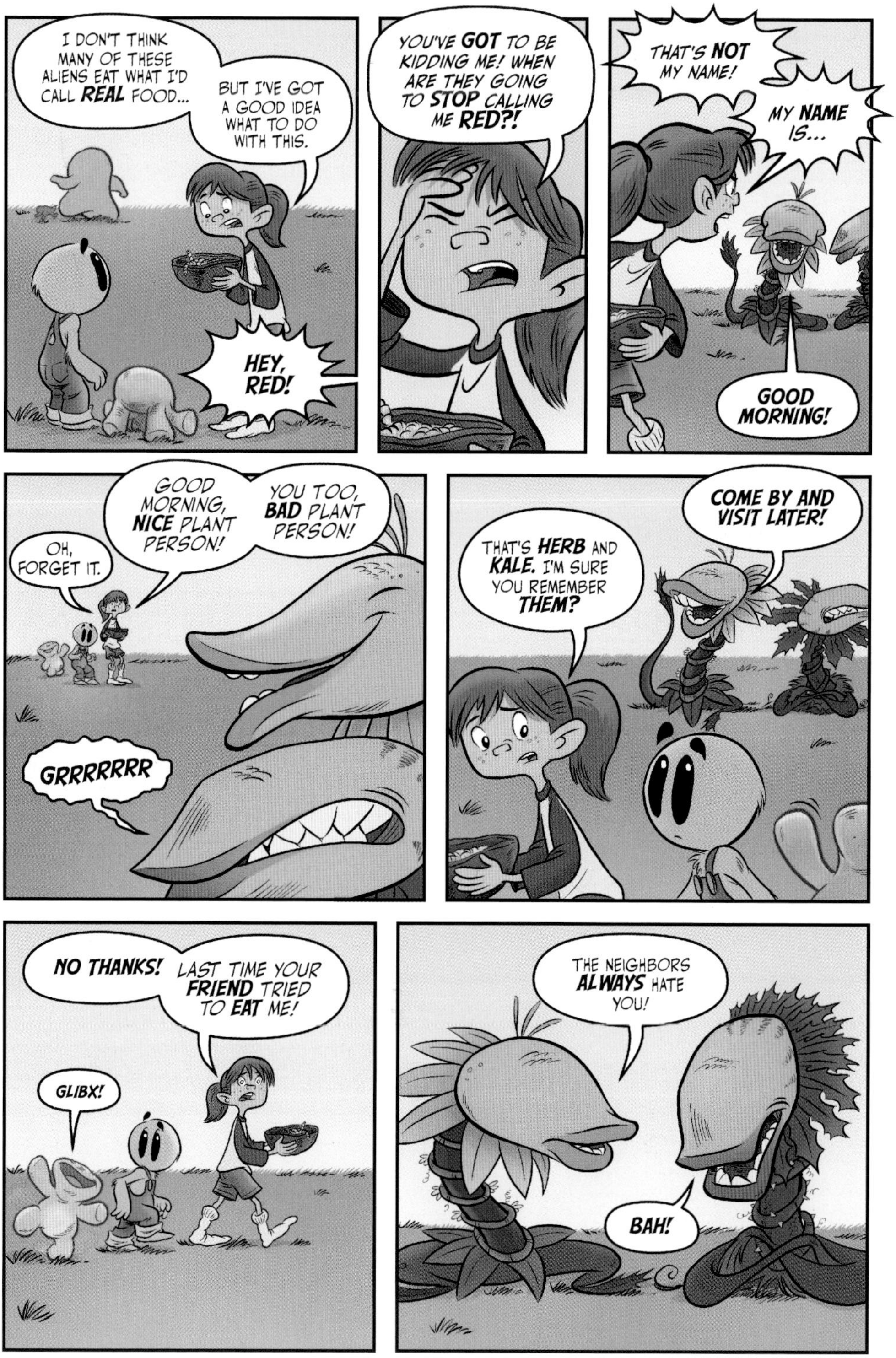
I DON'T THINK MANY OF THESE ALIENS EAT WHAT I'D CALL REAL FOOD...
BUT I'VE GOT A GOOD IDEA WHAT TO DO WITH THIS.
HEY, RED!
YOU'VE GOT TO BE KIDDING ME! WHEN ARE THEY GOING TO STOP CALLING ME RED?!
THAT'S NOT MY NAME!
MY NAME IS...
GOOD MORNING!
OH, FORGET IT.
GOOD MORNING, NICE PLANT PERSON!
YOU TOO, BAD PLANT PERSON!
GRRRRRRR
THAT'S HERB AND KALE. I'M SURE YOU REMEMBER THEM?
COME BY AND VISIT LATER!
NO THANKS!
LAST TIME YOUR FRIEND TRIED TO EAT ME!
GLIBX!
THE NEIGHBORS ALWAYS HATE YOU!
BAH!

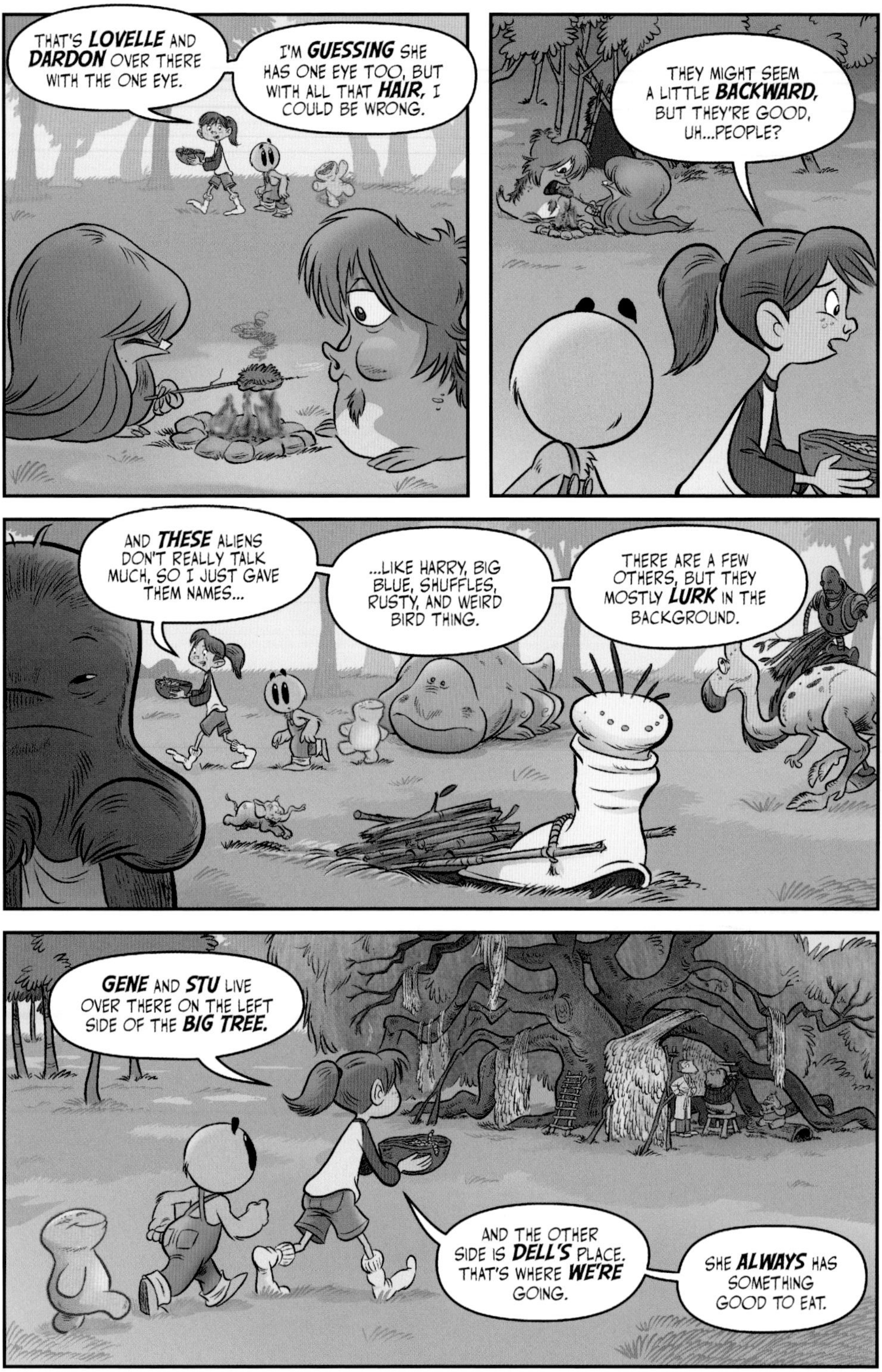
THAT'S LOVELLE AND DARDON OVER THERE WITH THE ONE EYE.
I'M GUESSING SHE HAS ONE EYE TOO, BUT WITH ALL THAT HAIR, I COULD BE WRONG.
THEY MIGHT SEEM A LITTLE BACKWARD, BUT THEY'RE GOOD, UH...PEOPLE?
AND THESE ALIENS DON'T REALLY TALK MUCH, SO I JUST GAVE THEM NAMES...
...LIKE HARRY, BIG BLUE, SHUFFLES, RUSTY, AND WEIRD BIRD THING.
THERE ARE A FEW OTHERS, BUT THEY MOSTLY LURK IN THE BACKGROUND.
GENE AND STU LIVE OVER THERE ON THE LEFT SIDE OF THE BIG TREE.
AND THE OTHER SIDE IS DELL'S PLACE. THAT'S WHERE WE'RE GOING.
SHE ALWAYS HAS SOMETHING GOOD TO EAT.

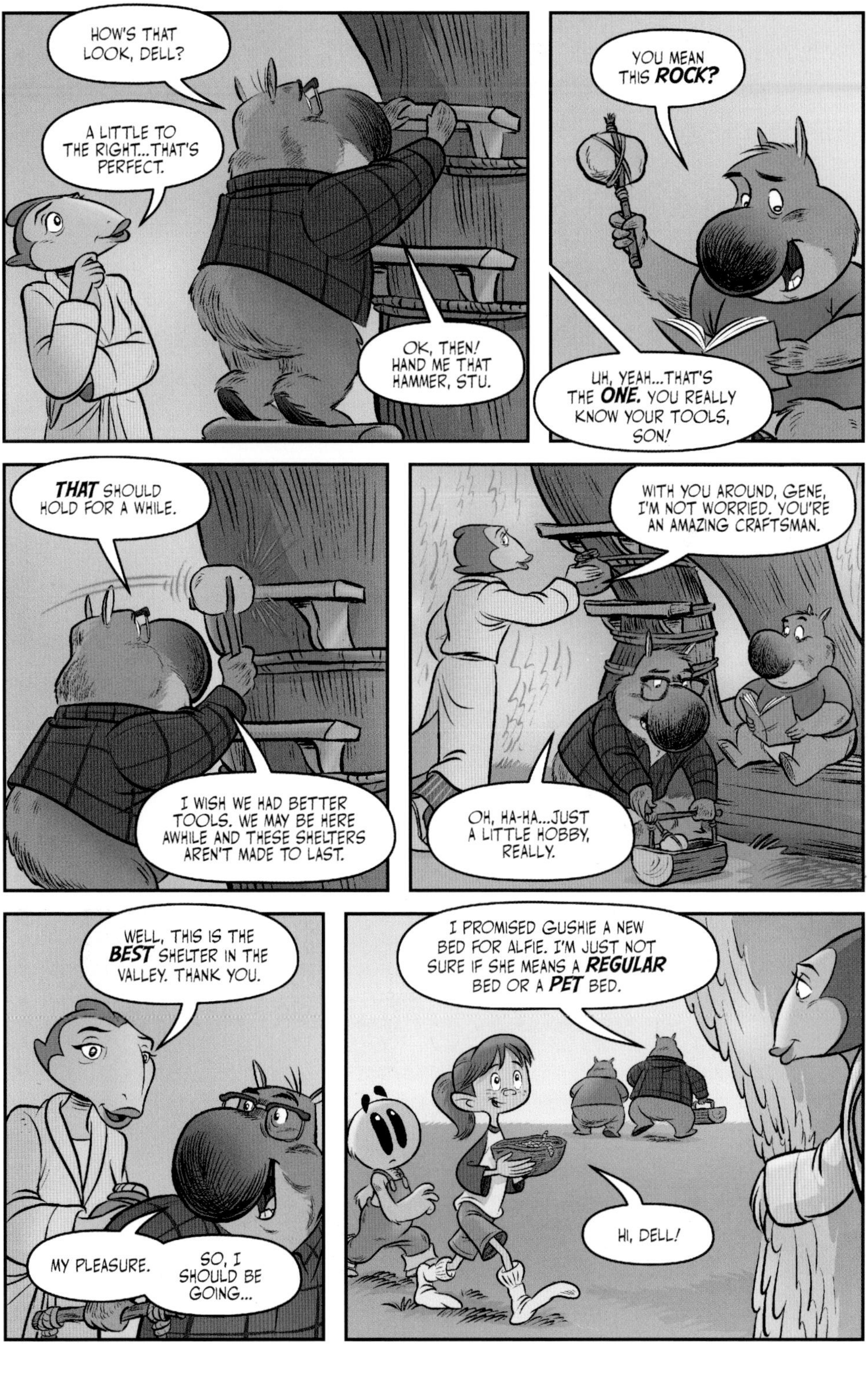
HOW'S THAT LOOK, DELL?
A LITTLE TO THE RIGHT...THAT'S PERFECT.
OK, THEN! HAND ME THAT HAMMER, STU.
YOU MEAN THIS **ROCK?**
UH, YEAH...THAT'S THE **ONE.** YOU REALLY KNOW YOUR TOOLS, SON!
THAT SHOULD HOLD FOR A WHILE.
I WISH WE HAD BETTER TOOLS. WE MAY BE HERE AWHILE AND THESE SHELTERS AREN'T MADE TO LAST.
WITH YOU AROUND, GENE, I'M NOT WORRIED. YOU'RE AN AMAZING CRAFTSMAN.
OH, HA-HA...JUST A LITTLE HOBBY, REALLY.
WELL, THIS IS THE **BEST** SHELTER IN THE VALLEY. THANK YOU.
MY PLEASURE.
SO, I SHOULD BE GOING...
I PROMISED GUSHIE A NEW BED FOR ALFIE. I'M JUST NOT SURE IF SHE MEANS A **REGULAR** BED OR A **PET** BED.
HI, DELL!

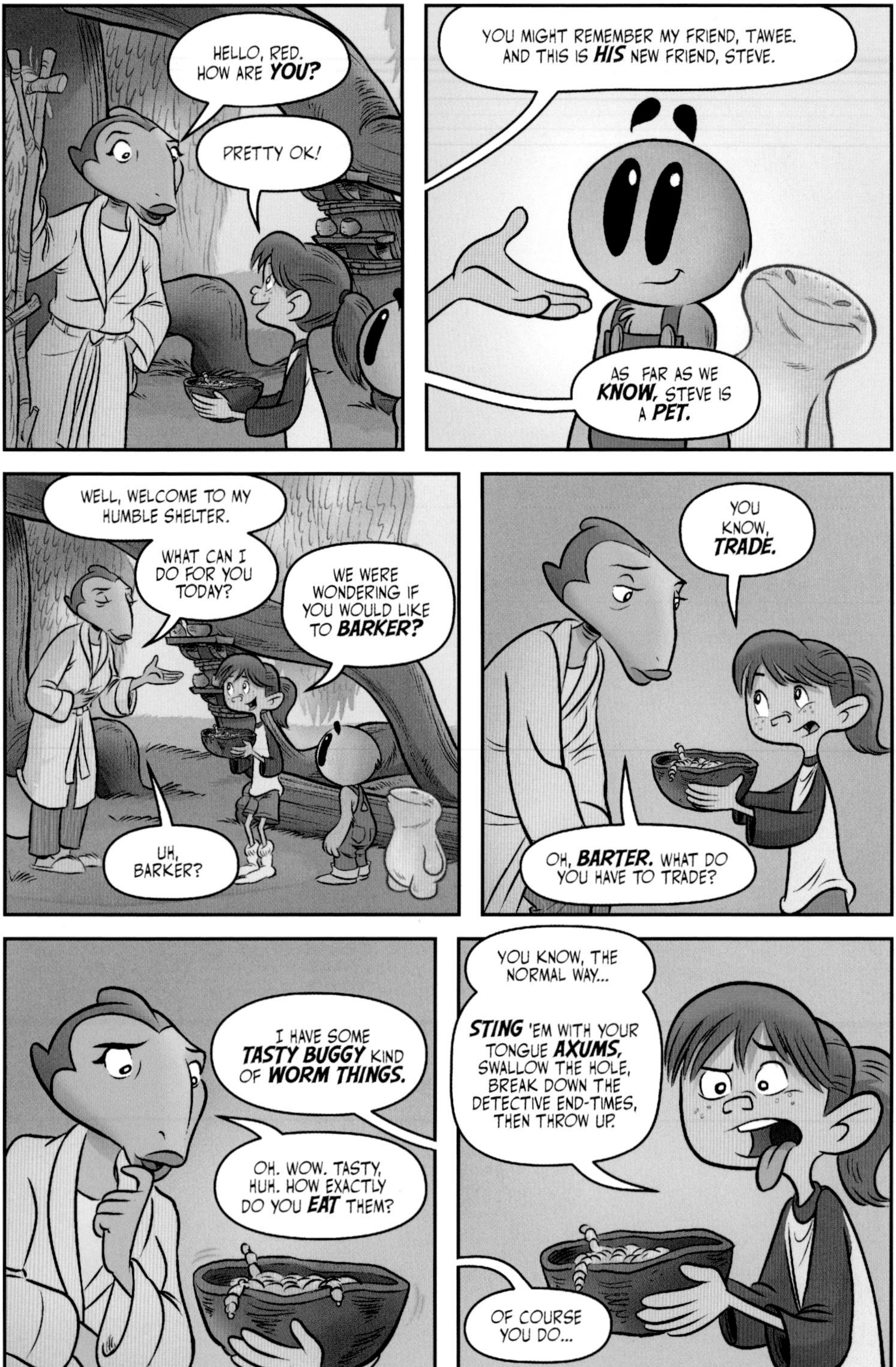
HELLO, RED.
HOW ARE **YOU?**
PRETTY OK!
YOU MIGHT REMEMBER MY FRIEND, TAWEE. AND THIS IS **HIS** NEW FRIEND, STEVE.
AS FAR AS WE **KNOW,** STEVE IS A **PET.**
WELL, WELCOME TO MY HUMBLE SHELTER.
WHAT CAN I DO FOR YOU TODAY?
WE WERE WONDERING IF YOU WOULD LIKE TO **BARKER?**
UH, BARKER?
YOU KNOW, **TRADE.**
OH, **BARTER.** WHAT DO YOU HAVE TO TRADE?
I HAVE SOME **TASTY BUGGY** KIND OF **WORM THINGS.**
OH. WOW. TASTY, HUH. HOW EXACTLY DO YOU **EAT** THEM?
YOU KNOW, THE NORMAL WAY...
STING 'EM WITH YOUR TONGUE **AXUMS,** SWALLOW THE HOLE, BREAK DOWN THE DETECTIVE END-TIMES, THEN THROW UP.
OF COURSE YOU DO...

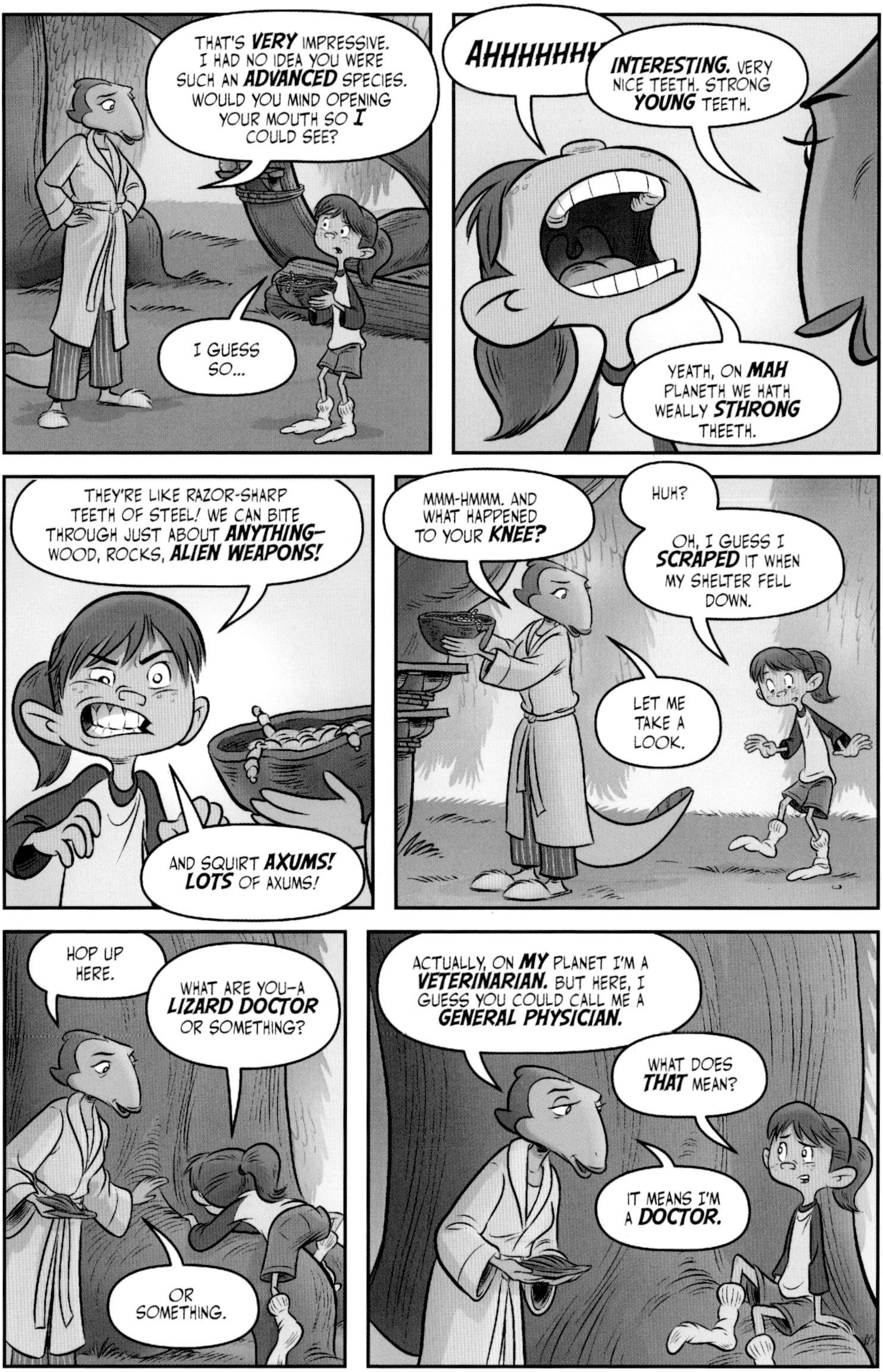
THAT'S VERY IMPRESSIVE. I HAD NO IDEA YOU WERE SUCH AN ADVANCED SPECIES. WOULD YOU MIND OPENING YOUR MOUTH SO I COULD SEE?
I GUESS SO...
AHHHHHHH
INTERESTING. VERY NICE TEETH. STRONG YOUNG TEETH.
YEATH, ON MAH PLANETH WE HATH WEALLY STHRONG THEETH.
THEY'RE LIKE RAZOR-SHARP TEETH OF STEEL! WE CAN BITE THROUGH JUST ABOUT ANYTHING—WOOD, ROCKS, ALIEN WEAPONS!
AND SQUIRT AXUMS! LOTS OF AXUMS!
MMM-HMMM. AND WHAT HAPPENED TO YOUR KNEE?
HUH?
OH, I GUESS I SCRAPED IT WHEN MY SHELTER FELL DOWN.
LET ME TAKE A LOOK.
HOP UP HERE.
WHAT ARE YOU—A LIZARD DOCTOR OR SOMETHING?
OR SOMETHING.
ACTUALLY, ON MY PLANET I'M A VETERINARIAN. BUT HERE, I GUESS YOU COULD CALL ME A GENERAL PHYSICIAN.
WHAT DOES THAT MEAN?
IT MEANS I'M A DOCTOR.

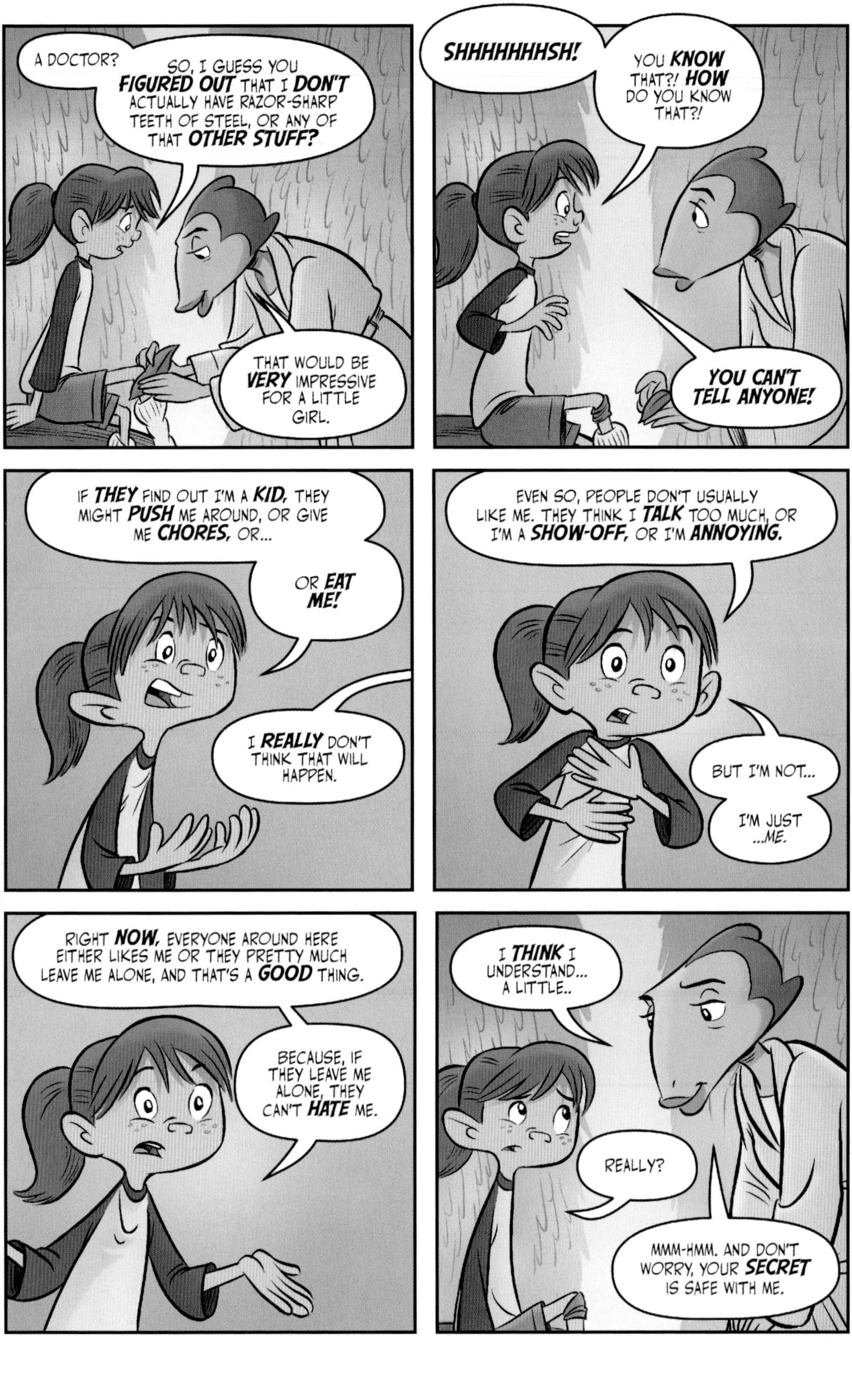
A DOCTOR?
SO, I GUESS YOU FIGURED OUT THAT I DON'T ACTUALLY HAVE RAZOR-SHARP TEETH OF STEEL, OR ANY OF THAT OTHER STUFF?
THAT WOULD BE VERY IMPRESSIVE FOR A LITTLE GIRL.
SHHHHHHHSH!
YOU KNOW THAT?! HOW DO YOU KNOW THAT?!
YOU CAN'T TELL ANYONE!
IF THEY FIND OUT I'M A KID, THEY MIGHT PUSH ME AROUND, OR GIVE ME CHORES, OR...
OR EAT ME!
I REALLY DON'T THINK THAT WILL HAPPEN.
EVEN SO, PEOPLE DON'T USUALLY LIKE ME. THEY THINK I TALK TOO MUCH, OR I'M A SHOW-OFF, OR I'M ANNOYING.
BUT I'M NOT...
I'M JUST ...ME.
RIGHT NOW, EVERYONE AROUND HERE EITHER LIKES ME OR THEY PRETTY MUCH LEAVE ME ALONE, AND THAT'S A GOOD THING.
BECAUSE, IF THEY LEAVE ME ALONE, THEY CAN'T HATE ME.
I THINK I UNDERSTAND... A LITTLE..
REALLY?
MMM-HMM. AND DON'T WORRY, YOUR SECRET IS SAFE WITH ME.

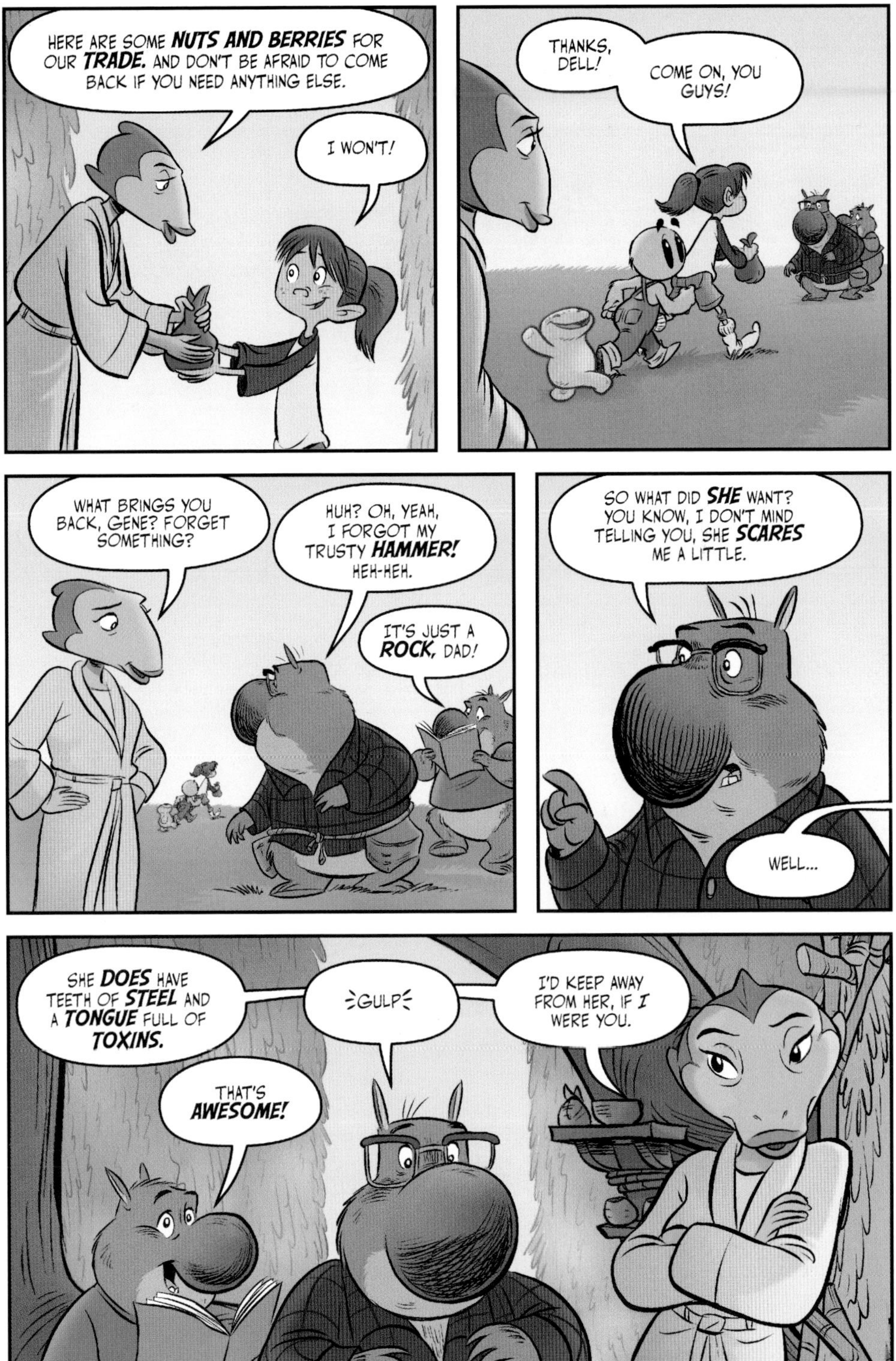
HERE ARE SOME **NUTS AND BERRIES** FOR OUR **TRADE.** AND DON'T BE AFRAID TO COME BACK IF YOU NEED ANYTHING ELSE.
I WON'T!
THANKS, DELL!
COME ON, YOU GUYS!
WHAT BRINGS YOU BACK, GENE? FORGET SOMETHING?
HUH? OH, YEAH, I FORGOT MY TRUSTY **HAMMER!** HEH-HEH.
IT'S JUST A **ROCK,** DAD!
SO WHAT DID **SHE** WANT? YOU KNOW, I DON'T MIND TELLING YOU, SHE **SCARES** ME A LITTLE.
WELL...
SHE **DOES** HAVE TEETH OF **STEEL** AND A **TONGUE** FULL OF **TOXINS.**
GULP
I'D KEEP AWAY FROM HER, IF *I* WERE YOU.
THAT'S **AWESOME!**

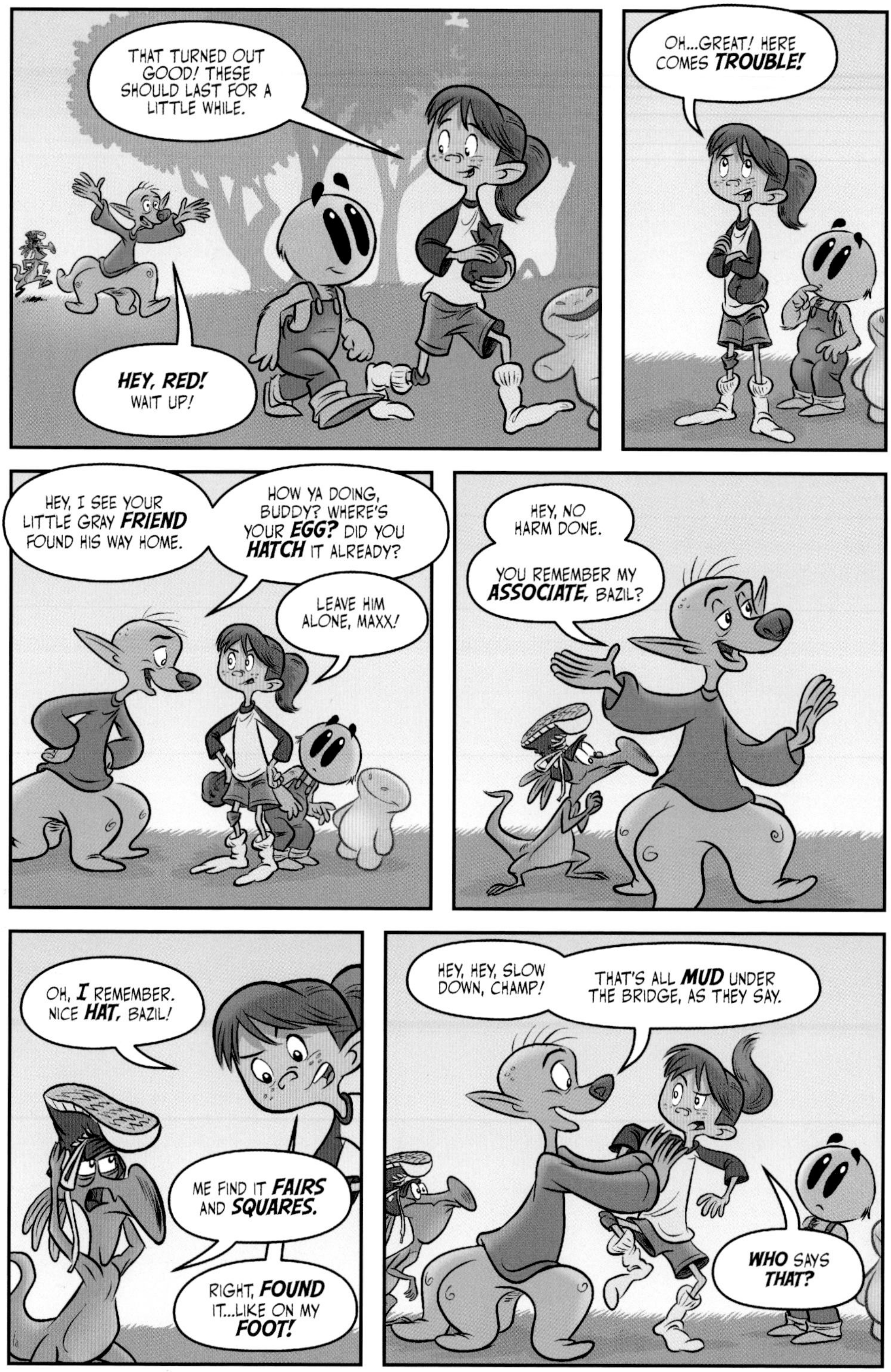
THAT TURNED OUT GOOD! THESE SHOULD LAST FOR A LITTLE WHILE.
HEY, RED! WAIT UP!
OH...GREAT! HERE COMES TROUBLE!
HEY, I SEE YOUR LITTLE GRAY FRIEND FOUND HIS WAY HOME.
HOW YA DOING, BUDDY? WHERE'S YOUR EGG? DID YOU HATCH IT ALREADY?
LEAVE HIM ALONE, MAXX!
HEY, NO HARM DONE.
YOU REMEMBER MY ASSOCIATE, BAZIL?
OH, I REMEMBER. NICE HAT, BAZIL!
ME FIND IT FAIRS AND SQUARES.
RIGHT, FOUND IT...LIKE ON MY FOOT!
HEY, HEY, SLOW DOWN, CHAMP!
THAT'S ALL MUD UNDER THE BRIDGE, AS THEY SAY.
WHO SAYS THAT?

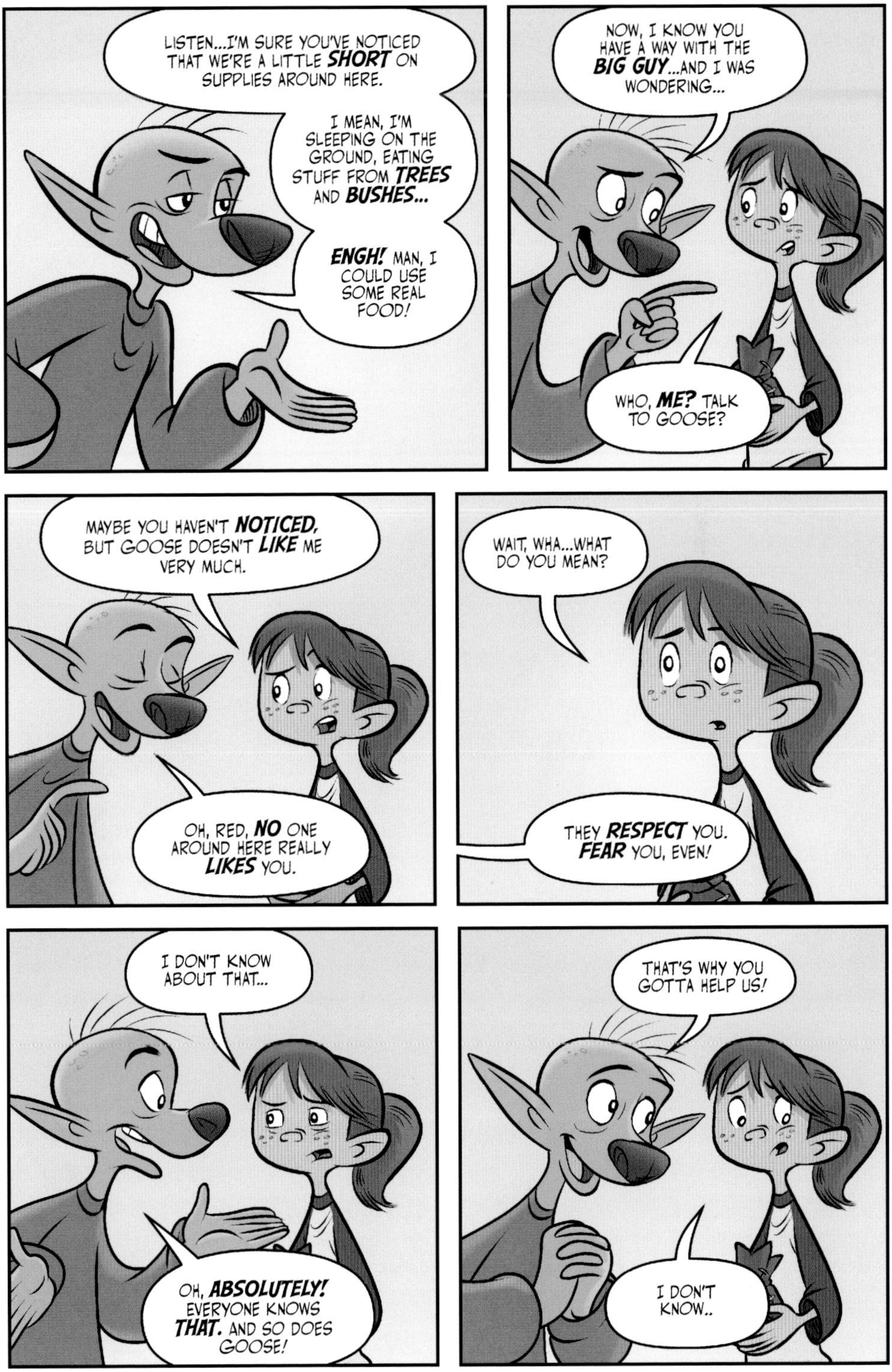

LISTEN...I'M SURE YOU'VE NOTICED THAT WE'RE A LITTLE SHORT ON SUPPLIES AROUND HERE.
I MEAN, I'M SLEEPING ON THE GROUND, EATING STUFF FROM TREES AND BUSHES...
ENGH! MAN, I COULD USE SOME REAL FOOD!
NOW, I KNOW YOU HAVE A WAY WITH THE BIG GUY...AND I WAS WONDERING...
WHO, ME? TALK TO GOOSE?
MAYBE YOU HAVEN'T NOTICED, BUT GOOSE DOESN'T LIKE ME VERY MUCH.
OH, RED, NO ONE AROUND HERE REALLY LIKES YOU.
WAIT, WHA...WHAT DO YOU MEAN?
THEY RESPECT YOU. FEAR YOU, EVEN!
I DON'T KNOW ABOUT THAT...
OH, ABSOLUTELY! EVERYONE KNOWS THAT. AND SO DOES GOOSE!
THAT'S WHY YOU GOTTA HELP US!
I DON'T KNOW..

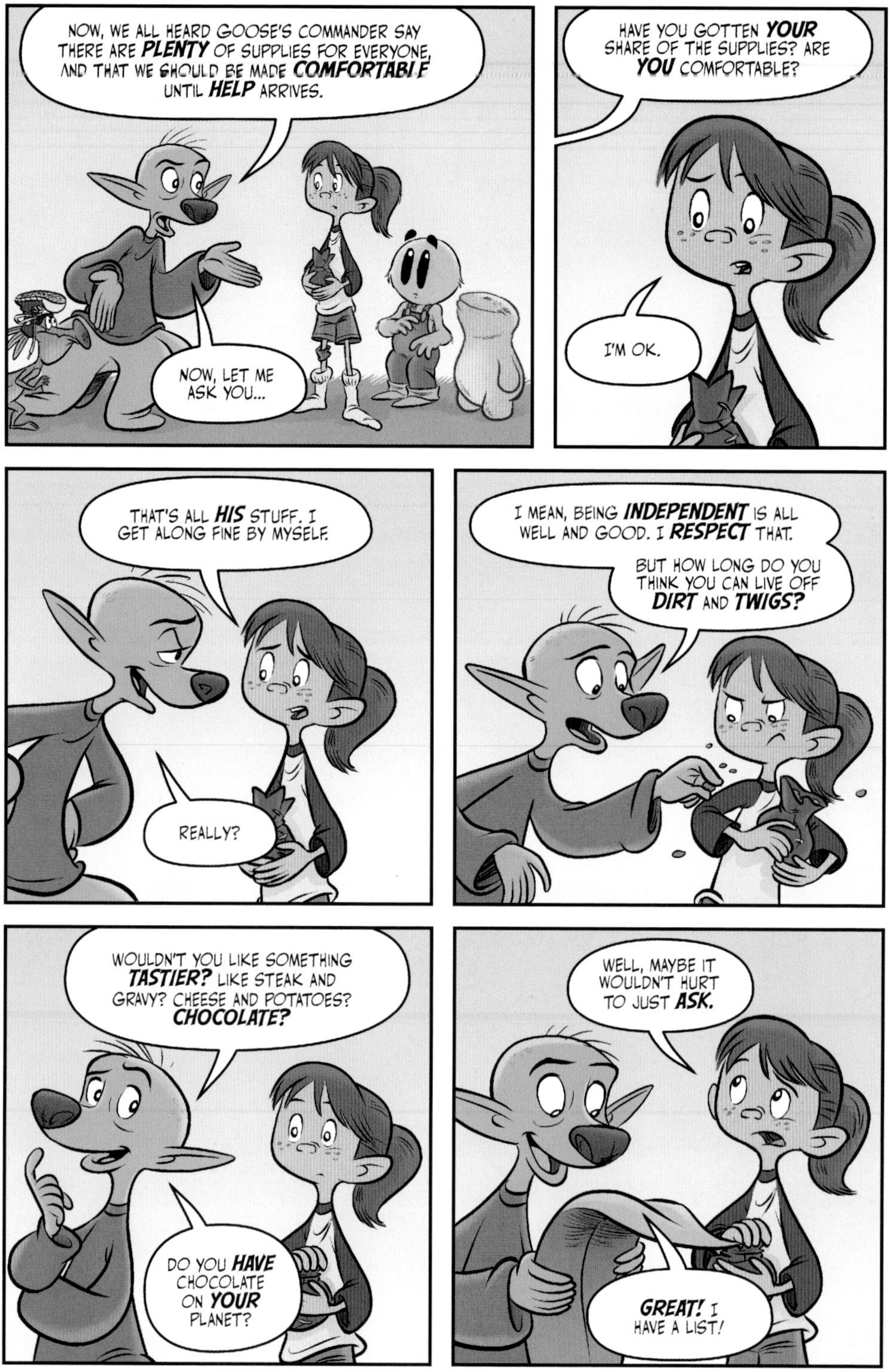
NOW, WE ALL HEARD GOOSE'S COMMANDER SAY THERE ARE PLENTY OF SUPPLIES FOR EVERYONE, AND THAT WE SHOULD BE MADE COMFORTABLE UNTIL HELP ARRIVES.
NOW, LET ME ASK YOU...
HAVE YOU GOTTEN YOUR SHARE OF THE SUPPLIES? ARE YOU COMFORTABLE?
I'M OK.
THAT'S ALL HIS STUFF. I GET ALONG FINE BY MYSELF.
REALLY?
I MEAN, BEING INDEPENDENT IS ALL WELL AND GOOD. I RESPECT THAT.
BUT HOW LONG DO YOU THINK YOU CAN LIVE OFF DIRT AND TWIGS?
WOULDN'T YOU LIKE SOMETHING TASTIER? LIKE STEAK AND GRAVY? CHEESE AND POTATOES? CHOCOLATE?
DO YOU HAVE CHOCOLATE ON YOUR PLANET?
WELL, MAYBE IT WOULDN'T HURT TO JUST ASK.
GREAT! I HAVE A LIST!

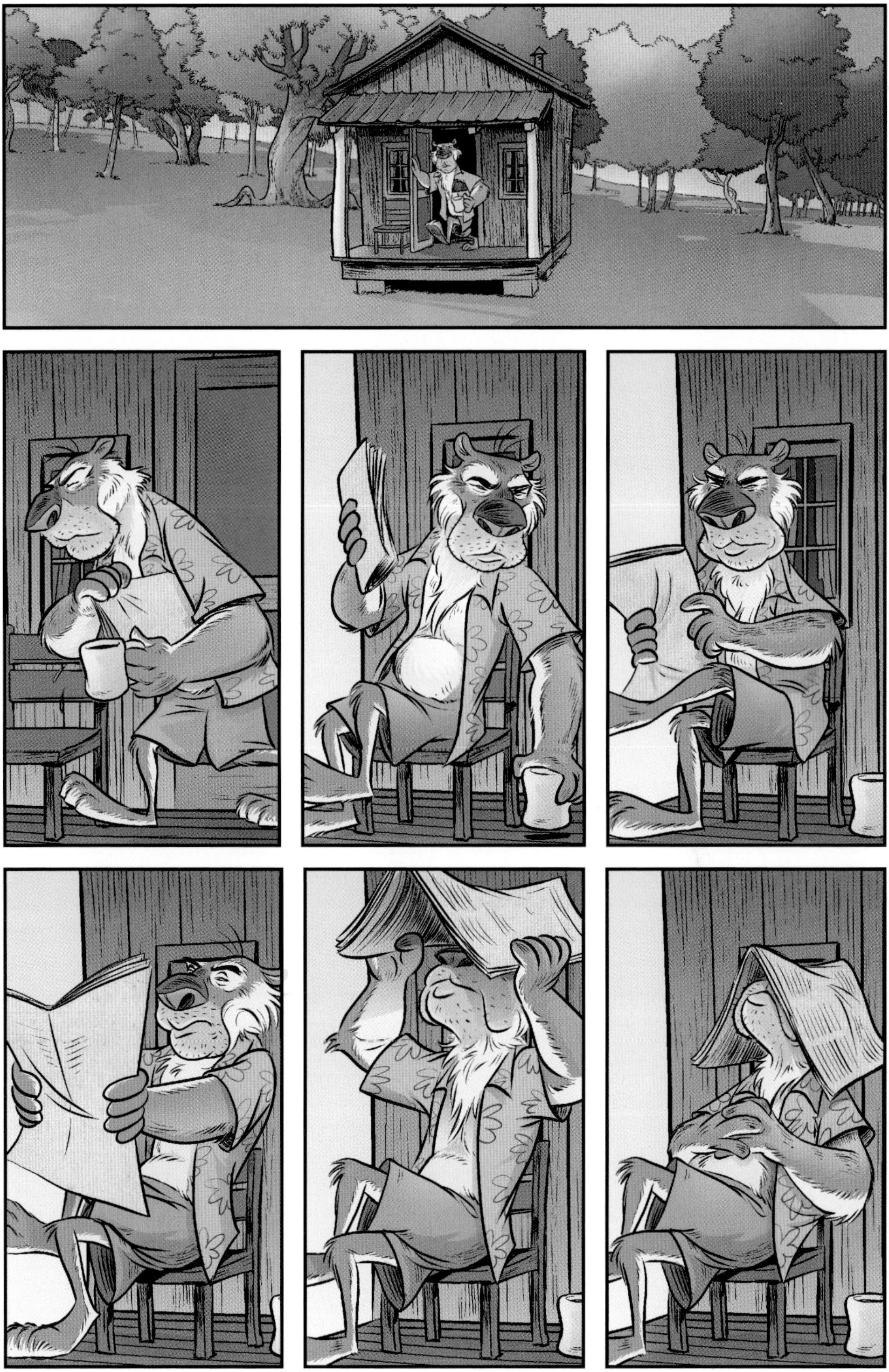

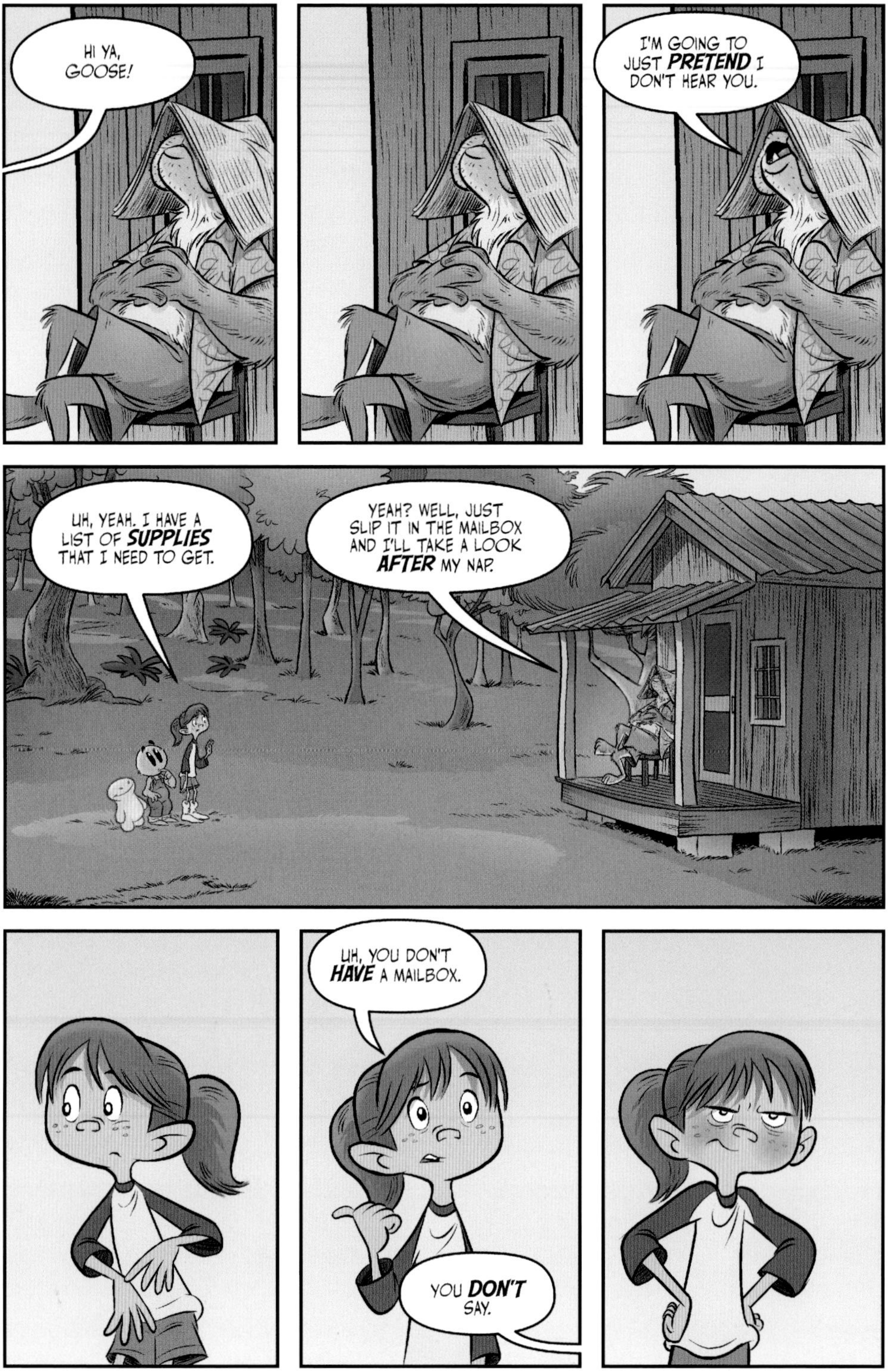
HI YA, GOOSE!
I'M GOING TO JUST PRETEND I DON'T HEAR YOU.
UH, YEAH. I HAVE A LIST OF SUPPLIES THAT I NEED TO GET.
YEAH? WELL, JUST SLIP IT IN THE MAILBOX AND I'LL TAKE A LOOK AFTER MY NAP.
UH, YOU DON'T HAVE A MAILBOX.
YOU DON'T SAY.

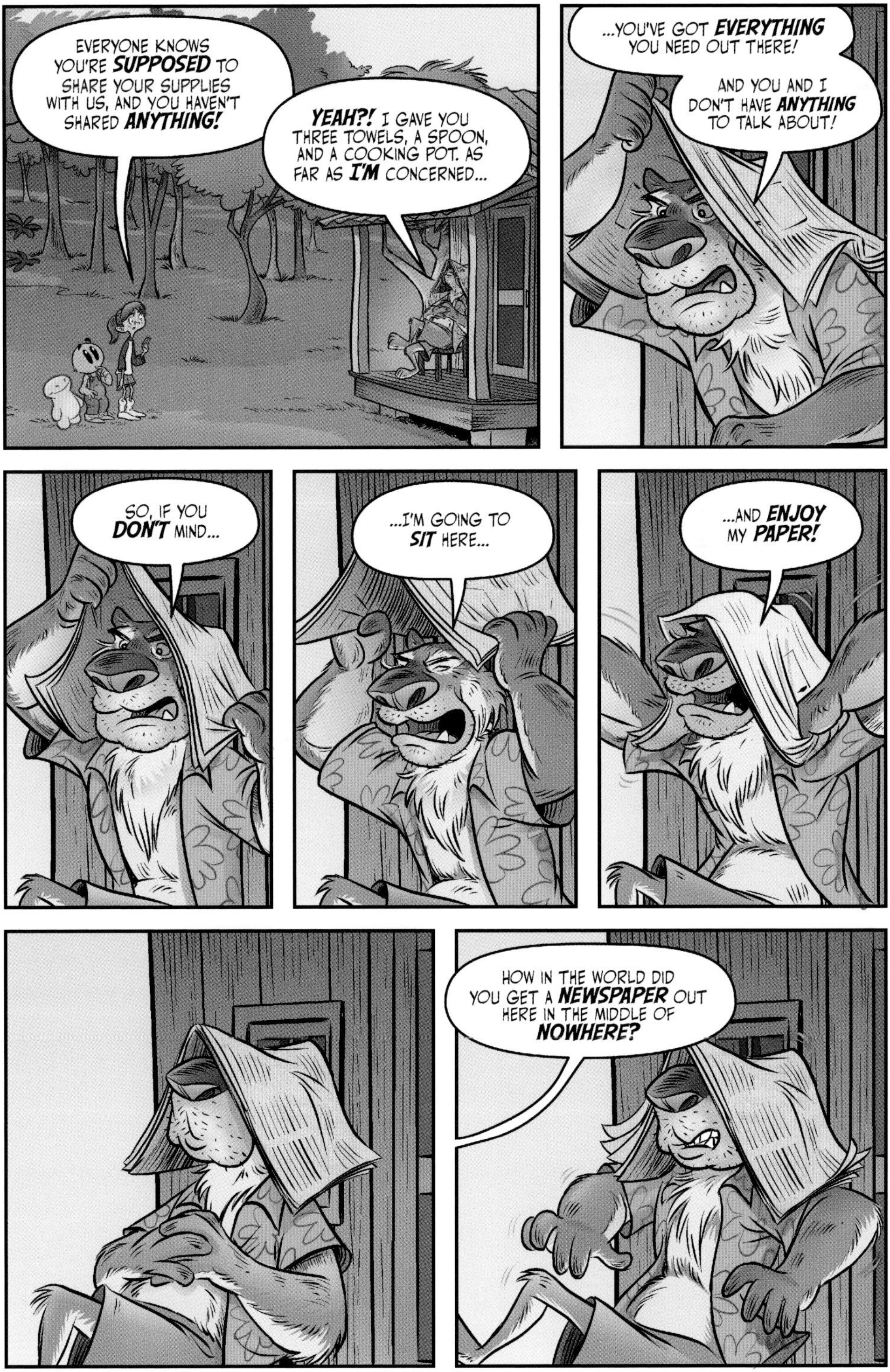
EVERYONE KNOWS YOU'RE SUPPOSED TO SHARE YOUR SUPPLIES WITH US, AND YOU HAVEN'T SHARED ANYTHING!
YEAH?! I GAVE YOU THREE TOWELS, A SPOON, AND A COOKING POT. AS FAR AS I'M CONCERNED...
...YOU'VE GOT EVERYTHING YOU NEED OUT THERE!
AND YOU AND I DON'T HAVE ANYTHING TO TALK ABOUT!
SO, IF YOU DON'T MIND...
...I'M GOING TO SIT HERE...
...AND ENJOY MY PAPER!
HOW IN THE WORLD DID YOU GET A NEWSPAPER OUT HERE IN THE MIDDLE OF NOWHERE?

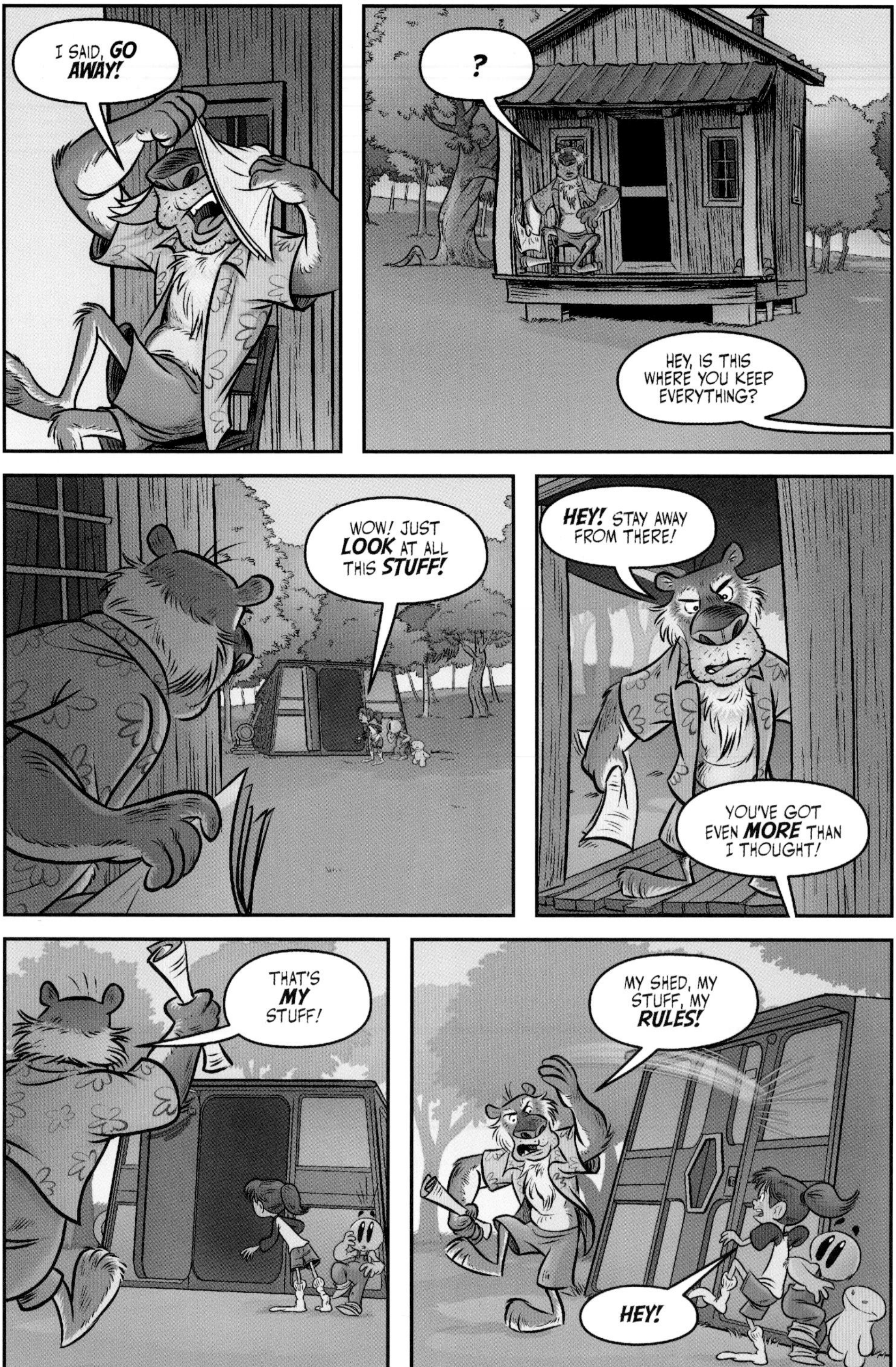
I SAID, GO AWAY!
?
HEY, IS THIS WHERE YOU KEEP EVERYTHING?
WOW! JUST LOOK AT ALL THIS STUFF!
HEY! STAY AWAY FROM THERE!
YOU'VE GOT EVEN MORE THAN I THOUGHT!
THAT'S MY STUFF!
MY SHED, MY STUFF, MY RULES!
HEY!

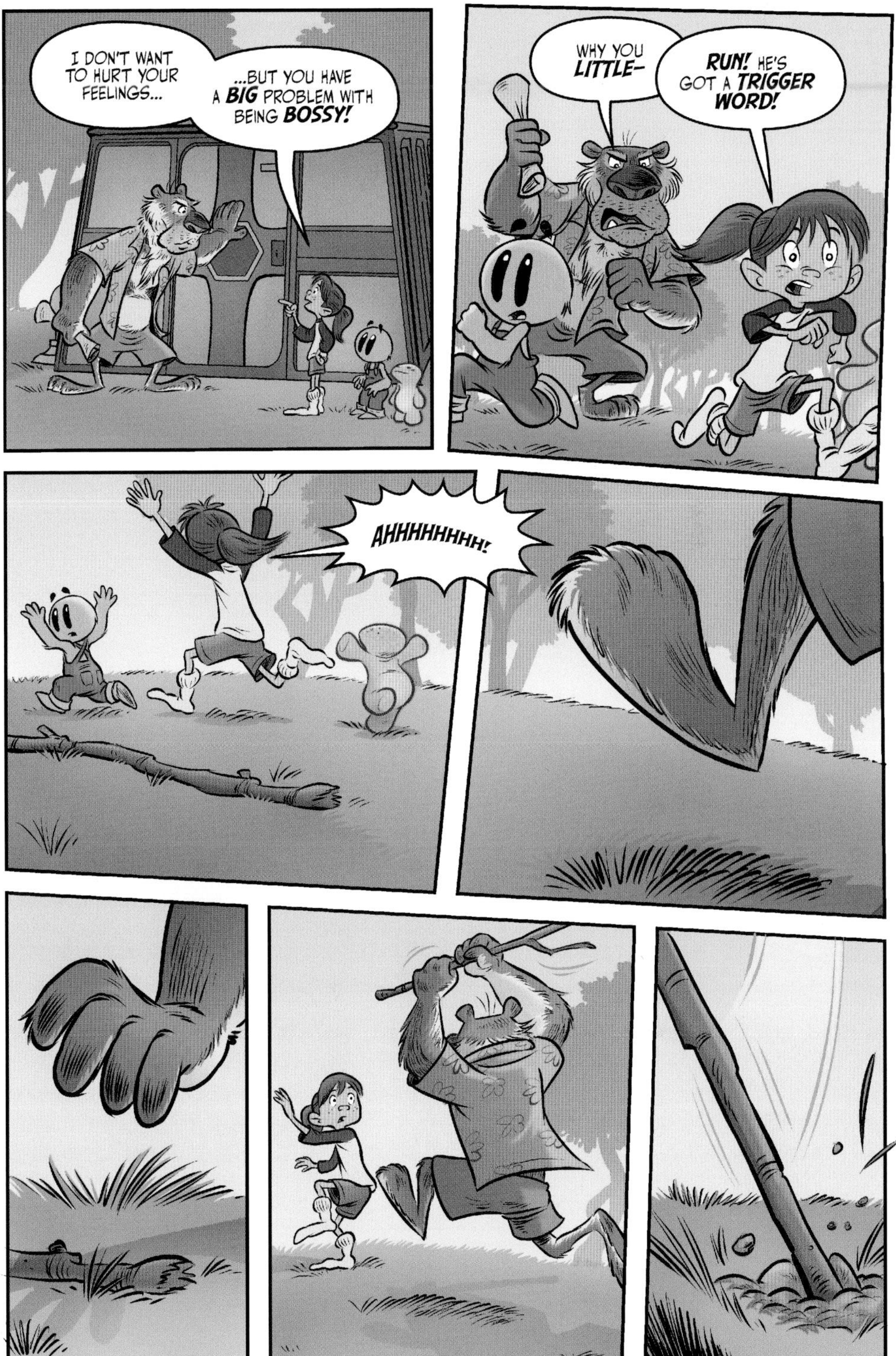
I DON'T WANT TO HURT YOUR FEELINGS...
...BUT YOU HAVE A BIG PROBLEM WITH BEING BOSSY!
WHY YOU LITTLE-
RUN! HE'S GOT A TRIGGER WORD!
AHHHHHHHH!

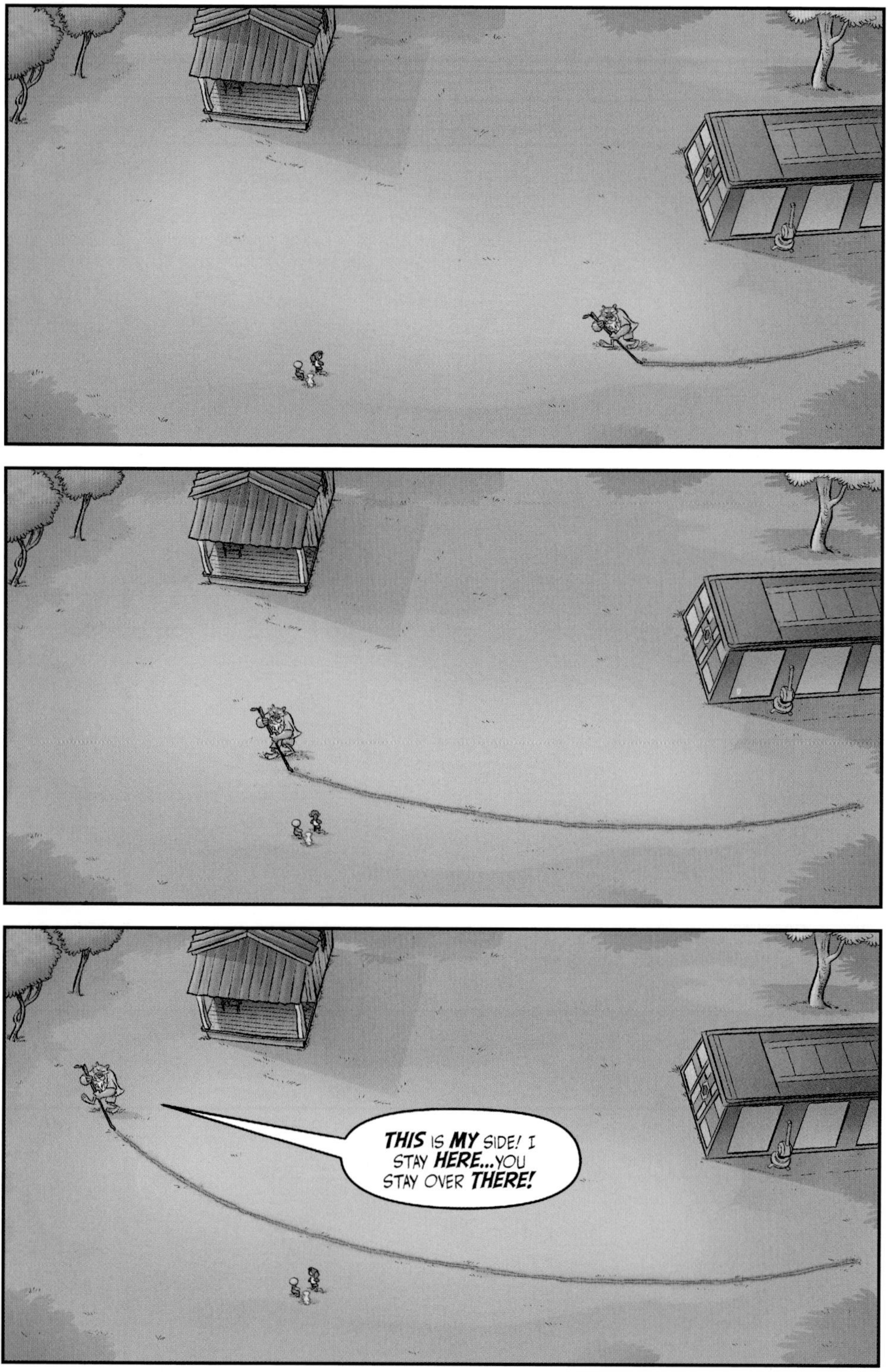
THIS IS MY SIDE! I STAY HERE...YOU STAY OVER THERE!

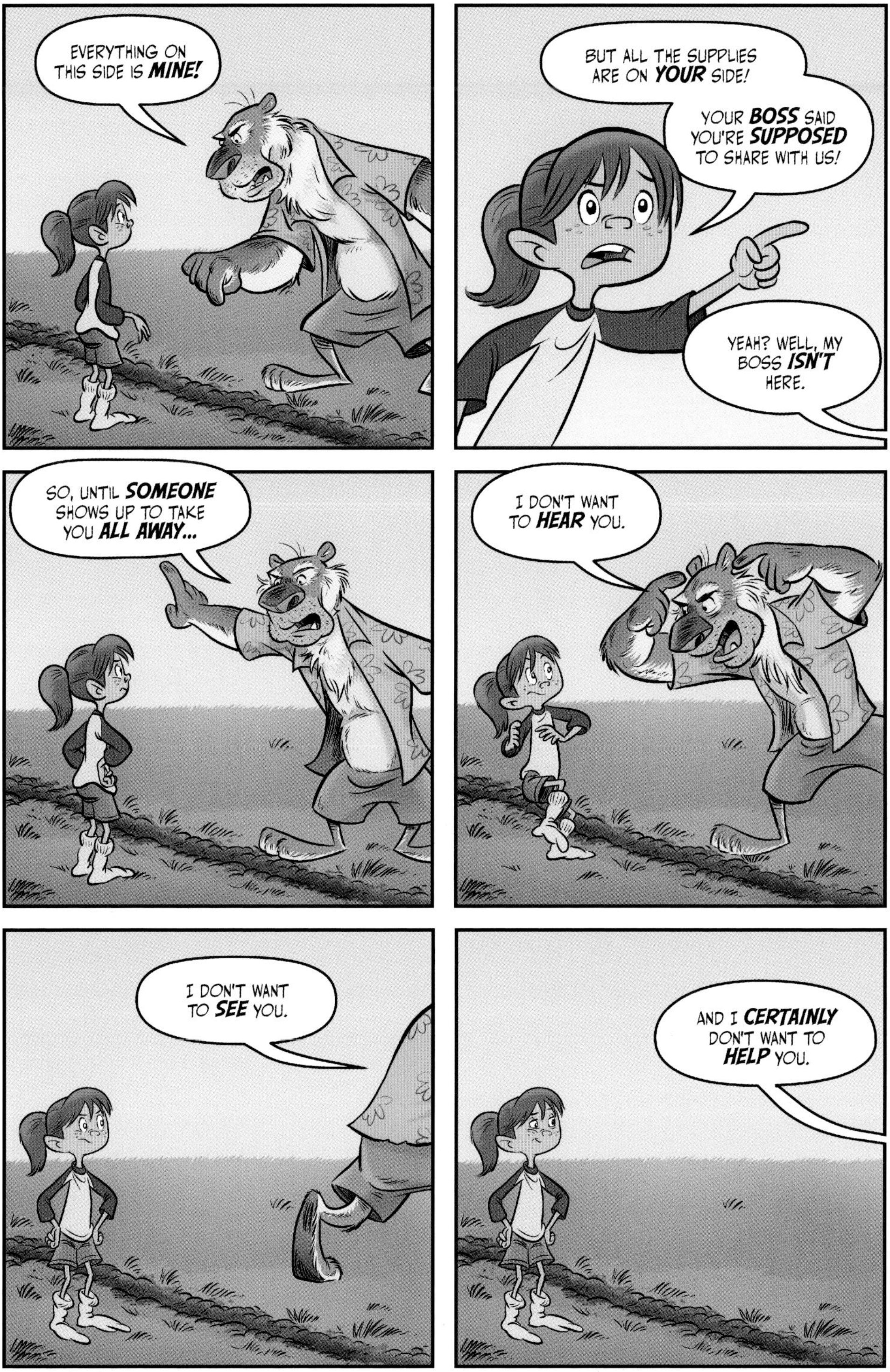
EVERYTHING ON THIS SIDE IS MINE!
BUT ALL THE SUPPLIES ARE ON YOUR SIDE!
YOUR BOSS SAID YOU'RE SUPPOSED TO SHARE WITH US!
YEAH? WELL, MY BOSS ISN'T HERE.
SO, UNTIL SOMEONE SHOWS UP TO TAKE YOU ALL AWAY...
I DON'T WANT TO HEAR YOU.
I DON'T WANT TO SEE YOU.
AND I CERTAINLY DON'T WANT TO HELP YOU.

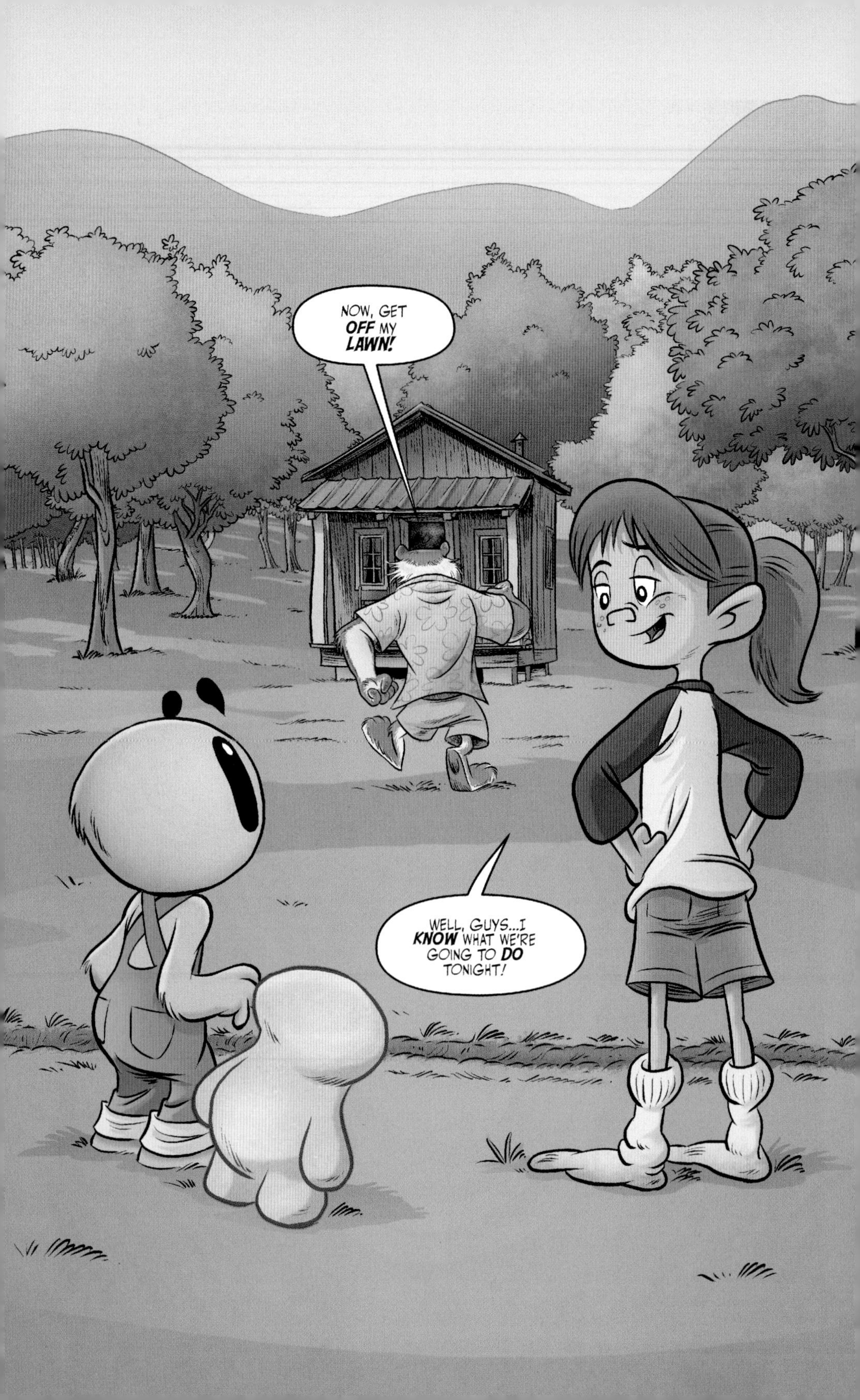
NOW, GET OFF MY LAWN!
WELL, GUYS...I KNOW WHAT WE'RE GOING TO DO TONIGHT!

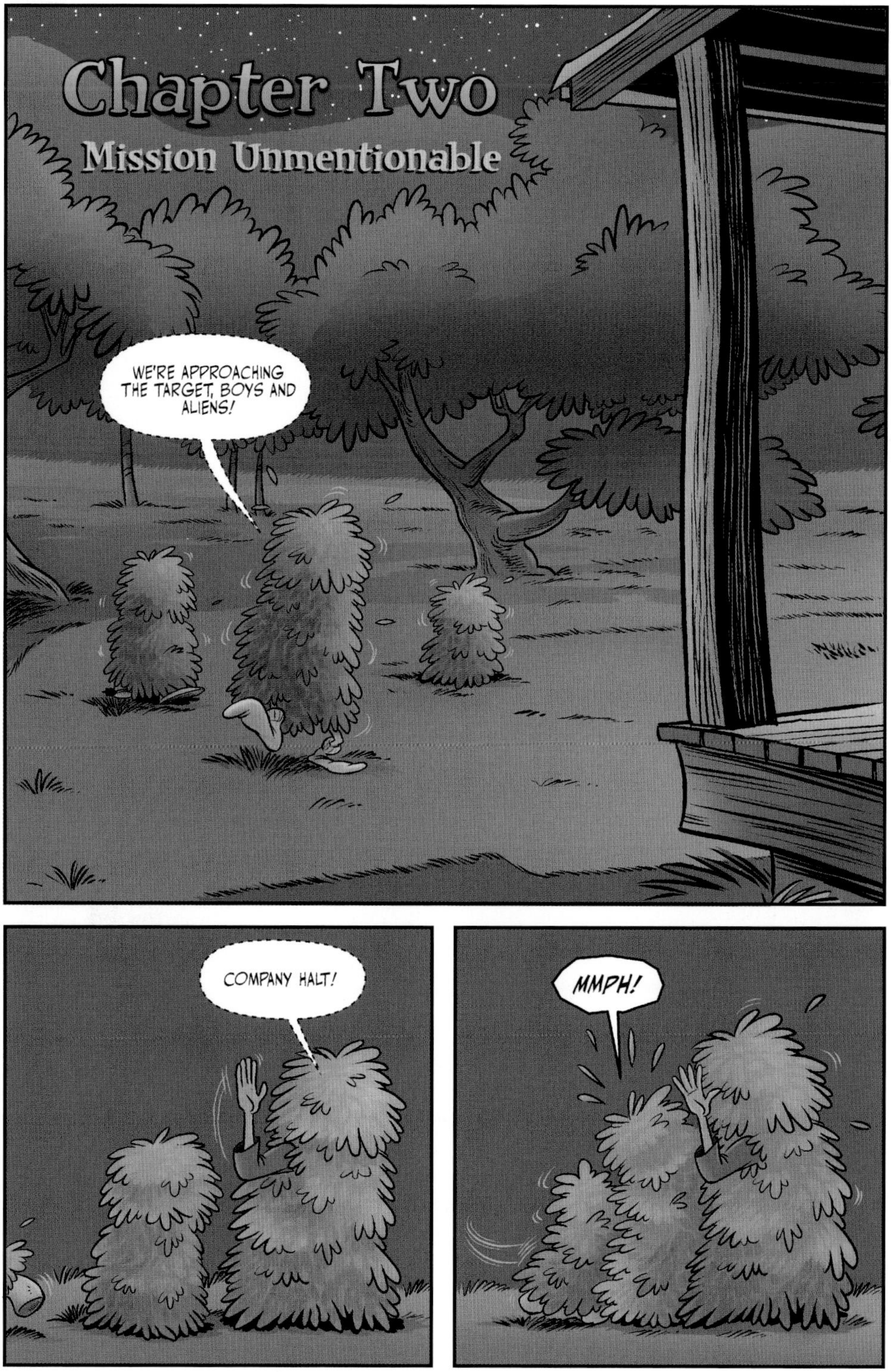
Chapter Two
Mission Unmentionable
WE'RE APPROACHING THE TARGET, BOYS AND ALIENS!
COMPANY HALT!
MMPH!

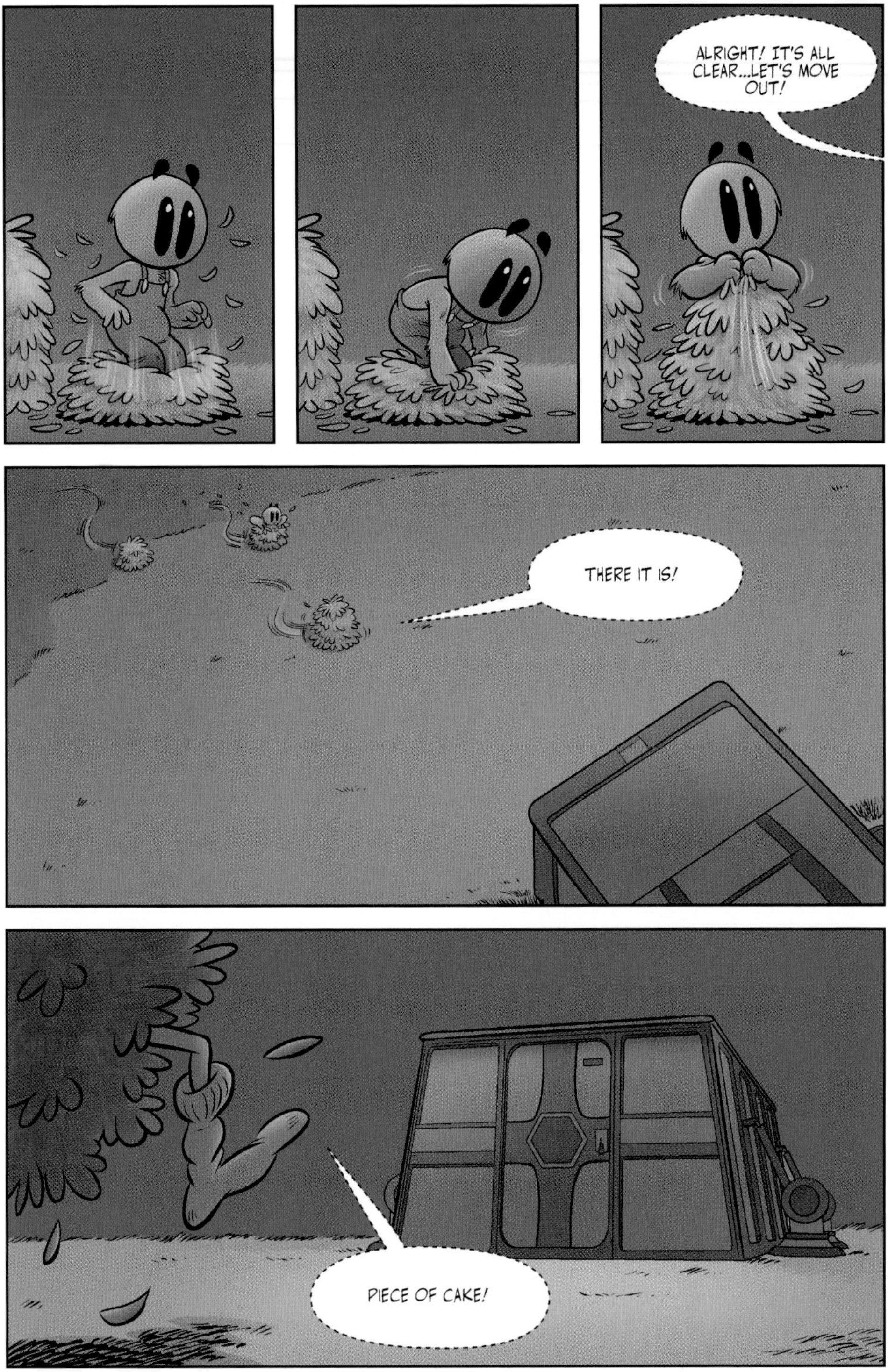
ALRIGHT! IT'S ALL CLEAR...LET'S MOVE OUT!
THERE IT IS!
PIECE OF CAKE!

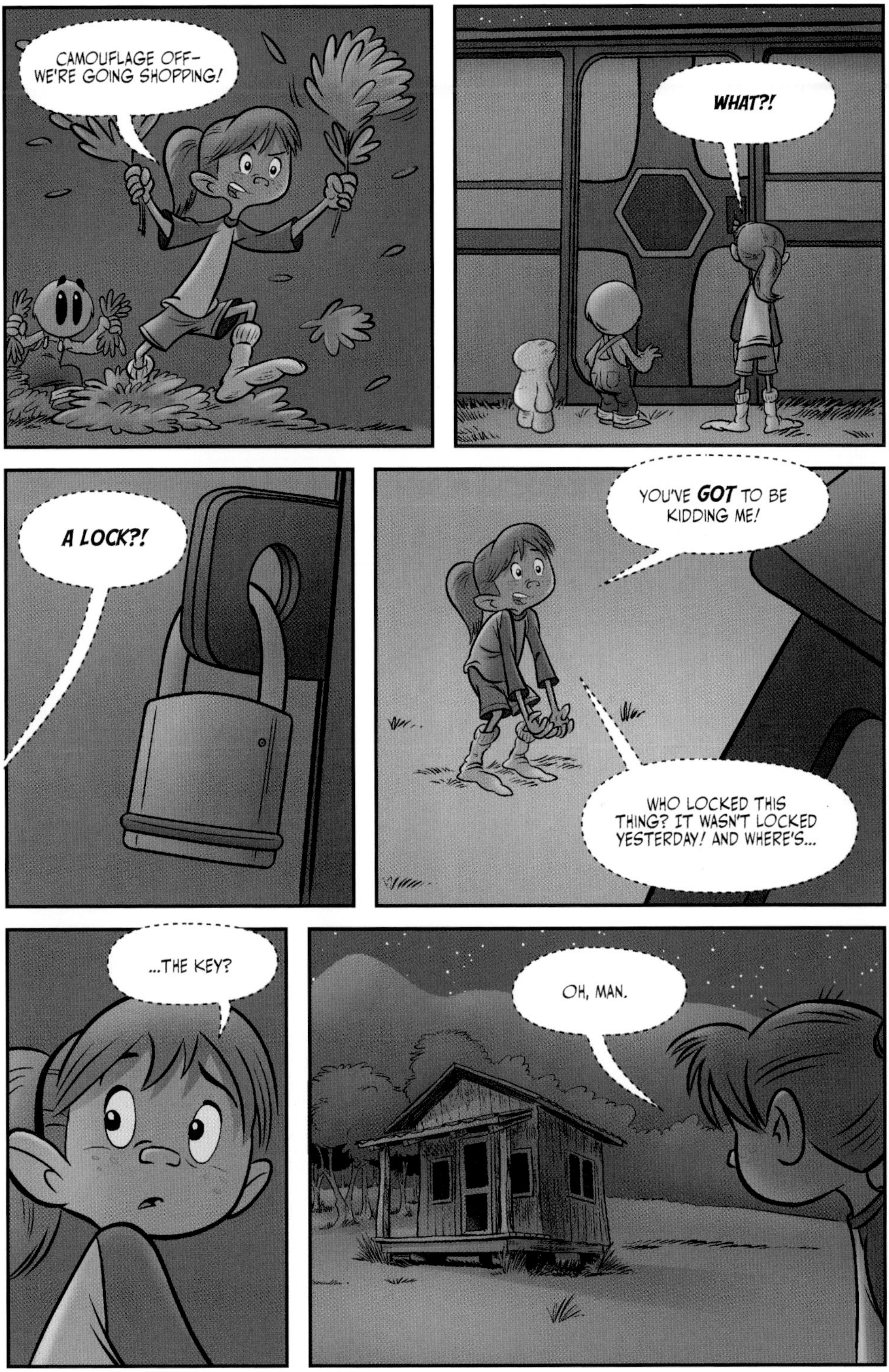
CAMOUFLAGE OFF–
WE'RE GOING SHOPPING!
WHAT?!
A LOCK?!
YOU'VE GOT TO BE KIDDING ME!
WHO LOCKED THIS THING? IT WASN'T LOCKED YESTERDAY! AND WHERE'S...
...THE KEY?
OH, MAN.

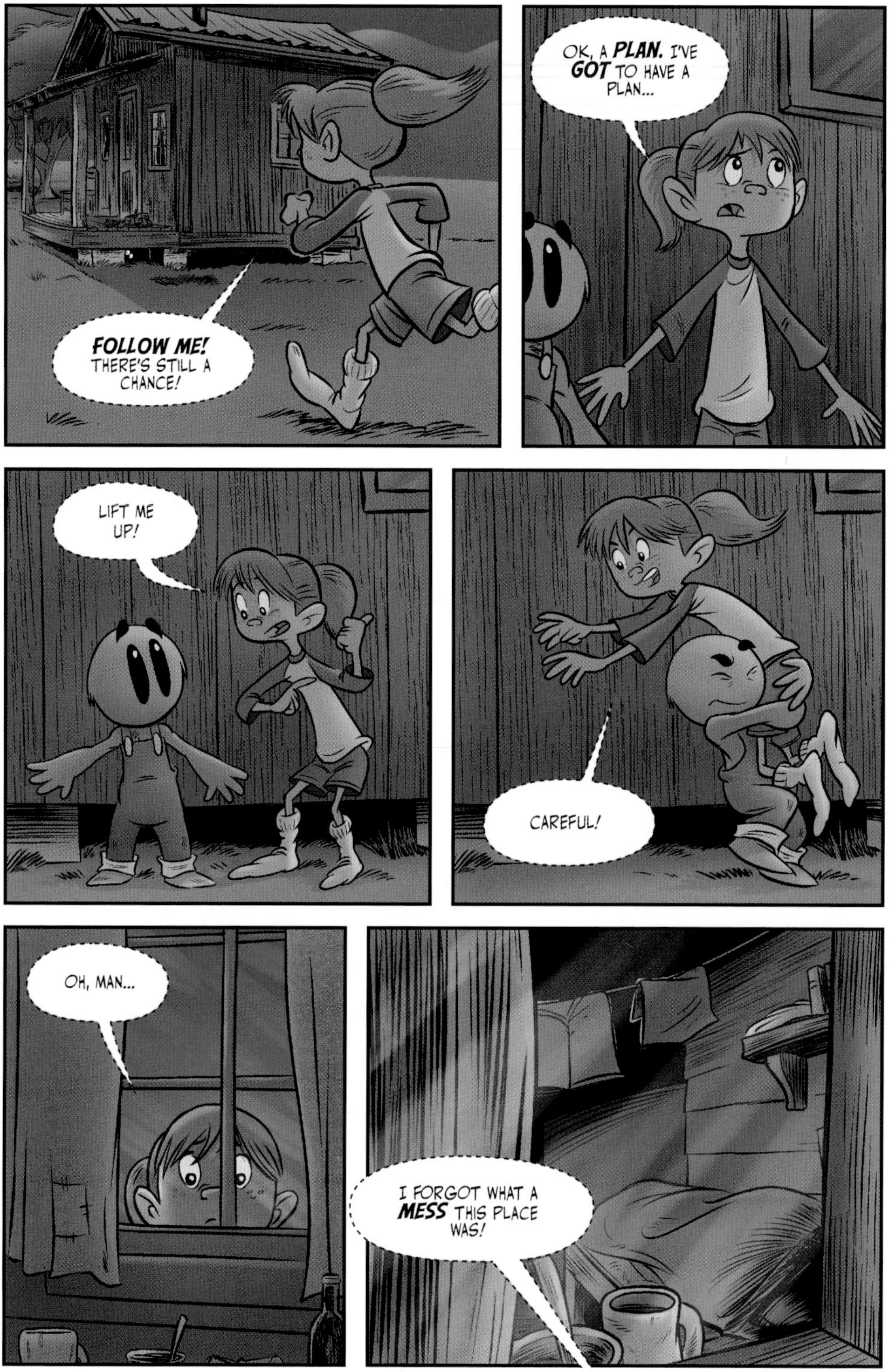
FOLLOW ME! THERE'S STILL A CHANCE!
OK, A PLAN. I'VE GOT TO HAVE A PLAN...
LIFT ME UP!
CAREFUL!
OH, MAN...
I FORGOT WHAT A MESS THIS PLACE WAS!

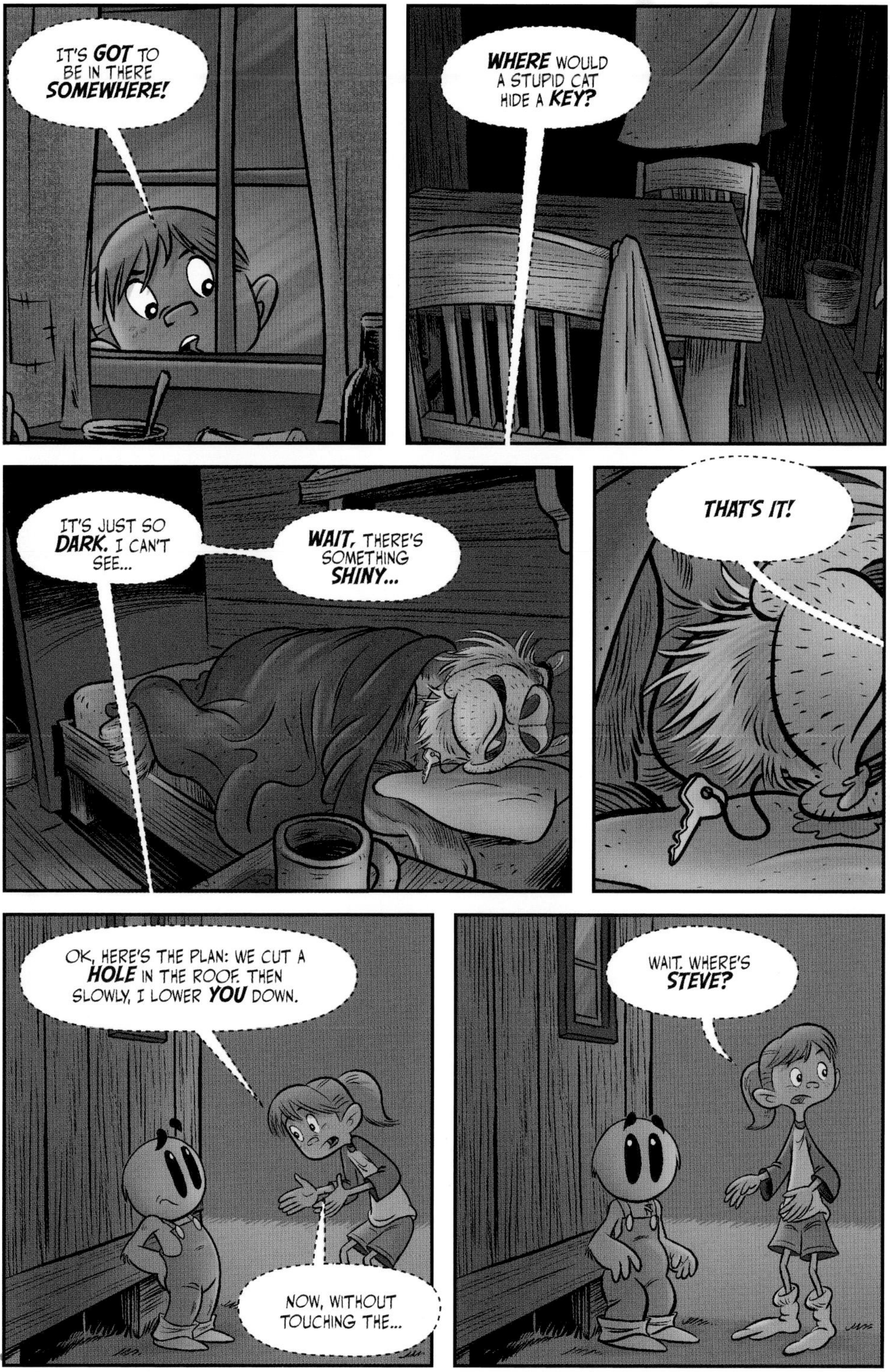
IT'S GOT TO BE IN THERE SOMEWHERE!
WHERE WOULD A STUPID CAT HIDE A KEY?
IT'S JUST SO DARK. I CAN'T SEE...
WAIT, THERE'S SOMETHING SHINY...
THAT'S IT!
OK, HERE'S THE PLAN: WE CUT A HOLE IN THE ROOF. THEN SLOWLY, I LOWER YOU DOWN.
NOW, WITHOUT TOUCHING THE...
WAIT. WHERE'S STEVE?

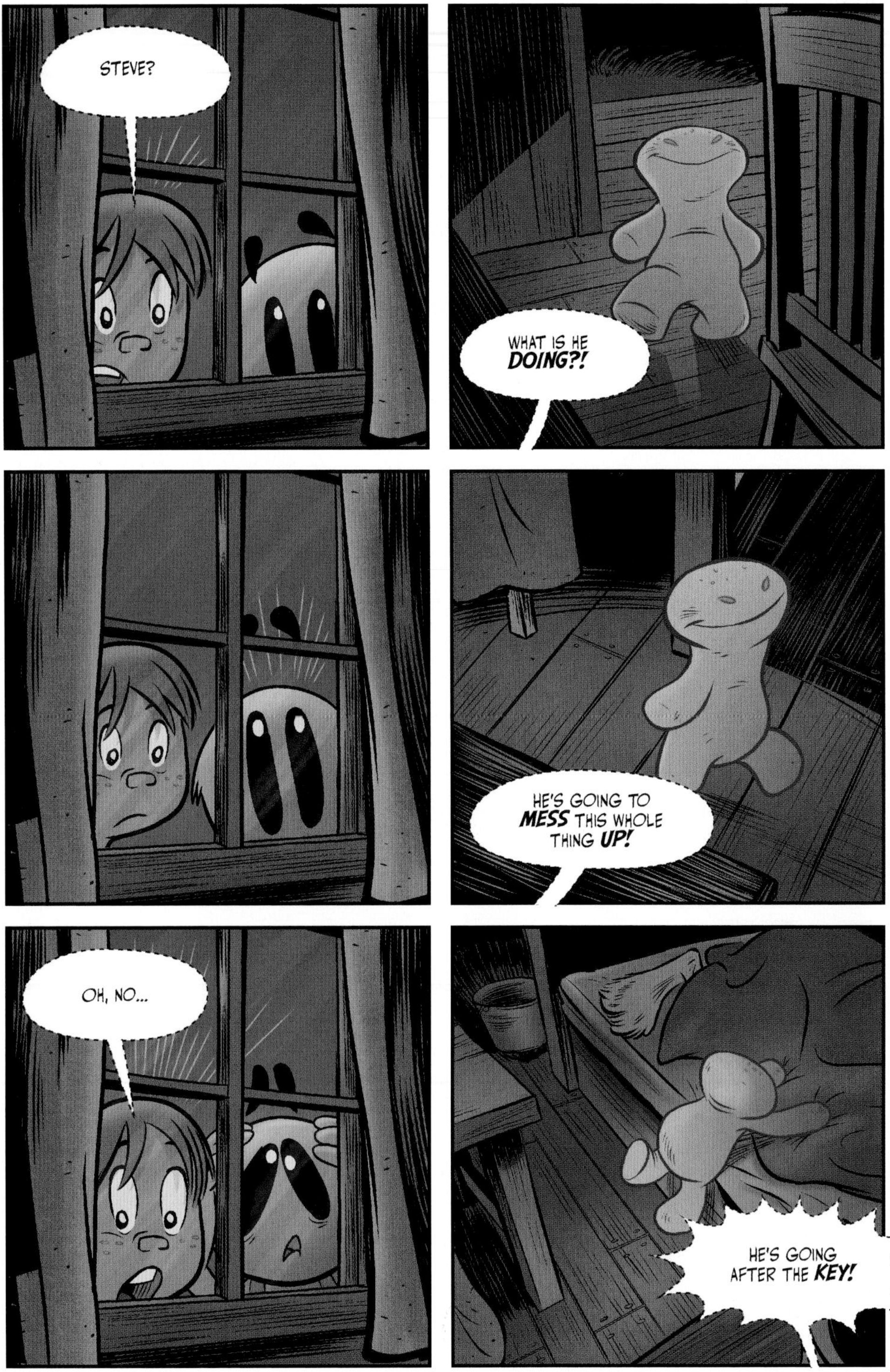

STEVE?
WHAT IS HE DOING?!
HE'S GOING TO MESS THIS WHOLE THING UP!
OH, NO...
HE'S GOING AFTER THE KEY!

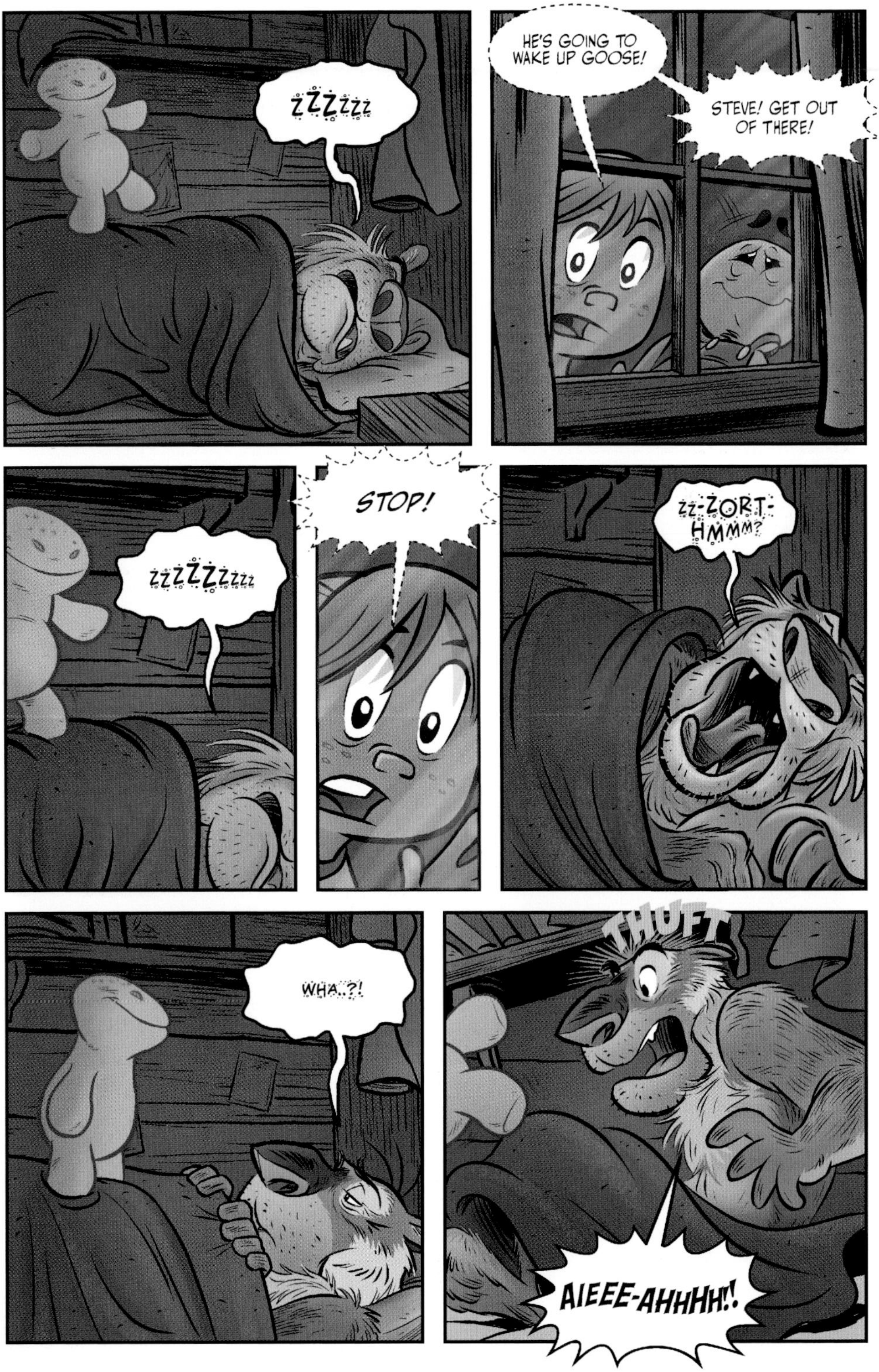
ZZZzzz
HE'S GOING TO WAKE UP GOOSE!
STEVE! GET OUT OF THERE!
zzZZZzzzz
STOP!
zz-ZORT-HMMM?
WHA..?!
THUFT
AIEEE-AHHHH!!

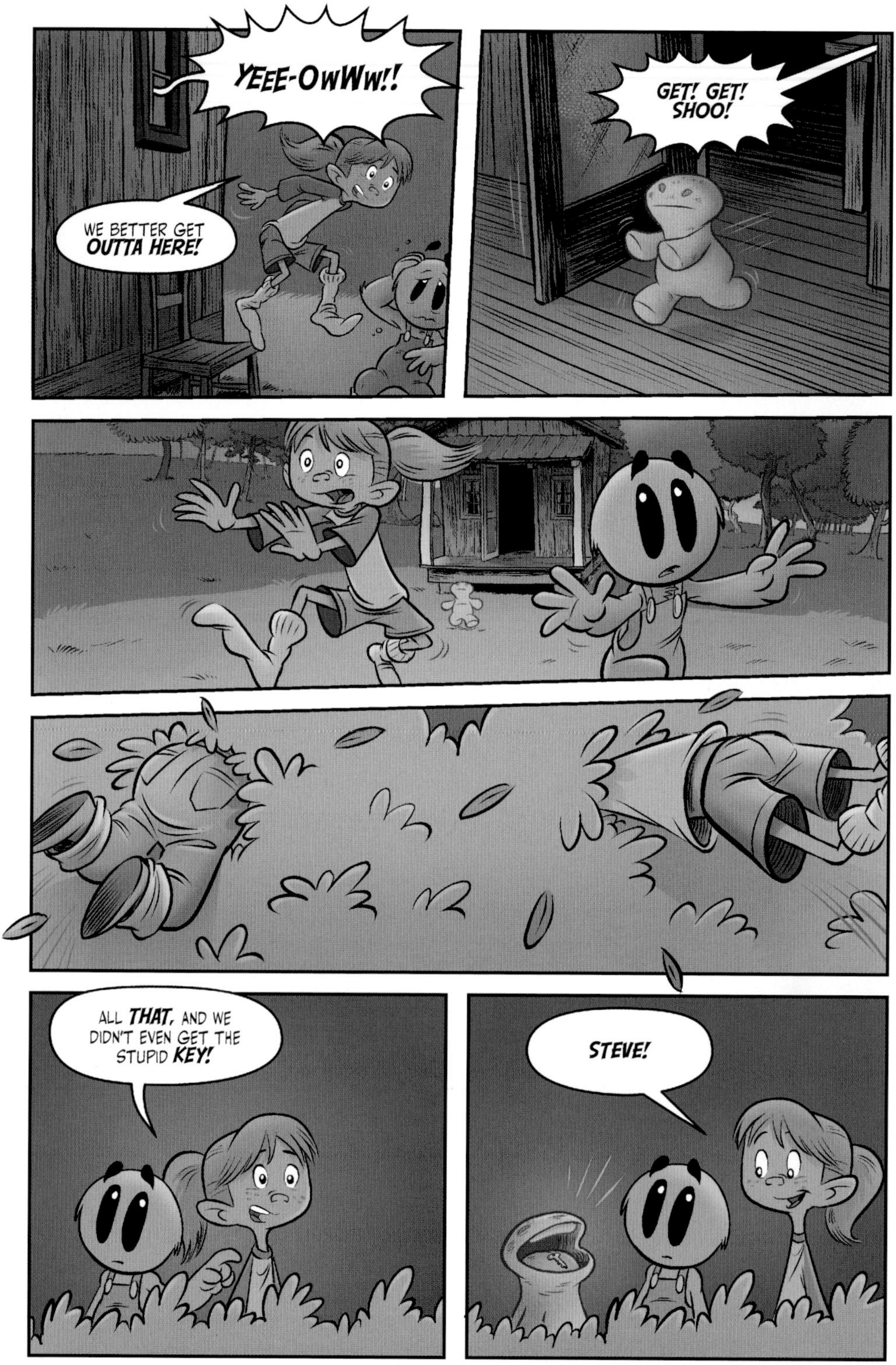
YEEE-OWWW!!
WE BETTER GET OUTTA HERE!
GET! GET! SHOO!
ALL THAT, AND WE DIDN'T EVEN GET THE STUPID KEY!
STEVE!

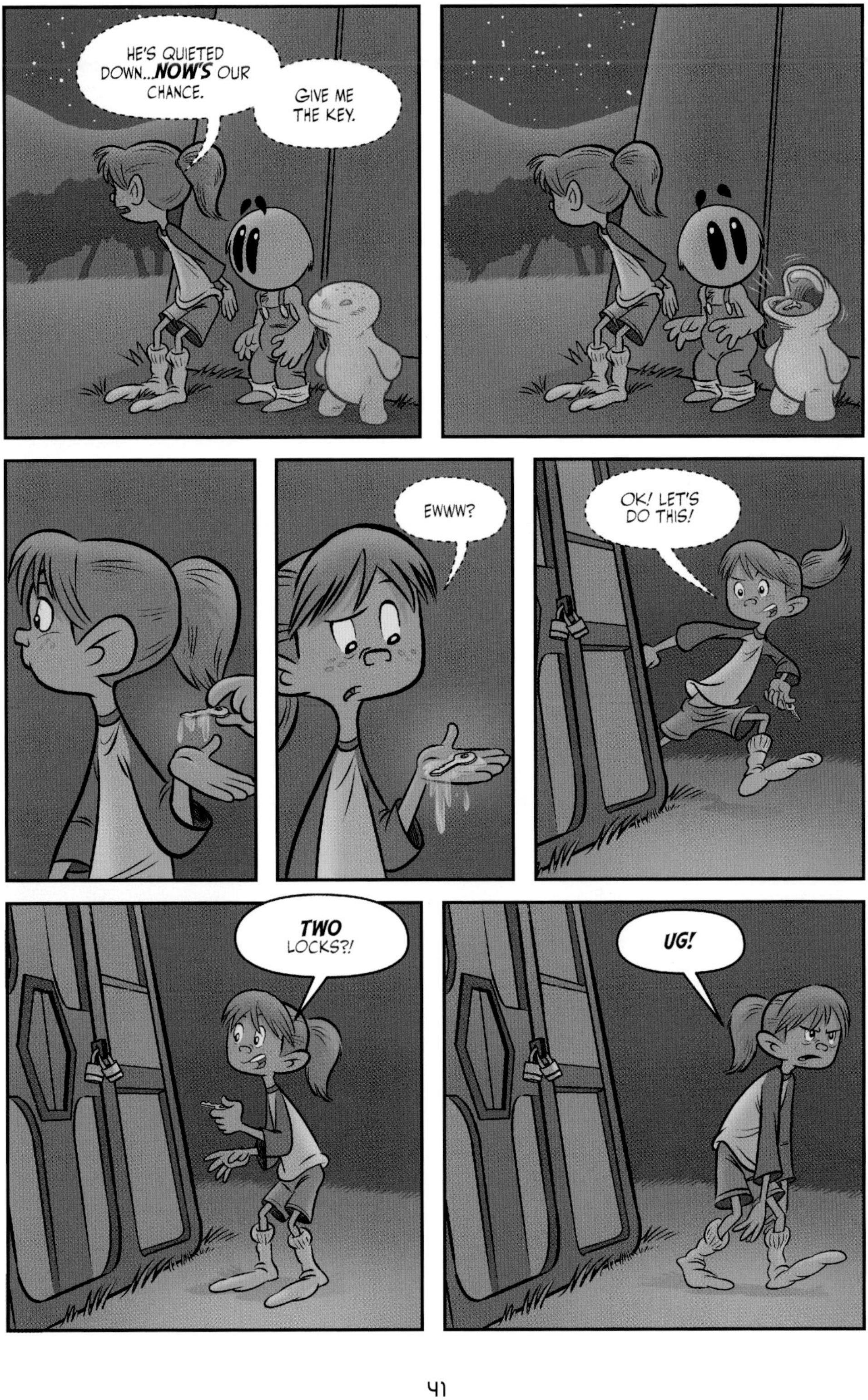
HE'S QUIETED DOWN...NOW'S OUR CHANCE.
GIVE ME THE KEY.
EWWW?
OK! LET'S DO THIS!
TWO LOCKS?!
UG!

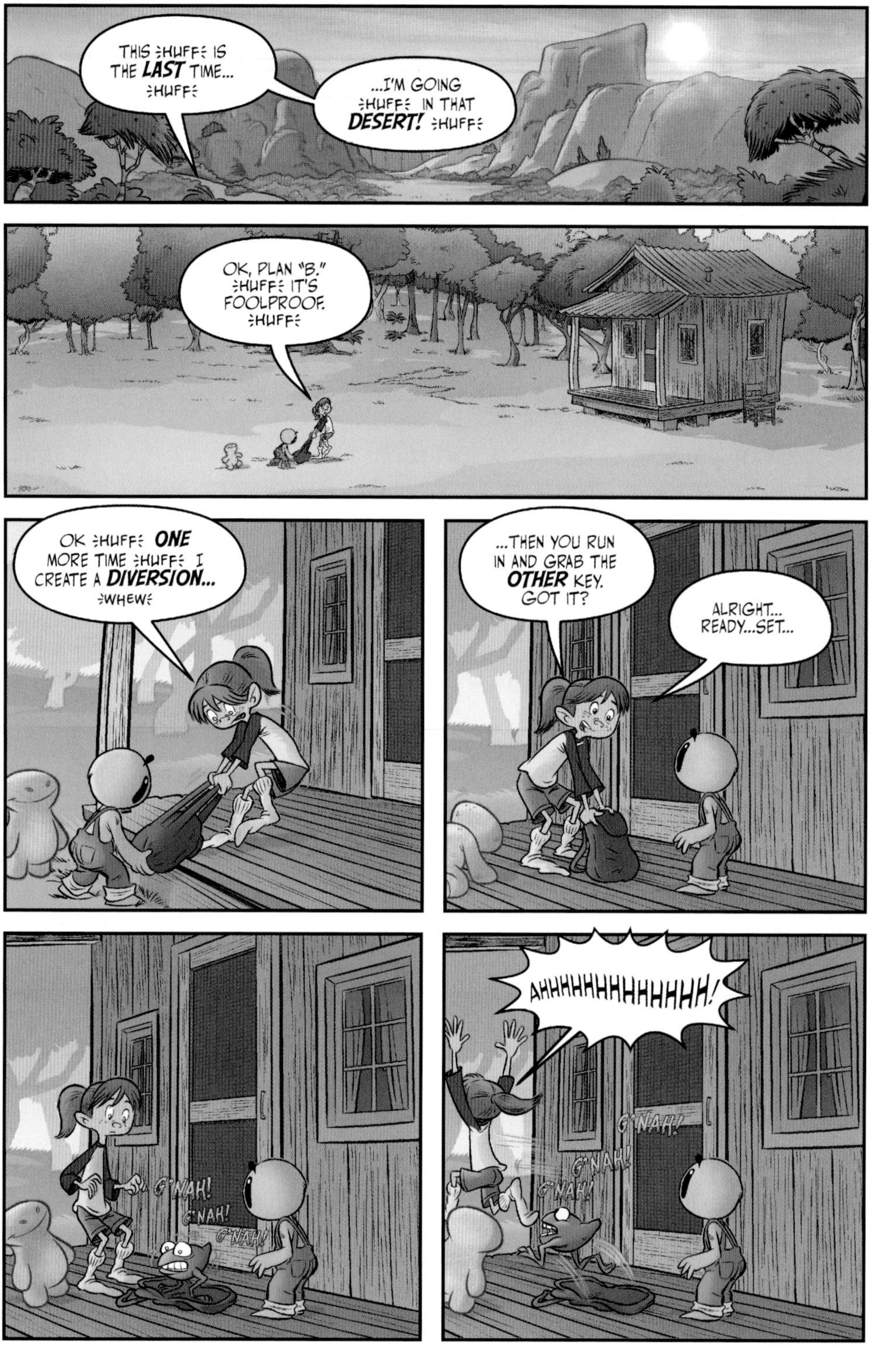

THIS ⁝HUFF⁝ IS THE **LAST** TIME... ⁝HUFF⁝
...I'M GOING ⁝HUFF⁝ IN THAT **DESERT!** ⁝HUFF⁝
OK, PLAN "B." ⁝HUFF⁝ IT'S FOOLPROOF. ⁝HUFF⁝
OK ⁝HUFF⁝ **ONE** MORE TIME ⁝HUFF⁝ I CREATE A **DIVERSION...** ⁝WHEW⁝
...THEN YOU RUN IN AND GRAB THE **OTHER** KEY. GOT IT?
ALRIGHT... READY...SET...
G'NAH!
G'NAH!
G'NAH!
AHHHHHHHHHHHHH!
G'NAH!
G'NAH!
G'NAH!

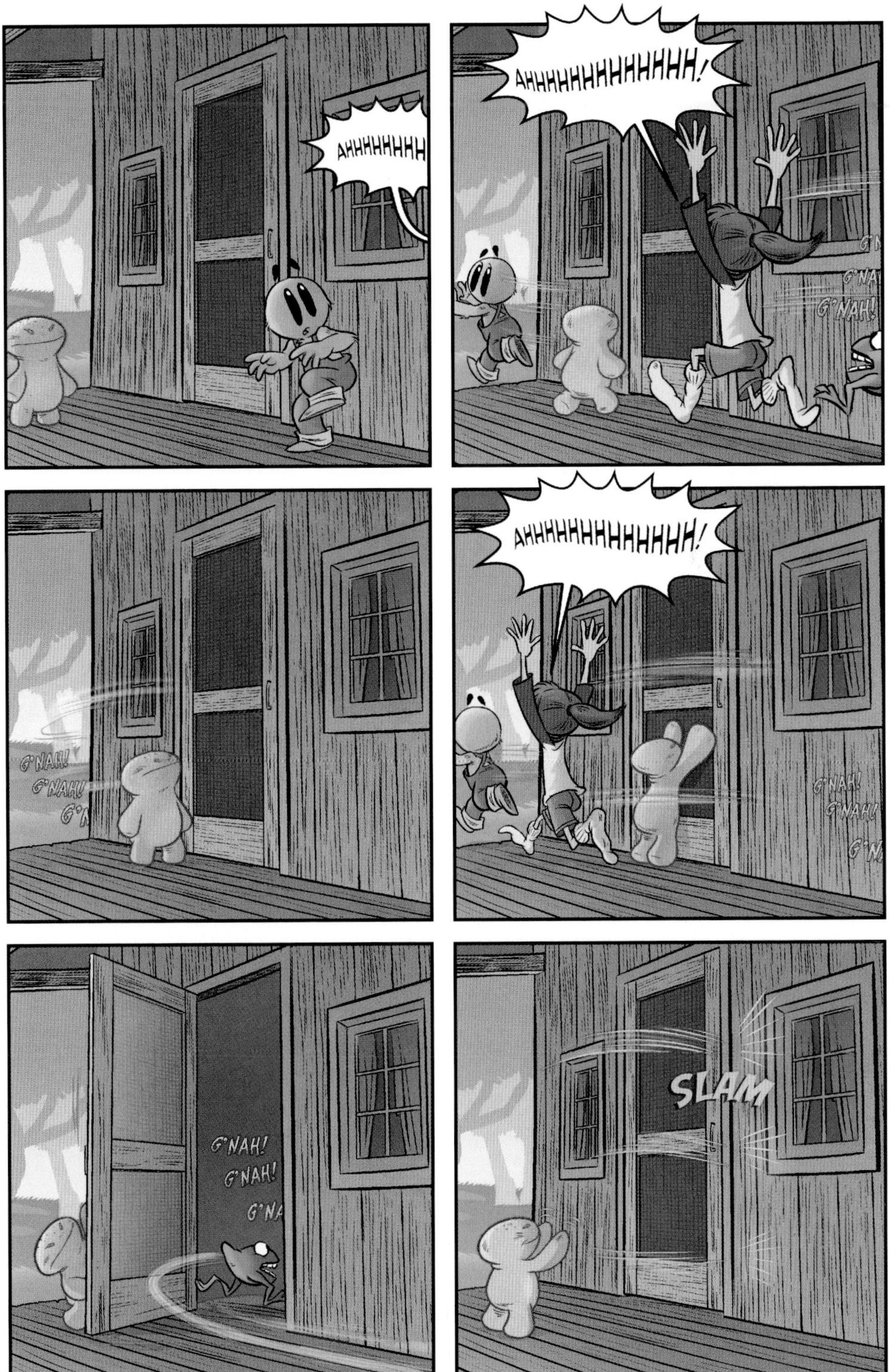
AHHHHHHHH
AHHHHHHHHHHHHH!
G'N
G'NAH
G'NAH!
G'NAH!
G'NAH!
G'N
AHHHHHHHHHHHHHH!
G'NAH!
G'NAH!
G'N
G'NAH!
G'NAH!
G'NA
SLAM

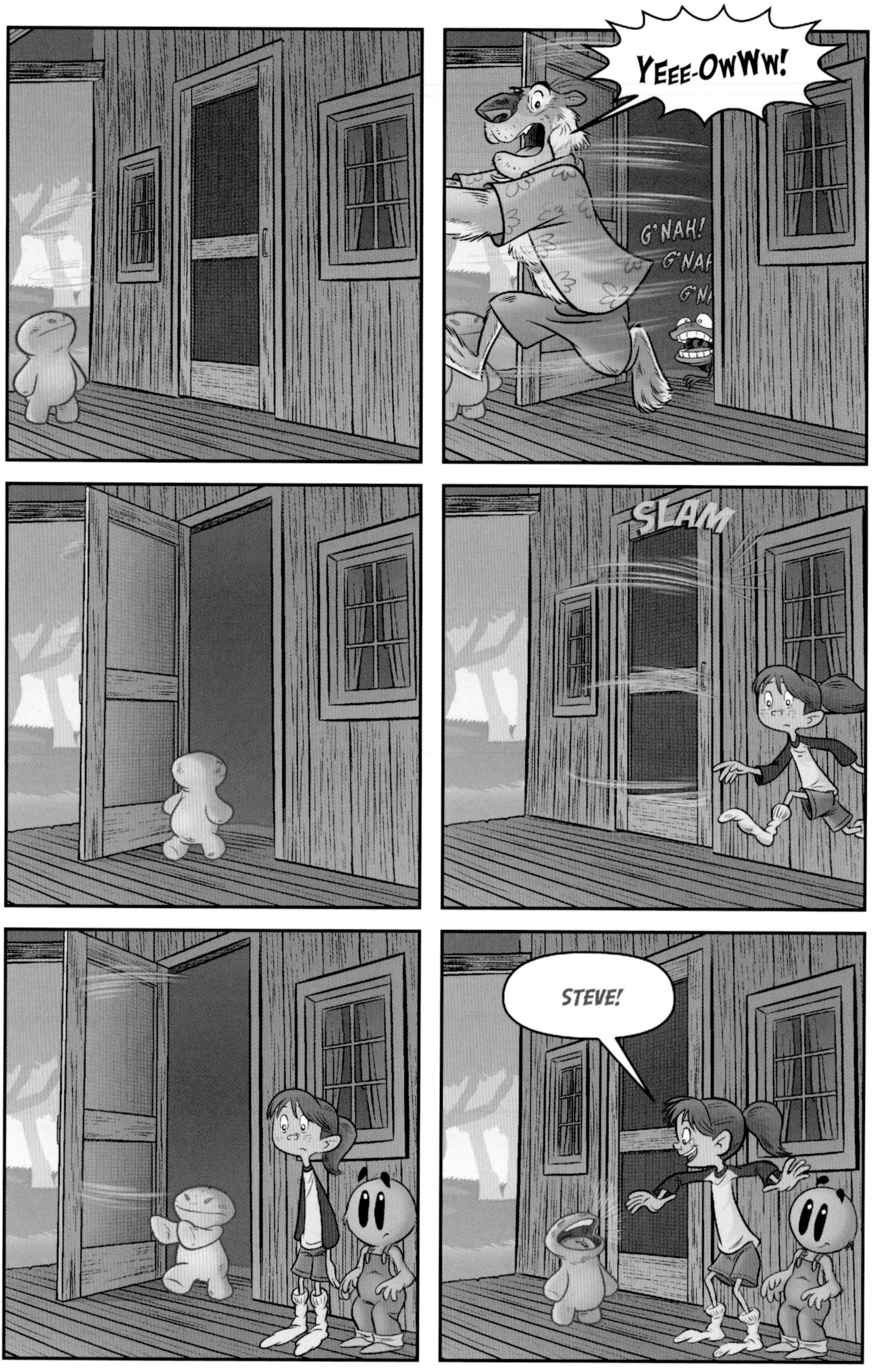
YEEE-OWWW!
G'NAH!
G'NAH
G'N
SLAM
STEVE!

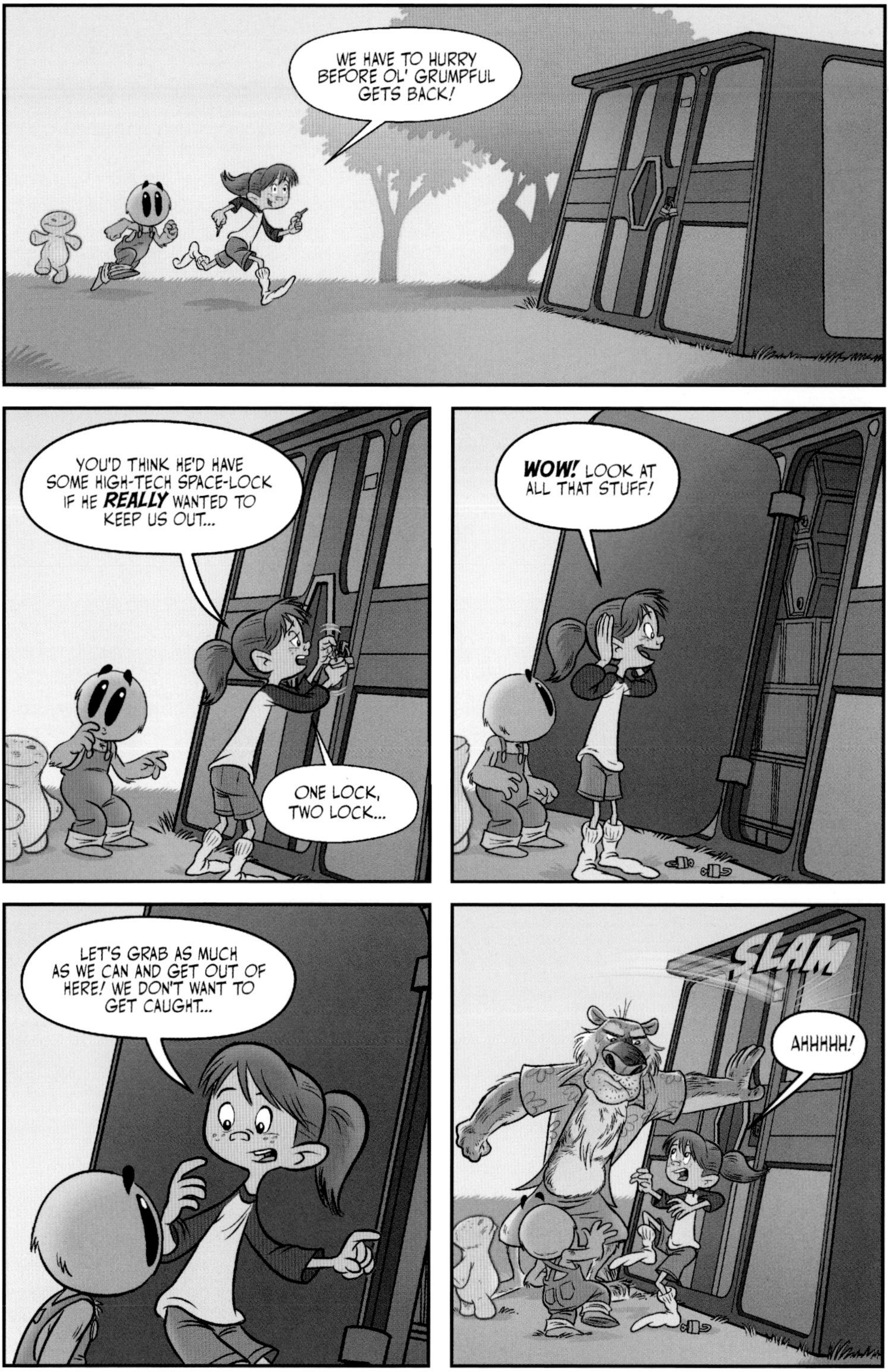
WE HAVE TO HURRY BEFORE OL' GRUMPFUL GETS BACK!
YOU'D THINK HE'D HAVE SOME HIGH-TECH SPACE-LOCK IF HE **REALLY** WANTED TO KEEP US OUT...
ONE LOCK, TWO LOCK...
WOW! LOOK AT ALL THAT STUFF!
LET'S GRAB AS MUCH AS WE CAN AND GET OUT OF HERE! WE DON'T WANT TO GET CAUGHT...
SLAM
AHHHHH!

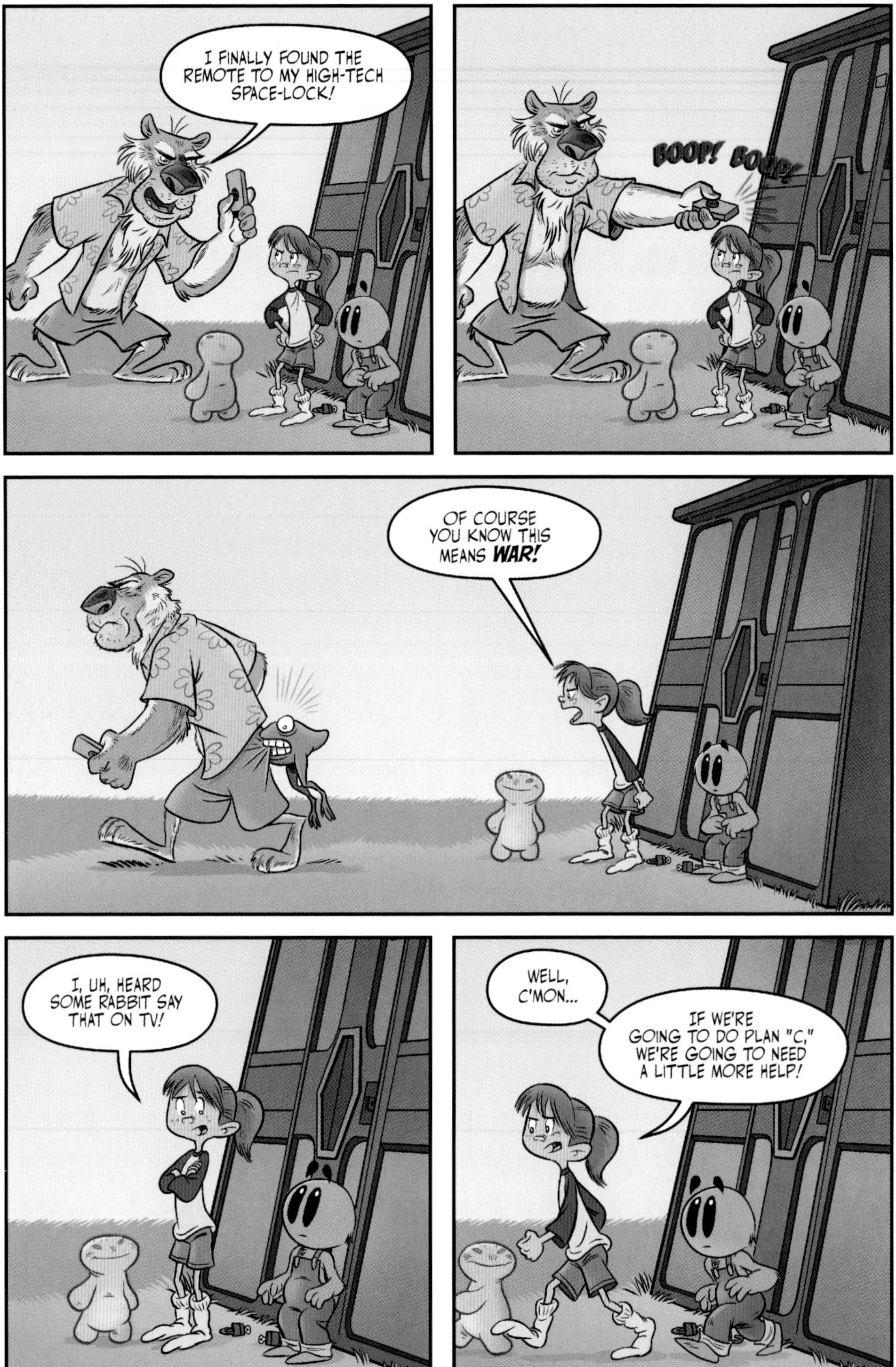

I FINALLY FOUND THE REMOTE TO MY HIGH-TECH SPACE-LOCK!
BOOP! BOOP!
OF COURSE YOU KNOW THIS MEANS WAR!
I, UH, HEARD SOME RABBIT SAY THAT ON TV!
WELL, C'MON...
IF WE'RE GOING TO DO PLAN "C," WE'RE GOING TO NEED A LITTLE MORE HELP!

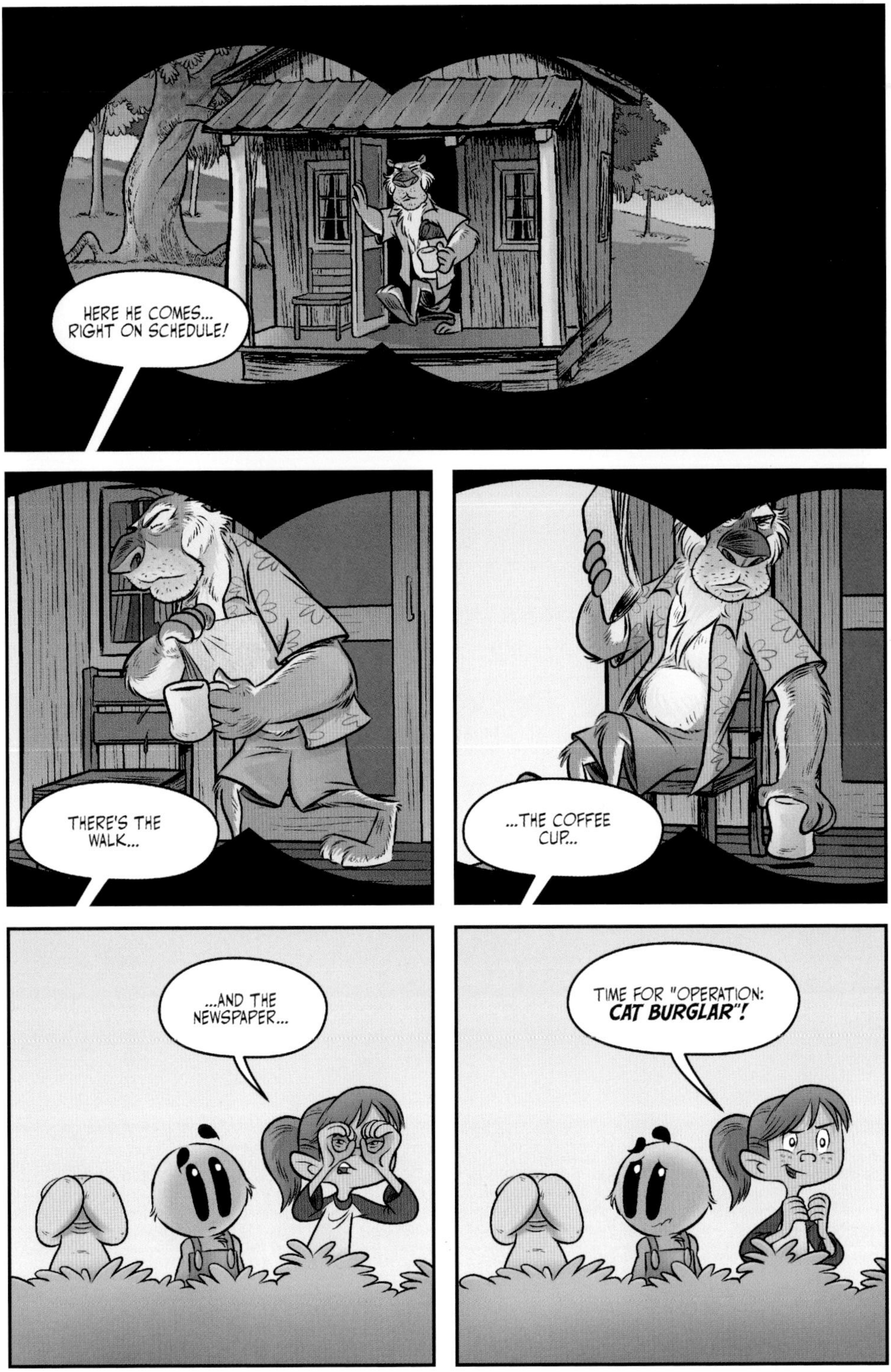
HERE HE COMES... RIGHT ON SCHEDULE!
THERE'S THE WALK...
...THE COFFEE CUP...
...AND THE NEWSPAPER...
TIME FOR "OPERATION: **CAT BURGLAR**"!

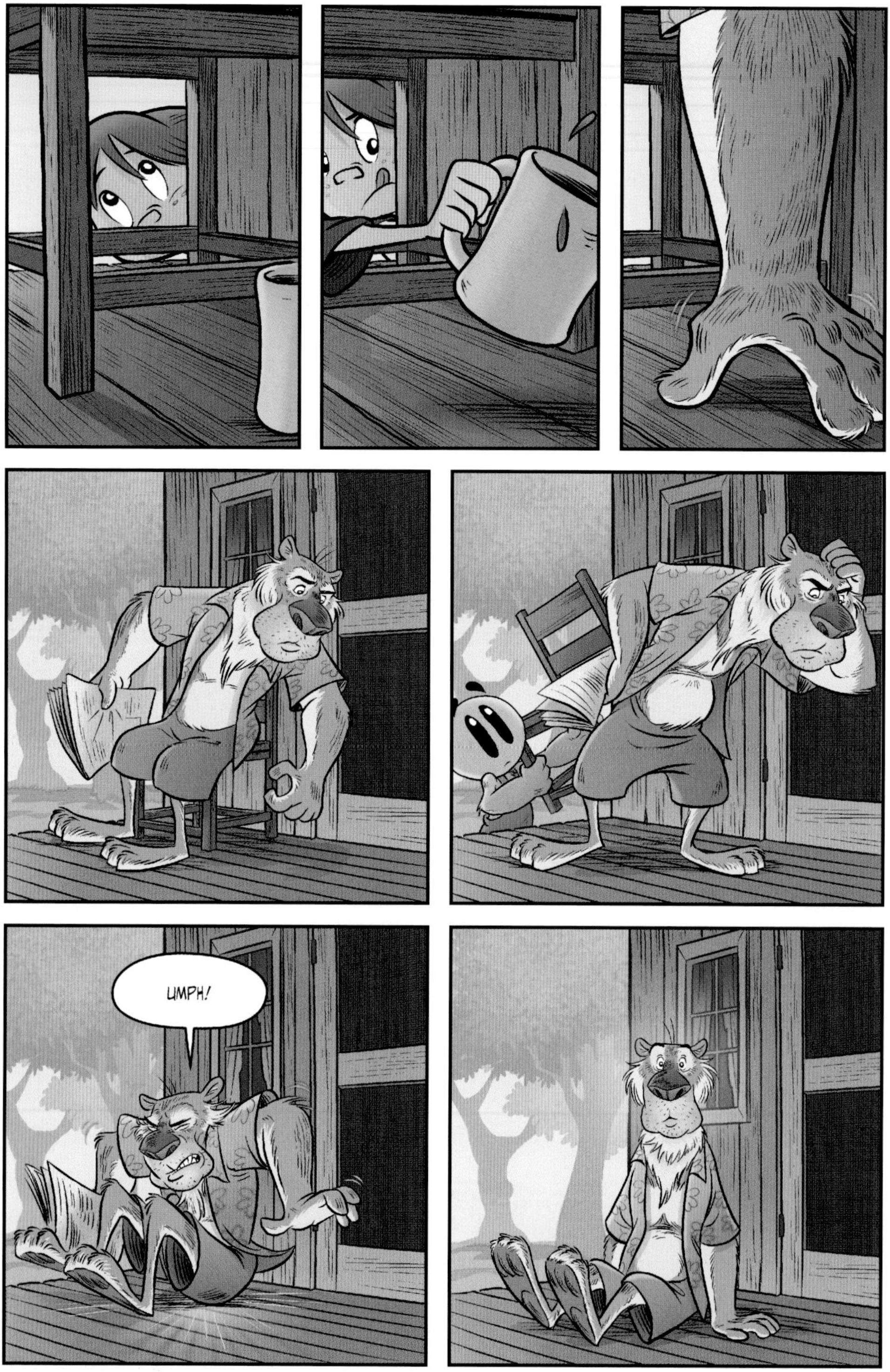
UMPH!

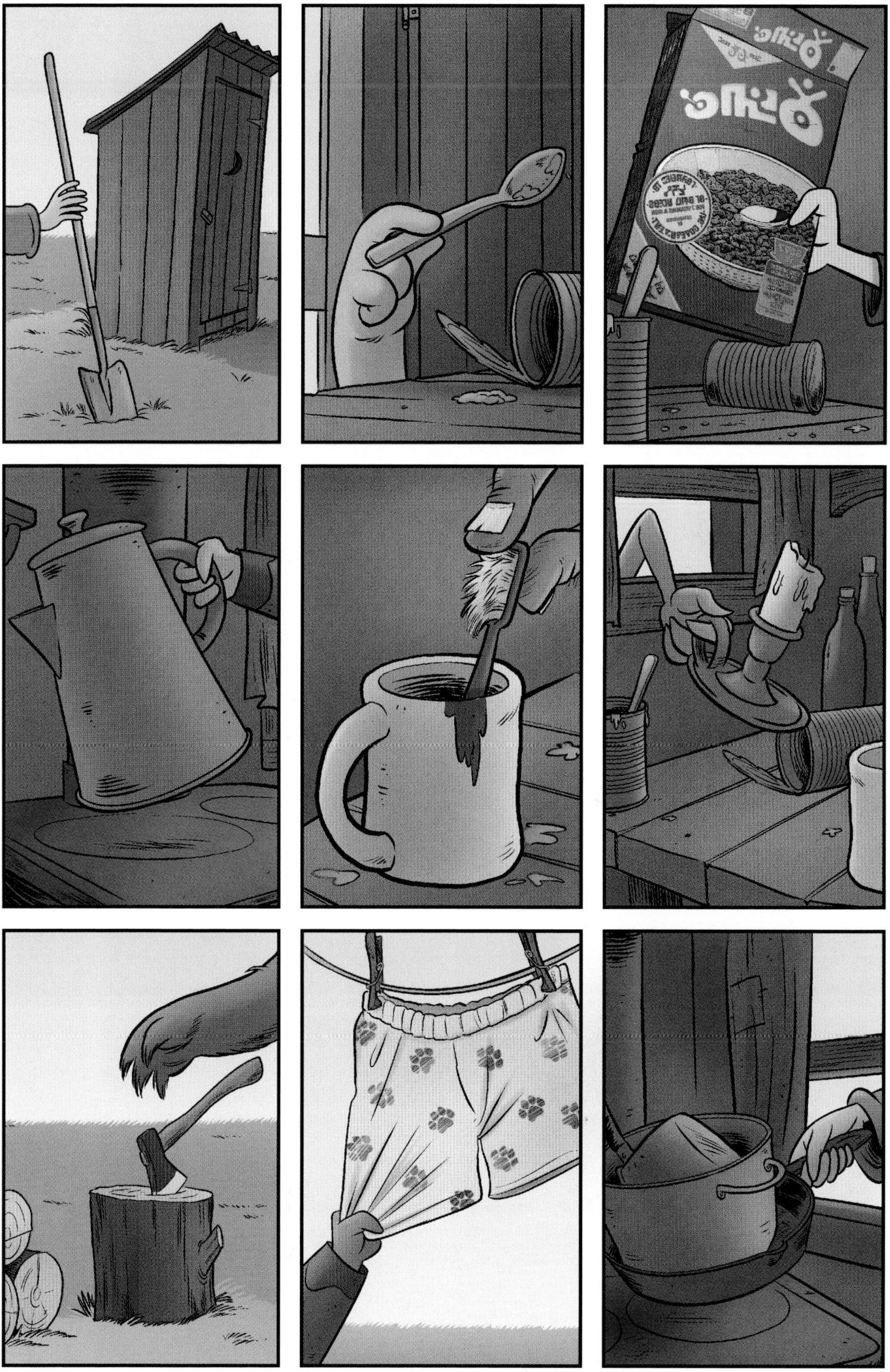

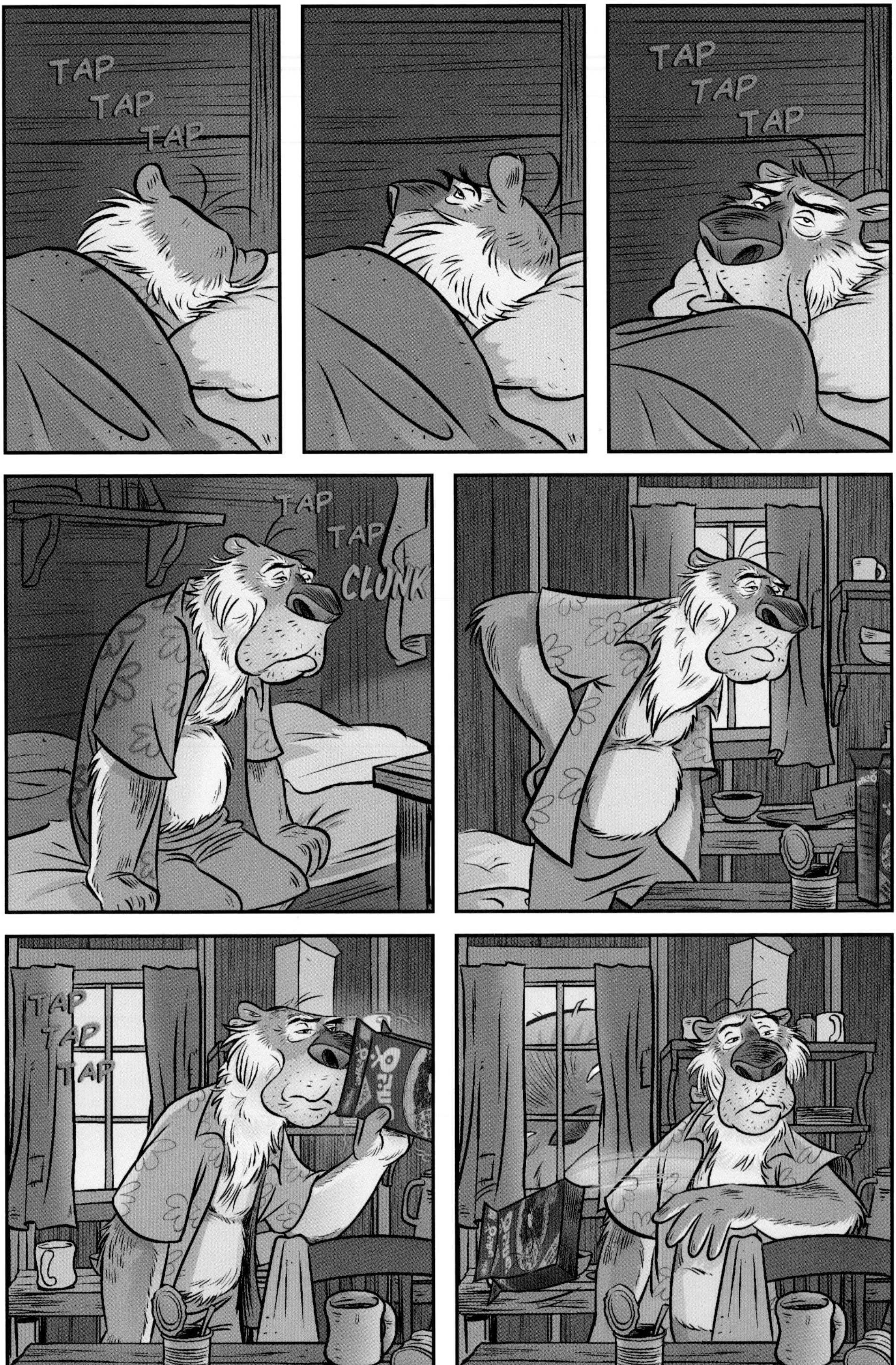
TAP
TAP
TAP
TAP
TAP
TAP
TAP
TAP
CLUNK
TAP
TAP
TAP

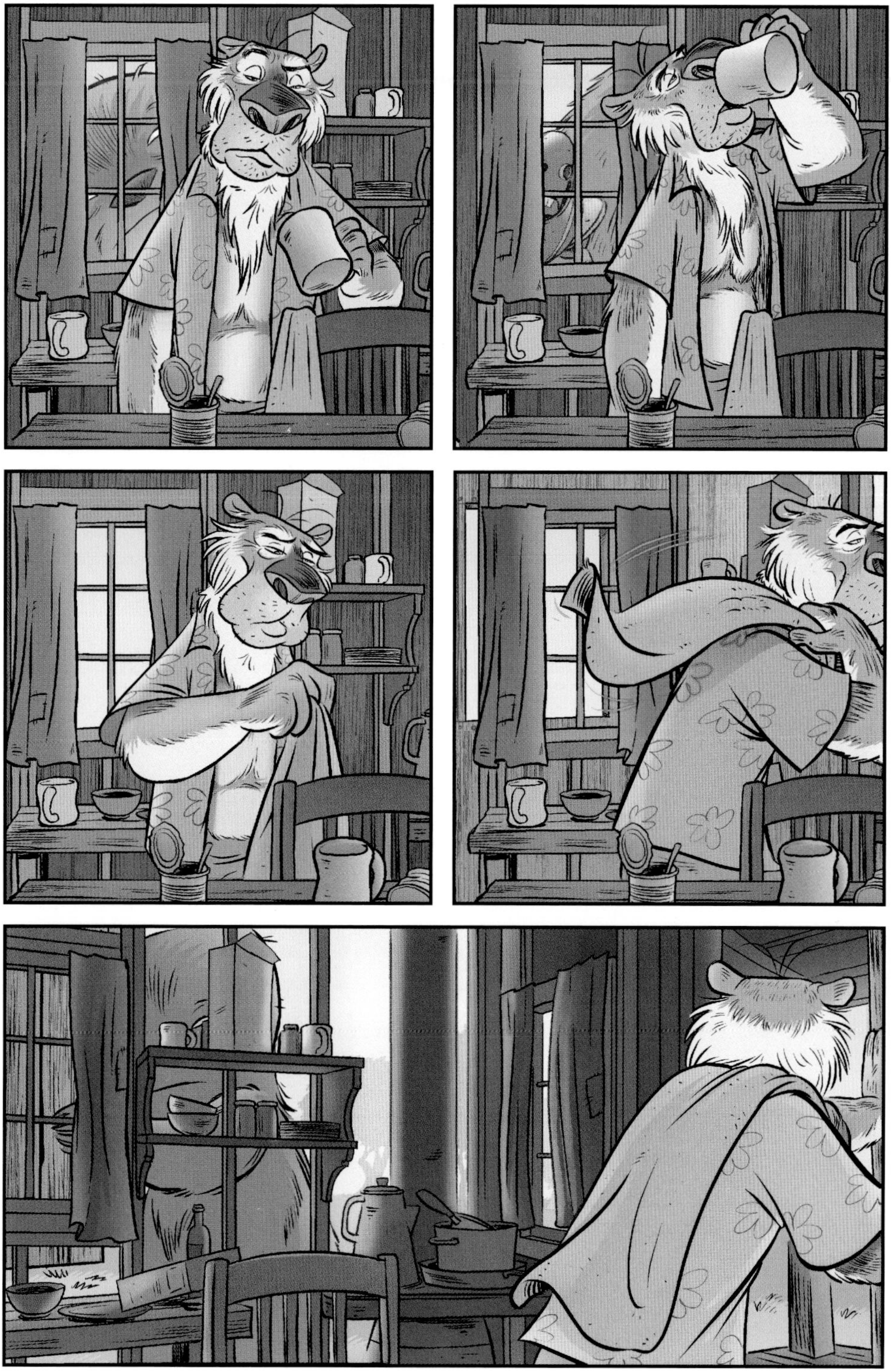

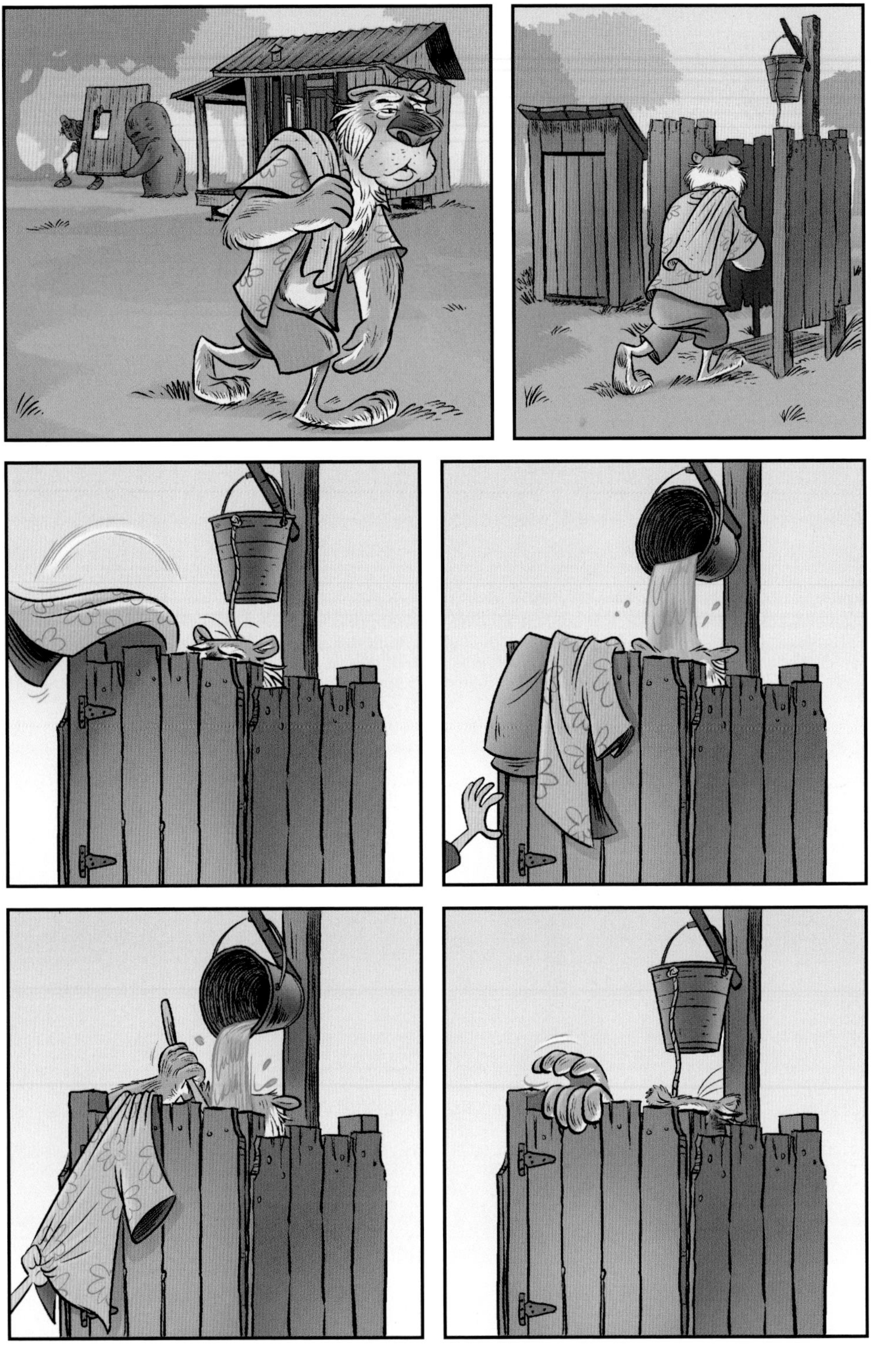

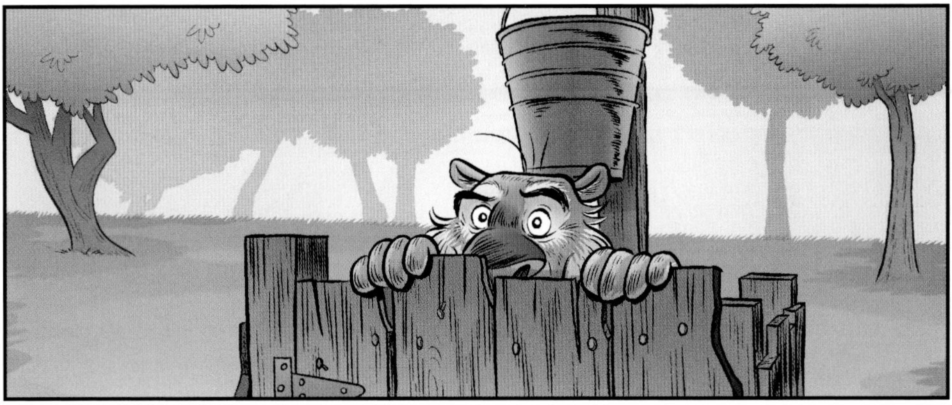

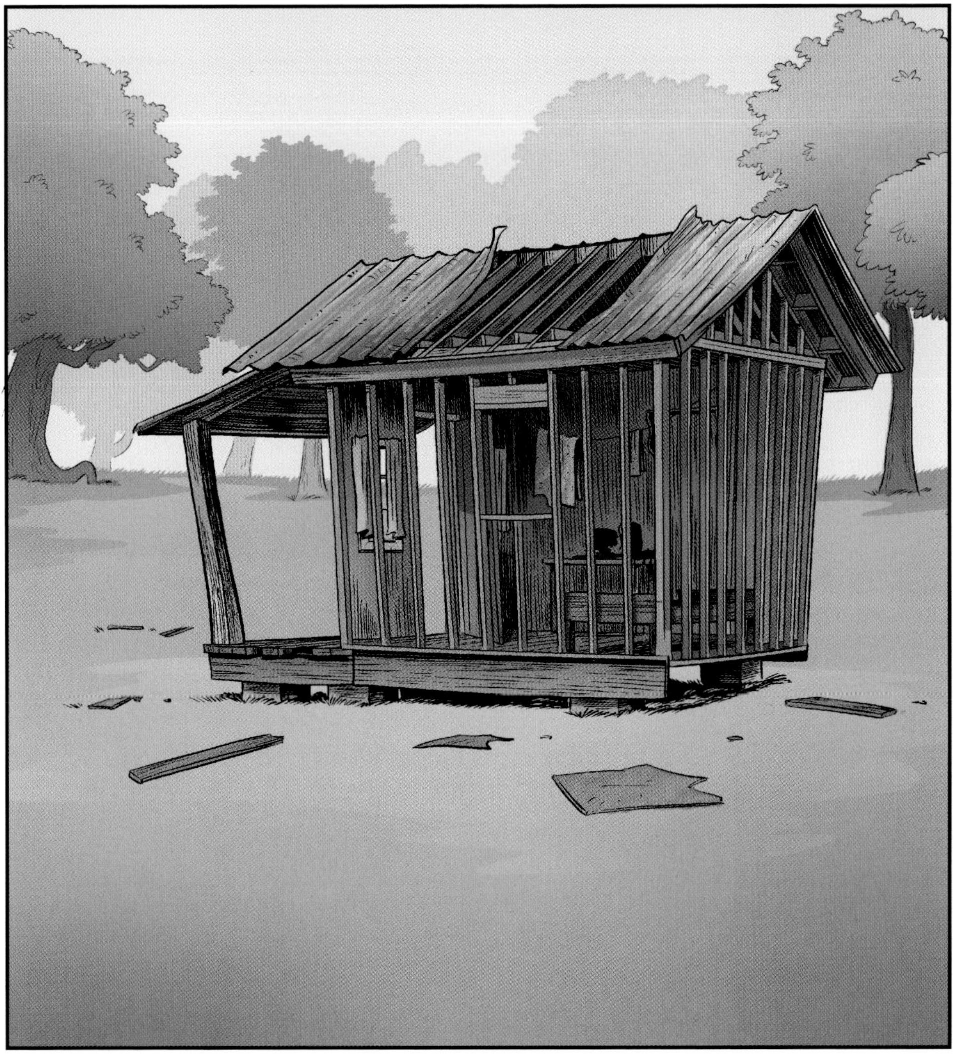

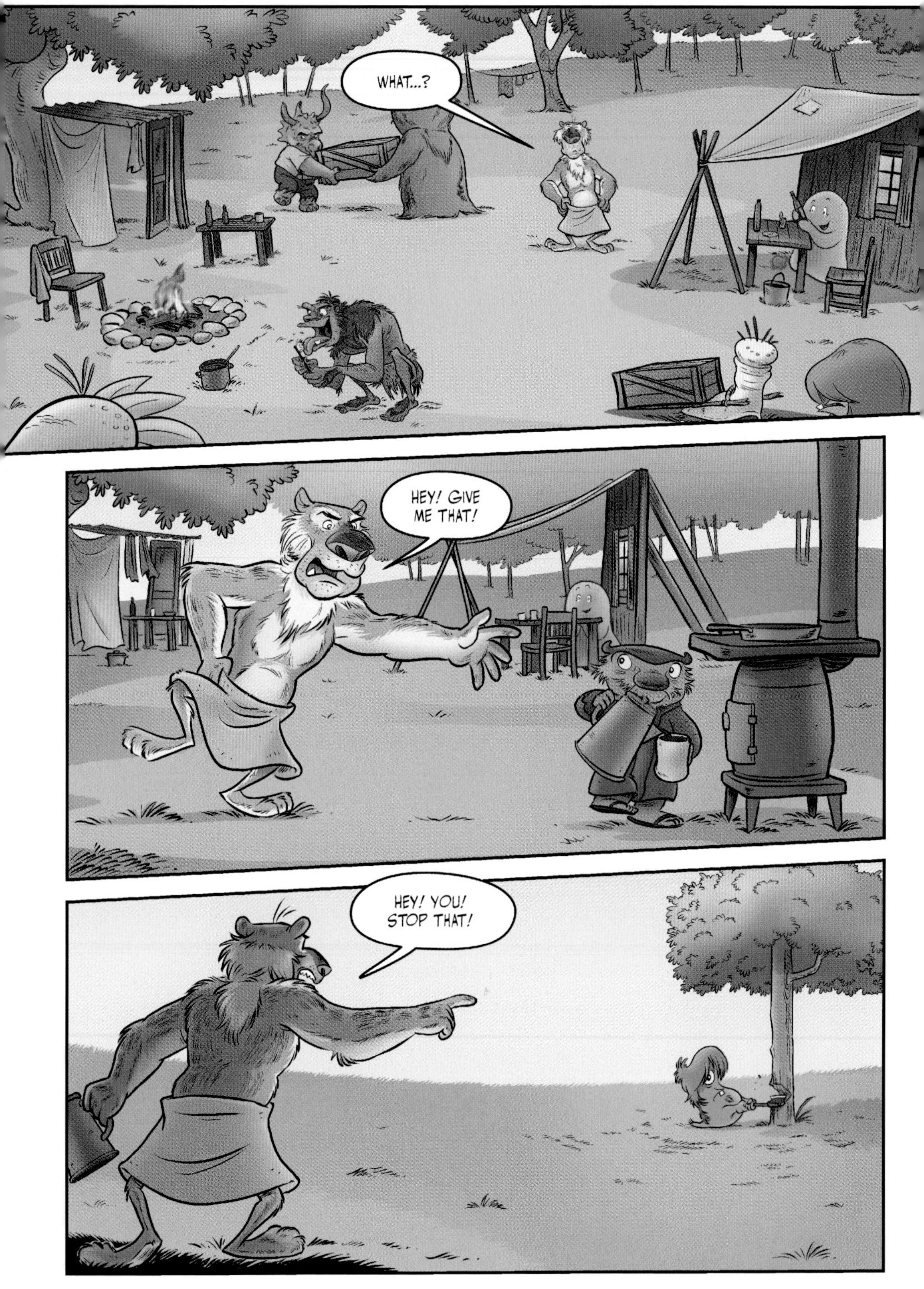
WHAT...?
HEY! GIVE ME THAT!
HEY! YOU! STOP THAT!

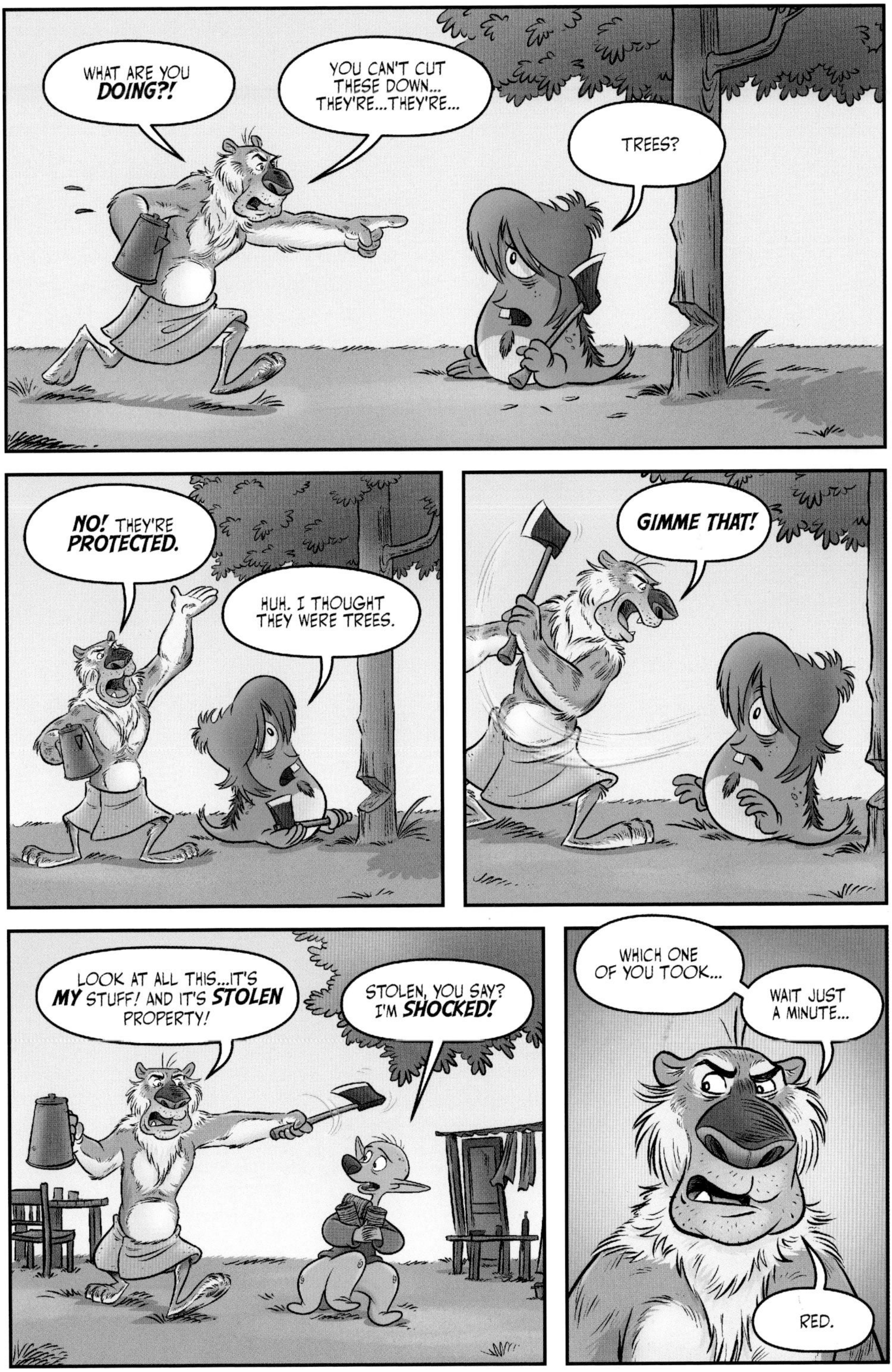
WHAT ARE YOU **DOING?!**
YOU CAN'T CUT THESE DOWN... THEY'RE...THEY'RE...
TREES?
NO! THEY'RE **PROTECTED.**
HUH. I THOUGHT THEY WERE TREES.
GIMME THAT!
LOOK AT ALL THIS...IT'S ***MY*** STUFF! AND IT'S **STOLEN** PROPERTY!
STOLEN, YOU SAY? I'M **SHOCKED!**
WHICH ONE OF YOU TOOK...
WAIT JUST A MINUTE...
RED.

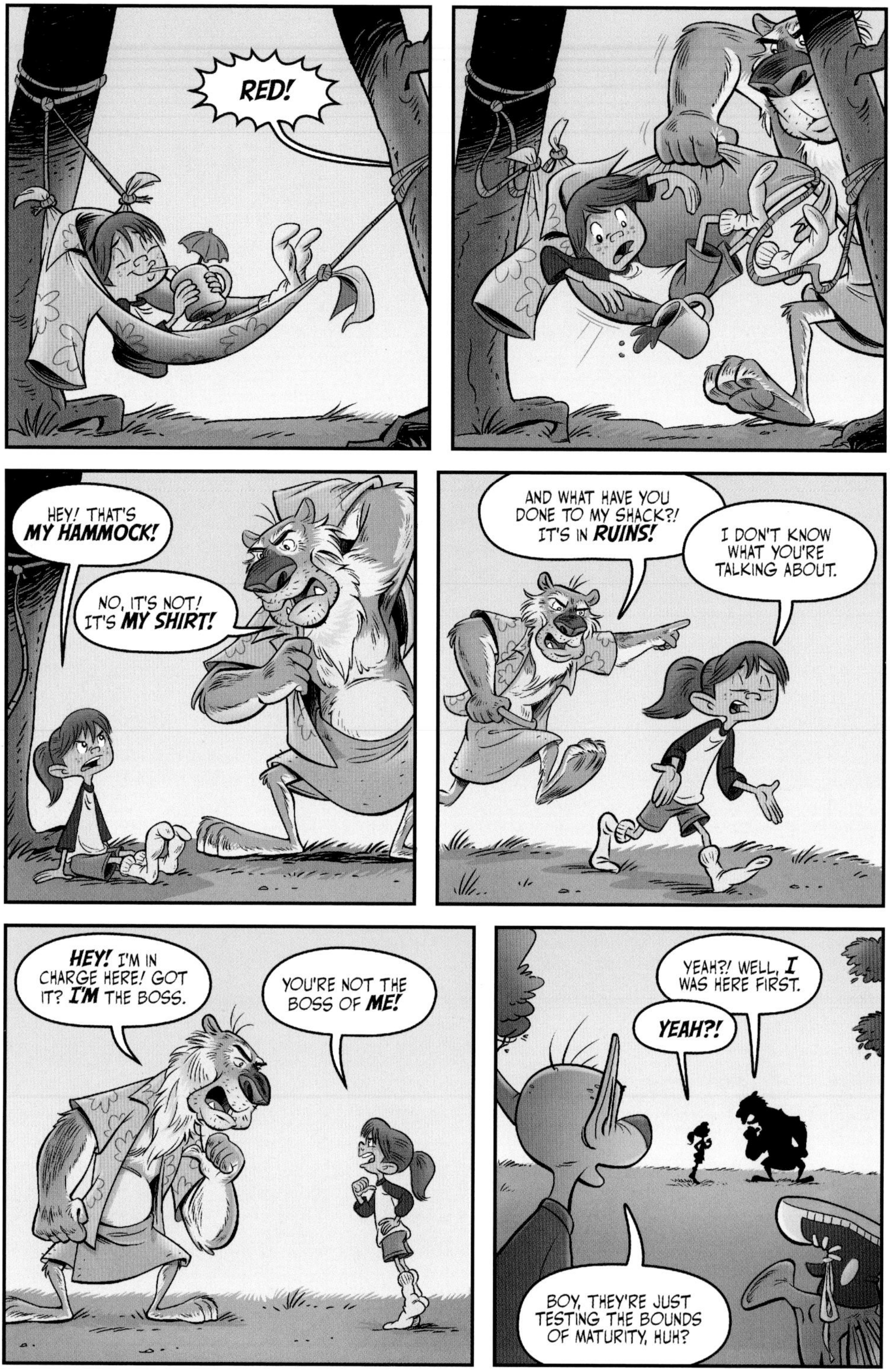

RED!
HEY! THAT'S MY HAMMOCK!
NO, IT'S NOT! IT'S MY SHIRT!
AND WHAT HAVE YOU DONE TO MY SHACK?! IT'S IN RUINS!
I DON'T KNOW WHAT YOU'RE TALKING ABOUT.
HEY! I'M IN CHARGE HERE! GOT IT? I'M THE BOSS.
YOU'RE NOT THE BOSS OF ME!
YEAH?! WELL, I WAS HERE FIRST.
YEAH?!
BOY, THEY'RE JUST TESTING THE BOUNDS OF MATURITY, HUH?

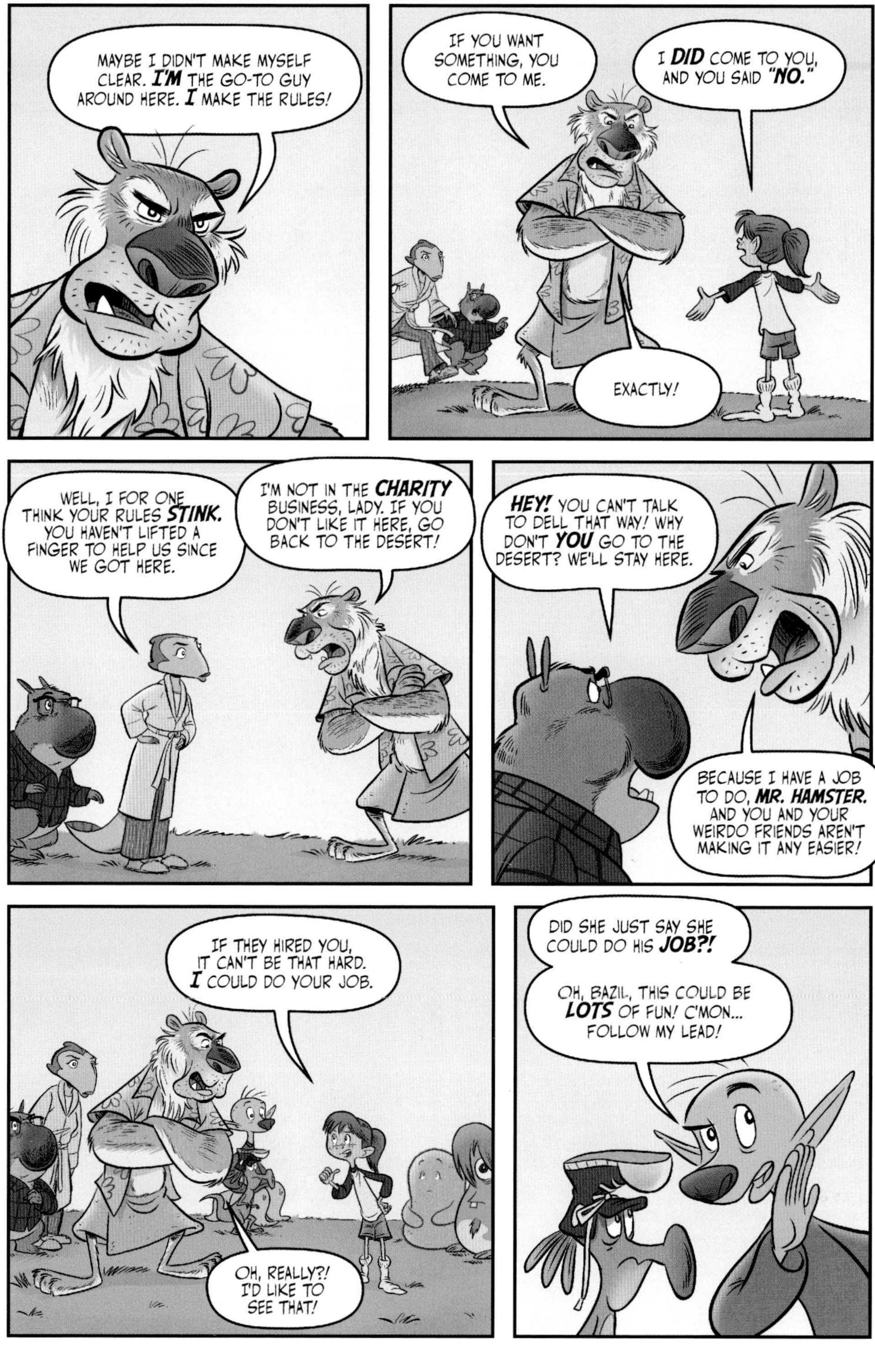
MAYBE I DIDN'T MAKE MYSELF CLEAR. **I'M** THE GO-TO GUY AROUND HERE. **I** MAKE THE RULES!
IF YOU WANT SOMETHING, YOU COME TO ME.
I **DID** COME TO YOU, AND YOU SAID **"NO."**
EXACTLY!
WELL, I FOR ONE THINK YOUR RULES **STINK.** YOU HAVEN'T LIFTED A FINGER TO HELP US SINCE WE GOT HERE.
I'M NOT IN THE **CHARITY** BUSINESS, LADY. IF YOU DON'T LIKE IT HERE, GO BACK TO THE DESERT!
HEY! YOU CAN'T TALK TO DELL THAT WAY! WHY DON'T **YOU** GO TO THE DESERT? WE'LL STAY HERE.
BECAUSE I HAVE A JOB TO DO, **MR. HAMSTER.** AND YOU AND YOUR WEIRDO FRIENDS AREN'T MAKING IT ANY EASIER!
IF THEY HIRED YOU, IT CAN'T BE THAT HARD. **I** COULD DO YOUR JOB.
OH, REALLY?! I'D LIKE TO SEE THAT!
DID SHE JUST SAY SHE COULD DO HIS **JOB?!**
OH, BAZIL, THIS COULD BE **LOTS** OF FUN! C'MON... FOLLOW MY LEAD!

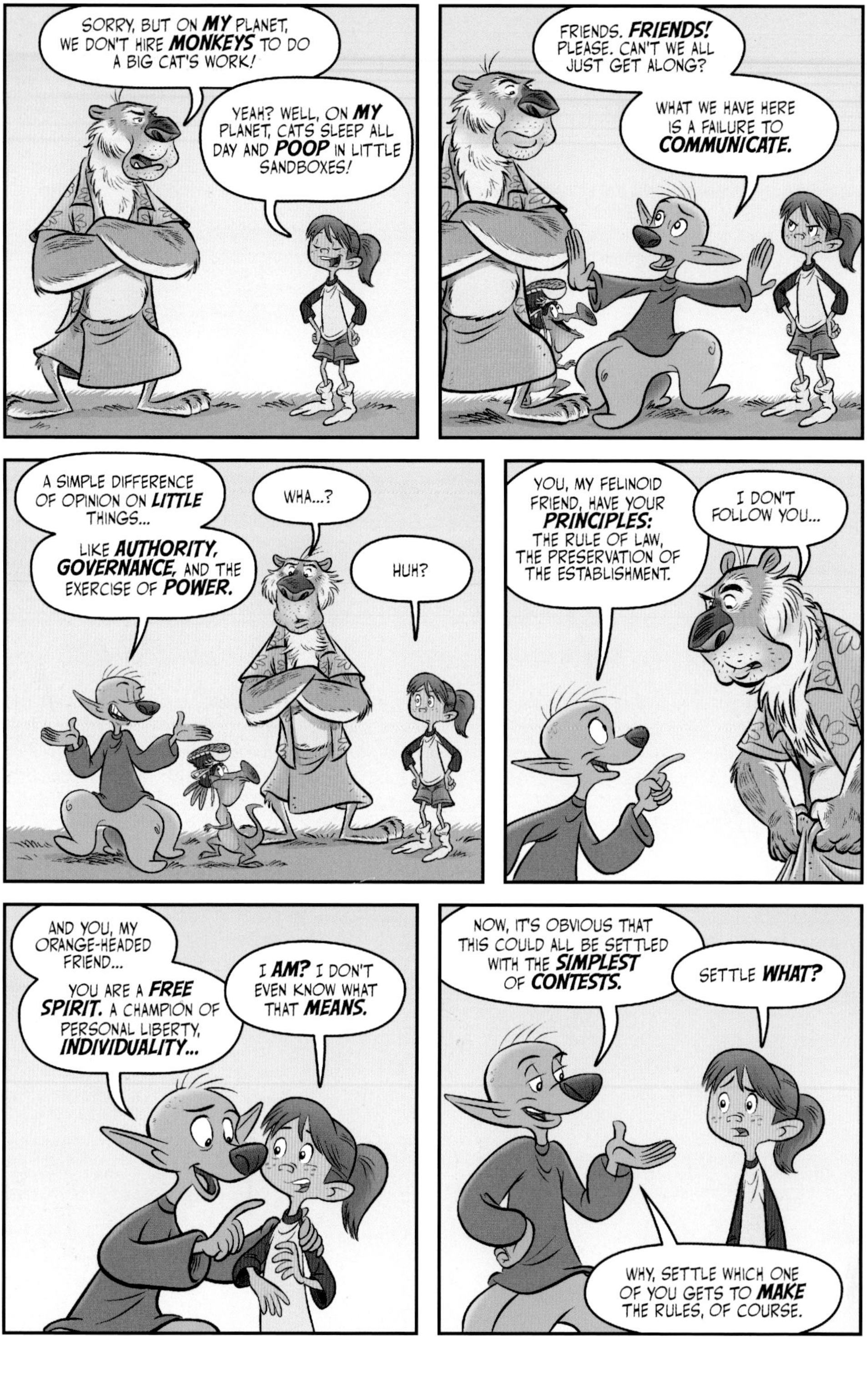

SORRY, BUT ON MY PLANET, WE DON'T HIRE MONKEYS TO DO A BIG CAT'S WORK!
YEAH? WELL, ON MY PLANET, CATS SLEEP ALL DAY AND POOP IN LITTLE SANDBOXES!
FRIENDS. FRIENDS! PLEASE. CAN'T WE ALL JUST GET ALONG?
WHAT WE HAVE HERE IS A FAILURE TO COMMUNICATE.
A SIMPLE DIFFERENCE OF OPINION ON LITTLE THINGS...
LIKE AUTHORITY, GOVERNANCE, AND THE EXERCISE OF POWER.
WHA...?
HUH?
YOU, MY FELINOID FRIEND, HAVE YOUR PRINCIPLES: THE RULE OF LAW, THE PRESERVATION OF THE ESTABLISHMENT.
I DON'T FOLLOW YOU...
AND YOU, MY ORANGE-HEADED FRIEND...
YOU ARE A FREE SPIRIT. A CHAMPION OF PERSONAL LIBERTY, INDIVIDUALITY...
I AM? I DON'T EVEN KNOW WHAT THAT MEANS.
NOW, IT'S OBVIOUS THAT THIS COULD ALL BE SETTLED WITH THE SIMPLEST OF CONTESTS.
SETTLE WHAT?
WHY, SETTLE WHICH ONE OF YOU GETS TO MAKE THE RULES, OF COURSE.

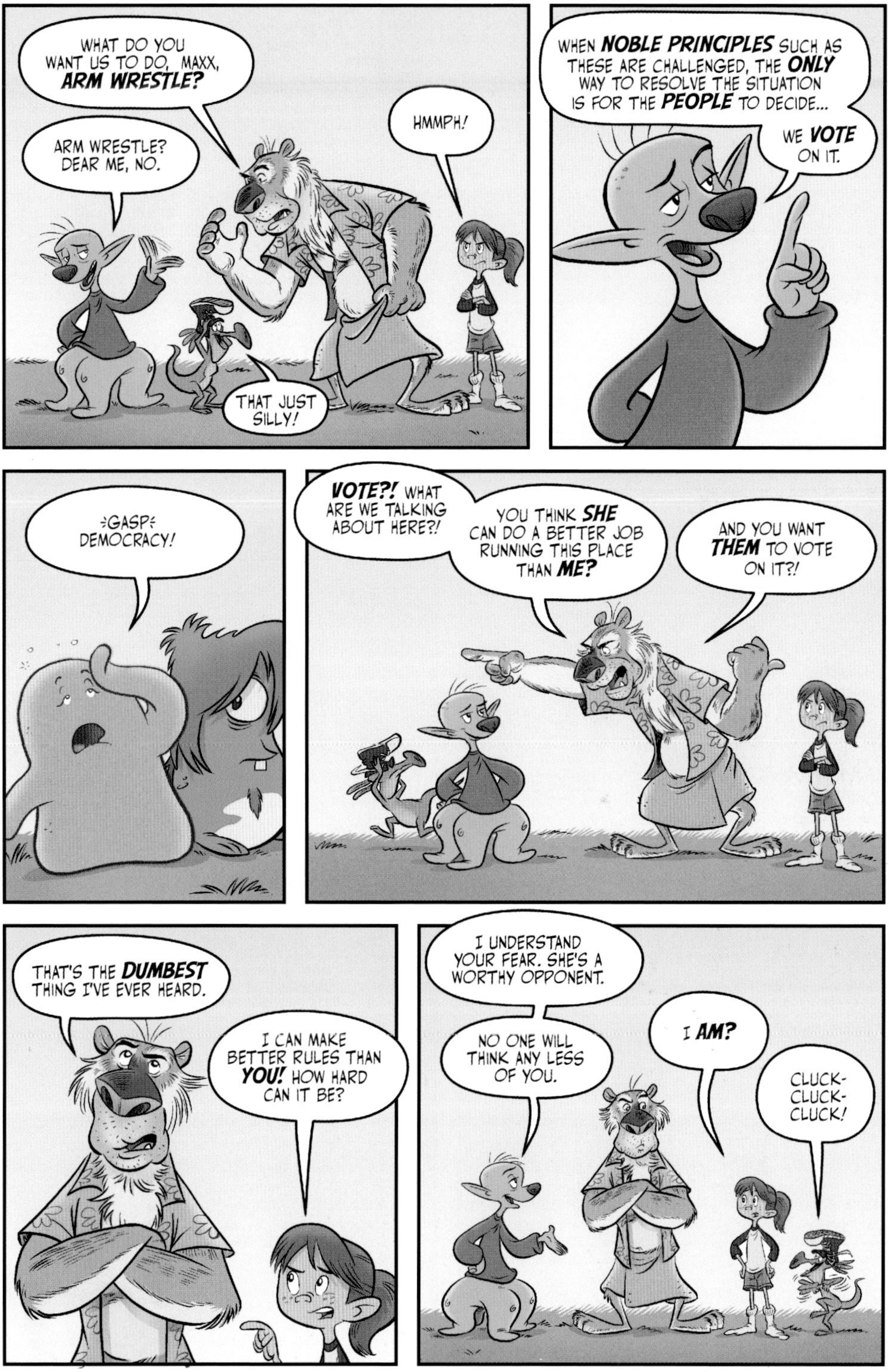
WHAT DO YOU WANT US TO DO, MAXX, ARM WRESTLE?
ARM WRESTLE? DEAR ME, NO.
HMMPH!
THAT JUST SILLY!
WHEN NOBLE PRINCIPLES SUCH AS THESE ARE CHALLENGED, THE ONLY WAY TO RESOLVE THE SITUATION IS FOR THE PEOPLE TO DECIDE...
WE VOTE ON IT.
GASP DEMOCRACY!
VOTE?! WHAT ARE WE TALKING ABOUT HERE?!
YOU THINK SHE CAN DO A BETTER JOB RUNNING THIS PLACE THAN ME?
AND YOU WANT THEM TO VOTE ON IT?!
THAT'S THE DUMBEST THING I'VE EVER HEARD.
I CAN MAKE BETTER RULES THAN YOU! HOW HARD CAN IT BE?
I UNDERSTAND YOUR FEAR. SHE'S A WORTHY OPPONENT.
NO ONE WILL THINK ANY LESS OF YOU.
I AM?
CLUCK-CLUCK-CLUCK!

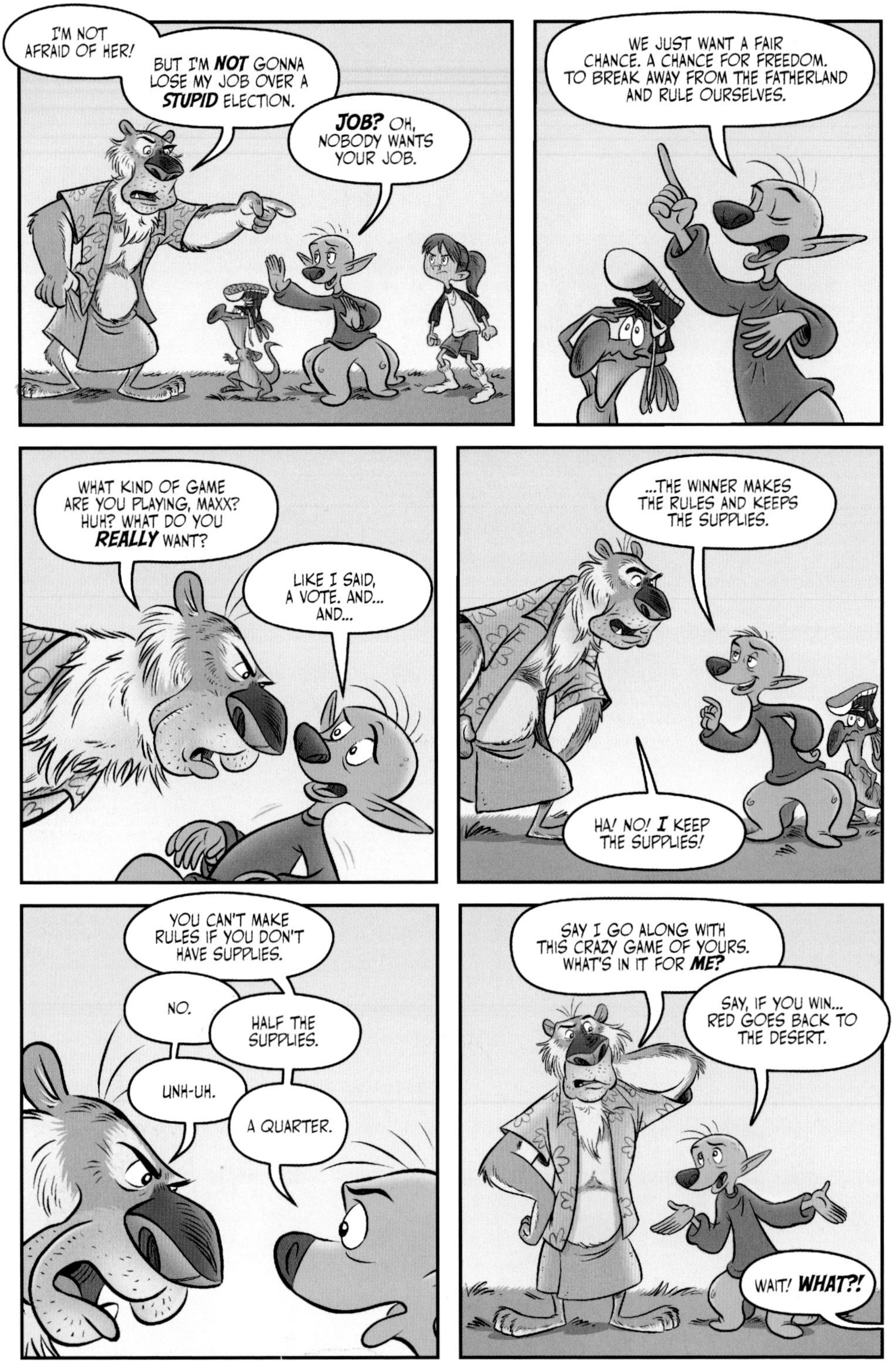
I'M NOT AFRAID OF HER!
BUT I'M NOT GONNA LOSE MY JOB OVER A STUPID ELECTION.
JOB? OH, NOBODY WANTS YOUR JOB.
WE JUST WANT A FAIR CHANCE. A CHANCE FOR FREEDOM. TO BREAK AWAY FROM THE FATHERLAND AND RULE OURSELVES.
WHAT KIND OF GAME ARE YOU PLAYING, MAXX? HUH? WHAT DO YOU REALLY WANT?
LIKE I SAID, A VOTE. AND... AND...
...THE WINNER MAKES THE RULES AND KEEPS THE SUPPLIES.
HA! NO! I KEEP THE SUPPLIES!
YOU CAN'T MAKE RULES IF YOU DON'T HAVE SUPPLIES.
NO.
HALF THE SUPPLIES.
UNH-UH.
A QUARTER.
SAY I GO ALONG WITH THIS CRAZY GAME OF YOURS. WHAT'S IN IT FOR ME?
SAY, IF YOU WIN... RED GOES BACK TO THE DESERT.
WAIT! WHAT?!

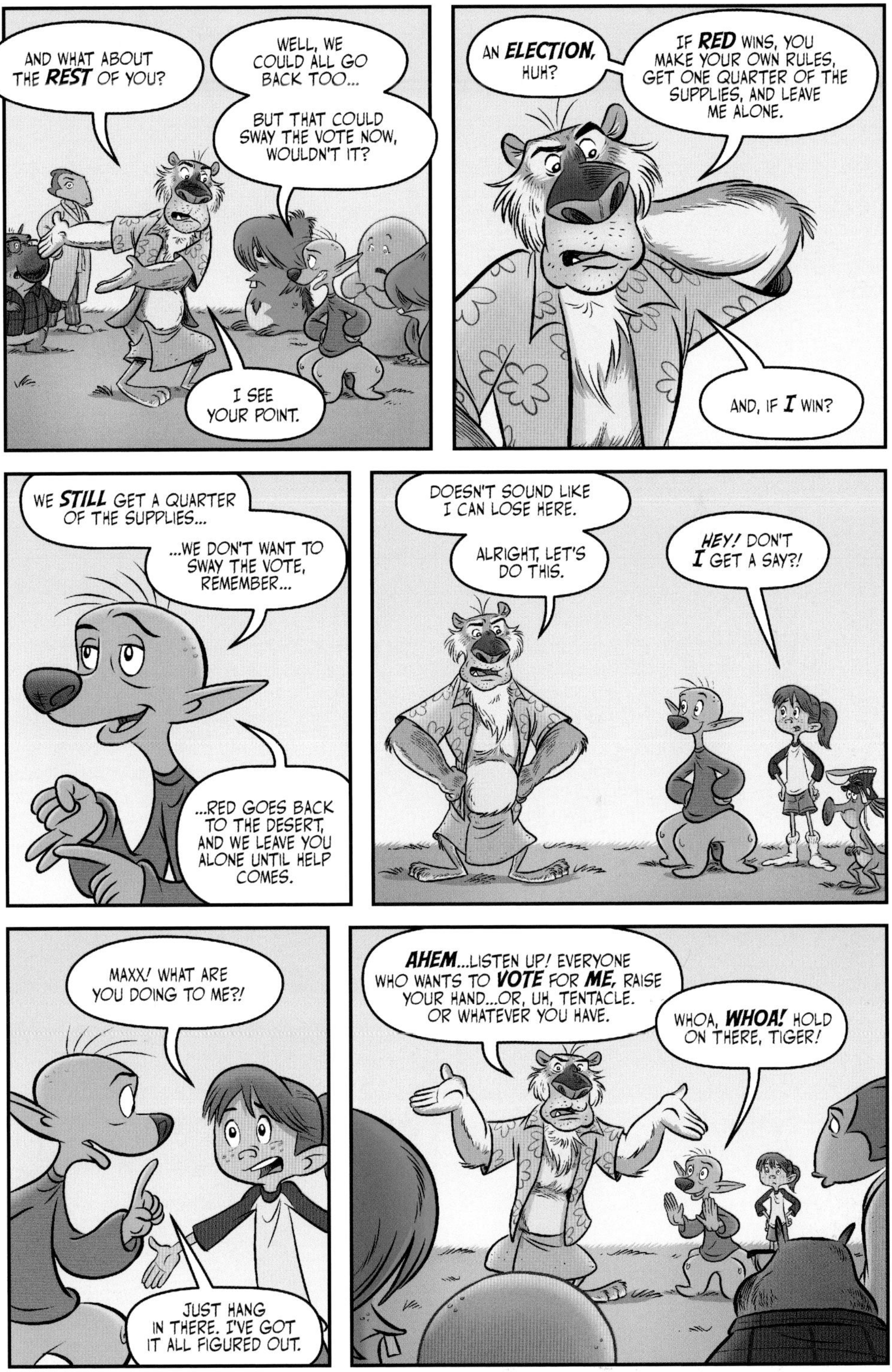
AND WHAT ABOUT THE **REST** OF YOU?
WELL, WE COULD ALL GO BACK TOO...
BUT THAT COULD SWAY THE VOTE NOW, WOULDN'T IT?
I SEE YOUR POINT.
AN **ELECTION,** HUH?
IF **RED** WINS, YOU MAKE YOUR OWN RULES, GET ONE QUARTER OF THE SUPPLIES, AND LEAVE ME ALONE.
AND, IF ***I*** WIN?
WE **STILL** GET A QUARTER OF THE SUPPLIES...
...WE DON'T WANT TO SWAY THE VOTE, REMEMBER...
...RED GOES BACK TO THE DESERT, AND WE LEAVE YOU ALONE UNTIL HELP COMES.
DOESN'T SOUND LIKE I CAN LOSE HERE.
ALRIGHT, LET'S DO THIS.
HEY! DON'T ***I*** GET A SAY?!
MAXX! WHAT ARE YOU DOING TO ME?!
JUST HANG IN THERE. I'VE GOT IT ALL FIGURED OUT.
AHEM...LISTEN UP! EVERYONE WHO WANTS TO **VOTE** FOR **ME,** RAISE YOUR HAND...OR, UH, TENTACLE. OR WHATEVER YOU HAVE.
WHOA, **WHOA!** HOLD ON THERE, TIGER!

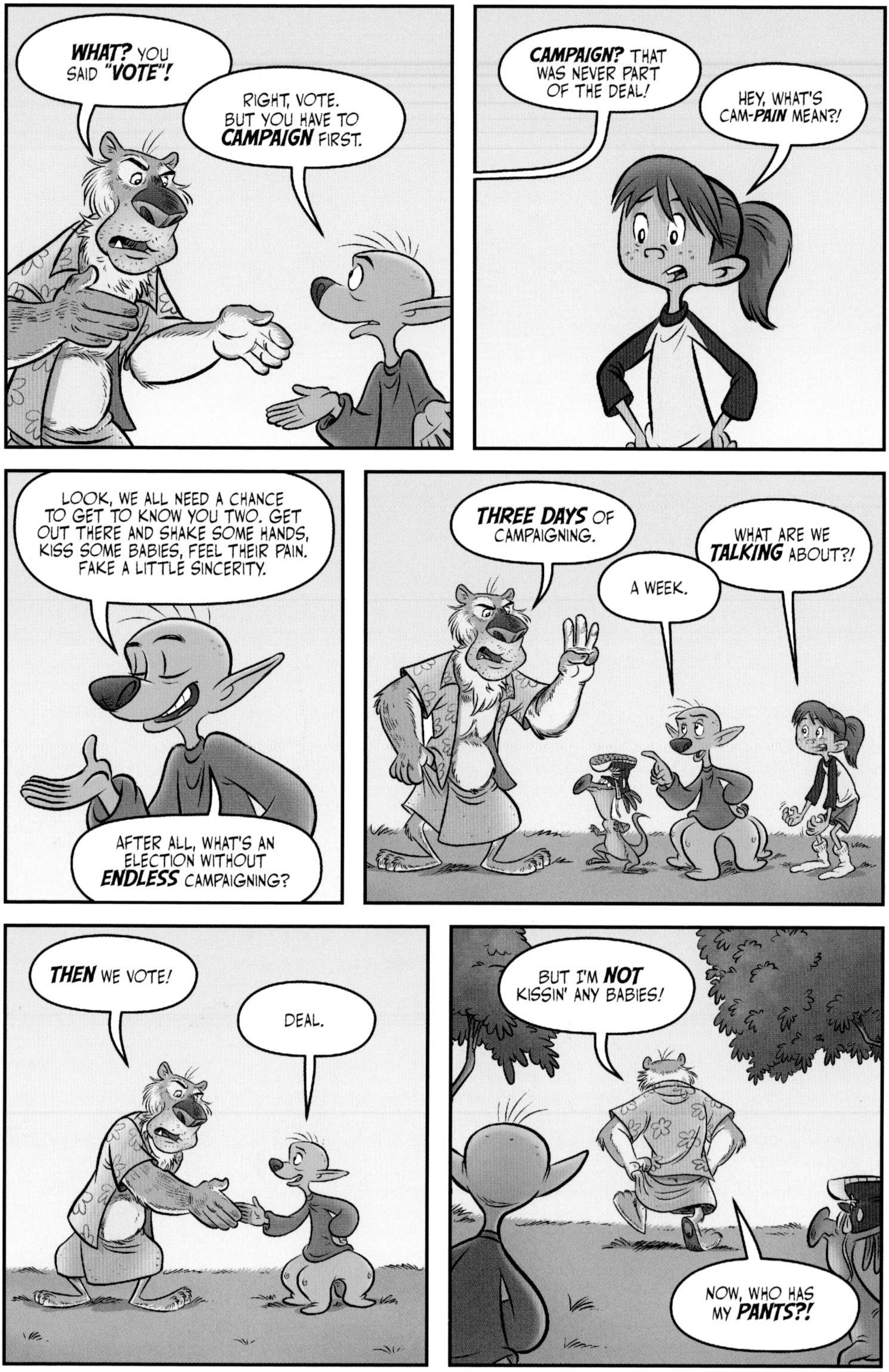
WHAT? YOU SAID "VOTE"!
RIGHT, VOTE. BUT YOU HAVE TO CAMPAIGN FIRST.
CAMPAIGN? THAT WAS NEVER PART OF THE DEAL!
HEY, WHAT'S CAM-PAIN MEAN?!
LOOK, WE ALL NEED A CHANCE TO GET TO KNOW YOU TWO. GET OUT THERE AND SHAKE SOME HANDS, KISS SOME BABIES, FEEL THEIR PAIN. FAKE A LITTLE SINCERITY.
AFTER ALL, WHAT'S AN ELECTION WITHOUT ENDLESS CAMPAIGNING?
THREE DAYS OF CAMPAIGNING.
A WEEK.
WHAT ARE WE TALKING ABOUT?!
THEN WE VOTE!
DEAL.
BUT I'M NOT KISSIN' ANY BABIES!
NOW, WHO HAS MY PANTS?!

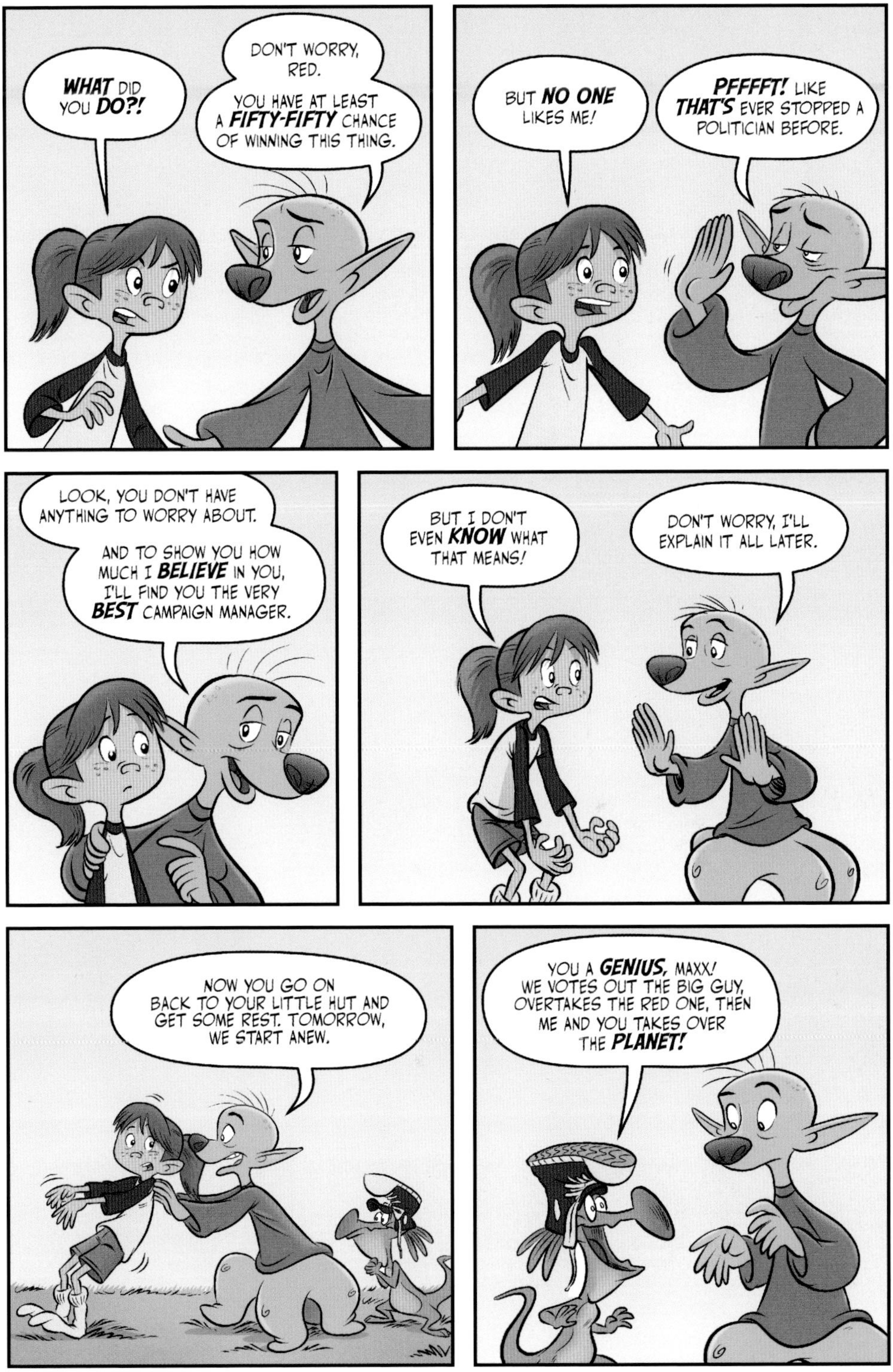
WHAT DID YOU DO?!
DON'T WORRY, RED.
YOU HAVE AT LEAST A FIFTY-FIFTY CHANCE OF WINNING THIS THING.
BUT NO ONE LIKES ME!
PFFFFT! LIKE THAT'S EVER STOPPED A POLITICIAN BEFORE.
LOOK, YOU DON'T HAVE ANYTHING TO WORRY ABOUT.
AND TO SHOW YOU HOW MUCH I BELIEVE IN YOU, I'LL FIND YOU THE VERY BEST CAMPAIGN MANAGER.
BUT I DON'T EVEN KNOW WHAT THAT MEANS!
DON'T WORRY, I'LL EXPLAIN IT ALL LATER.
NOW YOU GO ON BACK TO YOUR LITTLE HUT AND GET SOME REST. TOMORROW, WE START ANEW.
YOU A GENIUS, MAXX! WE VOTES OUT THE BIG GUY, OVERTAKES THE RED ONE, THEN ME AND YOU TAKES OVER THE PLANET!

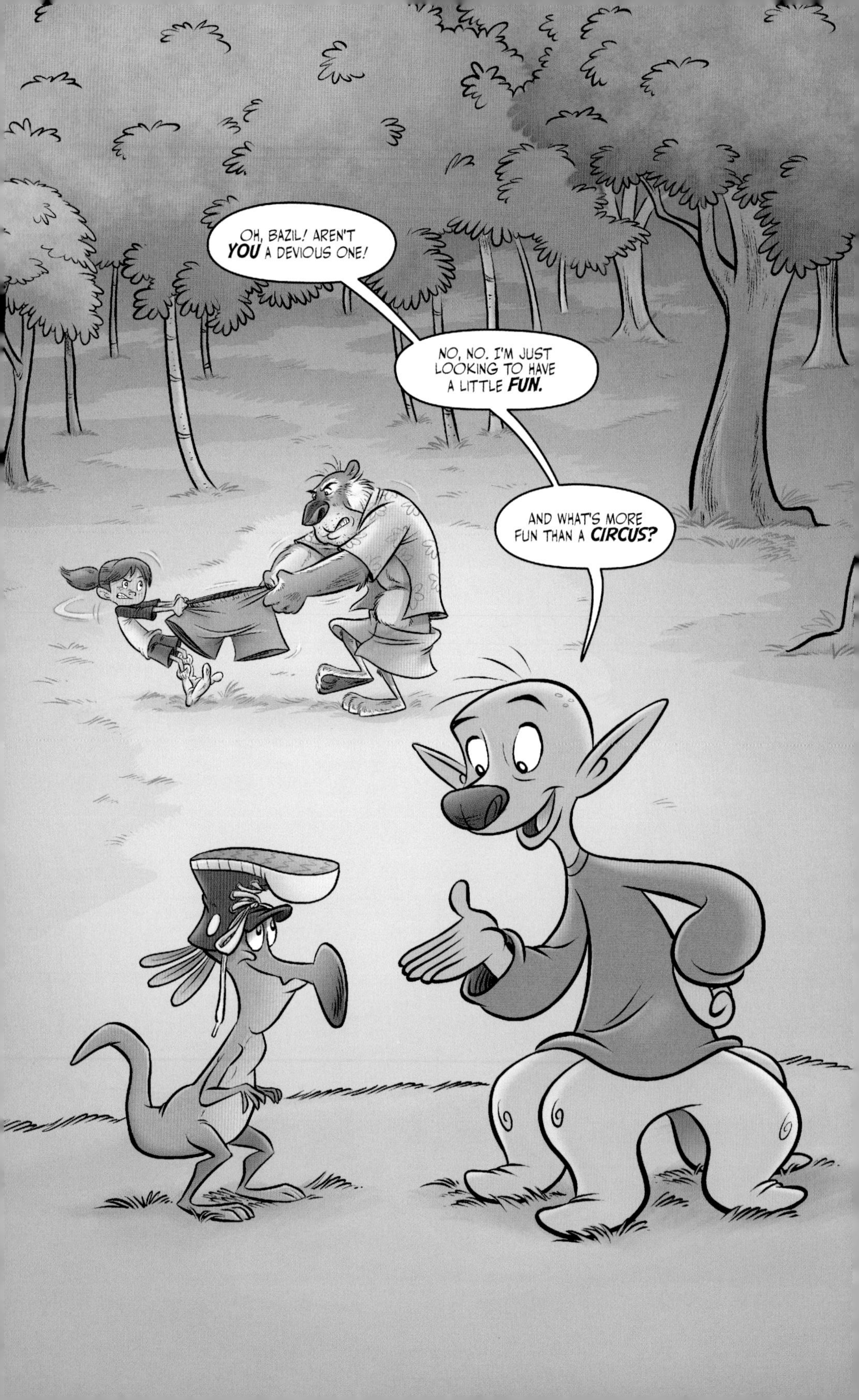
OH, BAZIL! AREN'T YOU A DEVIOUS ONE!
NO, NO. I'M JUST LOOKING TO HAVE A LITTLE FUN.
AND WHAT'S MORE FUN THAN A CIRCUS?

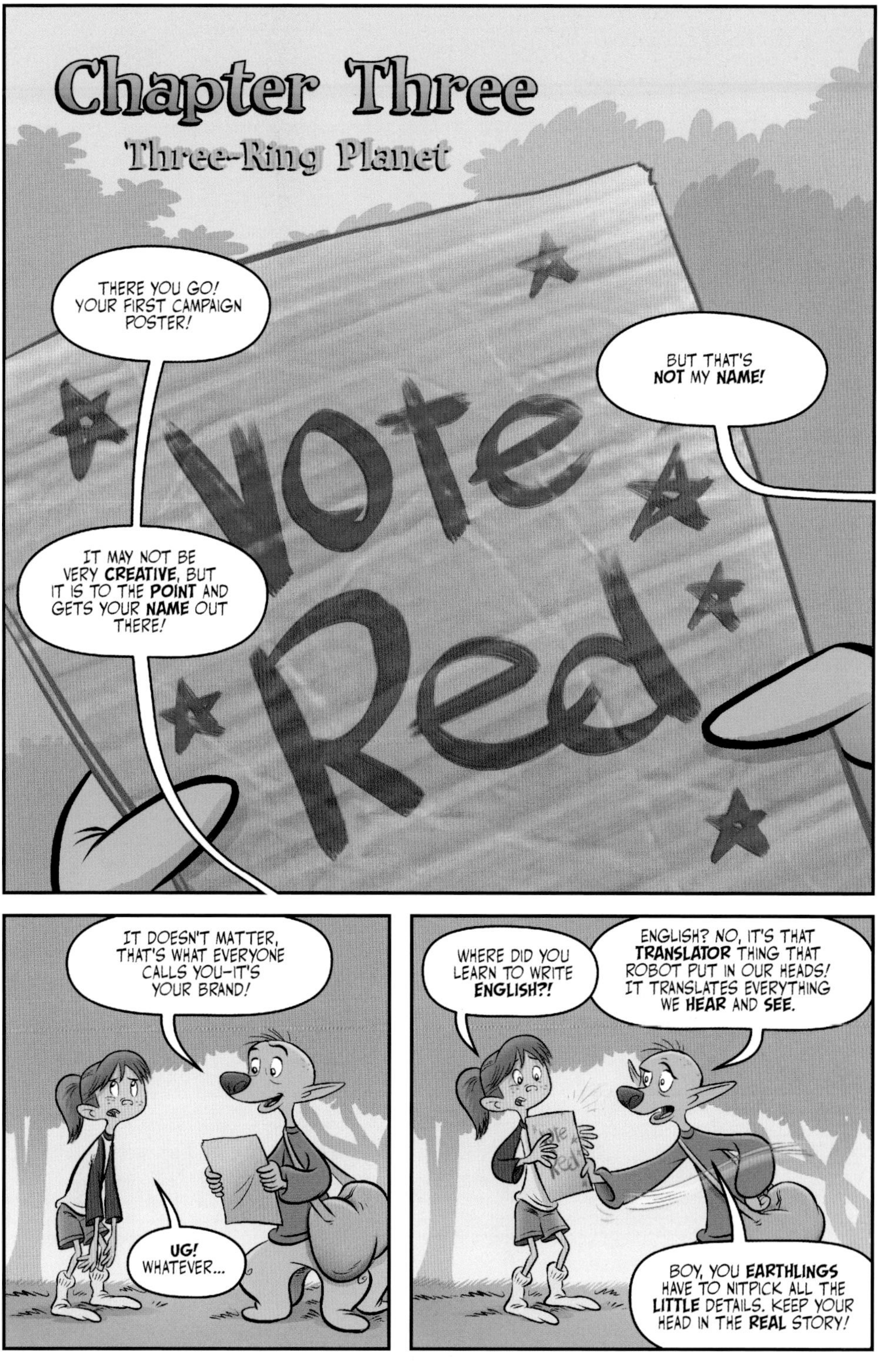
Chapter Three
Three-Ring Planet
THERE YOU GO! YOUR FIRST CAMPAIGN POSTER!
Vote Red
BUT THAT'S **NOT** MY **NAME!**
IT MAY NOT BE VERY **CREATIVE**, BUT IT IS TO THE **POINT** AND GETS YOUR **NAME** OUT THERE!
IT DOESN'T MATTER, THAT'S WHAT EVERYONE CALLS YOU—IT'S YOUR BRAND!
UG! WHATEVER...
WHERE DID YOU LEARN TO WRITE **ENGLISH?!**
ENGLISH? NO, IT'S THAT **TRANSLATOR** THING THAT ROBOT PUT IN OUR HEADS! IT TRANSLATES EVERYTHING WE **HEAR** AND **SEE.**
BOY, YOU **EARTHLINGS** HAVE TO NITPICK ALL THE **LITTLE** DETAILS. KEEP YOUR HEAD IN THE **REAL** STORY!

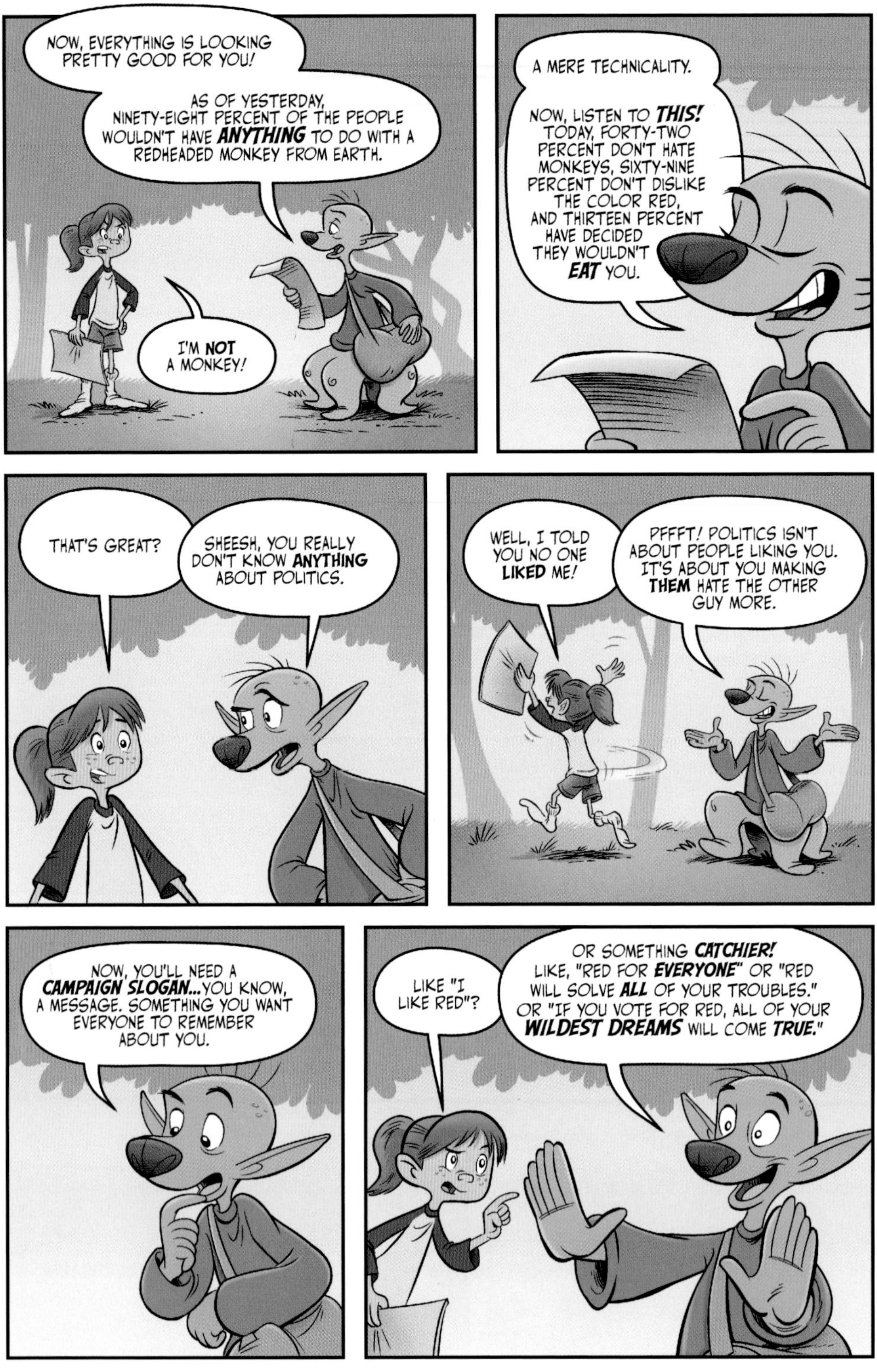
NOW, EVERYTHING IS LOOKING PRETTY GOOD FOR YOU!
AS OF YESTERDAY, NINETY-EIGHT PERCENT OF THE PEOPLE WOULDN'T HAVE ANYTHING TO DO WITH A REDHEADED MONKEY FROM EARTH.
I'M NOT A MONKEY!
A MERE TECHNICALITY.
NOW, LISTEN TO THIS! TODAY, FORTY-TWO PERCENT DON'T HATE MONKEYS, SIXTY-NINE PERCENT DON'T DISLIKE THE COLOR RED, AND THIRTEEN PERCENT HAVE DECIDED THEY WOULDN'T EAT YOU.
THAT'S GREAT?
SHEESH, YOU REALLY DON'T KNOW ANYTHING ABOUT POLITICS.
WELL, I TOLD YOU NO ONE LIKED ME!
PFFFT! POLITICS ISN'T ABOUT PEOPLE LIKING YOU. IT'S ABOUT YOU MAKING THEM HATE THE OTHER GUY MORE.
NOW, YOU'LL NEED A CAMPAIGN SLOGAN...YOU KNOW, A MESSAGE. SOMETHING YOU WANT EVERYONE TO REMEMBER ABOUT YOU.
LIKE "I LIKE RED"?
OR SOMETHING CATCHIER! LIKE, "RED FOR EVERYONE" OR "RED WILL SOLVE ALL OF YOUR TROUBLES." OR "IF YOU VOTE FOR RED, ALL OF YOUR WILDEST DREAMS WILL COME TRUE."

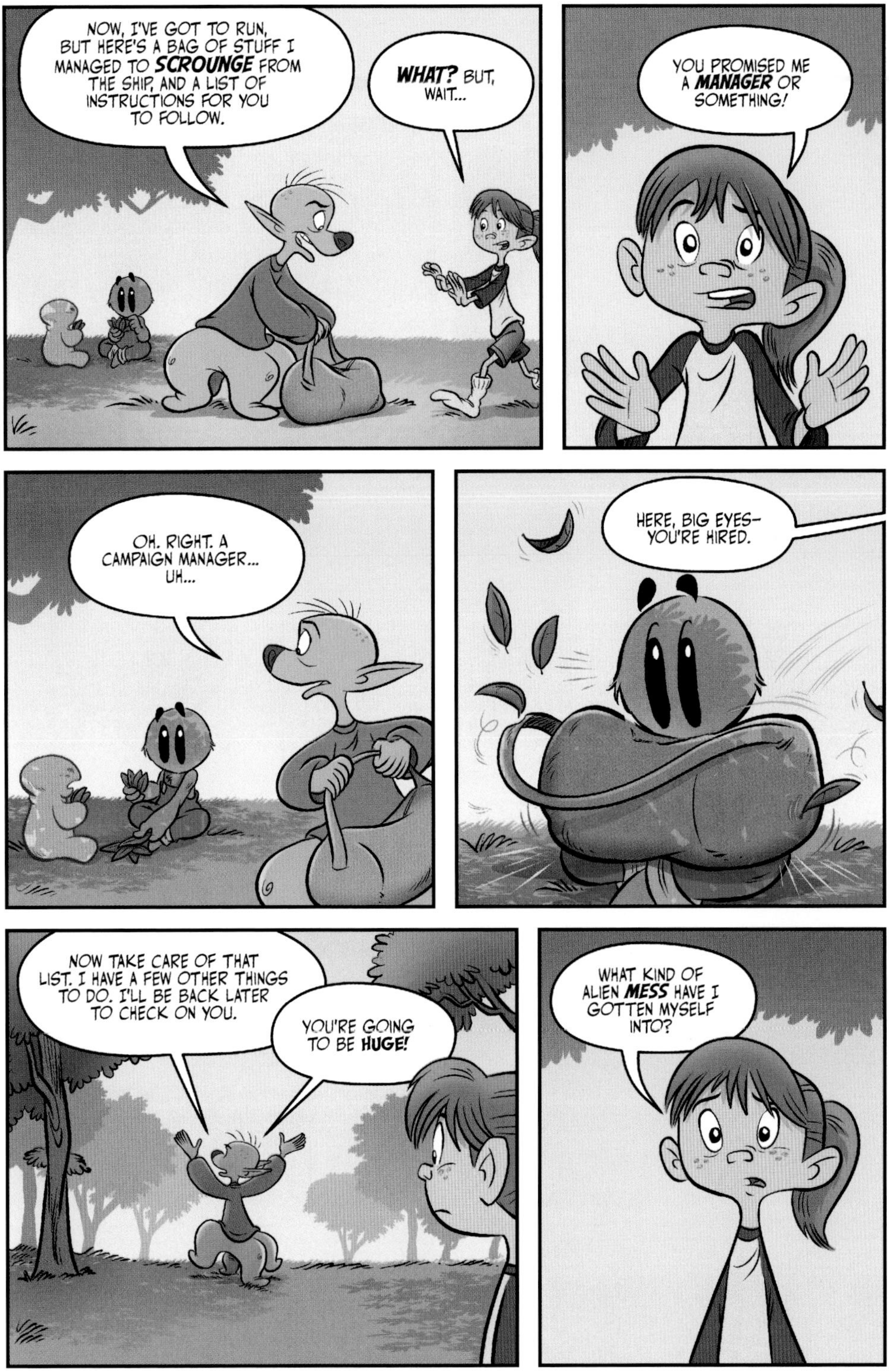
NOW, I'VE GOT TO RUN, BUT HERE'S A BAG OF STUFF I MANAGED TO SCROUNGE FROM THE SHIP, AND A LIST OF INSTRUCTIONS FOR YOU TO FOLLOW.
WHAT? BUT, WAIT...
YOU PROMISED ME A MANAGER OR SOMETHING!
OH. RIGHT. A CAMPAIGN MANAGER... UH...
HERE, BIG EYES– YOU'RE HIRED.
NOW TAKE CARE OF THAT LIST. I HAVE A FEW OTHER THINGS TO DO. I'LL BE BACK LATER TO CHECK ON YOU.
YOU'RE GOING TO BE HUGE!
WHAT KIND OF ALIEN MESS HAVE I GOTTEN MYSELF INTO?

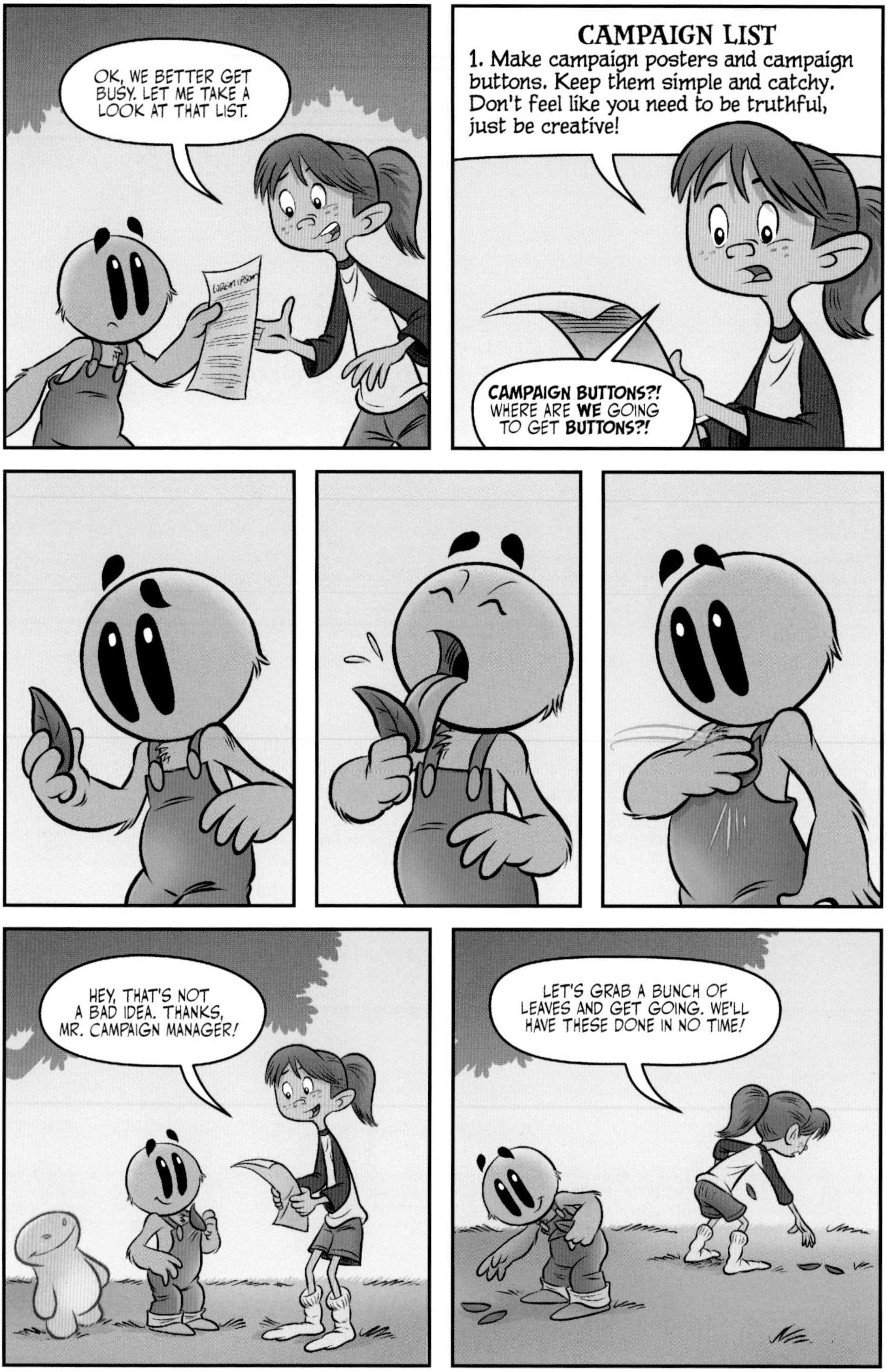
OK, WE BETTER GET BUSY. LET ME TAKE A LOOK AT THAT LIST.
CAMPAIGN LIST
1. Make campaign posters and campaign buttons. Keep them simple and catchy. Don't feel like you need to be truthful, just be creative!
CAMPAIGN BUTTONS?! WHERE ARE WE GOING TO GET BUTTONS?!
HEY, THAT'S NOT A BAD IDEA. THANKS, MR. CAMPAIGN MANAGER!
LET'S GRAB A BUNCH OF LEAVES AND GET GOING. WE'LL HAVE THESE DONE IN NO TIME!

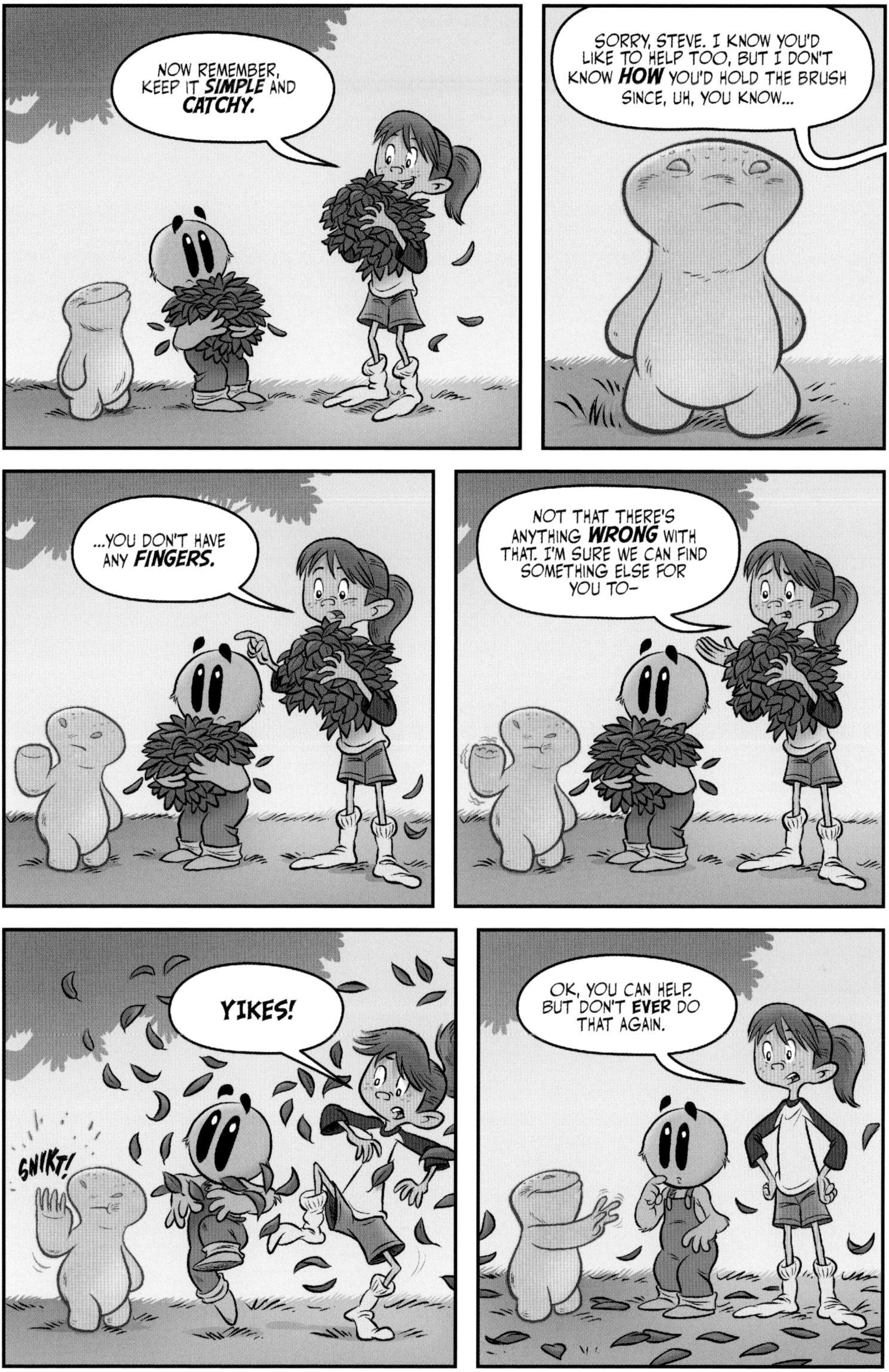
NOW REMEMBER, KEEP IT SIMPLE AND CATCHY.
SORRY, STEVE. I KNOW YOU'D LIKE TO HELP TOO, BUT I DON'T KNOW HOW YOU'D HOLD THE BRUSH SINCE, UH, YOU KNOW...
...YOU DON'T HAVE ANY FINGERS.
NOT THAT THERE'S ANYTHING WRONG WITH THAT. I'M SURE WE CAN FIND SOMETHING ELSE FOR YOU TO-
YIKES!
SNIKT!
OK, YOU CAN HELP. BUT DON'T EVER DO THAT AGAIN.

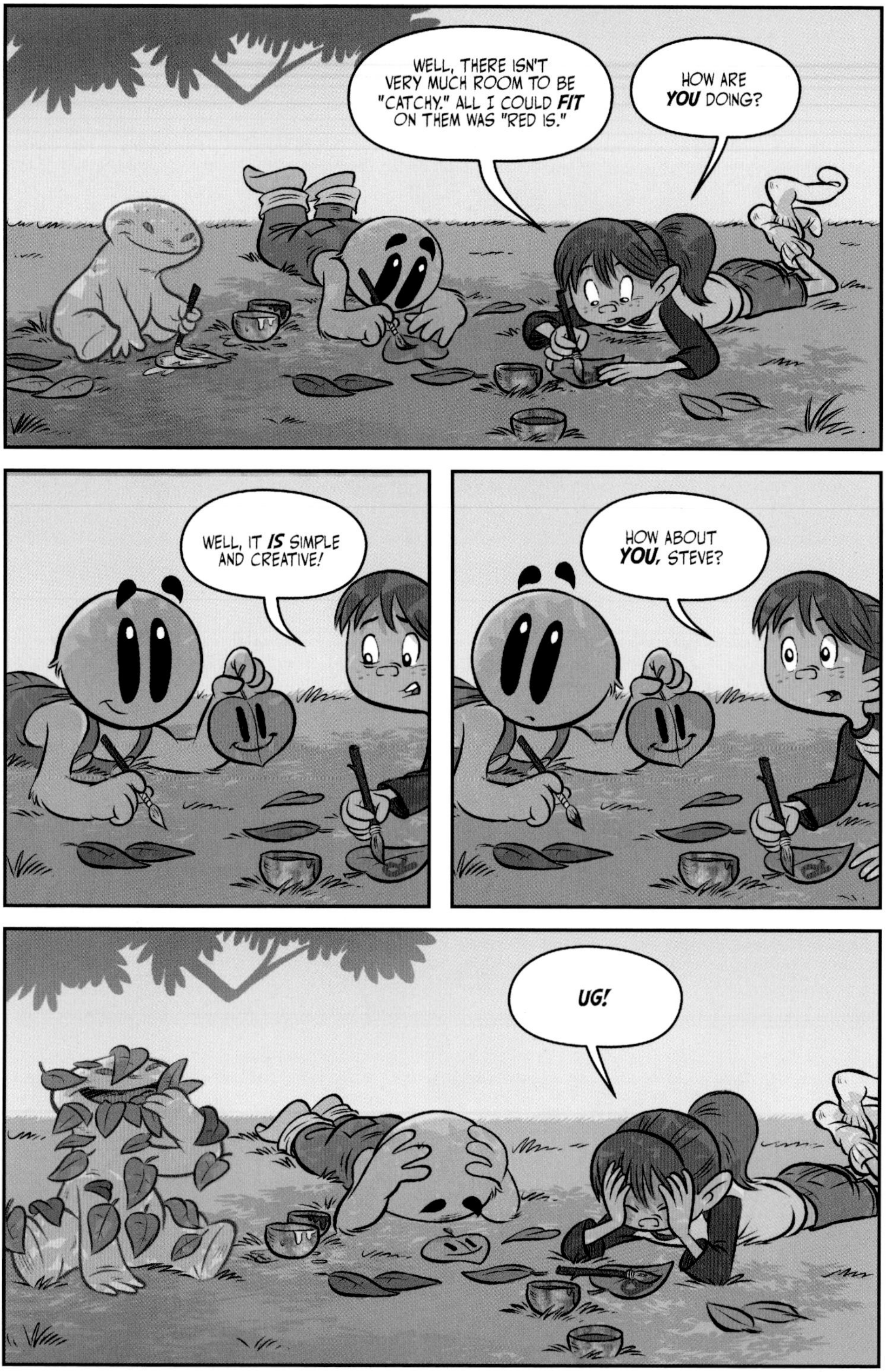
WELL, THERE ISN'T VERY MUCH ROOM TO BE "CATCHY." ALL I COULD FIT ON THEM WAS "RED IS."
HOW ARE YOU DOING?
WELL, IT IS SIMPLE AND CREATIVE!
HOW ABOUT YOU, STEVE?
UG!

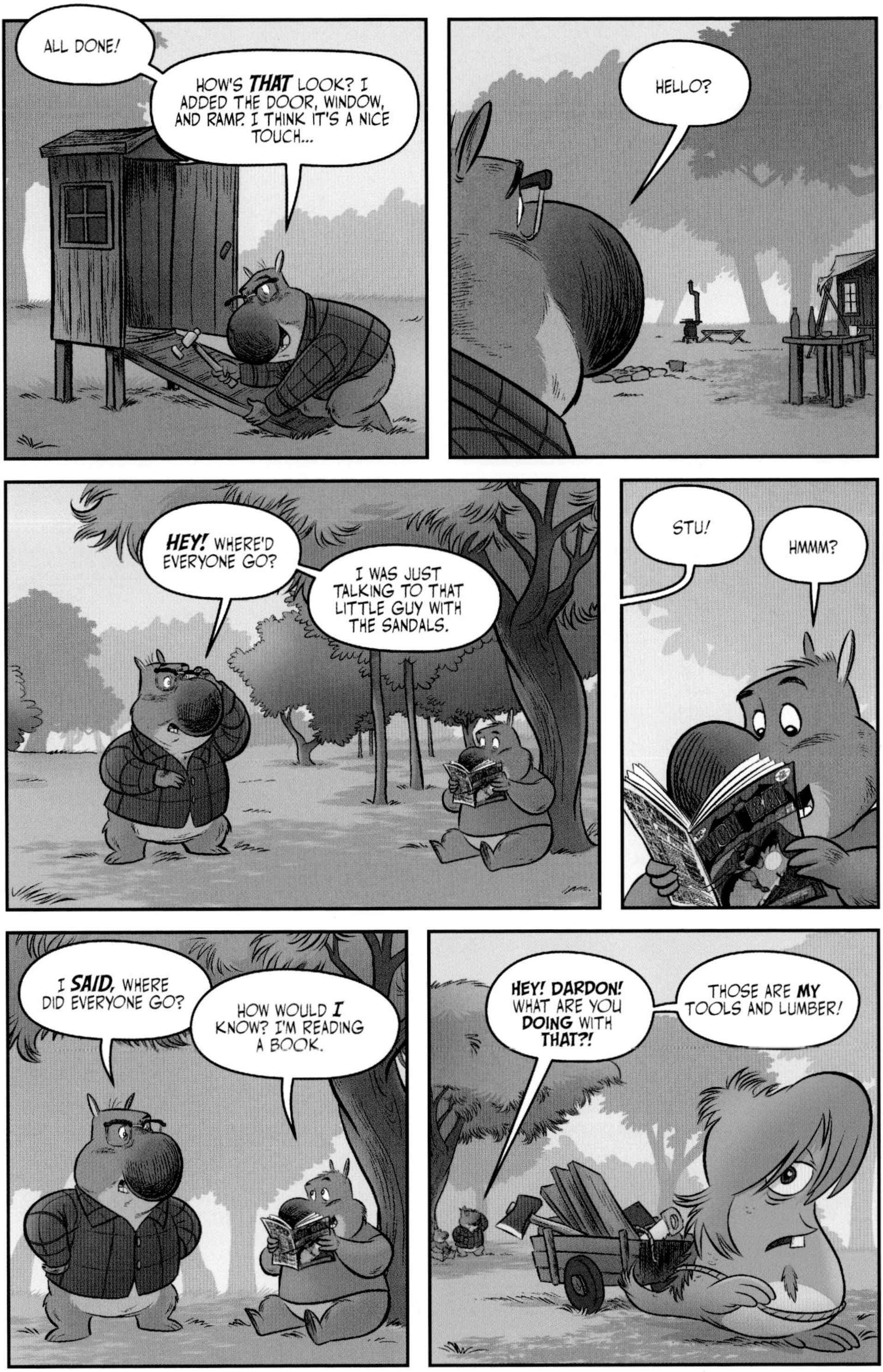
ALL DONE!
HOW'S **THAT** LOOK? I ADDED THE DOOR, WINDOW, AND RAMP. I THINK IT'S A NICE TOUCH...
HELLO?
HEY! WHERE'D EVERYONE GO?
I WAS JUST TALKING TO THAT LITTLE GUY WITH THE SANDALS.
STU!
HMMM?
I **SAID,** WHERE DID EVERYONE GO?
HOW WOULD **I** KNOW? I'M READING A BOOK.
HEY! DARDON! WHAT ARE YOU **DOING** WITH **THAT?!**
THOSE ARE **MY** TOOLS AND LUMBER!

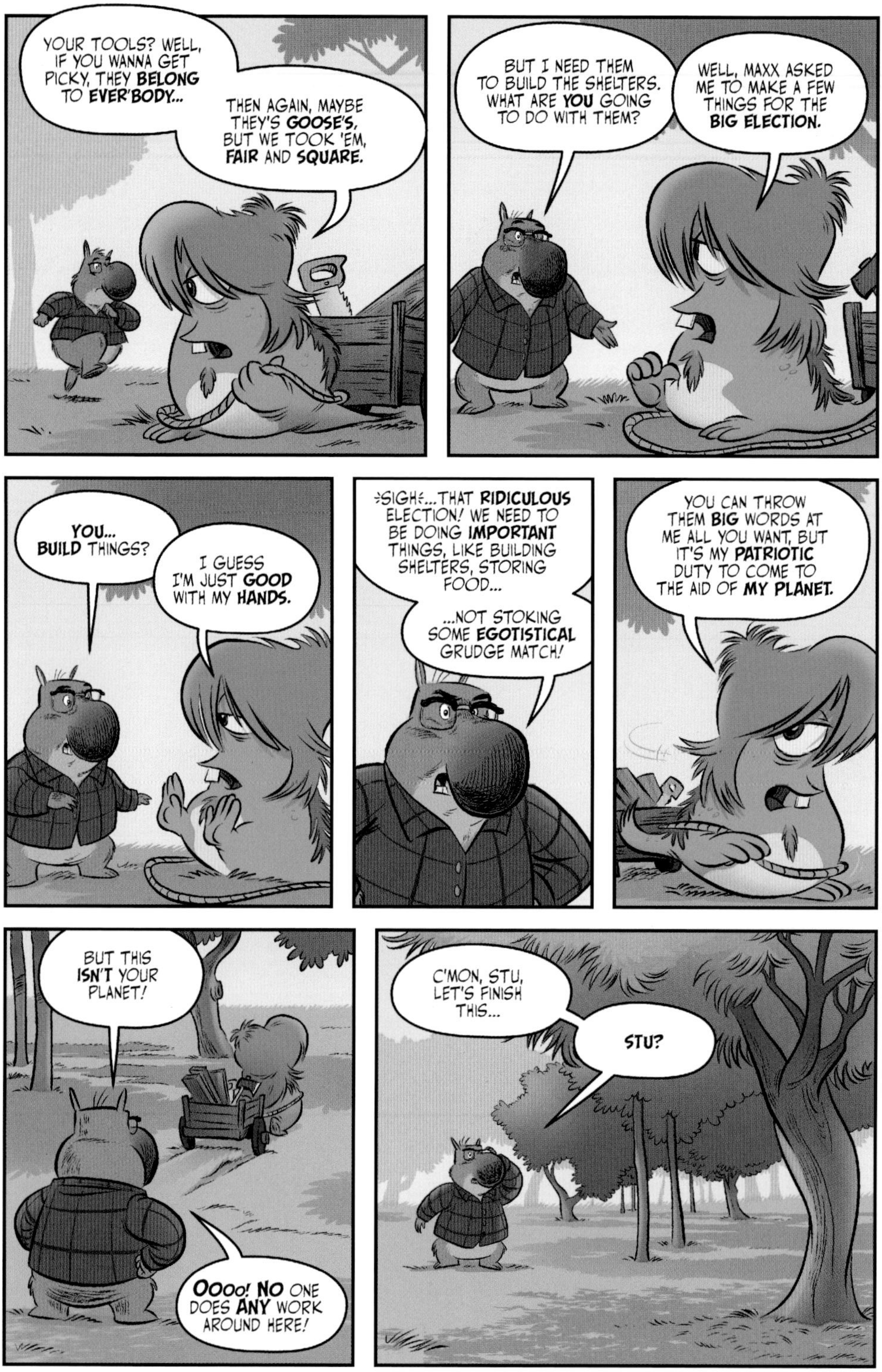

YOUR TOOLS? WELL, IF YOU WANNA GET PICKY, THEY **BELONG** TO **EVER'BODY...**
THEN AGAIN, MAYBE THEY'S **GOOSE'S,** BUT WE TOOK 'EM, **FAIR** AND **SQUARE.**
BUT I NEED THEM TO BUILD THE SHELTERS. WHAT ARE **YOU** GOING TO DO WITH THEM?
WELL, MAXX ASKED ME TO MAKE A FEW THINGS FOR THE **BIG ELECTION.**
YOU... BUILD THINGS?
I GUESS I'M JUST **GOOD** WITH MY **HANDS.**
SIGH... THAT **RIDICULOUS** ELECTION! WE NEED TO BE DOING **IMPORTANT** THINGS, LIKE BUILDING SHELTERS, STORING FOOD...
...NOT STOKING SOME **EGOTISTICAL** GRUDGE MATCH!
YOU CAN THROW THEM **BIG** WORDS AT ME ALL YOU WANT, BUT IT'S MY **PATRIOTIC** DUTY TO COME TO THE AID OF **MY PLANET.**
BUT THIS **ISN'T** YOUR PLANET!
OOOo! NO ONE DOES **ANY** WORK AROUND HERE!
C'MON, STU, LET'S FINISH THIS...
STU?

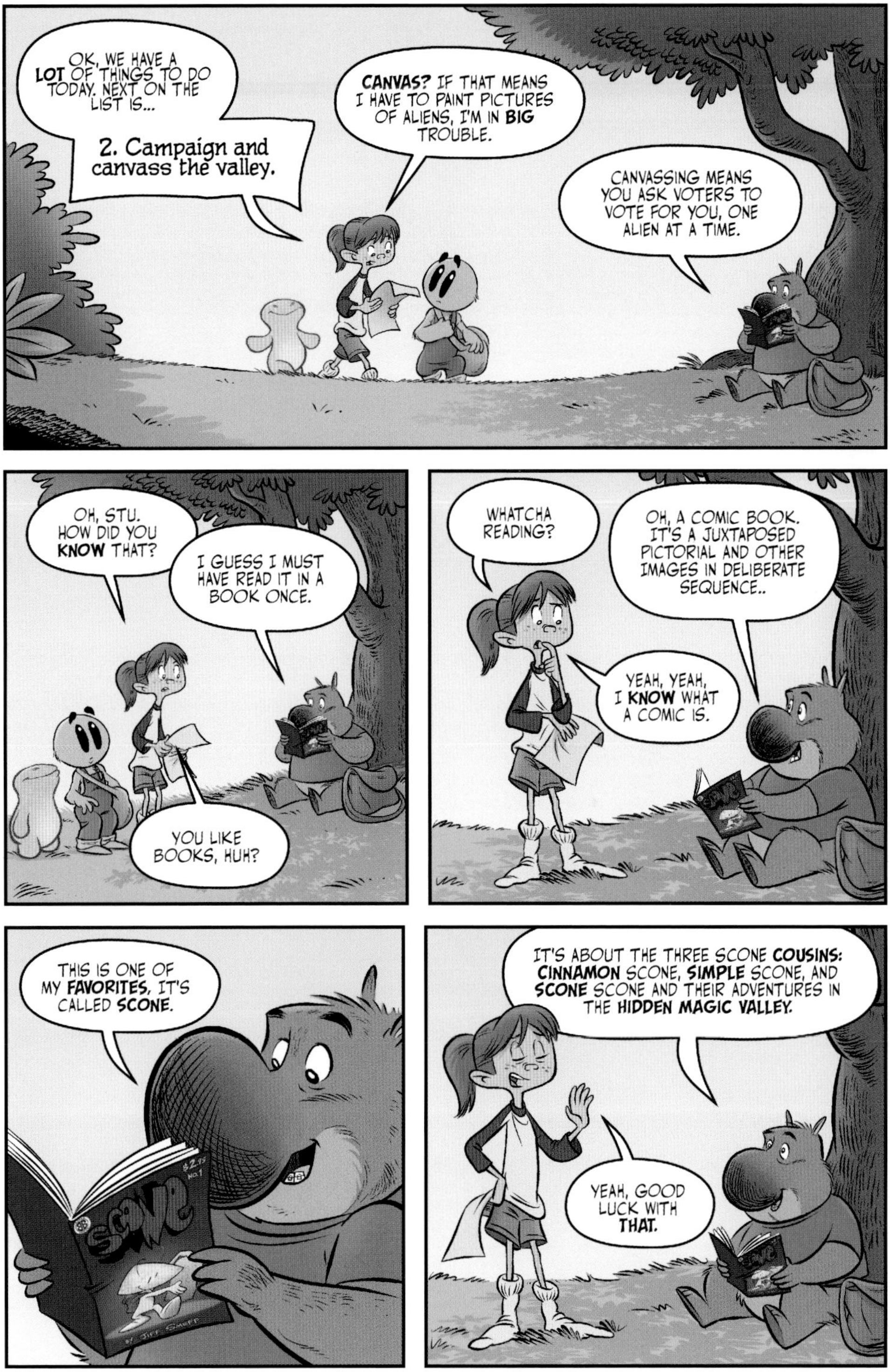
OK, WE HAVE A LOT OF THINGS TO DO TODAY. NEXT ON THE LIST IS...
2. Campaign and canvass the valley.
CANVAS? IF THAT MEANS I HAVE TO PAINT PICTURES OF ALIENS, I'M IN BIG TROUBLE.
CANVASSING MEANS YOU ASK VOTERS TO VOTE FOR YOU, ONE ALIEN AT A TIME.
OH, STU. HOW DID YOU KNOW THAT?
I GUESS I MUST HAVE READ IT IN A BOOK ONCE.
YOU LIKE BOOKS, HUH?
WHATCHA READING?
OH, A COMIC BOOK. IT'S A JUXTAPOSED PICTORIAL AND OTHER IMAGES IN DELIBERATE SEQUENCE..
YEAH, YEAH, I KNOW WHAT A COMIC IS.
THIS IS ONE OF MY FAVORITES, IT'S CALLED SCONE.
SCONE
IT'S ABOUT THE THREE SCONE COUSINS: CINNAMON SCONE, SIMPLE SCONE, AND SCONE SCONE AND THEIR ADVENTURES IN THE HIDDEN MAGIC VALLEY.
YEAH, GOOD LUCK WITH THAT.

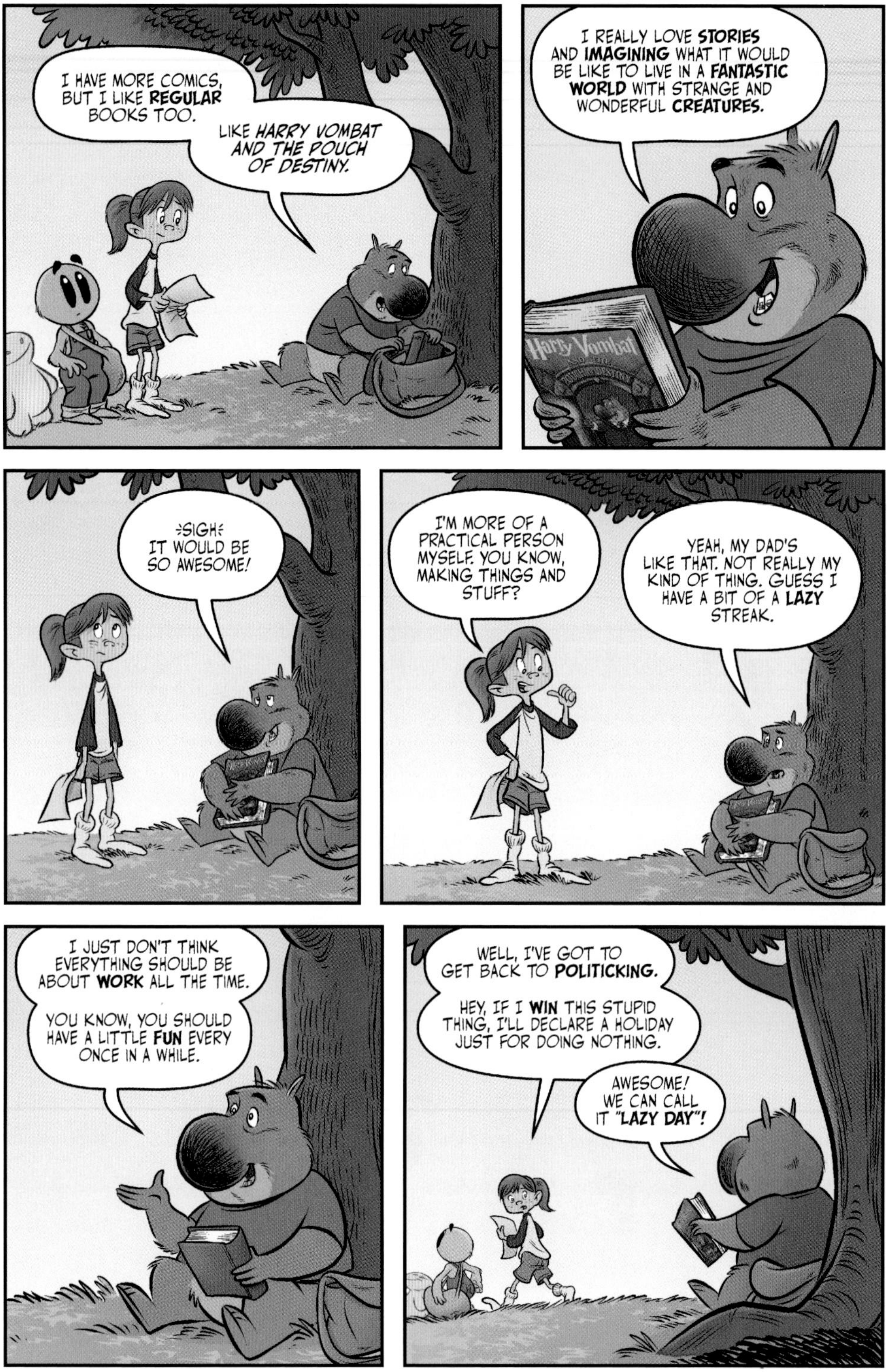
I HAVE MORE COMICS, BUT I LIKE **REGULAR** BOOKS TOO.
LIKE ***HARRY VOMBAT AND THE POUCH OF DESTINY.***
I REALLY LOVE **STORIES** AND **IMAGINING** WHAT IT WOULD BE LIKE TO LIVE IN A **FANTASTIC WORLD** WITH STRANGE AND WONDERFUL **CREATURES.**
Harry Vombat
SIGH IT WOULD BE SO AWESOME!
I'M MORE OF A PRACTICAL PERSON MYSELF. YOU KNOW, MAKING THINGS AND STUFF?
YEAH, MY DAD'S LIKE THAT. NOT REALLY MY KIND OF THING. GUESS I HAVE A BIT OF A **LAZY** STREAK.
I JUST DON'T THINK EVERYTHING SHOULD BE ABOUT **WORK** ALL THE TIME.
YOU KNOW, YOU SHOULD HAVE A LITTLE **FUN** EVERY ONCE IN A WHILE.
WELL, I'VE GOT TO GET BACK TO **POLITICKING.**
HEY, IF I **WIN** THIS STUPID THING, I'LL DECLARE A HOLIDAY JUST FOR DOING NOTHING.
AWESOME! WE CAN CALL IT **"LAZY DAY"!**

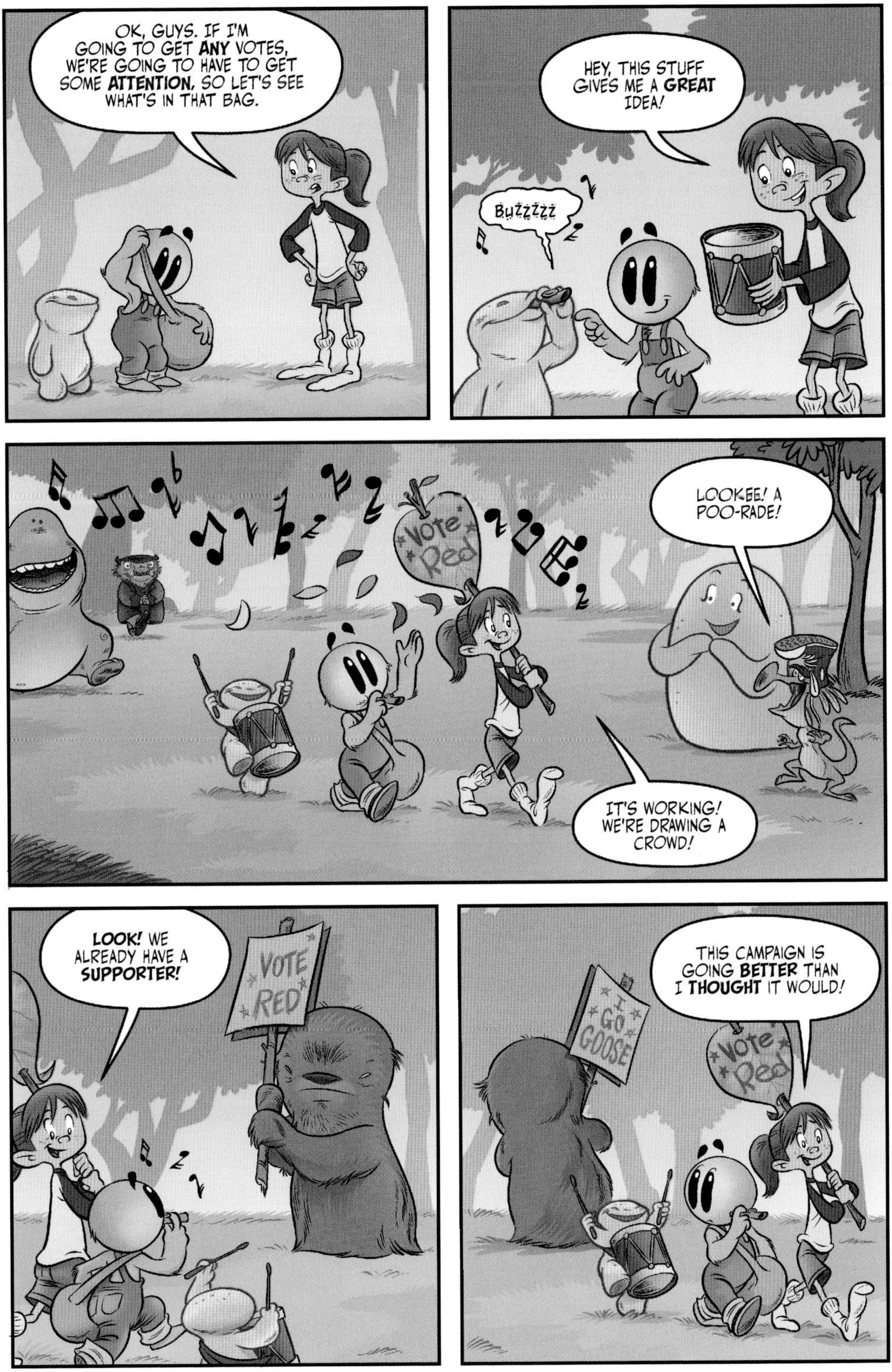
OK, GUYS. IF I'M GOING TO GET ANY VOTES, WE'RE GOING TO HAVE TO GET SOME ATTENTION, SO LET'S SEE WHAT'S IN THAT BAG.
HEY, THIS STUFF GIVES ME A GREAT IDEA!
BUZZZZZ
VOTE RED
LOOKEE! A POO-RADE!
IT'S WORKING! WE'RE DRAWING A CROWD!
LOOK! WE ALREADY HAVE A SUPPORTER!
VOTE RED
THIS CAMPAIGN IS GOING BETTER THAN I THOUGHT IT WOULD!
I GO GOOSE
VOTE RED

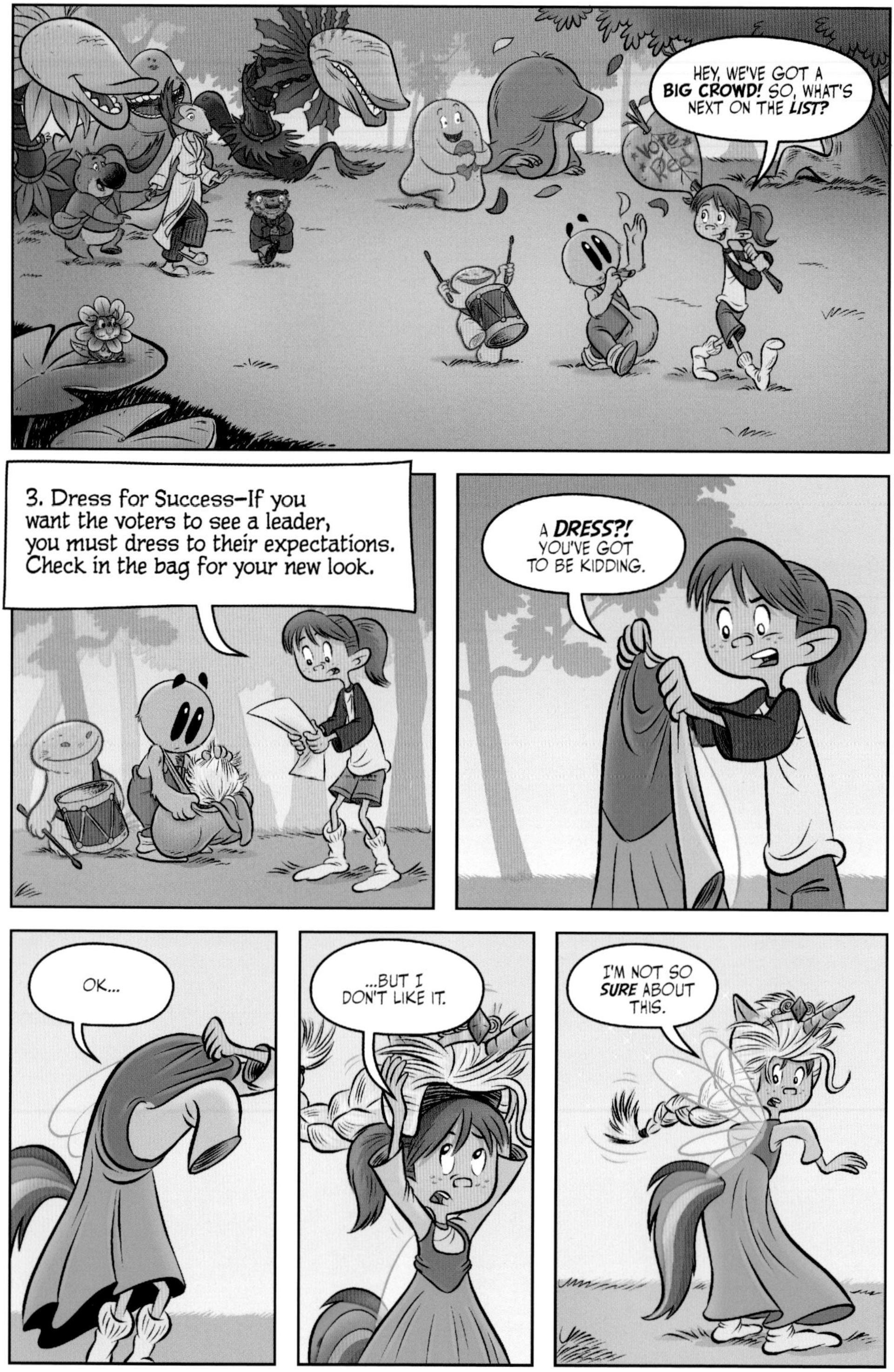
HEY, WE'VE GOT A BIG CROWD! SO, WHAT'S NEXT ON THE LIST?
VOTE RED
3. Dress for Success–If you want the voters to see a leader, you must dress to their expectations. Check in the bag for your new look.
A DRESS?! YOU'VE GOT TO BE KIDDING.
OK...
...BUT I DON'T LIKE IT.
I'M NOT SO SURE ABOUT THIS.

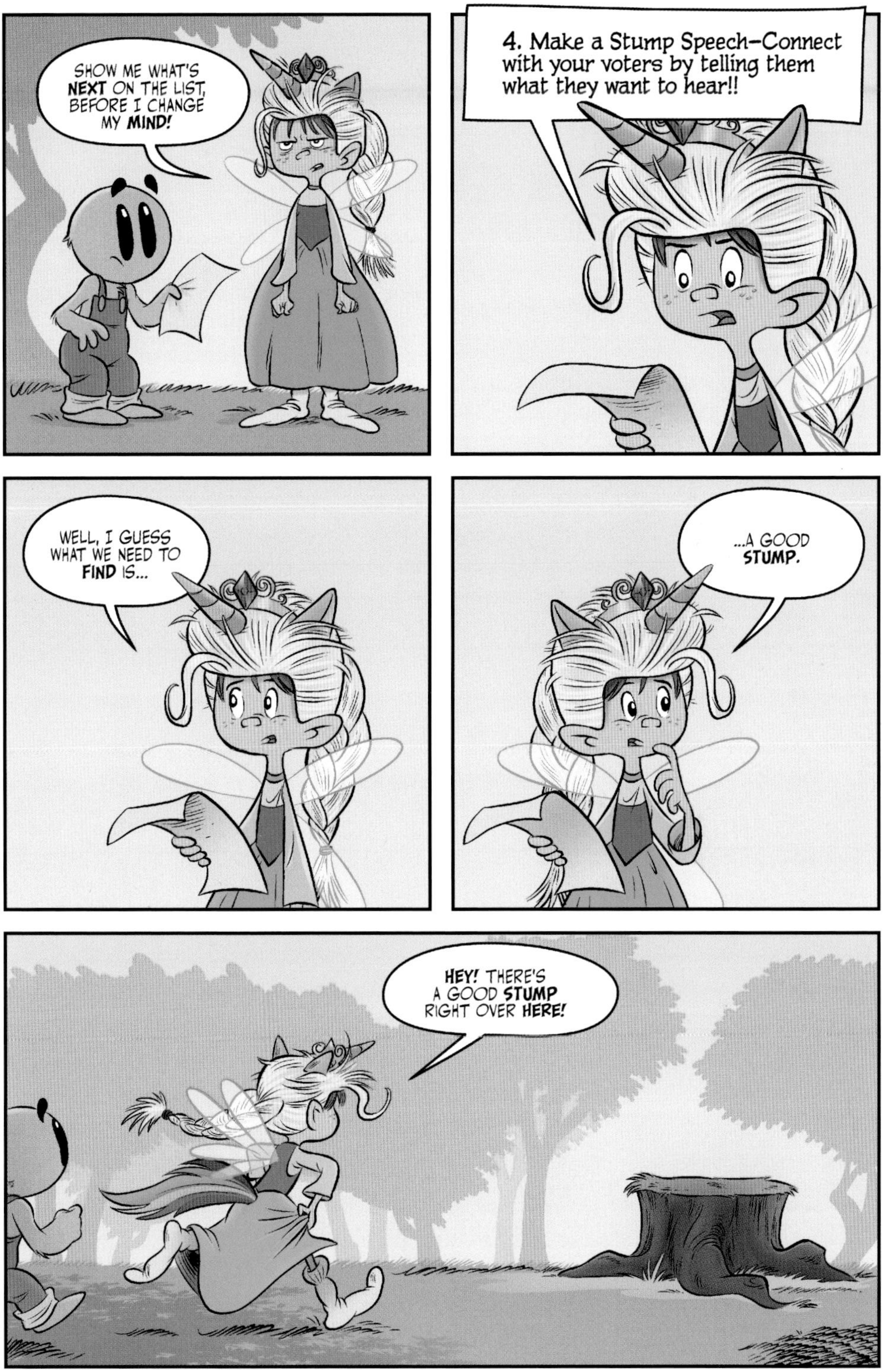
SHOW ME WHAT'S NEXT ON THE LIST, BEFORE I CHANGE MY MIND!
4. Make a Stump Speech–Connect with your voters by telling them what they want to hear!!
WELL, I GUESS WHAT WE NEED TO FIND IS...
...A GOOD STUMP.
HEY! THERE'S A GOOD STUMP RIGHT OVER HERE!

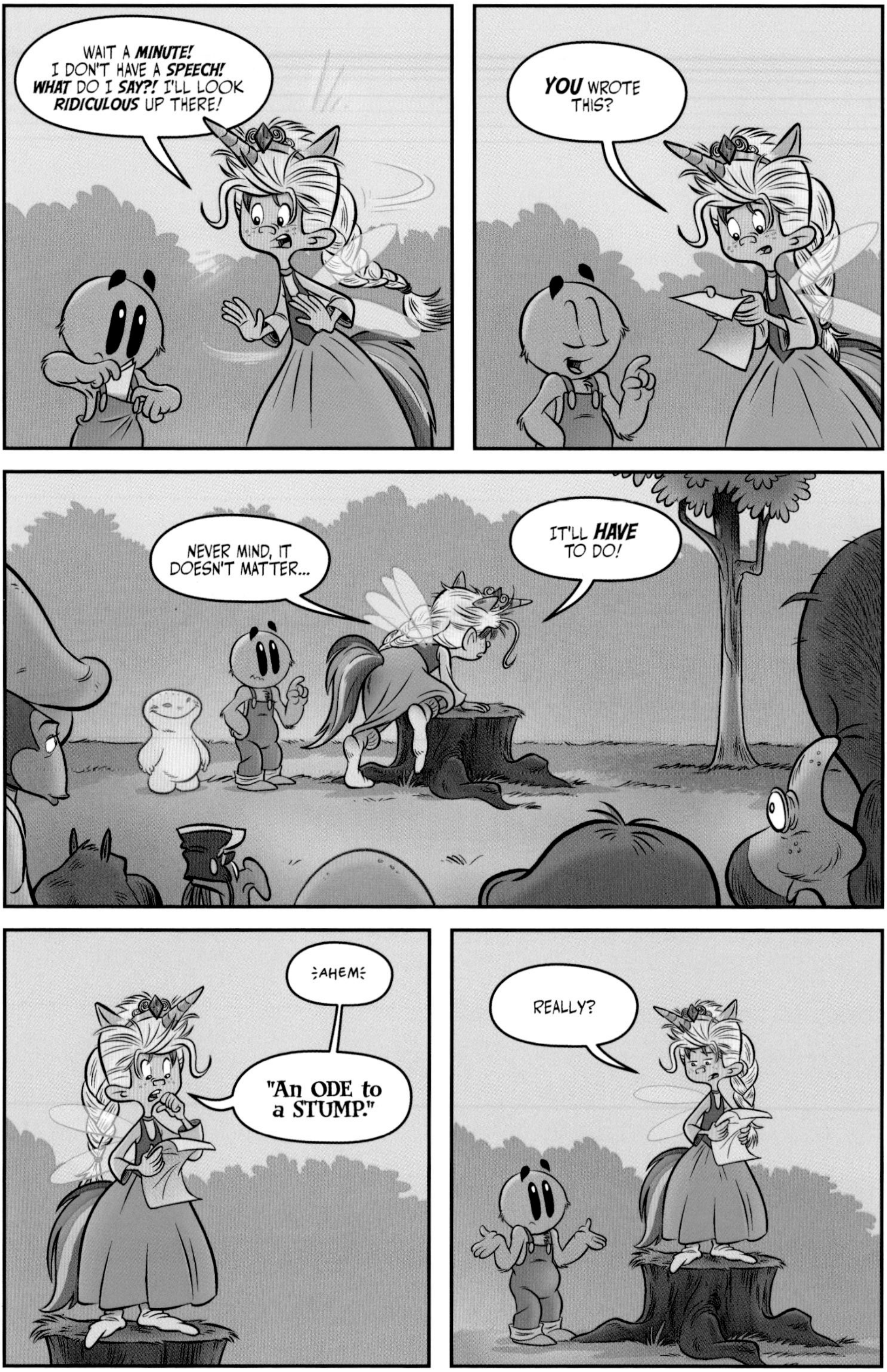

WAIT A **MINUTE!** I DON'T HAVE A **SPEECH!** **WHAT** DO I **SAY?!** I'LL LOOK **RIDICULOUS** UP THERE!
YOU WROTE THIS?
NEVER MIND, IT DOESN'T MATTER...
IT'LL **HAVE** TO DO!
AHEM
"An ODE to a STUMP."
REALLY?

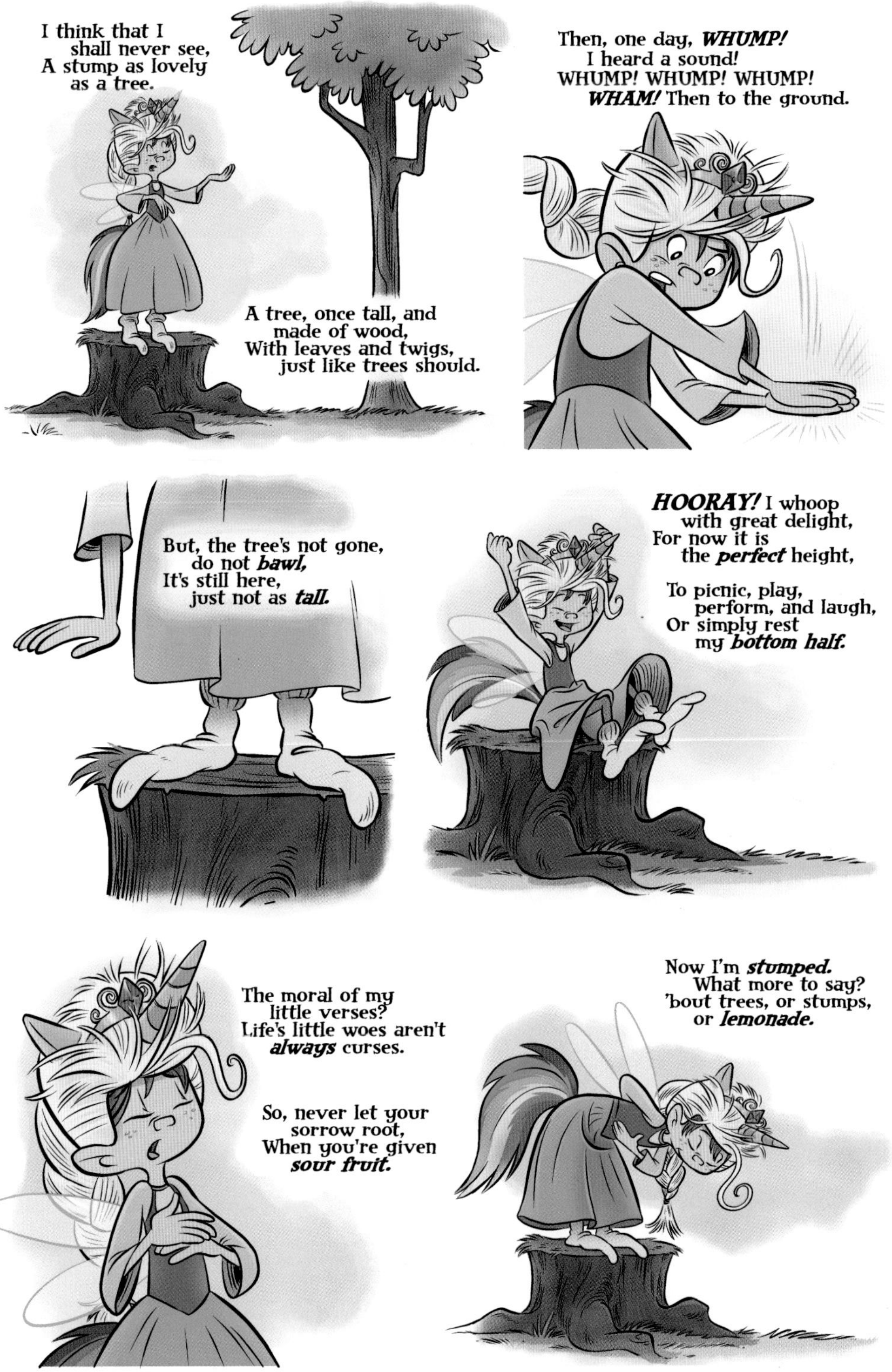
I think that I shall never see, A stump as lovely as a tree.
A tree, once tall, and made of wood, With leaves and twigs, just like trees should.
Then, one day, *WHUMP!* I heard a sound! WHUMP! WHUMP! WHUMP! *WHAM!* Then to the ground.
But, the tree's not gone, do not *bawl,* It's still here, just not as *tall.*
HOORAY! I whoop with great delight, For now it is the *perfect* height,
To picnic, play, perform, and laugh, Or simply rest my *bottom half.*
The moral of my little verses? Life's little woes aren't *always* curses.
So, never let your sorrow root, When you're given *sour fruit.*
Now I'm *stumped.* What more to say? 'bout trees, or stumps, or *lemonade.*

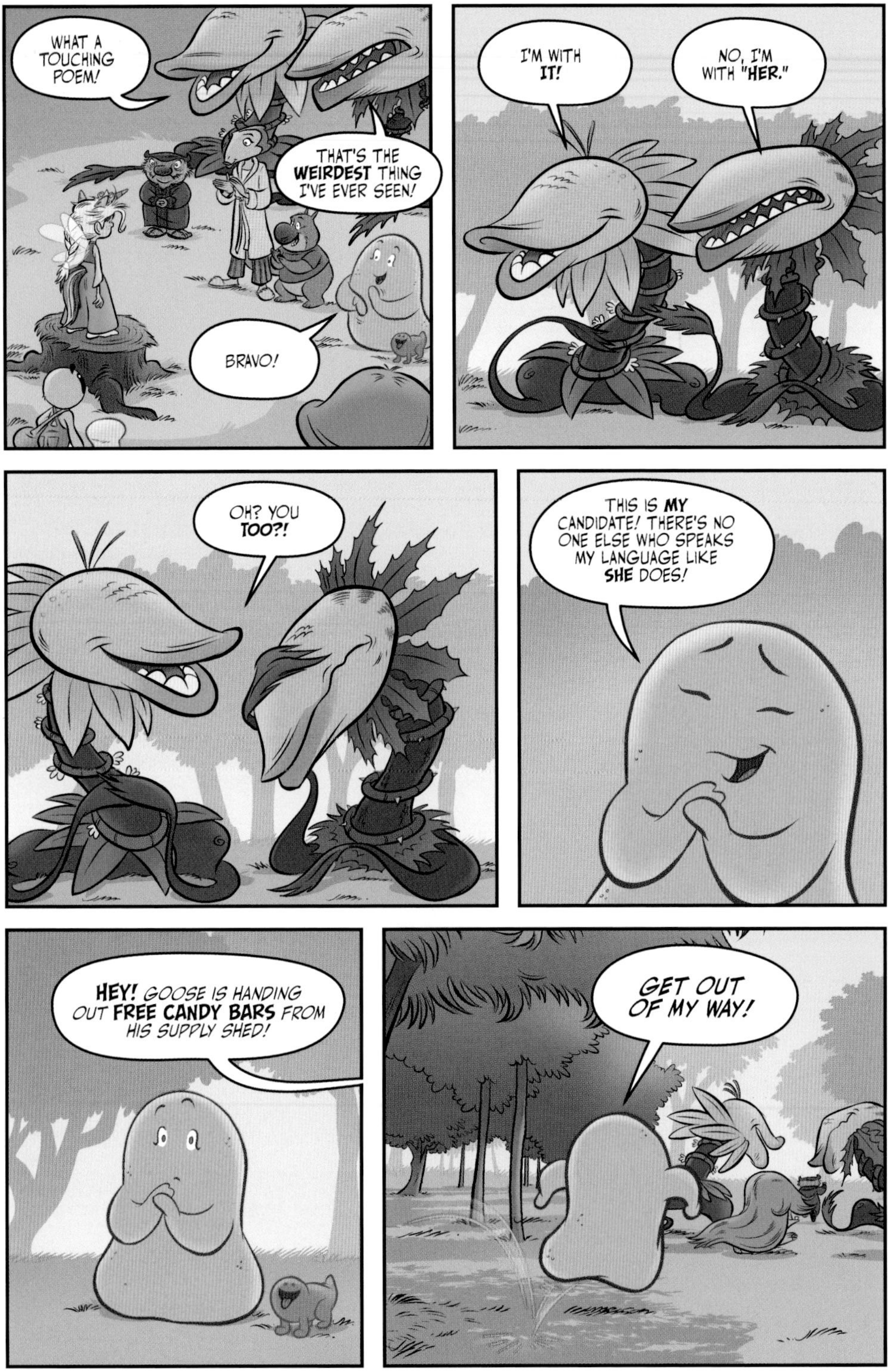
WHAT A TOUCHING POEM!
THAT'S THE WEIRDEST THING I'VE EVER SEEN!
BRAVO!
I'M WITH IT!
NO, I'M WITH "HER."
OH? YOU TOO?!
THIS IS MY CANDIDATE! THERE'S NO ONE ELSE WHO SPEAKS MY LANGUAGE LIKE SHE DOES!
HEY! GOOSE IS HANDING OUT FREE CANDY BARS FROM HIS SUPPLY SHED!
GET OUT OF MY WAY!

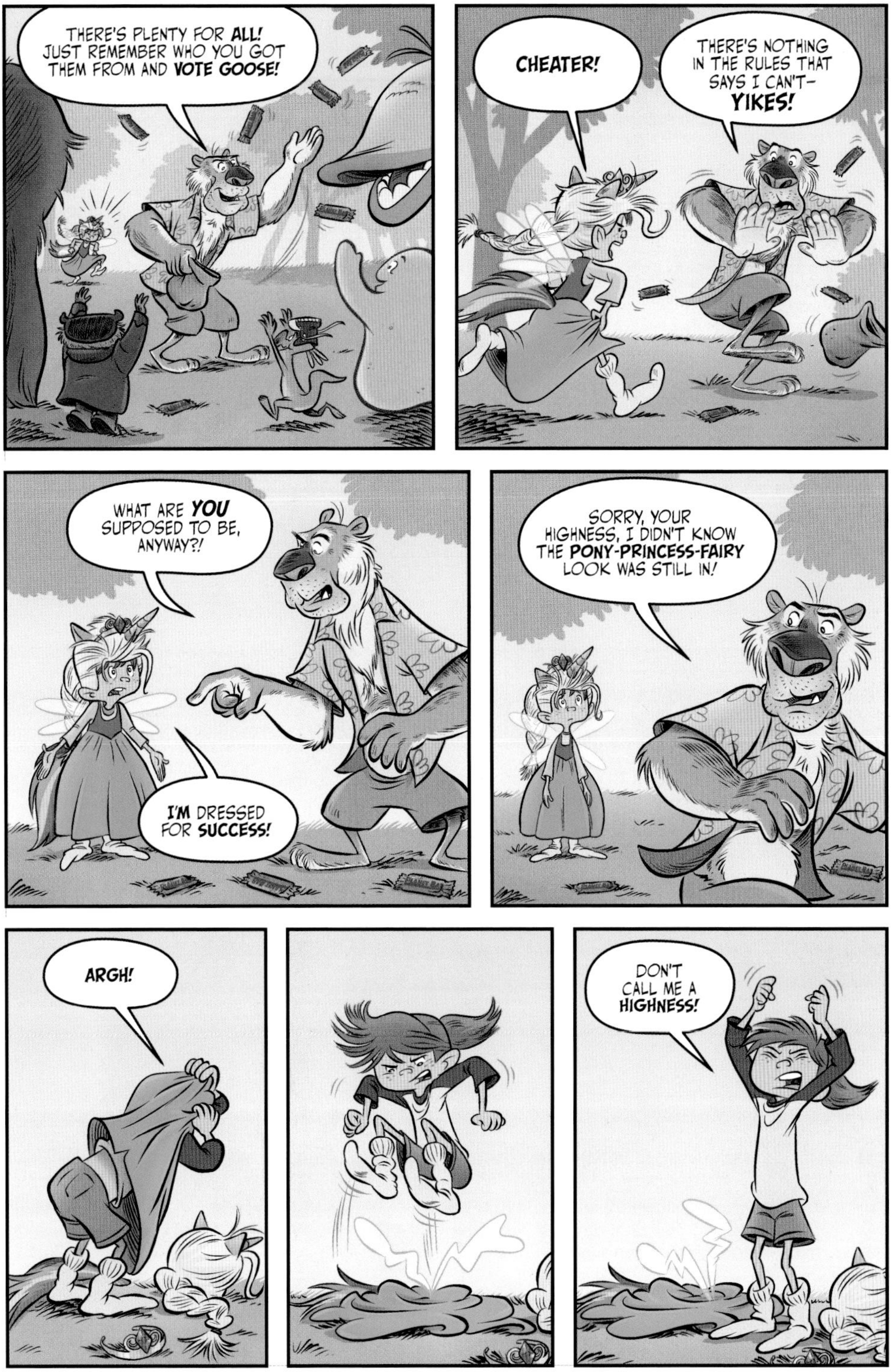
THERE'S PLENTY FOR ALL! JUST REMEMBER WHO YOU GOT THEM FROM AND VOTE GOOSE!
CHEATER!
THERE'S NOTHING IN THE RULES THAT SAYS I CAN'T— YIKES!
WHAT ARE YOU SUPPOSED TO BE, ANYWAY?!
I'M DRESSED FOR SUCCESS!
SORRY, YOUR HIGHNESS, I DIDN'T KNOW THE PONY-PRINCESS-FAIRY LOOK WAS STILL IN!
ARGH!
DON'T CALL ME A HIGHNESS!

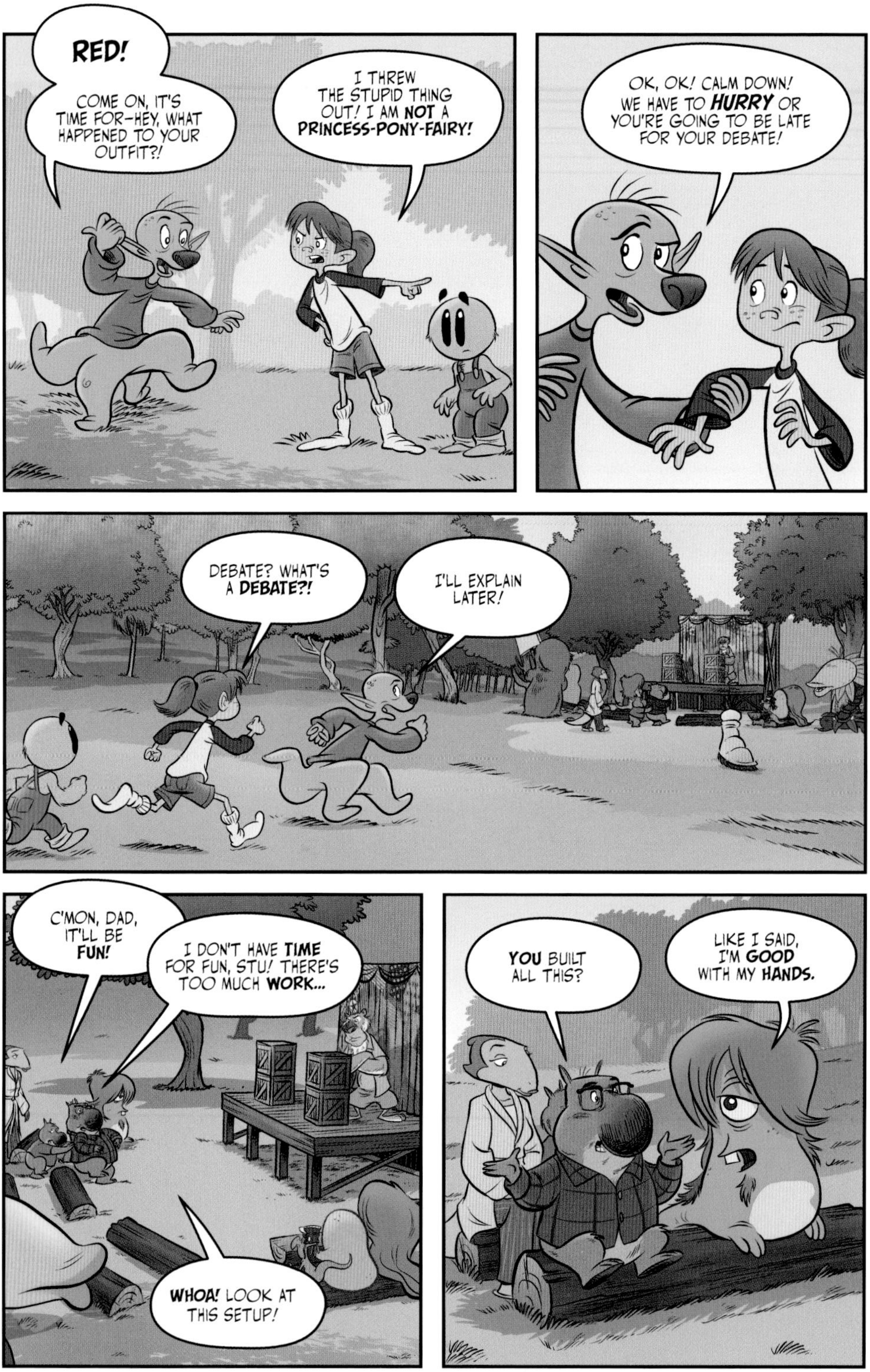
RED!
COME ON, IT'S TIME FOR—HEY, WHAT HAPPENED TO YOUR OUTFIT?!
I THREW THE STUPID THING OUT! I AM **NOT** A **PRINCESS-PONY-FAIRY!**
OK, OK! CALM DOWN! WE HAVE TO **HURRY** OR YOU'RE GOING TO BE LATE FOR YOUR DEBATE!
DEBATE? WHAT'S A **DEBATE?!**
I'LL EXPLAIN LATER!
C'MON, DAD, IT'LL BE **FUN!**
I DON'T HAVE **TIME** FOR FUN, STU! THERE'S TOO MUCH **WORK...**
WHOA! LOOK AT THIS SETUP!
YOU BUILT ALL THIS?
LIKE I SAID, I'M **GOOD** WITH MY **HANDS.**

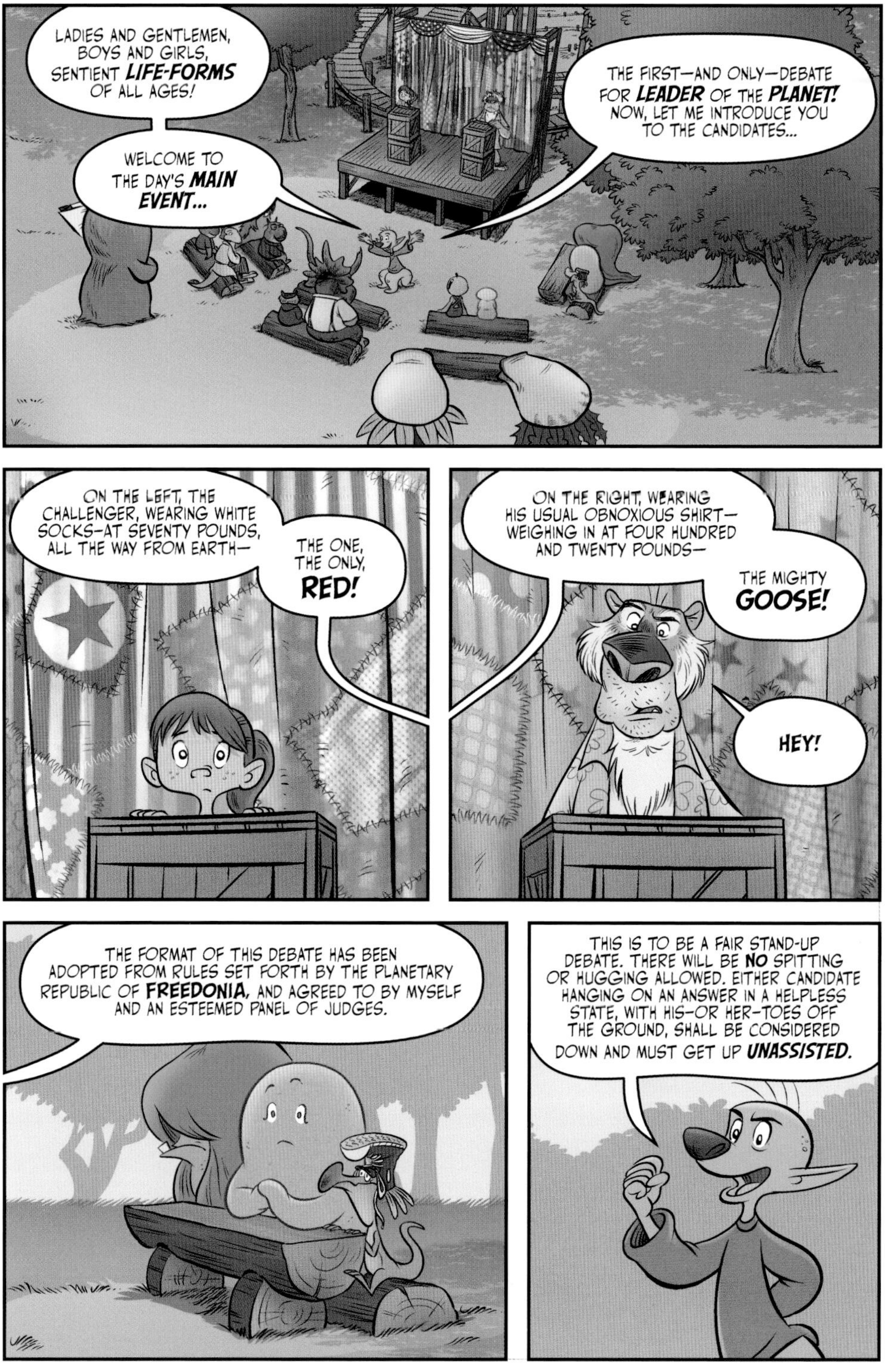

LADIES AND GENTLEMEN, BOYS AND GIRLS, SENTIENT **LIFE-FORMS** OF ALL AGES!
WELCOME TO THE DAY'S **MAIN EVENT...**
THE FIRST—AND ONLY—DEBATE FOR **LEADER** OF THE **PLANET!** NOW, LET ME INTRODUCE YOU TO THE CANDIDATES...
ON THE LEFT, THE CHALLENGER, WEARING WHITE SOCKS—AT SEVENTY POUNDS, ALL THE WAY FROM EARTH—
THE ONE, THE ONLY, **RED!**
ON THE RIGHT, WEARING HIS USUAL OBNOXIOUS SHIRT—WEIGHING IN AT FOUR HUNDRED AND TWENTY POUNDS—
THE MIGHTY **GOOSE!**
HEY!
THE FORMAT OF THIS DEBATE HAS BEEN ADOPTED FROM RULES SET FORTH BY THE PLANETARY REPUBLIC OF **FREEDONIA,** AND AGREED TO BY MYSELF AND AN ESTEEMED PANEL OF JUDGES.
THIS IS TO BE A FAIR STAND-UP DEBATE. THERE WILL BE **NO** SPITTING OR HUGGING ALLOWED. EITHER CANDIDATE HANGING ON AN ANSWER IN A HELPLESS STATE, WITH HIS—OR HER—TOES OFF THE GROUND, SHALL BE CONSIDERED DOWN AND MUST GET UP **UNASSISTED.**

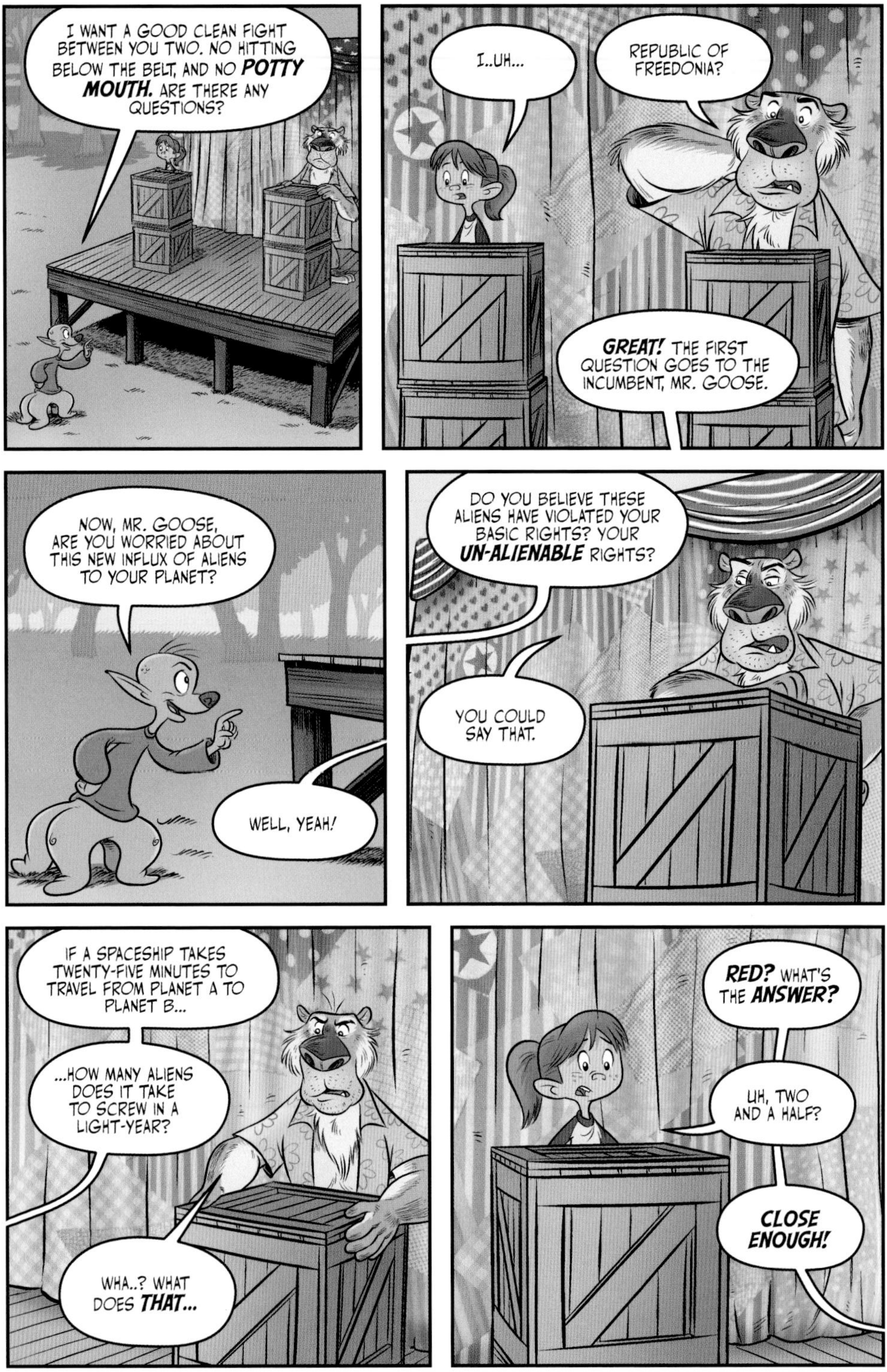
I WANT A GOOD CLEAN FIGHT BETWEEN YOU TWO. NO HITTING BELOW THE BELT, AND NO POTTY MOUTH. ARE THERE ANY QUESTIONS?
I..UH...
REPUBLIC OF FREEDONIA?
GREAT! THE FIRST QUESTION GOES TO THE INCUMBENT, MR. GOOSE.
NOW, MR. GOOSE, ARE YOU WORRIED ABOUT THIS NEW INFLUX OF ALIENS TO YOUR PLANET?
WELL, YEAH!
DO YOU BELIEVE THESE ALIENS HAVE VIOLATED YOUR BASIC RIGHTS? YOUR UN-ALIENABLE RIGHTS?
YOU COULD SAY THAT.
IF A SPACESHIP TAKES TWENTY-FIVE MINUTES TO TRAVEL FROM PLANET A TO PLANET B...
...HOW MANY ALIENS DOES IT TAKE TO SCREW IN A LIGHT-YEAR?
WHA..? WHAT DOES THAT...
RED? WHAT'S THE ANSWER?
UH, TWO AND A HALF?
CLOSE ENOUGH!

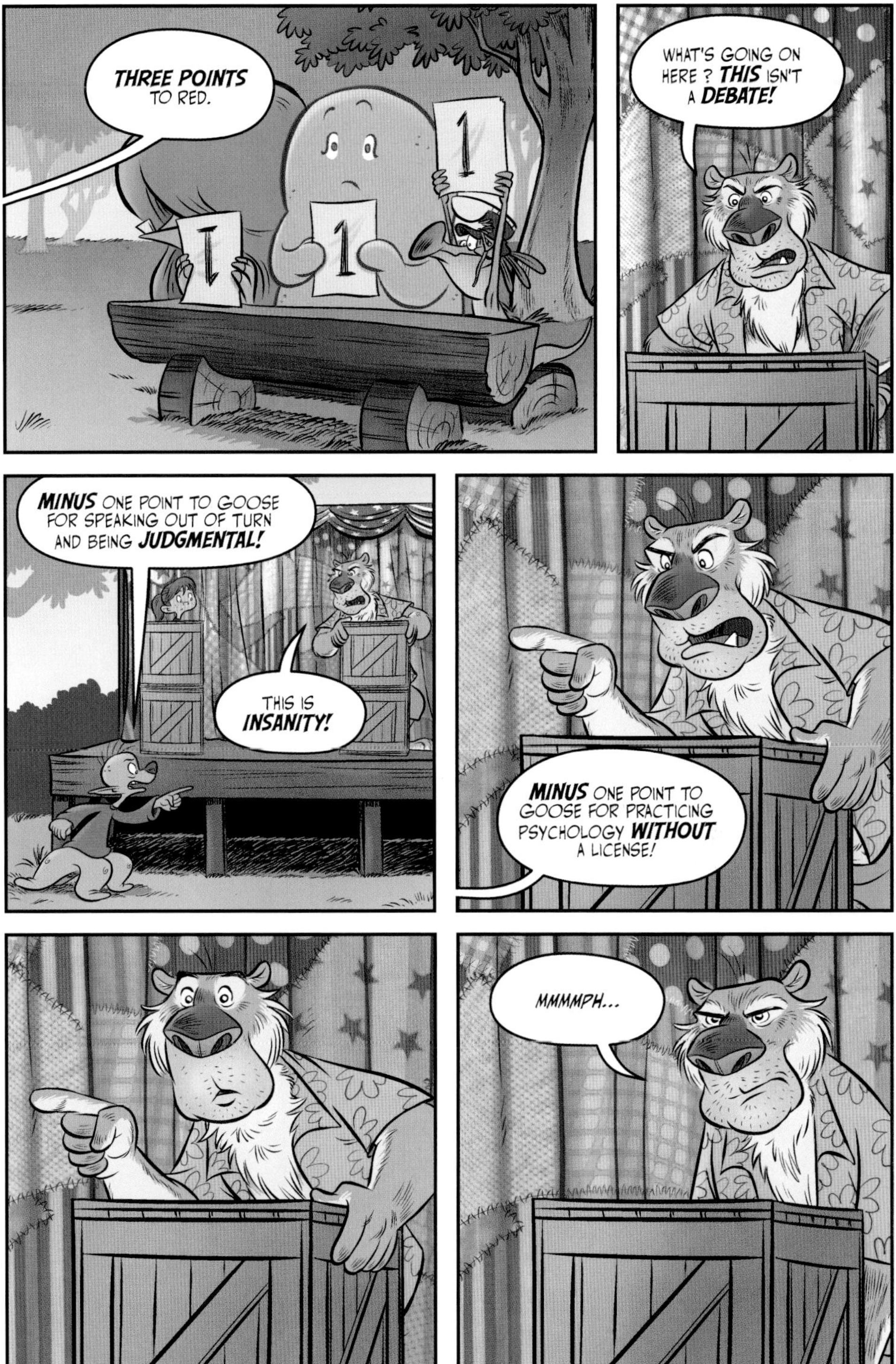
THREE POINTS TO RED.
WHAT'S GOING ON HERE ? THIS ISN'T A DEBATE!
MINUS ONE POINT TO GOOSE FOR SPEAKING OUT OF TURN AND BEING JUDGMENTAL!
THIS IS INSANITY!
MINUS ONE POINT TO GOOSE FOR PRACTICING PSYCHOLOGY WITHOUT A LICENSE!
MMMMPH...

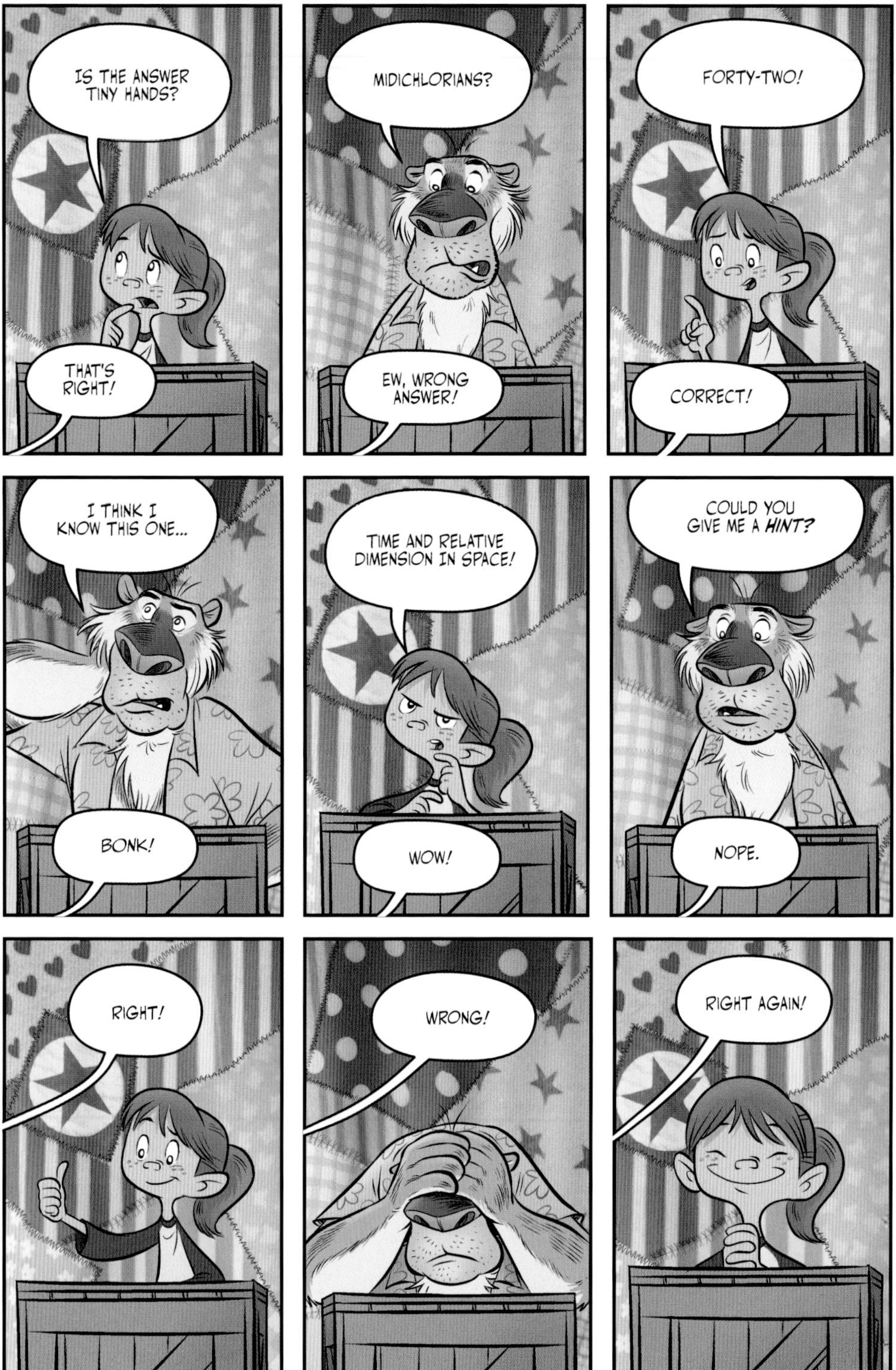
IS THE ANSWER TINY HANDS?
THAT'S RIGHT!
MIDICHLORIANS?
EW, WRONG ANSWER!
FORTY-TWO!
CORRECT!
I THINK I KNOW THIS ONE...
BONK!
TIME AND RELATIVE DIMENSION IN SPACE!
WOW!
COULD YOU GIVE ME A *HINT?*
NOPE.
RIGHT!
WRONG!
RIGHT AGAIN!

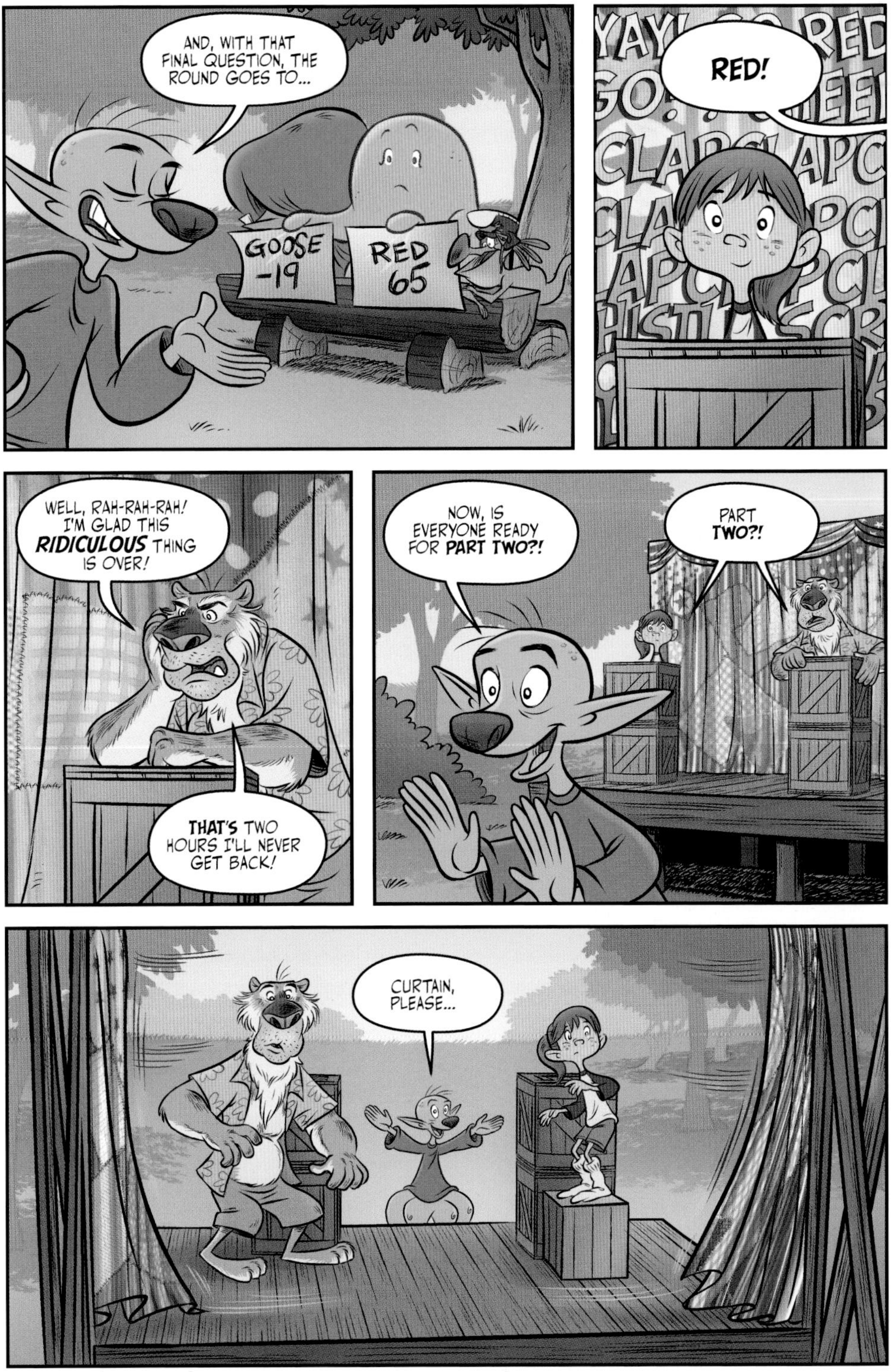
AND, WITH THAT FINAL QUESTION, THE ROUND GOES TO...
GOOSE -19
RED 65
RED!
WELL, RAH-RAH-RAH! I'M GLAD THIS **RIDICULOUS** THING IS OVER!
THAT'S TWO HOURS I'LL NEVER GET BACK!
NOW, IS EVERYONE READY FOR **PART TWO?!**
PART **TWO?!**
CURTAIN, PLEASE...

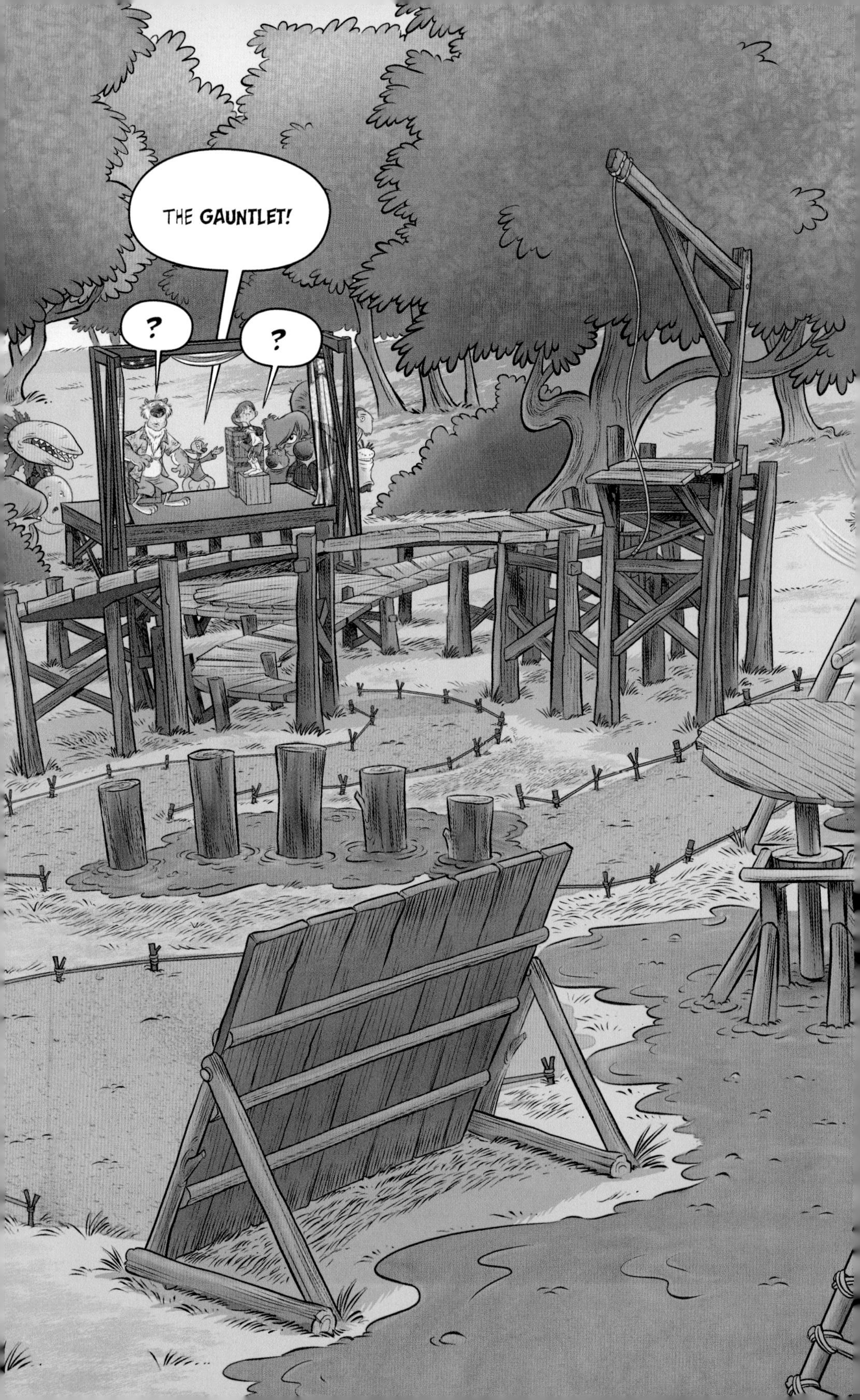
?
THE GAUNTLET!
?

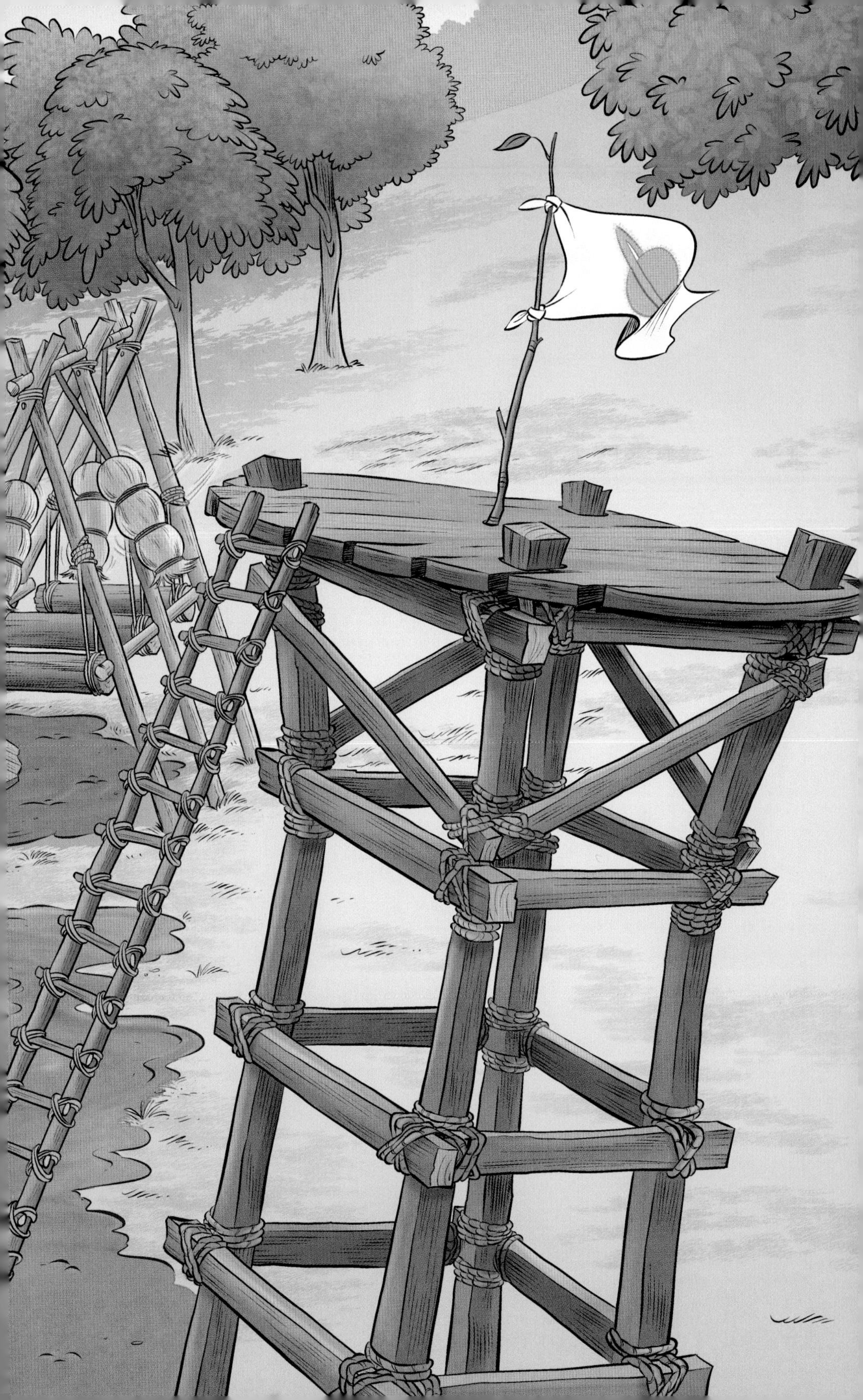

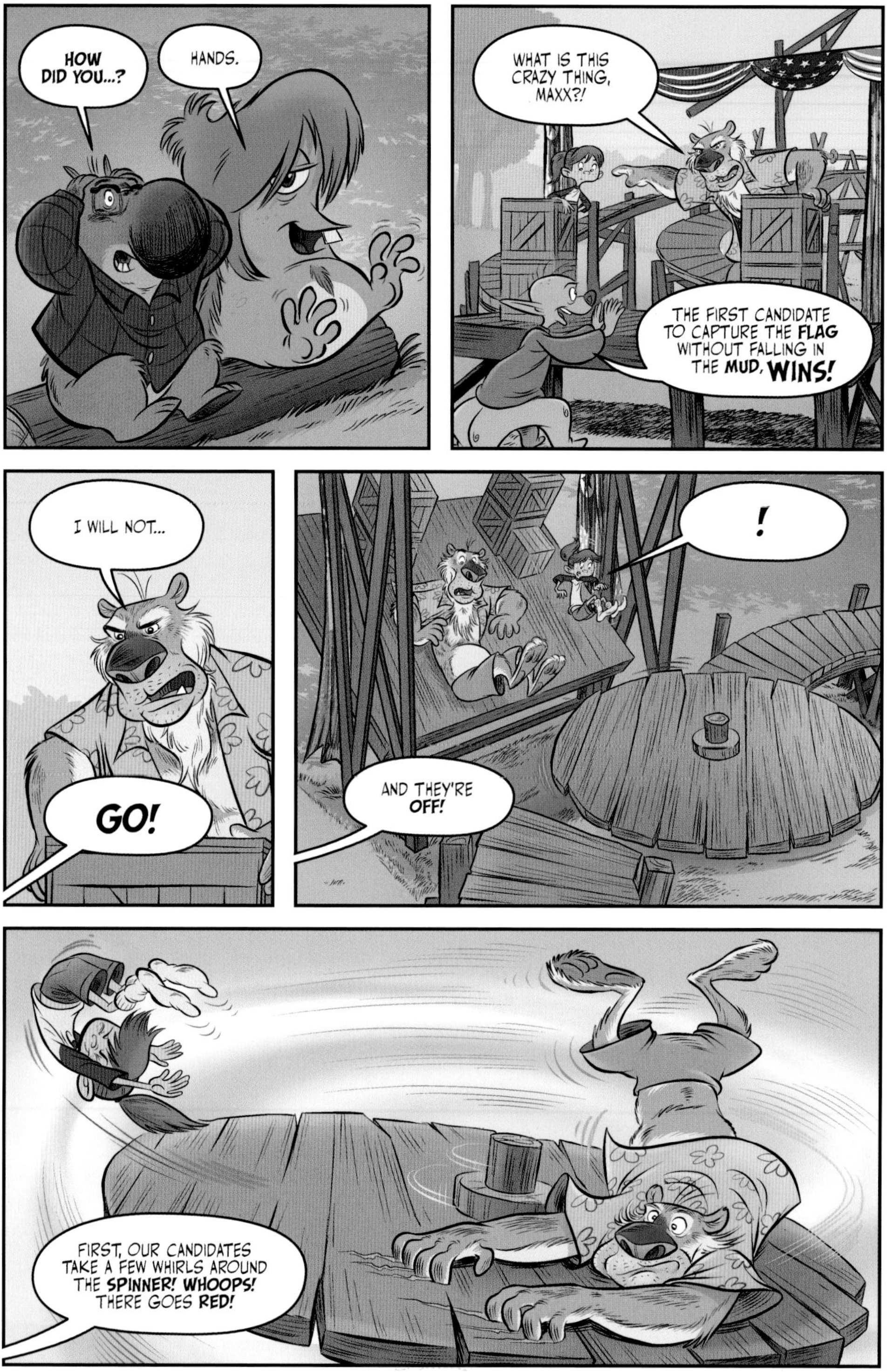
HOW DID YOU...?
HANDS.
WHAT IS THIS CRAZY THING, MAXX?!
THE FIRST CANDIDATE TO CAPTURE THE FLAG WITHOUT FALLING IN THE MUD, WINS!
I WILL NOT...
GO!
!
AND THEY'RE OFF!
FIRST, OUR CANDIDATES TAKE A FEW WHIRLS AROUND THE SPINNER! WHOOPS! THERE GOES RED!

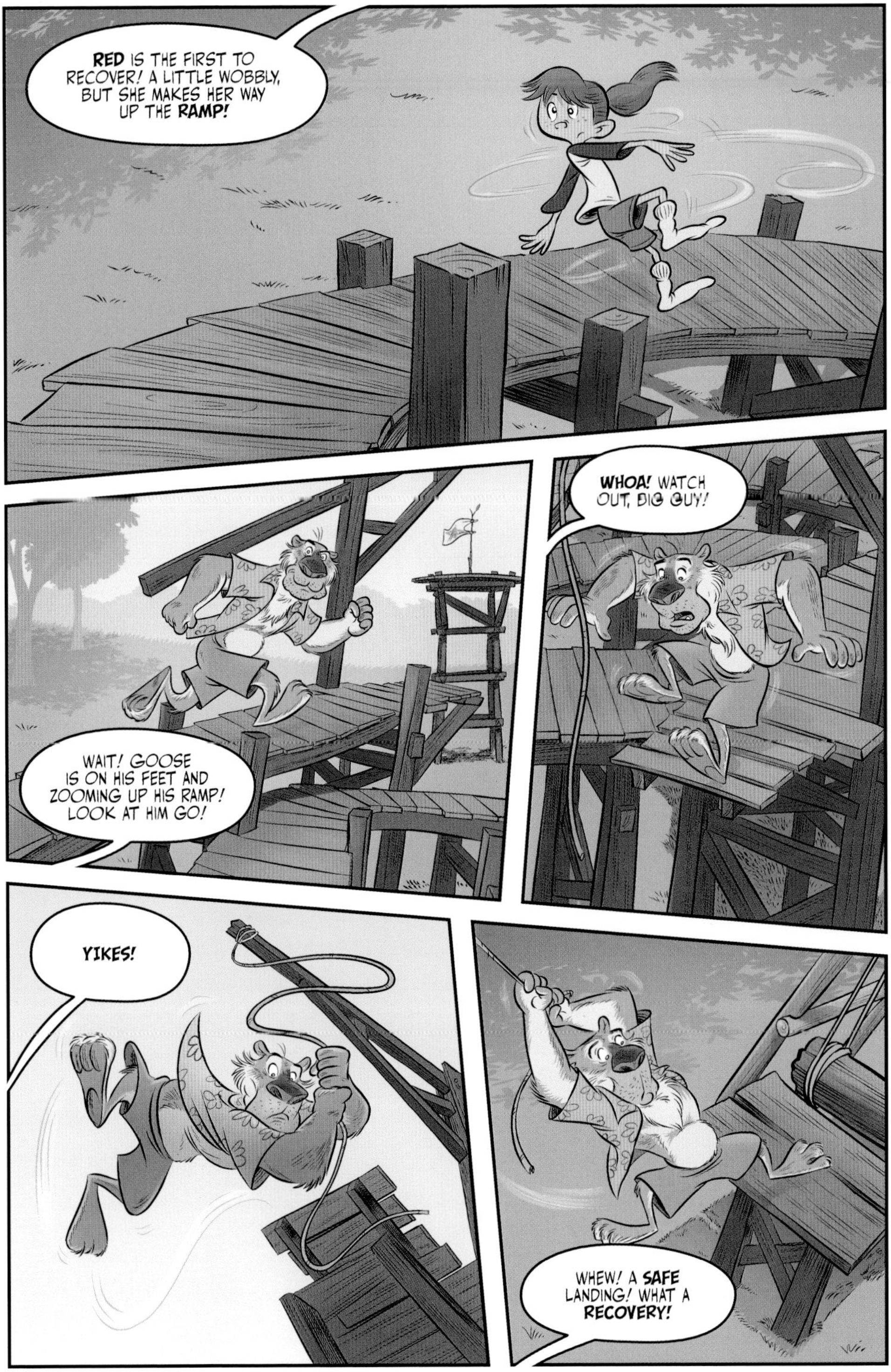
RED IS THE FIRST TO RECOVER! A LITTLE WOBBLY, BUT SHE MAKES HER WAY UP THE RAMP!
WAIT! GOOSE IS ON HIS FEET AND ZOOMING UP HIS RAMP! LOOK AT HIM GO!
WHOA! WATCH OUT, BIG GUY!
YIKES!
WHEW! A SAFE LANDING! WHAT A RECOVERY!

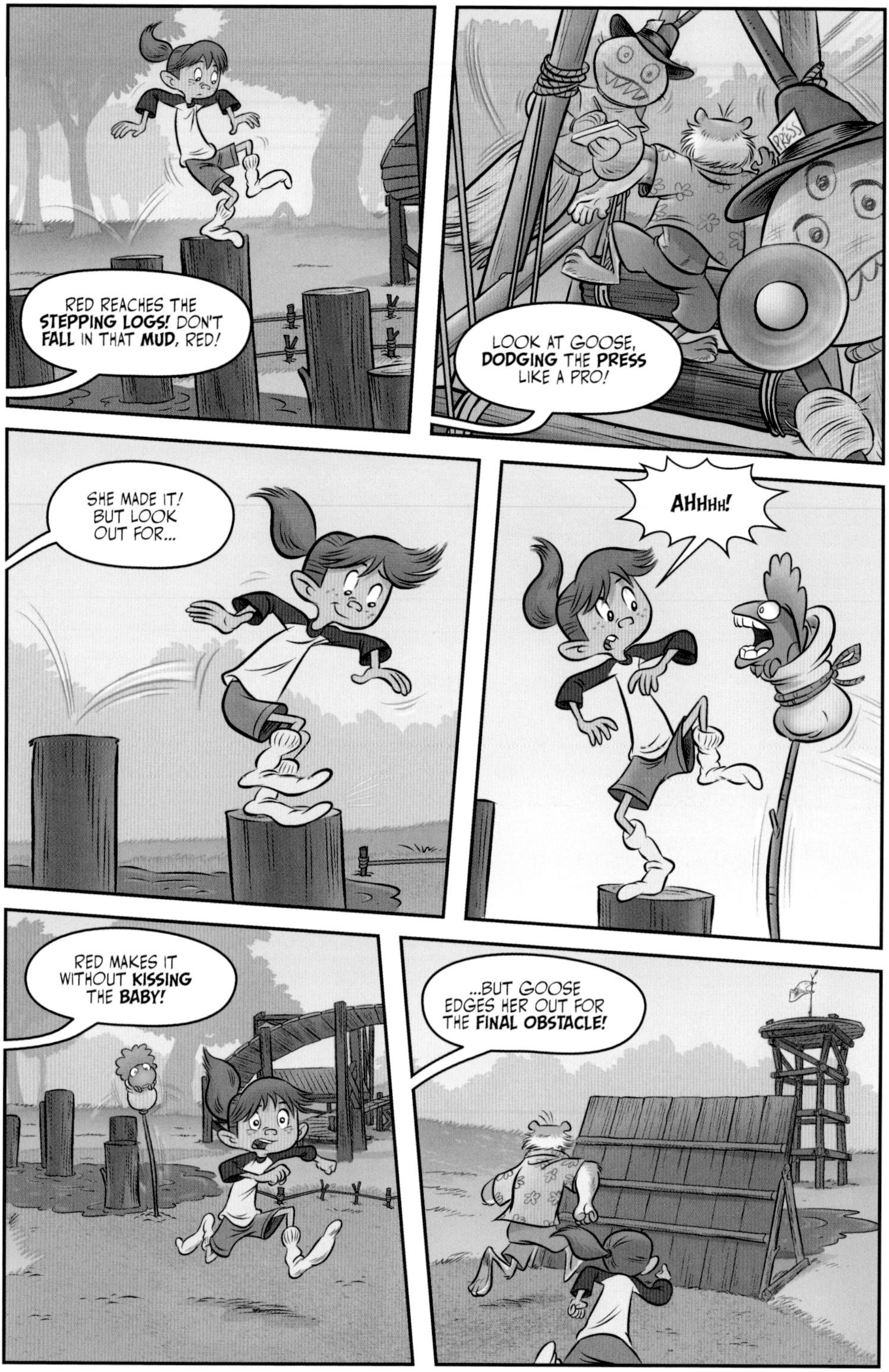
RED REACHES THE **STEPPING LOGS!** DON'T **FALL** IN THAT **MUD**, RED!
PRESS
LOOK AT GOOSE, **DODGING** THE **PRESS** LIKE A PRO!
SHE MADE IT! BUT LOOK OUT FOR...
AHHHH!
RED MAKES IT WITHOUT **KISSING** THE **BABY!**
...BUT GOOSE EDGES HER OUT FOR THE **FINAL OBSTACLE!**

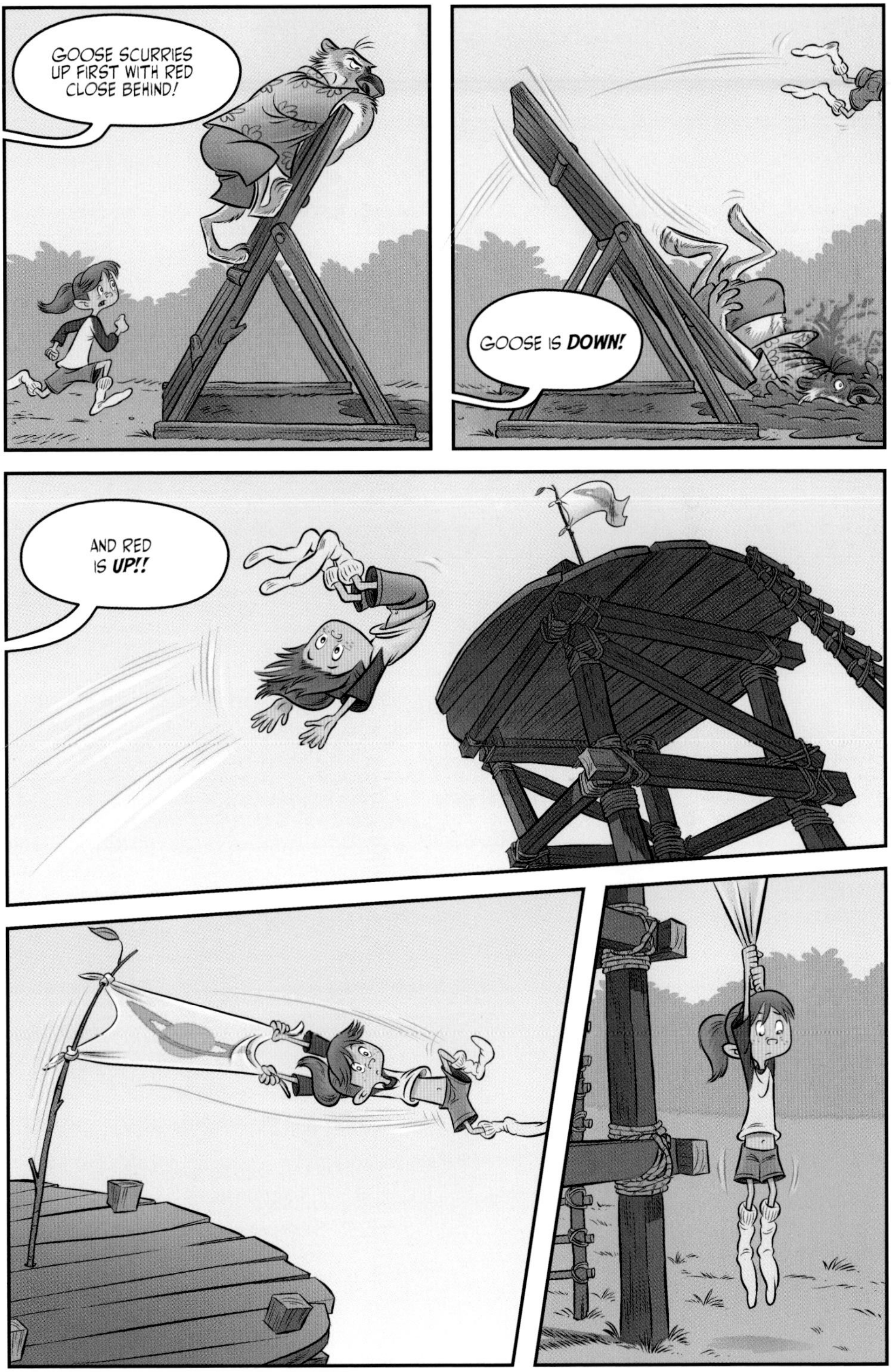
GOOSE SCURRIES UP FIRST WITH RED CLOSE BEHIND!
GOOSE IS **DOWN!**
AND RED IS **UP!!**

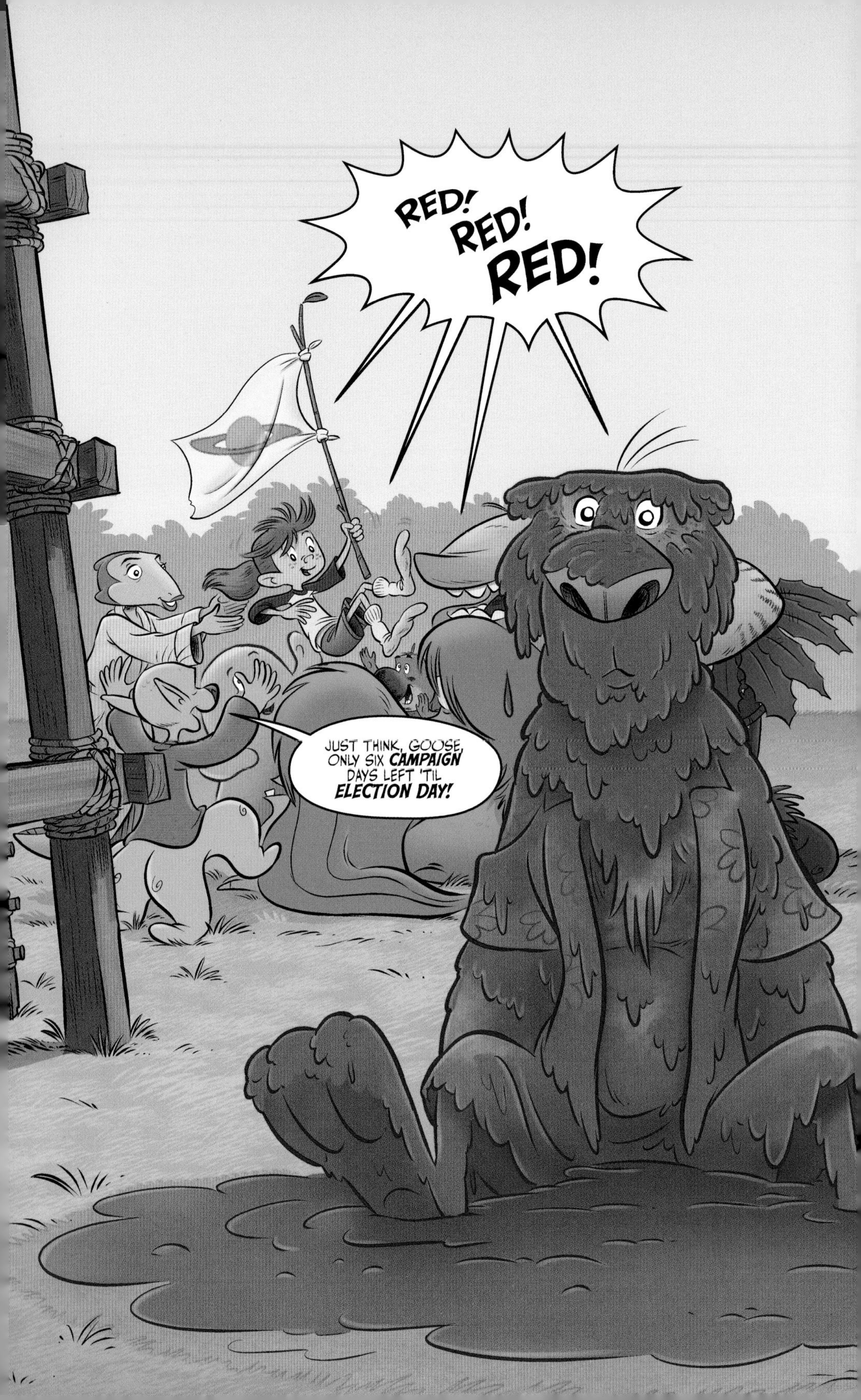
RED! RED! RED!
JUST THINK, GOOSE, ONLY SIX CAMPAIGN DAYS LEFT 'TIL ELECTION DAY!

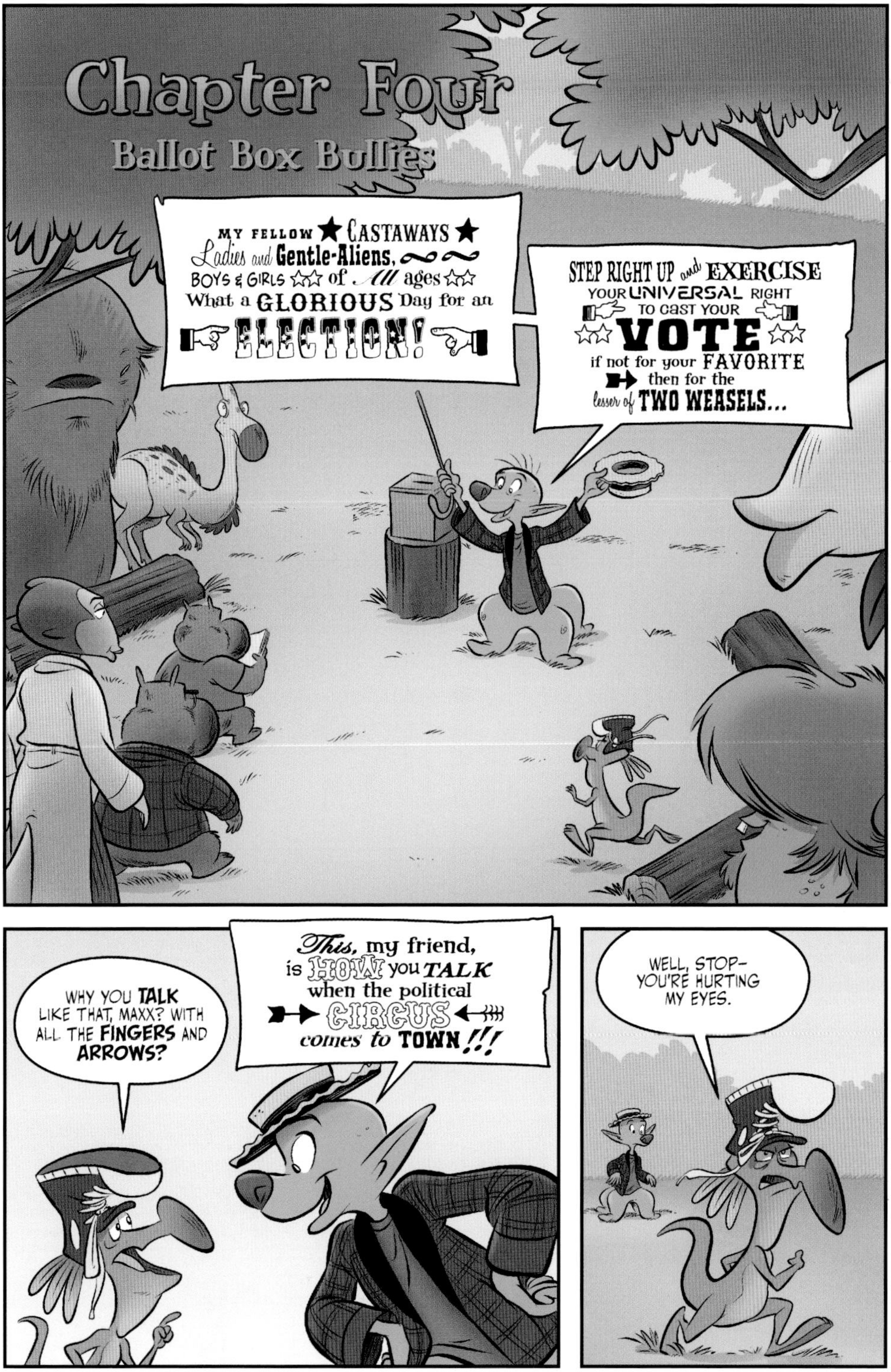
Chapter Four
Ballot Box Bullies
MY FELLOW ★ CASTAWAYS ★ Ladies and Gentle-Aliens, BOYS & GIRLS ☆☆ of All ages ☆☆ What a GLORIOUS Day for an ELECTION!
STEP RIGHT UP and EXERCISE YOUR UNIVERSAL RIGHT TO CAST YOUR VOTE if not for your FAVORITE then for the lesser of TWO WEASELS...
WHY YOU TALK LIKE THAT, MAXX? WITH ALL THE FINGERS AND ARROWS?
This, my friend, is HOW you TALK when the political CIRCUS comes to TOWN!!!
WELL, STOP– YOU'RE HURTING MY EYES.

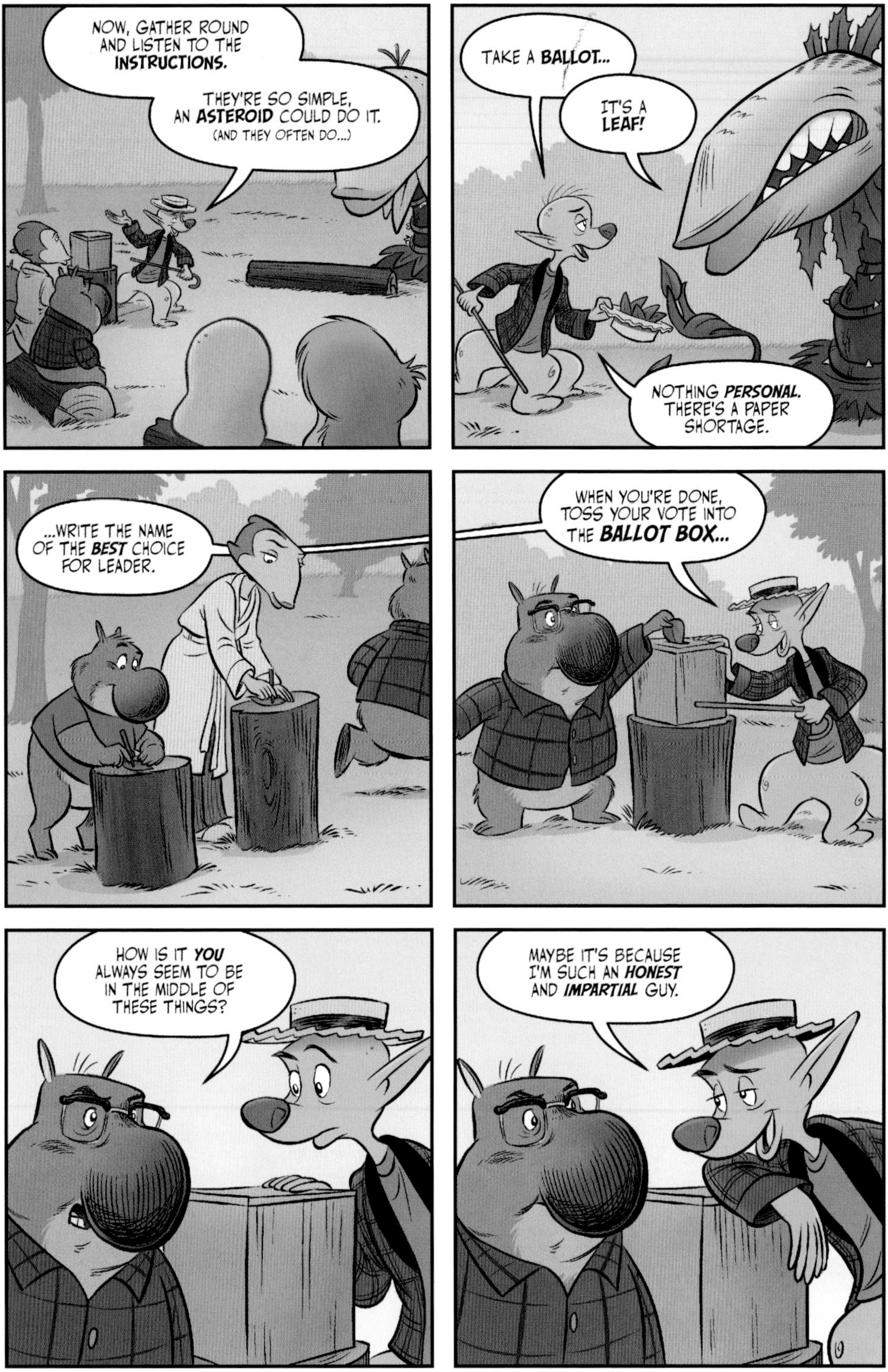
NOW, GATHER ROUND AND LISTEN TO THE **INSTRUCTIONS.**
THEY'RE SO SIMPLE, AN **ASTEROID** COULD DO IT. (AND THEY OFTEN DO...)
TAKE A **BALLOT...**
IT'S A **LEAF!**
NOTHING ***PERSONAL.*** THERE'S A PAPER SHORTAGE.
...WRITE THE NAME OF THE ***BEST*** CHOICE FOR LEADER.
WHEN YOU'RE DONE, TOSS YOUR VOTE INTO THE ***BALLOT BOX...***
HOW IS IT ***YOU*** ALWAYS SEEM TO BE IN THE MIDDLE OF THESE THINGS?
MAYBE IT'S BECAUSE I'M SUCH AN ***HONEST*** AND ***IMPARTIAL*** GUY.

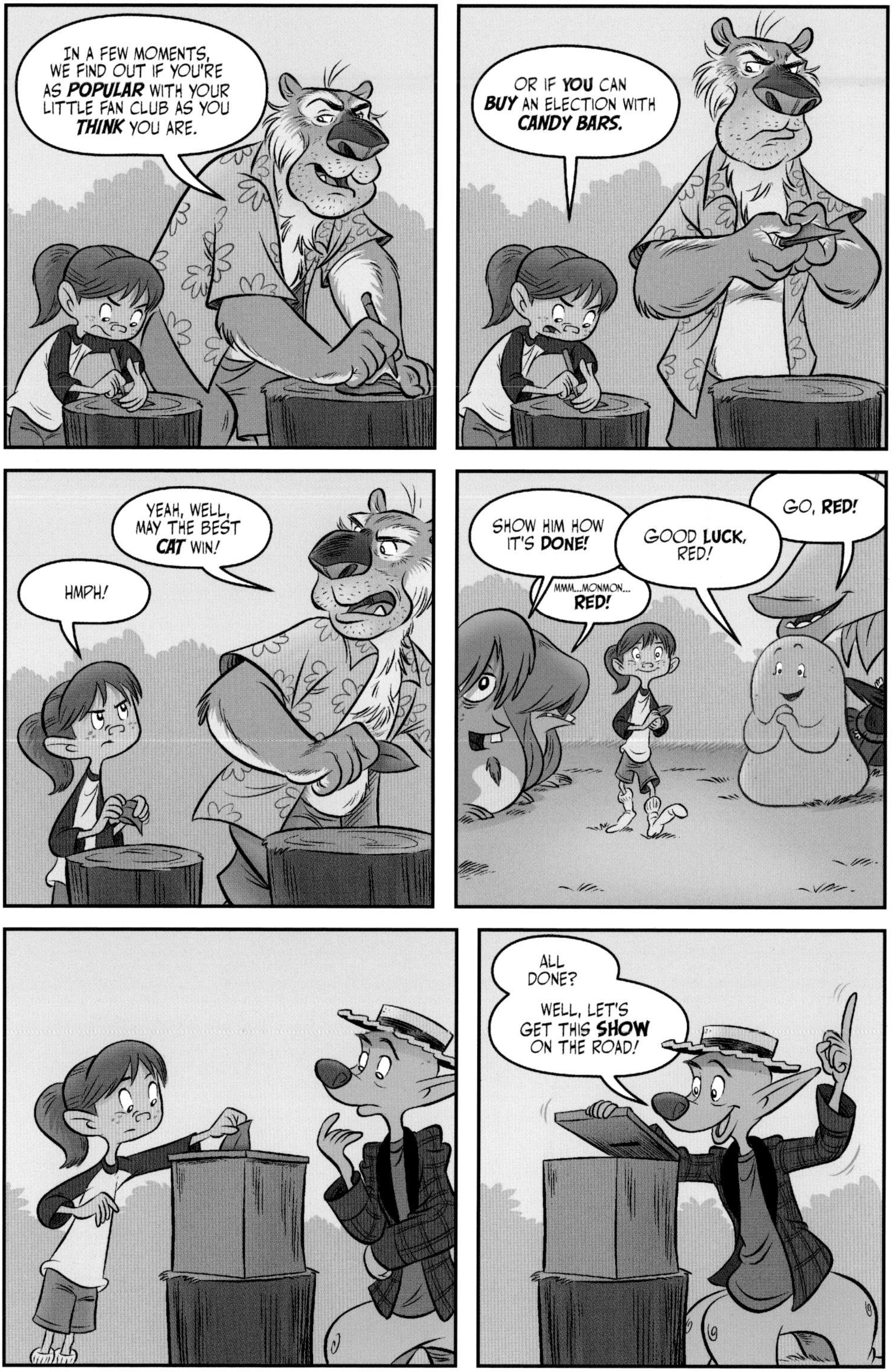
IN A FEW MOMENTS, WE FIND OUT IF YOU'RE AS POPULAR WITH YOUR LITTLE FAN CLUB AS YOU THINK YOU ARE.
OR IF YOU CAN BUY AN ELECTION WITH CANDY BARS.
YEAH, WELL, MAY THE BEST CAT WIN!
HMPH!
SHOW HIM HOW IT'S DONE!
MMM...MONMON... RED!
GOOD LUCK, RED!
GO, RED!
ALL DONE?
WELL, LET'S GET THIS SHOW ON THE ROAD!

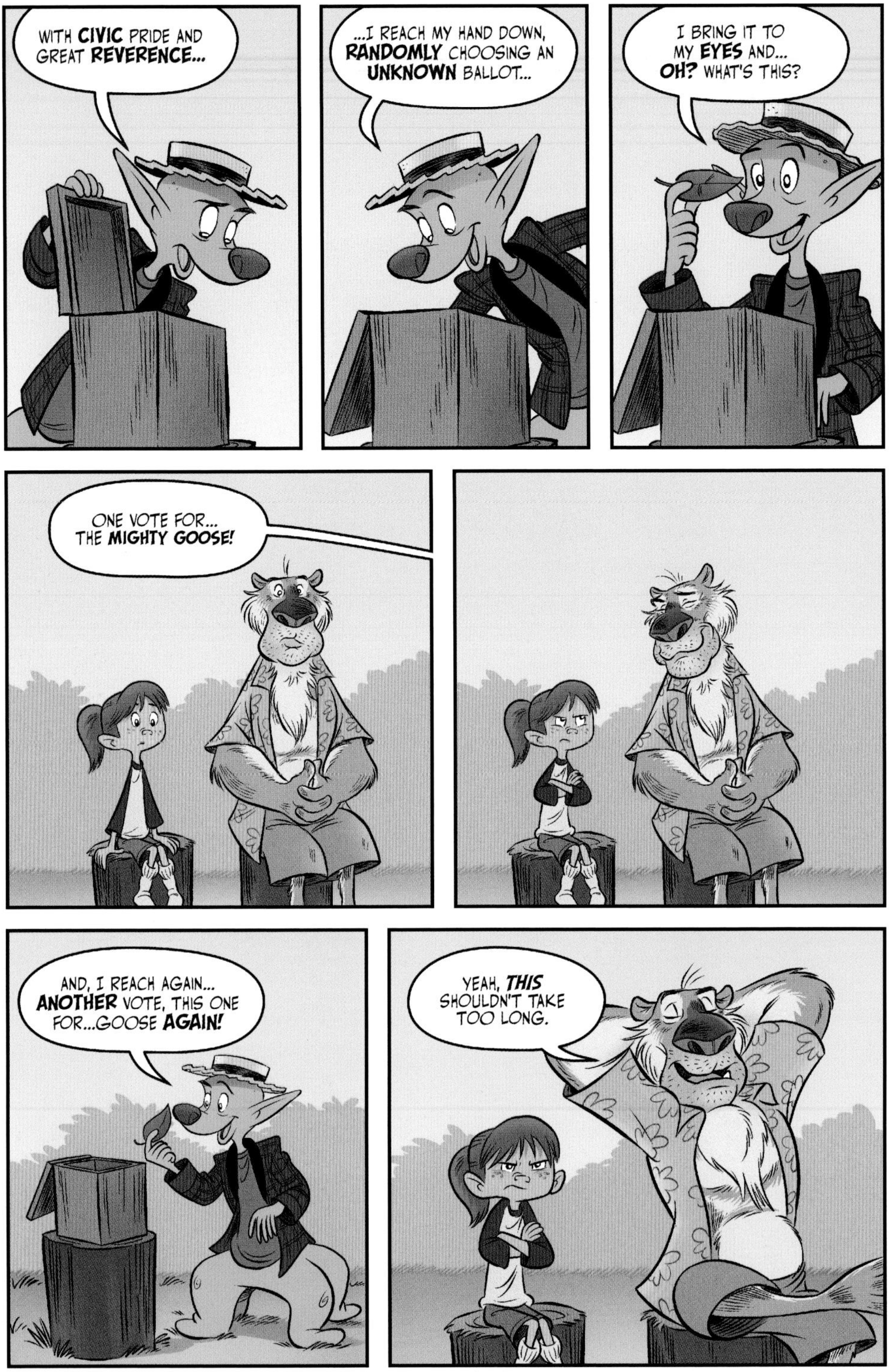
WITH CIVIC PRIDE AND GREAT REVERENCE...
...I REACH MY HAND DOWN, RANDOMLY CHOOSING AN UNKNOWN BALLOT...
I BRING IT TO MY EYES AND... OH? WHAT'S THIS?
ONE VOTE FOR... THE MIGHTY GOOSE!
AND, I REACH AGAIN... ANOTHER VOTE, THIS ONE FOR...GOOSE AGAIN!
YEAH, THIS SHOULDN'T TAKE TOO LONG.

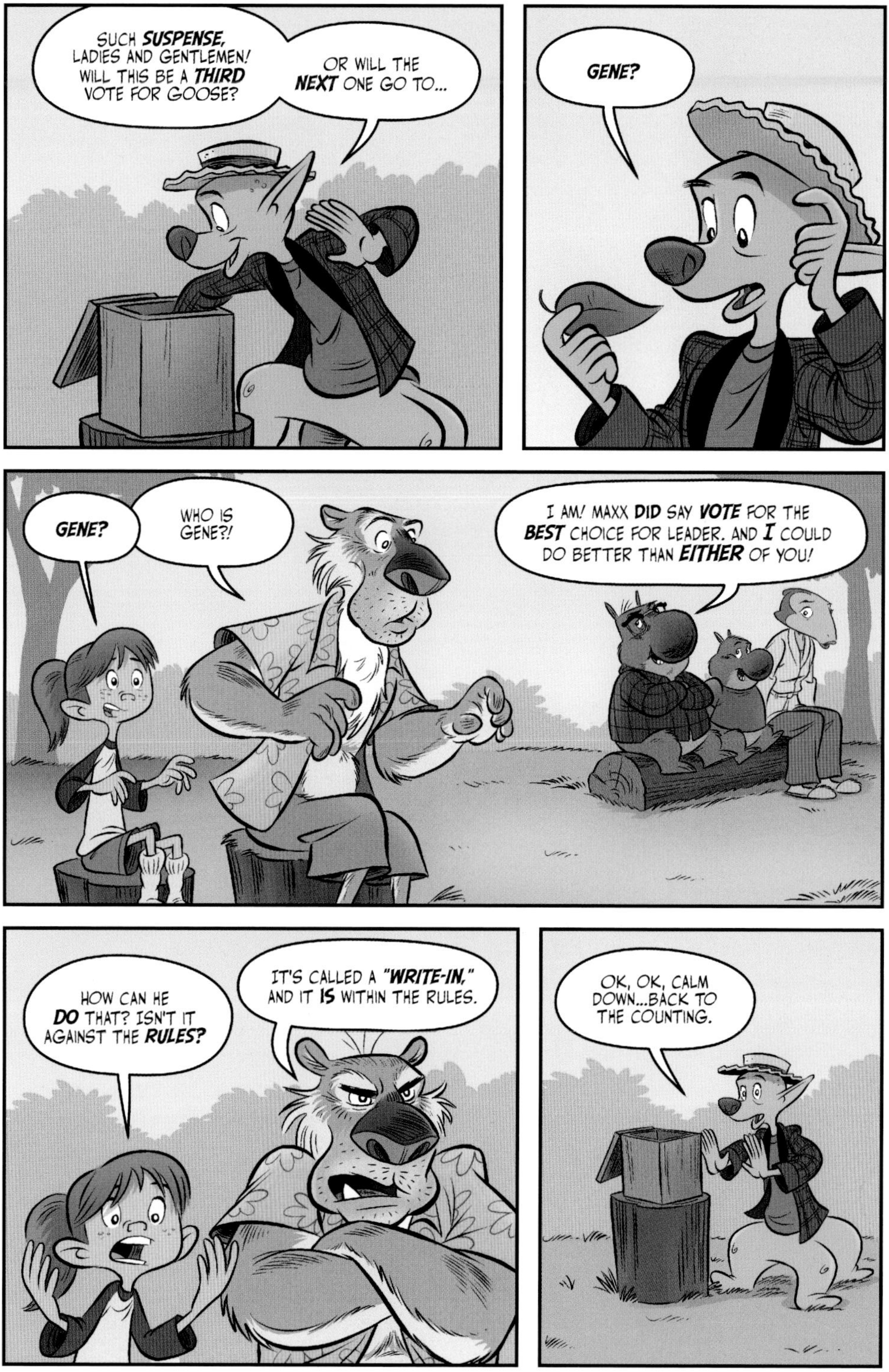
SUCH SUSPENSE, LADIES AND GENTLEMEN! WILL THIS BE A THIRD VOTE FOR GOOSE?
OR WILL THE NEXT ONE GO TO...
GENE?
GENE?
WHO IS GENE?!
I AM! MAXX DID SAY VOTE FOR THE BEST CHOICE FOR LEADER. AND I COULD DO BETTER THAN EITHER OF YOU!
HOW CAN HE DO THAT? ISN'T IT AGAINST THE RULES?
IT'S CALLED A "WRITE-IN," AND IT IS WITHIN THE RULES.
OK, OK, CALM DOWN...BACK TO THE COUNTING.

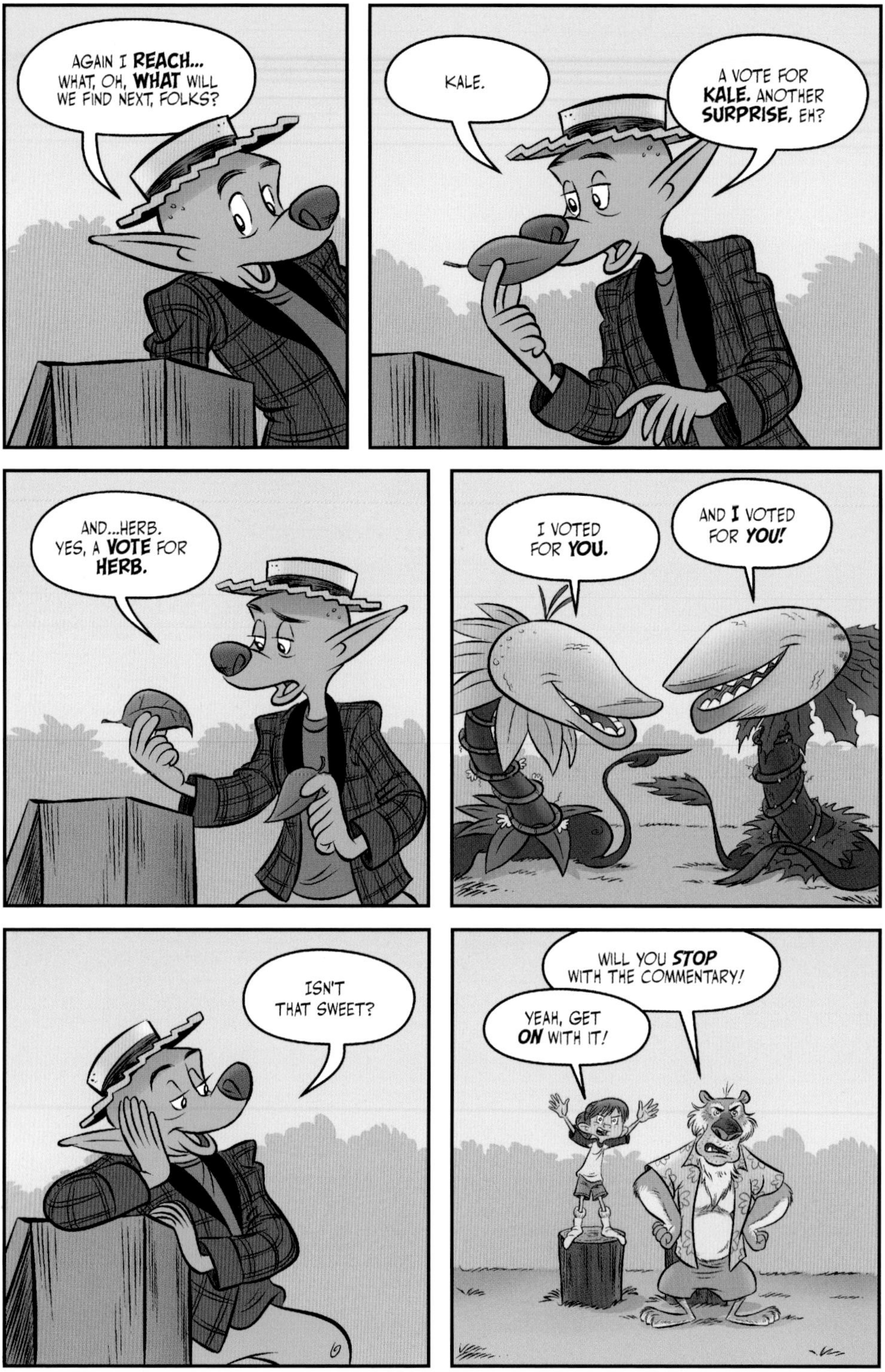
AGAIN I REACH... WHAT, OH, WHAT WILL WE FIND NEXT, FOLKS?
KALE.
A VOTE FOR KALE. ANOTHER SURPRISE, EH?
AND...HERB. YES, A VOTE FOR HERB.
I VOTED FOR YOU.
AND I VOTED FOR YOU!
ISN'T THAT SWEET?
WILL YOU STOP WITH THE COMMENTARY!
YEAH, GET ON WITH IT!

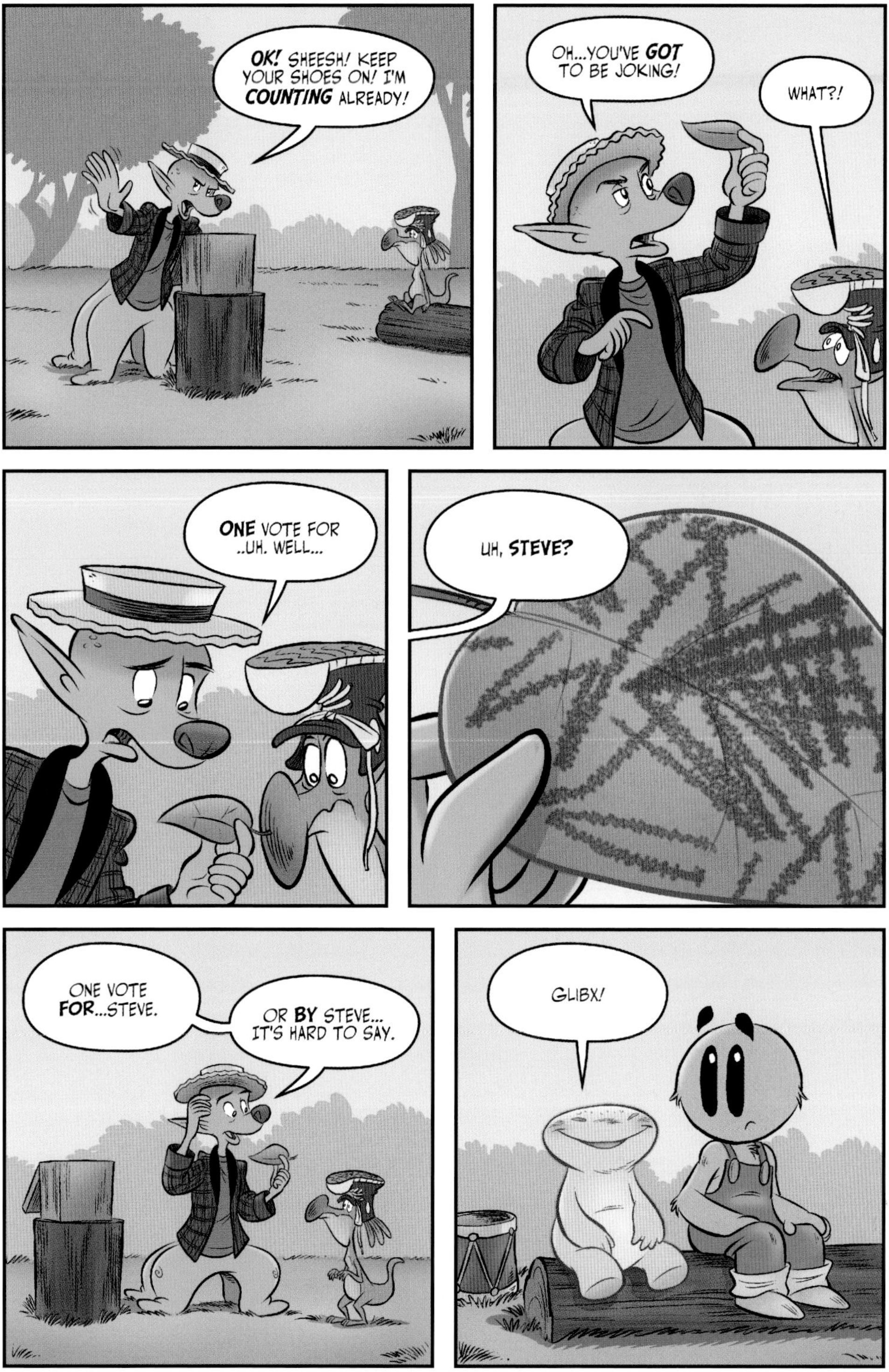
OK! SHEESH! KEEP YOUR SHOES ON! I'M COUNTING ALREADY!
OH...YOU'VE GOT TO BE JOKING!
WHAT?!
ONE VOTE FOR ..UH. WELL...
UH, STEVE?
ONE VOTE FOR...STEVE.
OR BY STEVE... IT'S HARD TO SAY.
GLIBX!

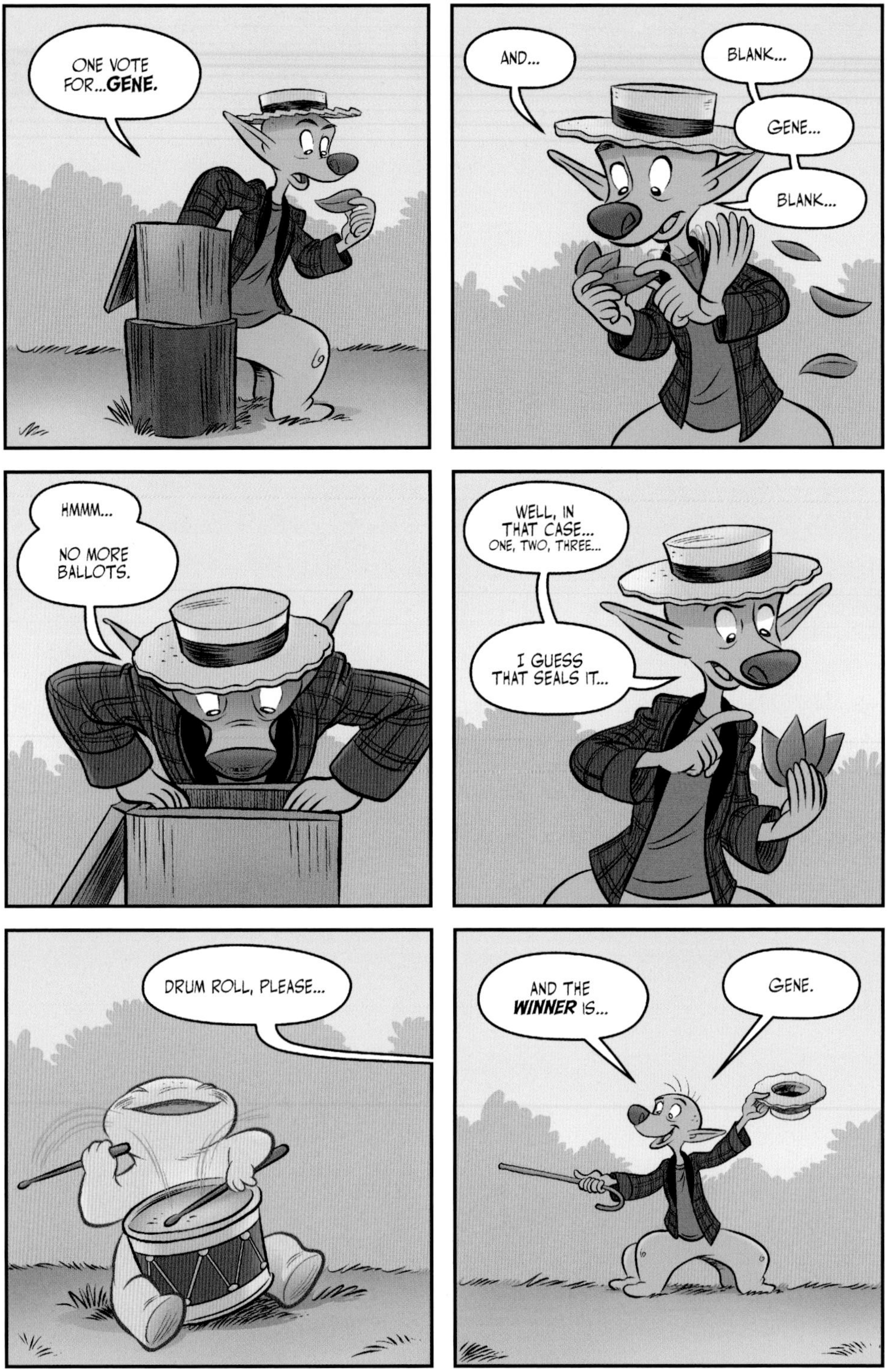
ONE VOTE FOR...GENE.
AND...
BLANK...
GENE...
BLANK...
HMMM...
NO MORE BALLOTS.
WELL, IN THAT CASE... ONE, TWO, THREE...
I GUESS THAT SEALS IT...
DRUM ROLL, PLEASE...
AND THE WINNER IS...
GENE.

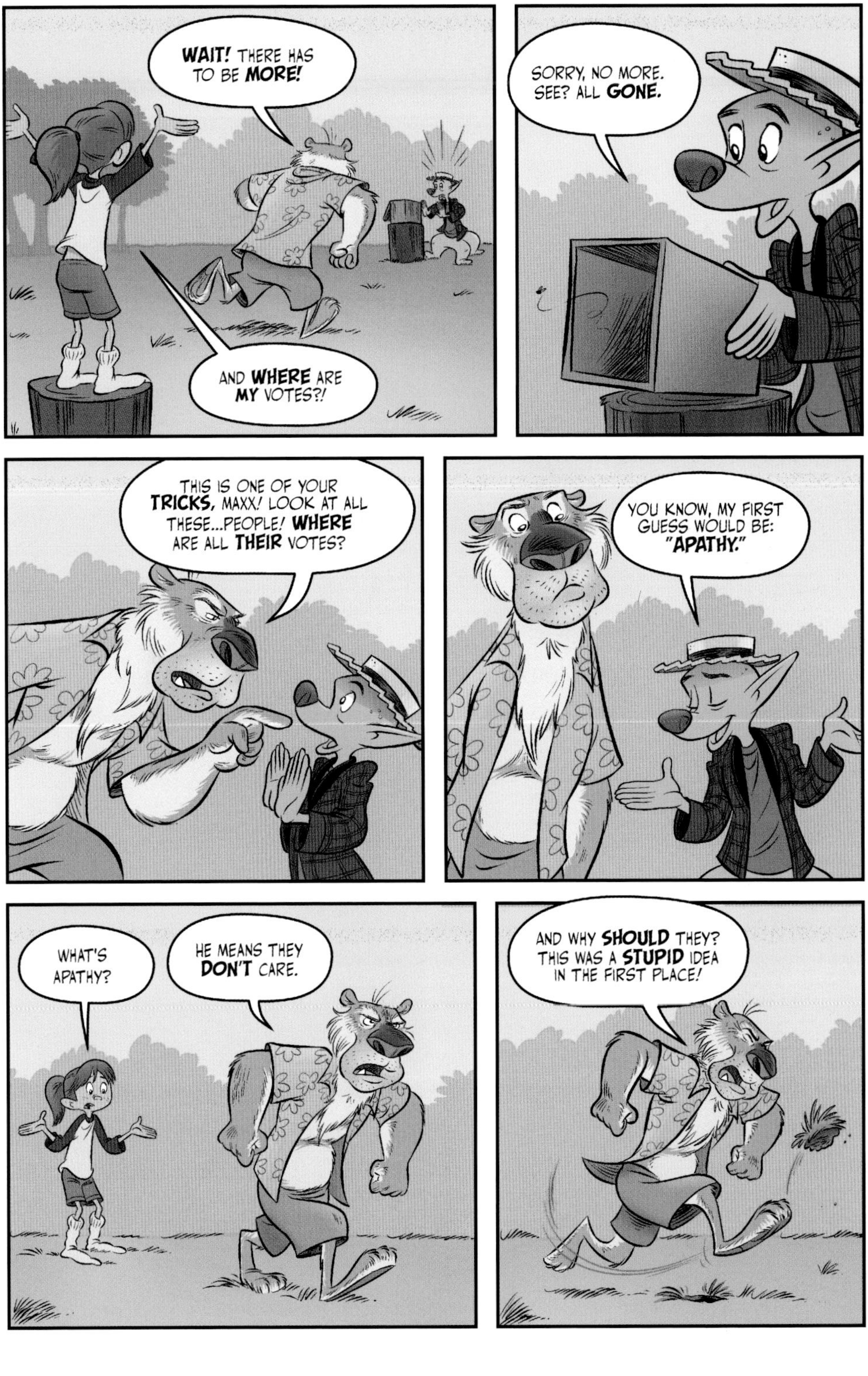
WAIT! THERE HAS TO BE MORE!
AND WHERE ARE MY VOTES?!
SORRY, NO MORE. SEE? ALL GONE.
THIS IS ONE OF YOUR TRICKS, MAXX! LOOK AT ALL THESE...PEOPLE! WHERE ARE ALL THEIR VOTES?
YOU KNOW, MY FIRST GUESS WOULD BE: "APATHY."
WHAT'S APATHY?
HE MEANS THEY DON'T CARE.
AND WHY SHOULD THEY? THIS WAS A STUPID IDEA IN THE FIRST PLACE!

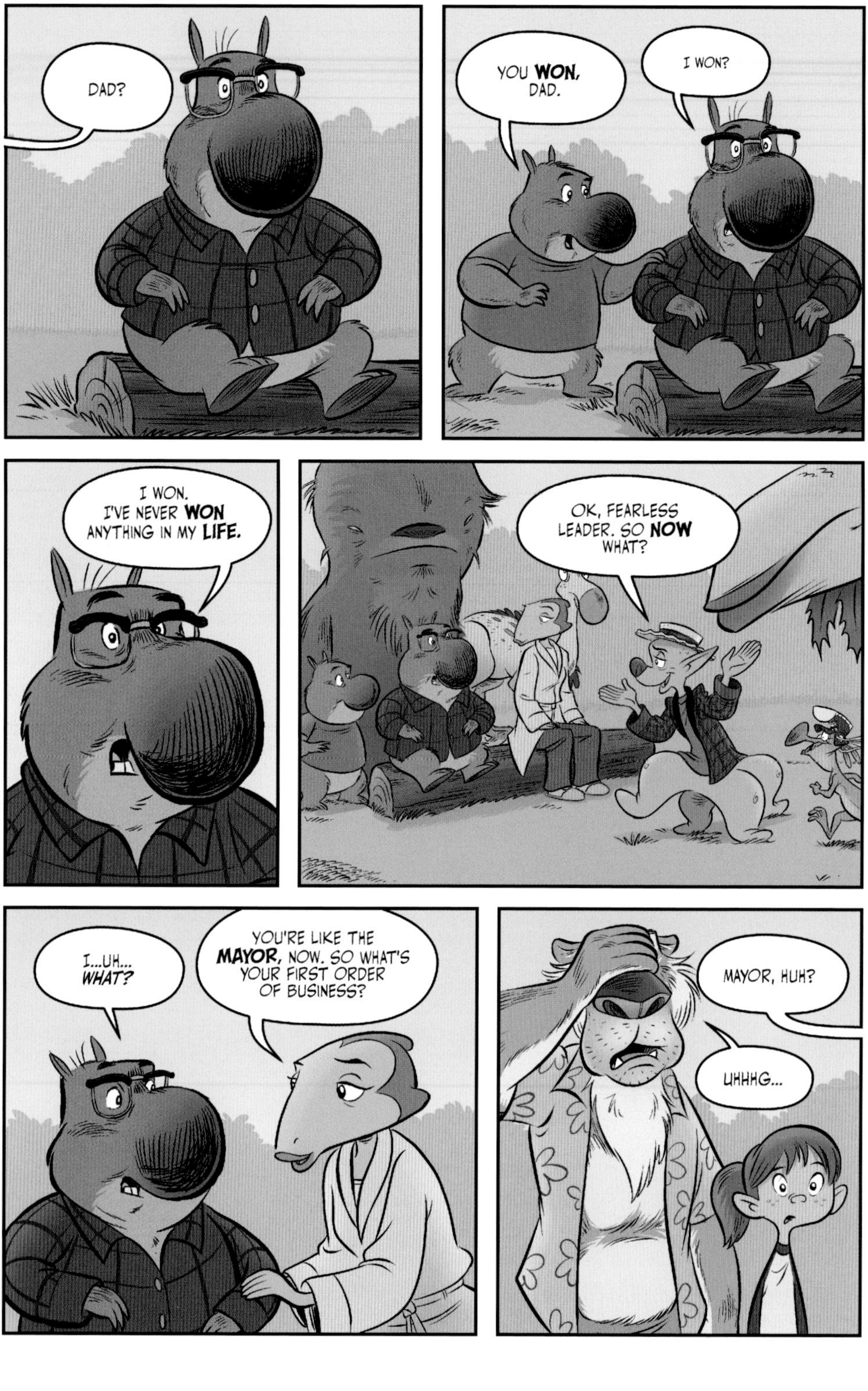
DAD?
YOU WON, DAD.
I WON?
I WON. I'VE NEVER WON ANYTHING IN MY LIFE.
OK, FEARLESS LEADER. SO NOW WHAT?
I...UH... WHAT?
YOU'RE LIKE THE MAYOR, NOW. SO WHAT'S YOUR FIRST ORDER OF BUSINESS?
MAYOR, HUH?
UHHHG...

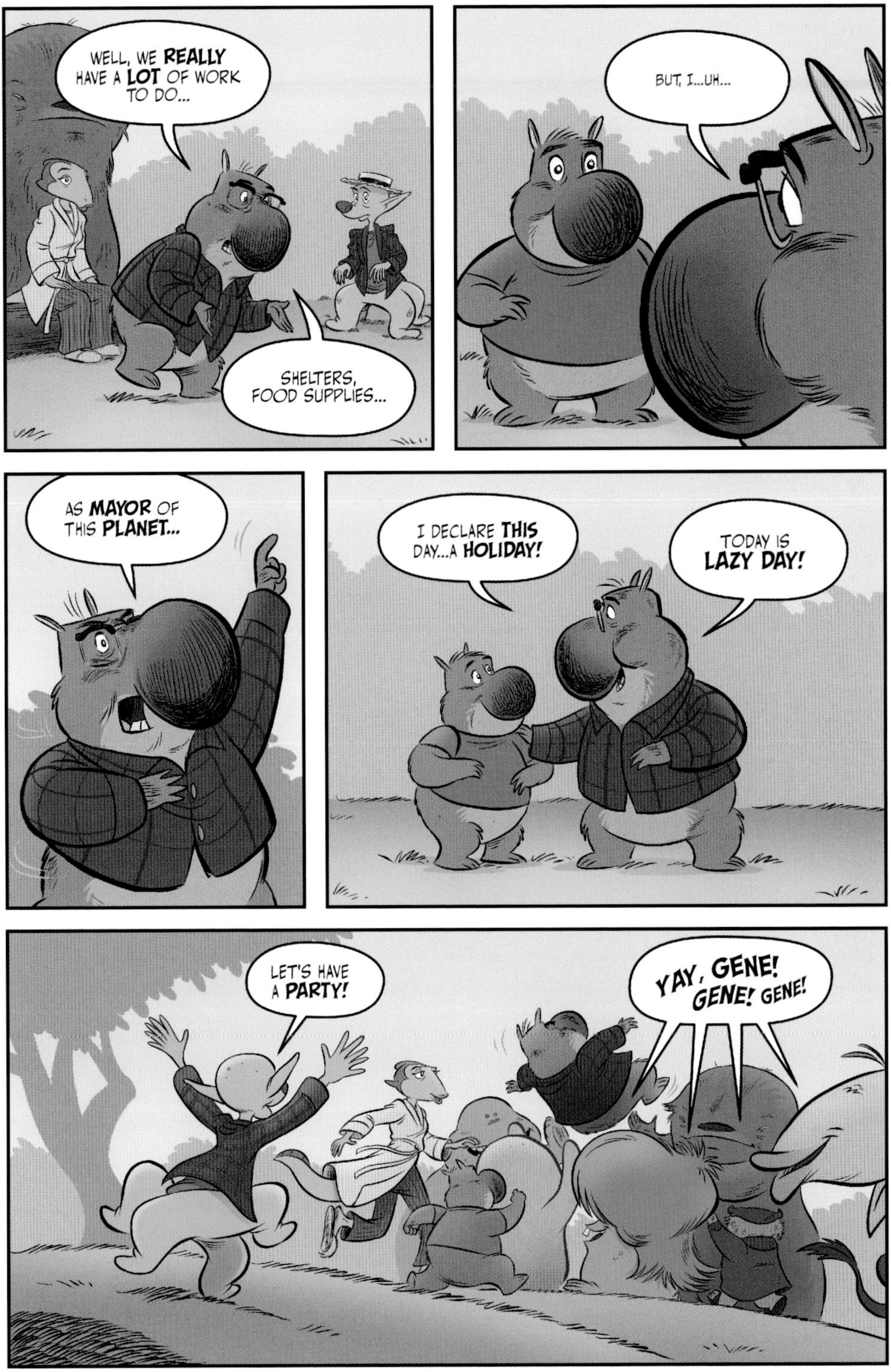
WELL, WE REALLY HAVE A LOT OF WORK TO DO...
SHELTERS, FOOD SUPPLIES...
BUT, I...UH...
AS MAYOR OF THIS PLANET...
I DECLARE THIS DAY...A HOLIDAY!
TODAY IS LAZY DAY!
LET'S HAVE A PARTY!
YAY, GENE! GENE! GENE!

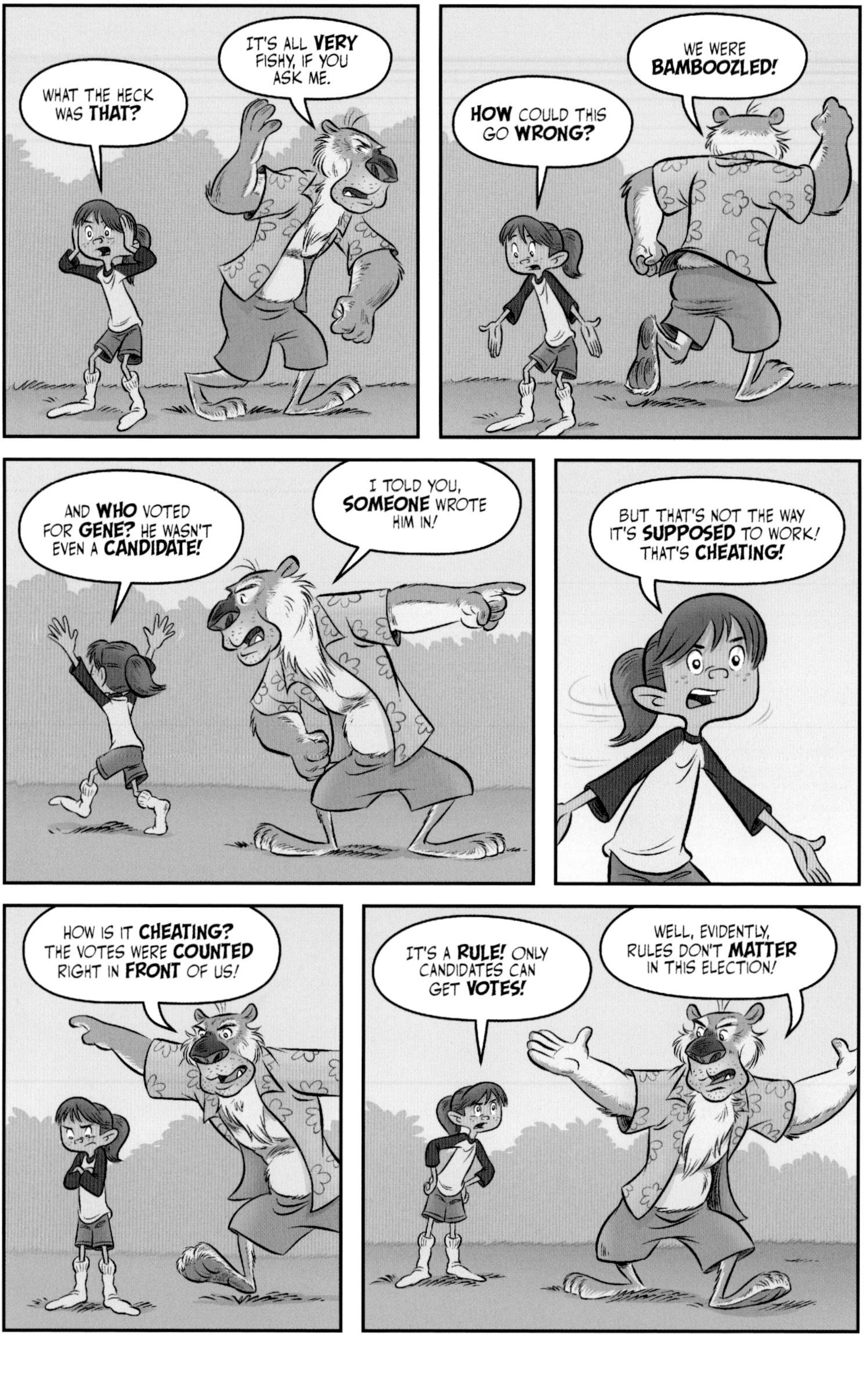
WHAT THE HECK WAS THAT?
IT'S ALL VERY FISHY, IF YOU ASK ME.
HOW COULD THIS GO WRONG?
WE WERE BAMBOOZLED!
AND WHO VOTED FOR GENE? HE WASN'T EVEN A CANDIDATE!
I TOLD YOU, SOMEONE WROTE HIM IN!
BUT THAT'S NOT THE WAY IT'S SUPPOSED TO WORK! THAT'S CHEATING!
HOW IS IT CHEATING? THE VOTES WERE COUNTED RIGHT IN FRONT OF US!
IT'S A RULE! ONLY CANDIDATES CAN GET VOTES!
WELL, EVIDENTLY, RULES DON'T MATTER IN THIS ELECTION!

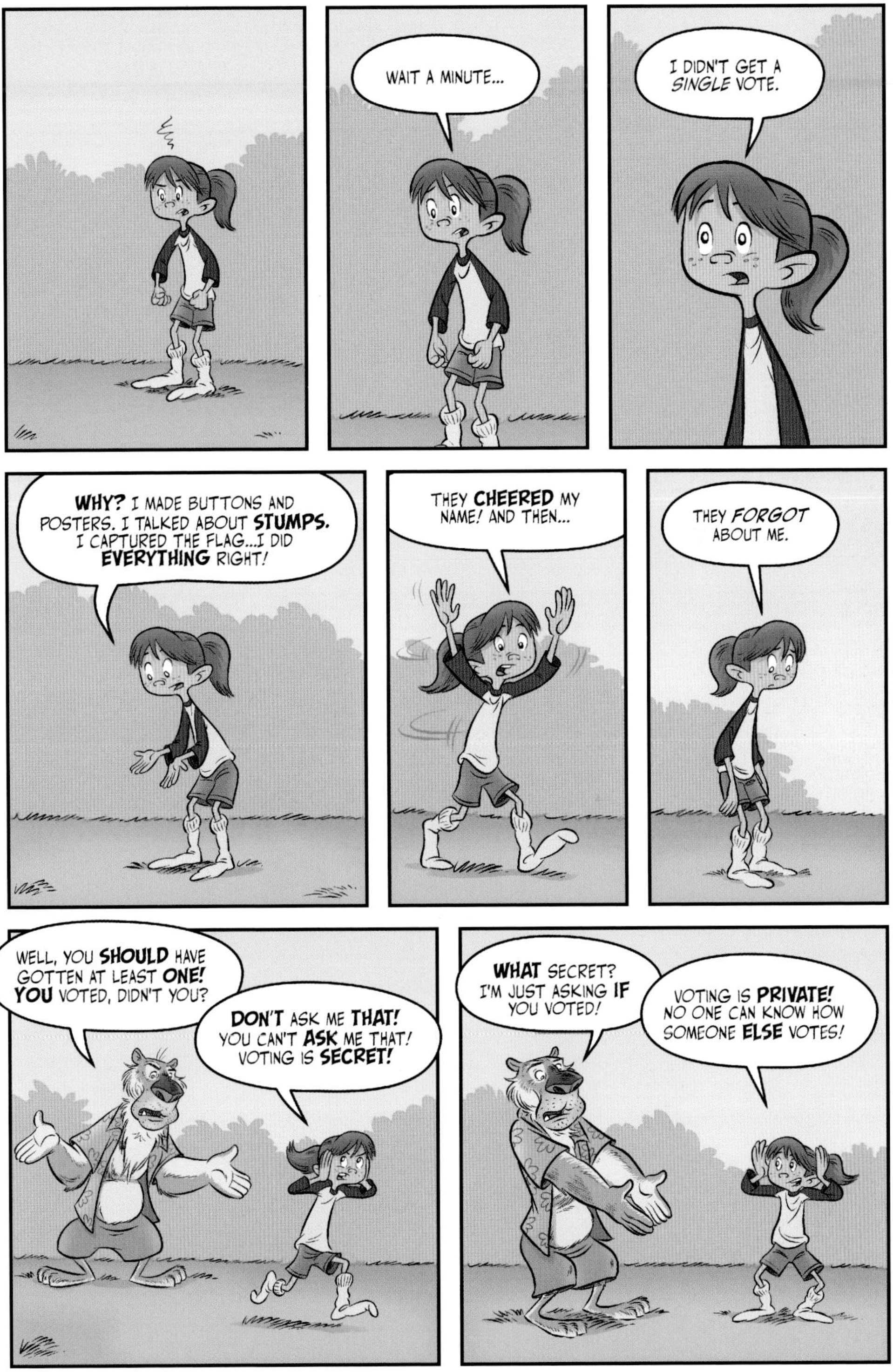
WAIT A MINUTE...
I DIDN'T GET A *SINGLE* VOTE.
WHY? I MADE BUTTONS AND POSTERS. I TALKED ABOUT **STUMPS.** I CAPTURED THE FLAG...I DID **EVERYTHING** RIGHT!
THEY **CHEERED** MY NAME! AND THEN...
THEY *FORGOT* ABOUT ME.
WELL, YOU **SHOULD** HAVE GOTTEN AT LEAST **ONE! YOU** VOTED, DIDN'T YOU?
DON'T ASK ME **THAT!** YOU CAN'T **ASK** ME THAT! VOTING IS **SECRET!**
WHAT SECRET? I'M JUST ASKING **IF** YOU VOTED!
VOTING IS **PRIVATE!** NO ONE CAN KNOW HOW SOMEONE **ELSE** VOTES!

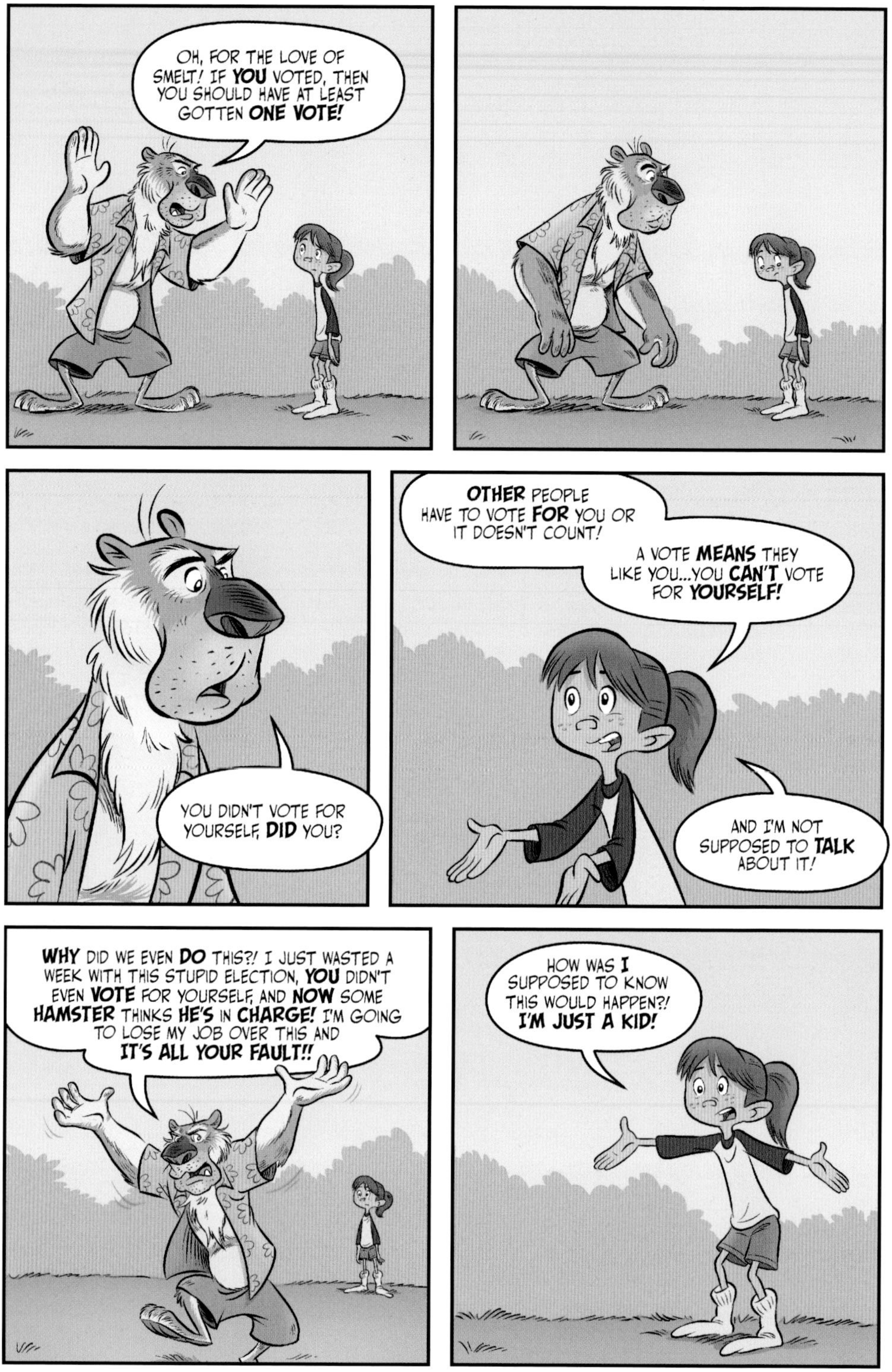
OH, FOR THE LOVE OF SMELT! IF YOU VOTED, THEN YOU SHOULD HAVE AT LEAST GOTTEN ONE VOTE!
YOU DIDN'T VOTE FOR YOURSELF, DID YOU?
OTHER PEOPLE HAVE TO VOTE FOR YOU OR IT DOESN'T COUNT!
A VOTE MEANS THEY LIKE YOU...YOU CAN'T VOTE FOR YOURSELF!
AND I'M NOT SUPPOSED TO TALK ABOUT IT!
WHY DID WE EVEN DO THIS?! I JUST WASTED A WEEK WITH THIS STUPID ELECTION, YOU DIDN'T EVEN VOTE FOR YOURSELF, AND NOW SOME HAMSTER THINKS HE'S IN CHARGE! I'M GOING TO LOSE MY JOB OVER THIS AND IT'S ALL YOUR FAULT!!
HOW WAS I SUPPOSED TO KNOW THIS WOULD HAPPEN?! I'M JUST A KID!

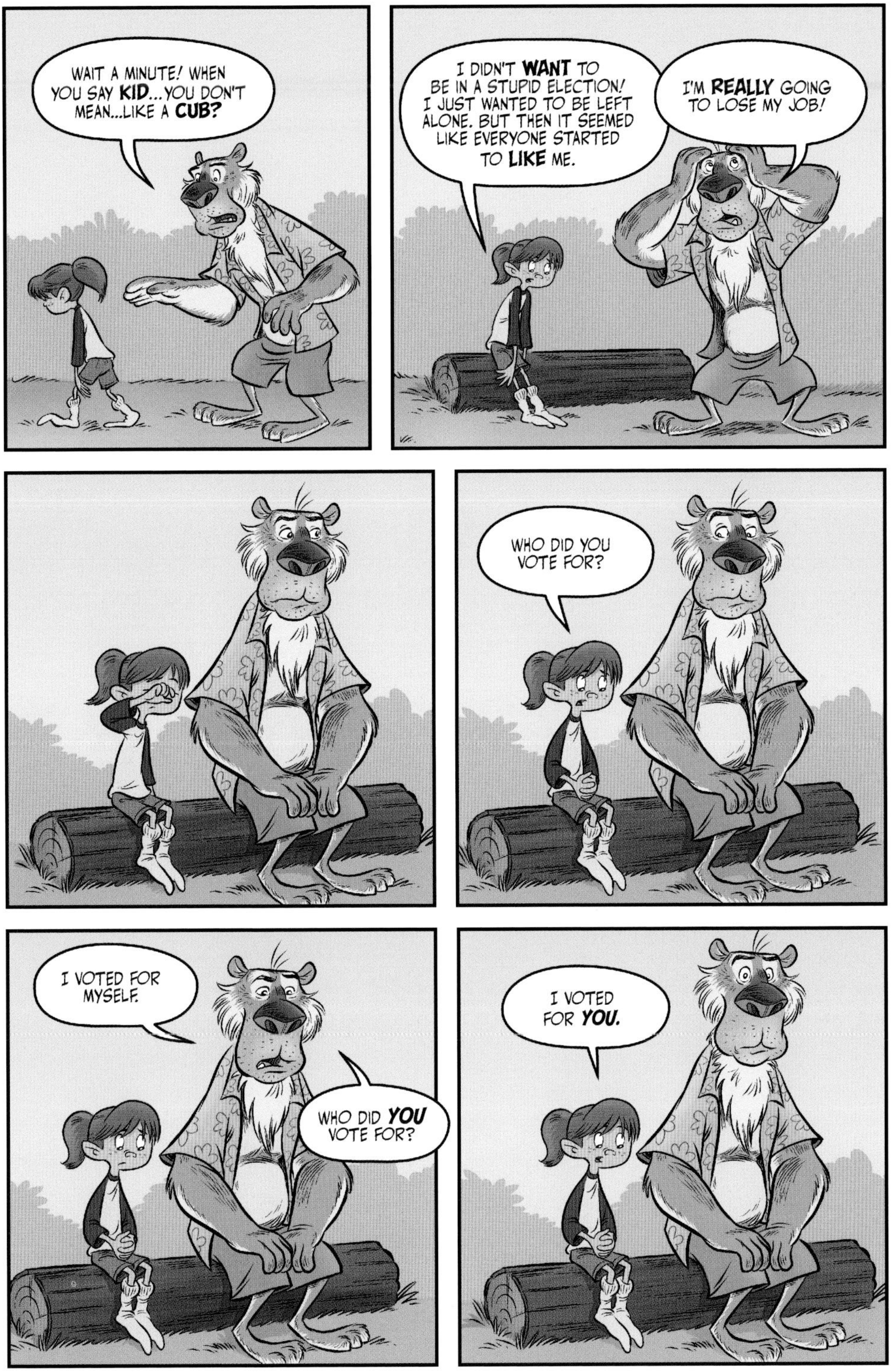
WAIT A MINUTE! WHEN YOU SAY KID...YOU DON'T MEAN...LIKE A CUB?
I DIDN'T WANT TO BE IN A STUPID ELECTION! I JUST WANTED TO BE LEFT ALONE. BUT THEN IT SEEMED LIKE EVERYONE STARTED TO LIKE ME.
I'M REALLY GOING TO LOSE MY JOB!
WHO DID YOU VOTE FOR?
I VOTED FOR MYSELF.
WHO DID YOU VOTE FOR?
I VOTED FOR YOU.

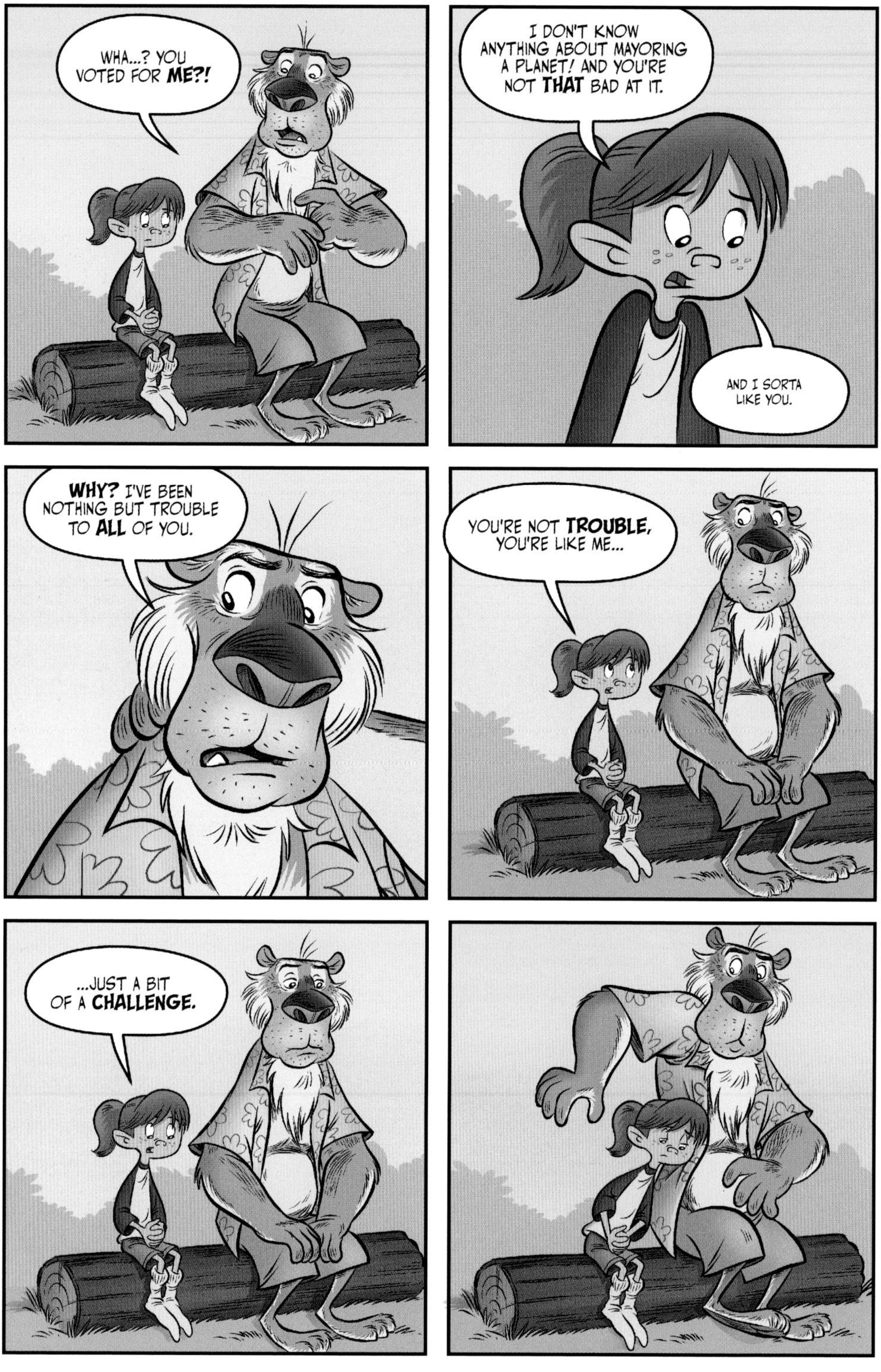
WHA...? YOU VOTED FOR **ME?!**
I DON'T KNOW ANYTHING ABOUT MAYORING A PLANET! AND YOU'RE NOT **THAT** BAD AT IT.
AND I SORTA LIKE YOU.
WHY? I'VE BEEN NOTHING BUT TROUBLE TO **ALL** OF YOU.
YOU'RE NOT **TROUBLE,** YOU'RE LIKE ME...
...JUST A BIT OF A **CHALLENGE.**

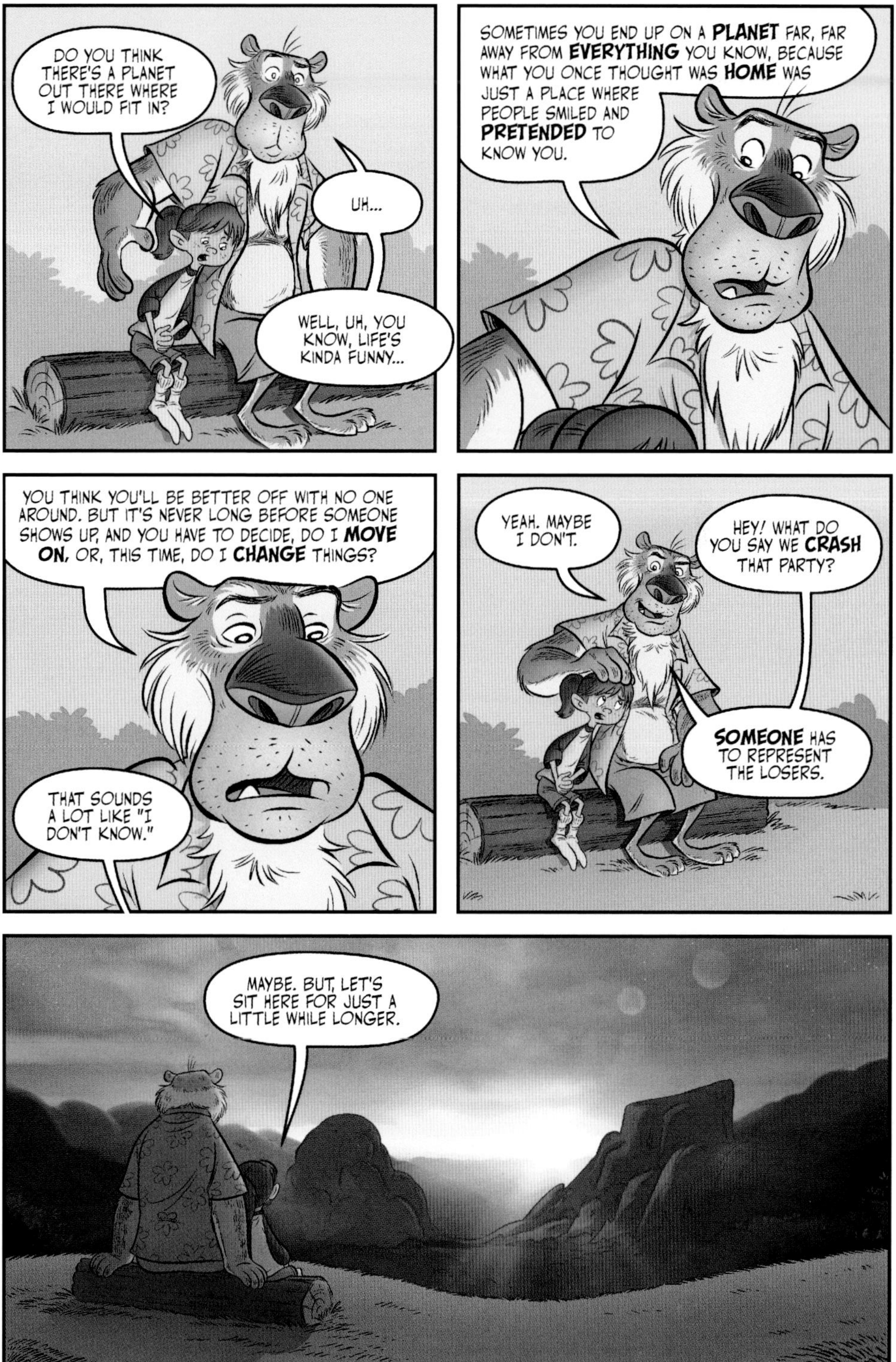
DO YOU THINK THERE'S A PLANET OUT THERE WHERE I WOULD FIT IN?
UH...
WELL, UH, YOU KNOW, LIFE'S KINDA FUNNY...
SOMETIMES YOU END UP ON A **PLANET** FAR, FAR AWAY FROM **EVERYTHING** YOU KNOW, BECAUSE WHAT YOU ONCE THOUGHT WAS **HOME** WAS JUST A PLACE WHERE PEOPLE SMILED AND **PRETENDED** TO KNOW YOU.
YOU THINK YOU'LL BE BETTER OFF WITH NO ONE AROUND. BUT IT'S NEVER LONG BEFORE SOMEONE SHOWS UP, AND YOU HAVE TO DECIDE, DO I **MOVE ON**, OR, THIS TIME, DO I **CHANGE** THINGS?
THAT SOUNDS A LOT LIKE "I DON'T KNOW."
YEAH. MAYBE I DON'T.
HEY! WHAT DO YOU SAY WE **CRASH** THAT PARTY?
SOMEONE HAS TO REPRESENT THE LOSERS.
MAYBE. BUT, LET'S SIT HERE FOR JUST A LITTLE WHILE LONGER.

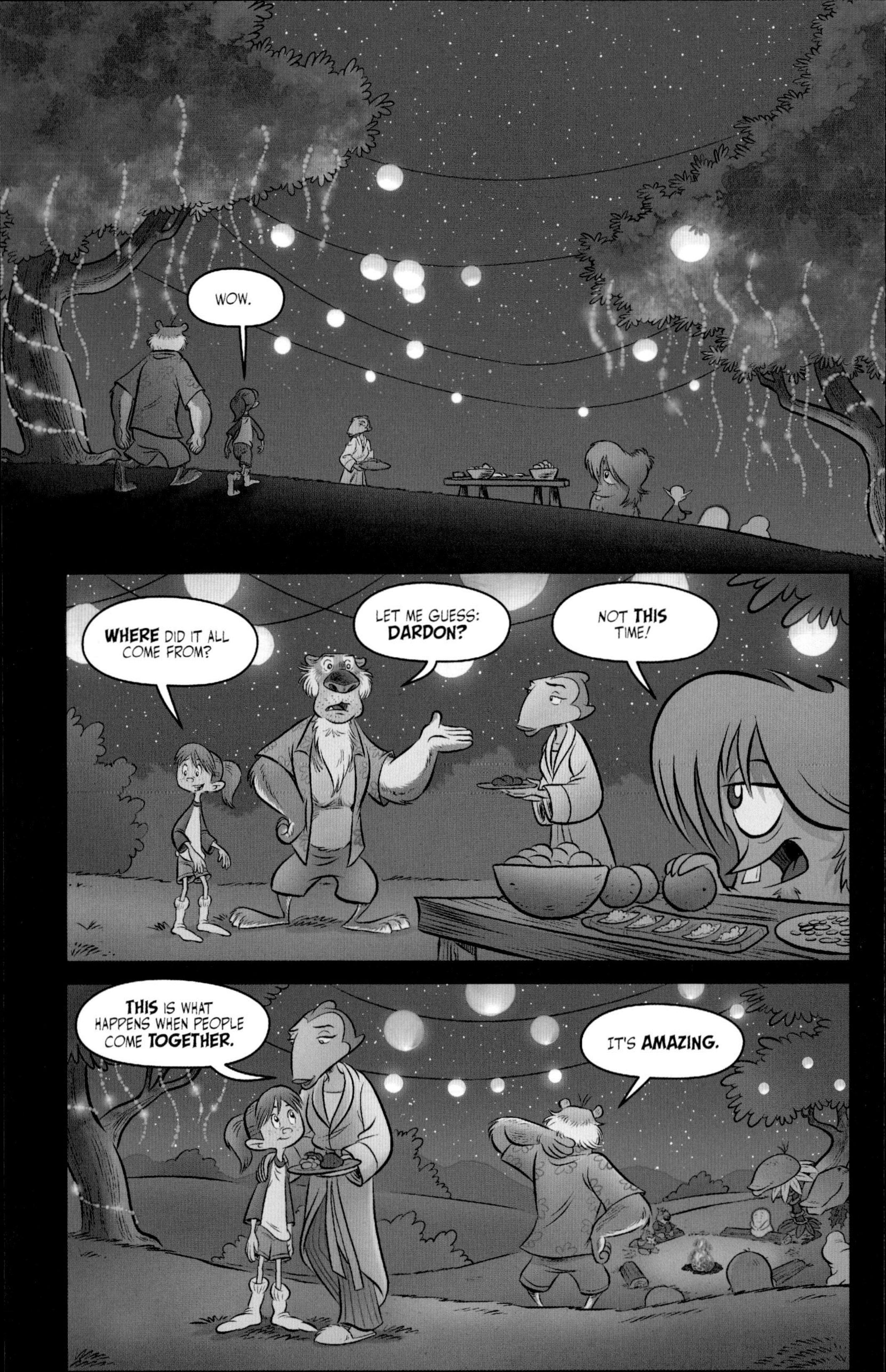
WOW.
WHERE DID IT ALL COME FROM?
LET ME GUESS: **DARDON?**
NOT **THIS** TIME!
THIS IS WHAT HAPPENS WHEN PEOPLE COME **TOGETHER.**
IT'S **AMAZING.**

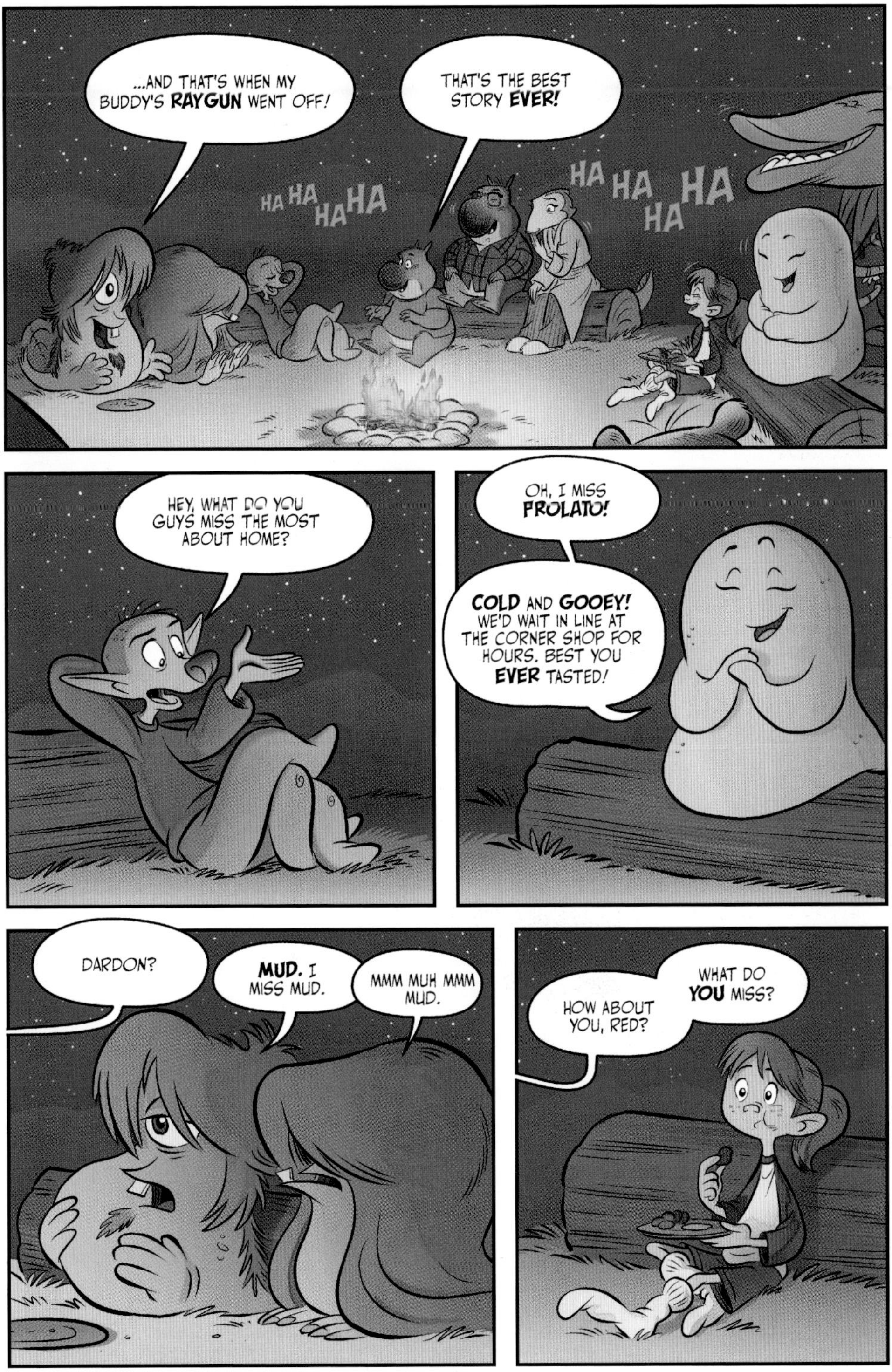
...AND THAT'S WHEN MY BUDDY'S **RAYGUN** WENT OFF!
THAT'S THE BEST STORY **EVER!**
HA HA HA HA
HA HA HA HA
HEY, WHAT DO YOU GUYS MISS THE MOST ABOUT HOME?
OH, I MISS **PROLATO!**
COLD AND **GOOEY!** WE'D WAIT IN LINE AT THE CORNER SHOP FOR HOURS. BEST YOU **EVER** TASTED!
DARDON?
MUD. I MISS MUD.
MMM MUH MMM MUD.
HOW ABOUT YOU, RED?
WHAT DO **YOU** MISS?

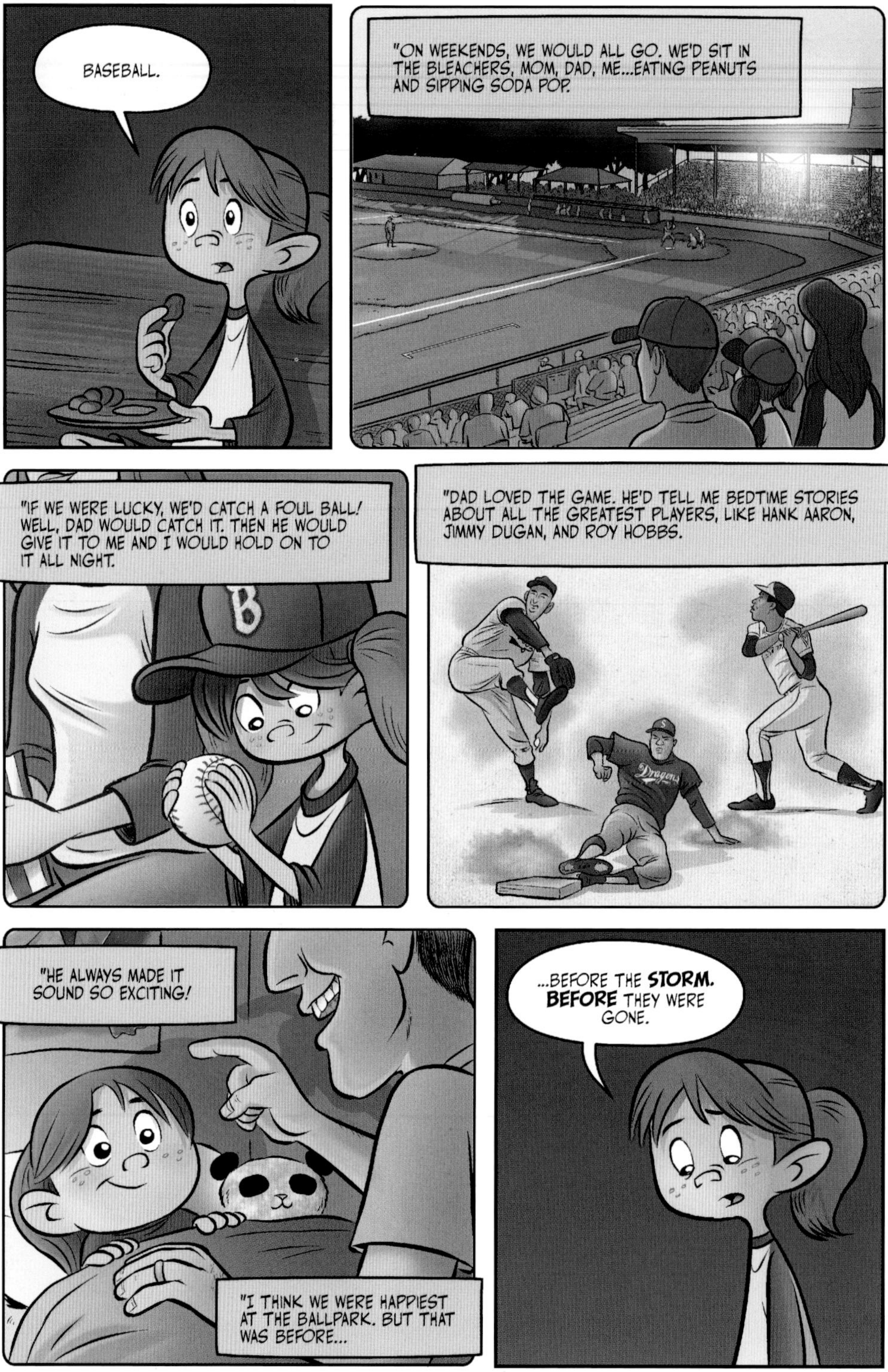
BASEBALL.
"ON WEEKENDS, WE WOULD ALL GO. WE'D SIT IN THE BLEACHERS, MOM, DAD, ME...EATING PEANUTS AND SIPPING SODA POP.
"IF WE WERE LUCKY, WE'D CATCH A FOUL BALL! WELL, DAD WOULD CATCH IT. THEN HE WOULD GIVE IT TO ME AND I WOULD HOLD ON TO IT ALL NIGHT.
"DAD LOVED THE GAME. HE'D TELL ME BEDTIME STORIES ABOUT ALL THE GREATEST PLAYERS, LIKE HANK AARON, JIMMY DUGAN, AND ROY HOBBS.
"HE ALWAYS MADE IT SOUND SO EXCITING!
"I THINK WE WERE HAPPIEST AT THE BALLPARK. BUT THAT WAS BEFORE...
...BEFORE THE **STORM.** **BEFORE** THEY WERE GONE.

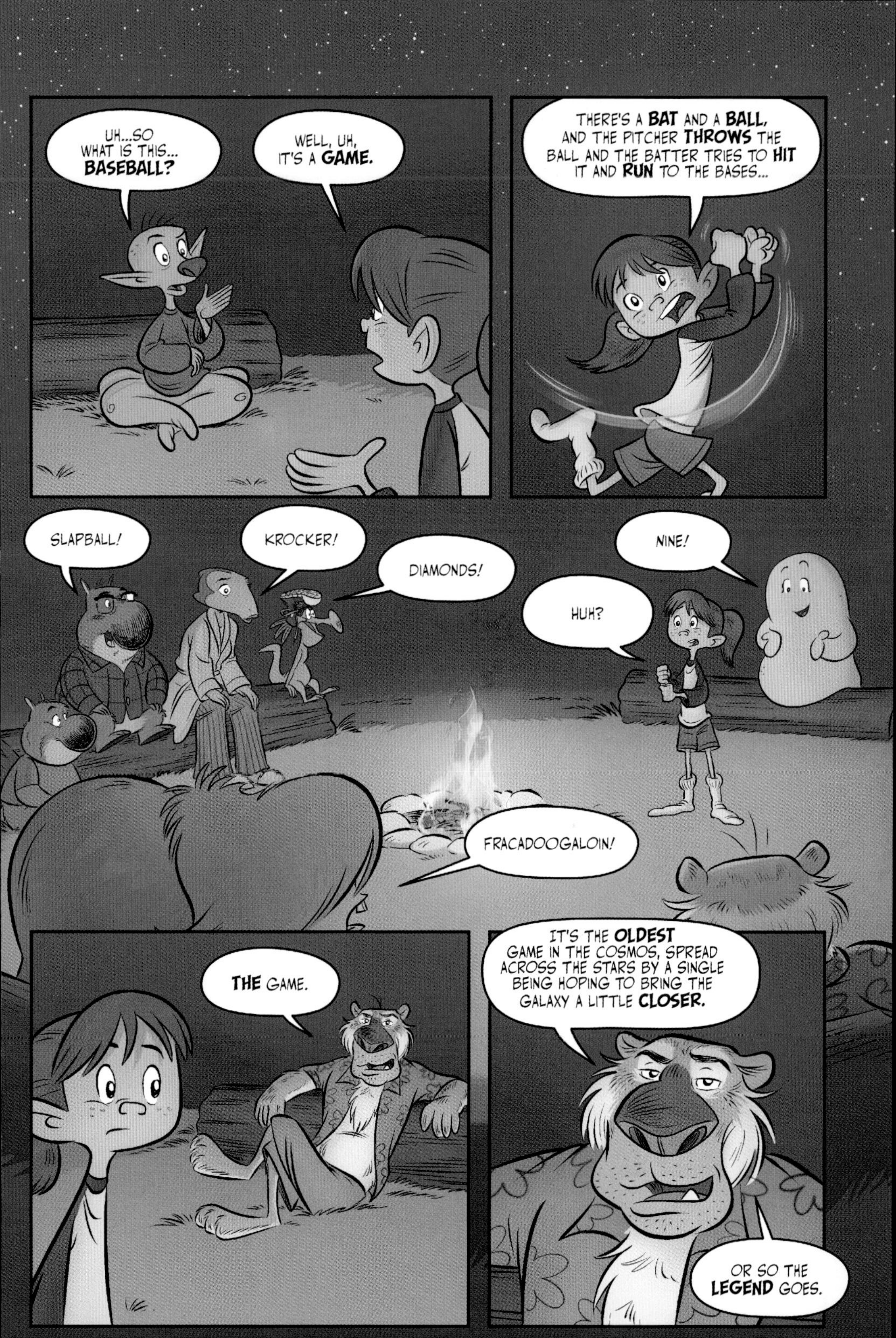
UH...SO WHAT IS THIS... **BASEBALL?**
WELL, UH, IT'S A **GAME.**
THERE'S A **BAT** AND A **BALL,** AND THE PITCHER **THROWS** THE BALL AND THE BATTER TRIES TO **HIT** IT AND **RUN** TO THE BASES...
SLAPBALL!
KROCKER!
DIAMONDS!
NINE!
HUH?
FRACADOOGALOIN!
THE GAME.
IT'S THE **OLDEST** GAME IN THE COSMOS, SPREAD ACROSS THE STARS BY A SINGLE BEING HOPING TO BRING THE GALAXY A LITTLE **CLOSER.**
OR SO THE **LEGEND** GOES.

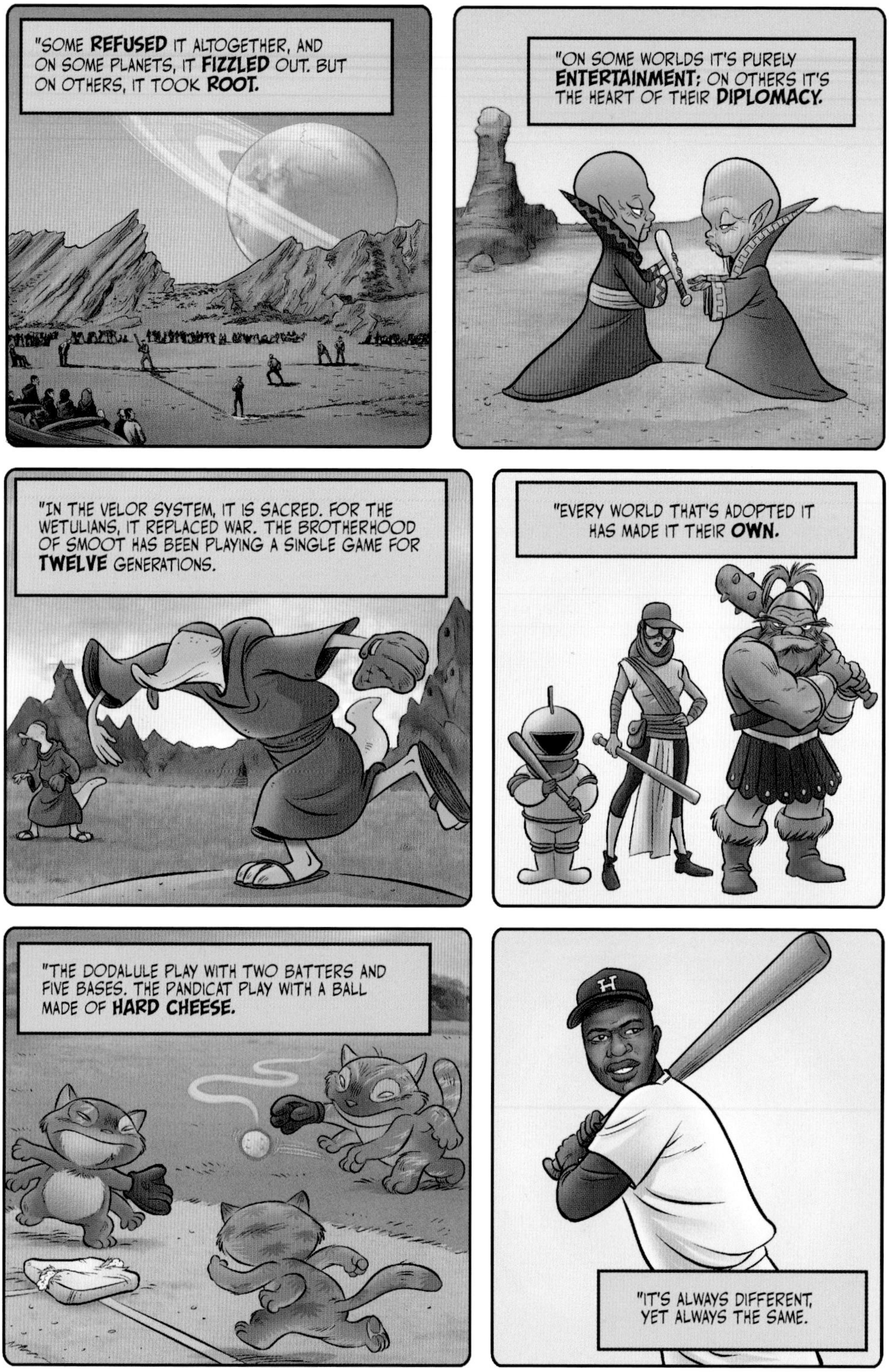
"SOME REFUSED IT ALTOGETHER, AND ON SOME PLANETS, IT FIZZLED OUT. BUT ON OTHERS, IT TOOK ROOT.
"ON SOME WORLDS IT'S PURELY ENTERTAINMENT; ON OTHERS IT'S THE HEART OF THEIR DIPLOMACY.
"IN THE VELOR SYSTEM, IT IS SACRED. FOR THE WETULIANS, IT REPLACED WAR. THE BROTHERHOOD OF SMOOT HAS BEEN PLAYING A SINGLE GAME FOR TWELVE GENERATIONS.
"EVERY WORLD THAT'S ADOPTED IT HAS MADE IT THEIR OWN.
"THE DODALULE PLAY WITH TWO BATTERS AND FIVE BASES. THE PANDICAT PLAY WITH A BALL MADE OF HARD CHEESE.
"IT'S ALWAYS DIFFERENT, YET ALWAYS THE SAME.

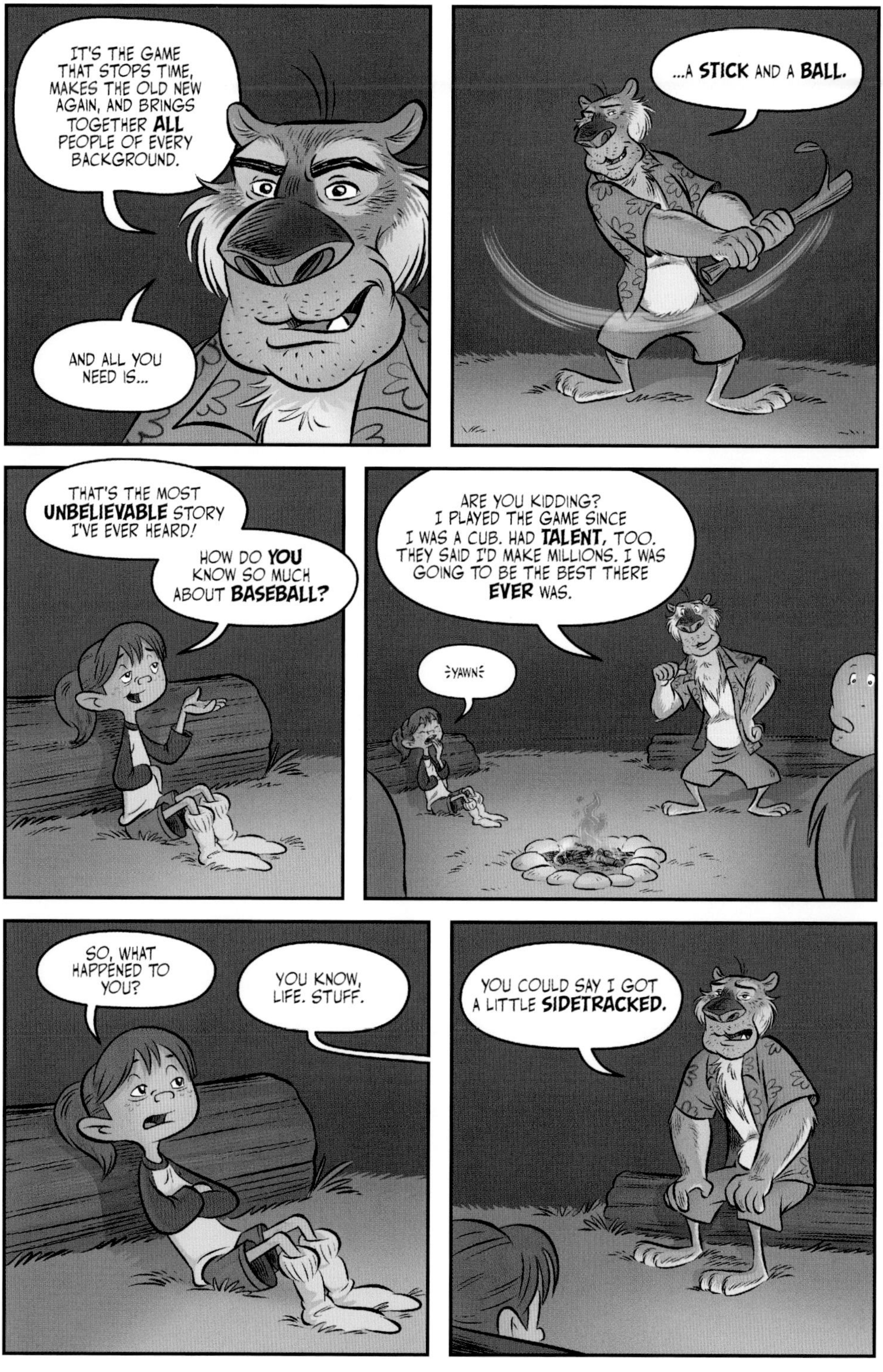
IT'S THE GAME THAT STOPS TIME, MAKES THE OLD NEW AGAIN, AND BRINGS TOGETHER ALL PEOPLE OF EVERY BACKGROUND.
AND ALL YOU NEED IS...
...A STICK AND A BALL.
THAT'S THE MOST UNBELIEVABLE STORY I'VE EVER HEARD!
HOW DO YOU KNOW SO MUCH ABOUT BASEBALL?
ARE YOU KIDDING? I PLAYED THE GAME SINCE I WAS A CUB. HAD TALENT, TOO. THEY SAID I'D MAKE MILLIONS. I WAS GOING TO BE THE BEST THERE EVER WAS.
YAWN
SO, WHAT HAPPENED TO YOU?
YOU KNOW, LIFE. STUFF.
YOU COULD SAY I GOT A LITTLE SIDETRACKED.

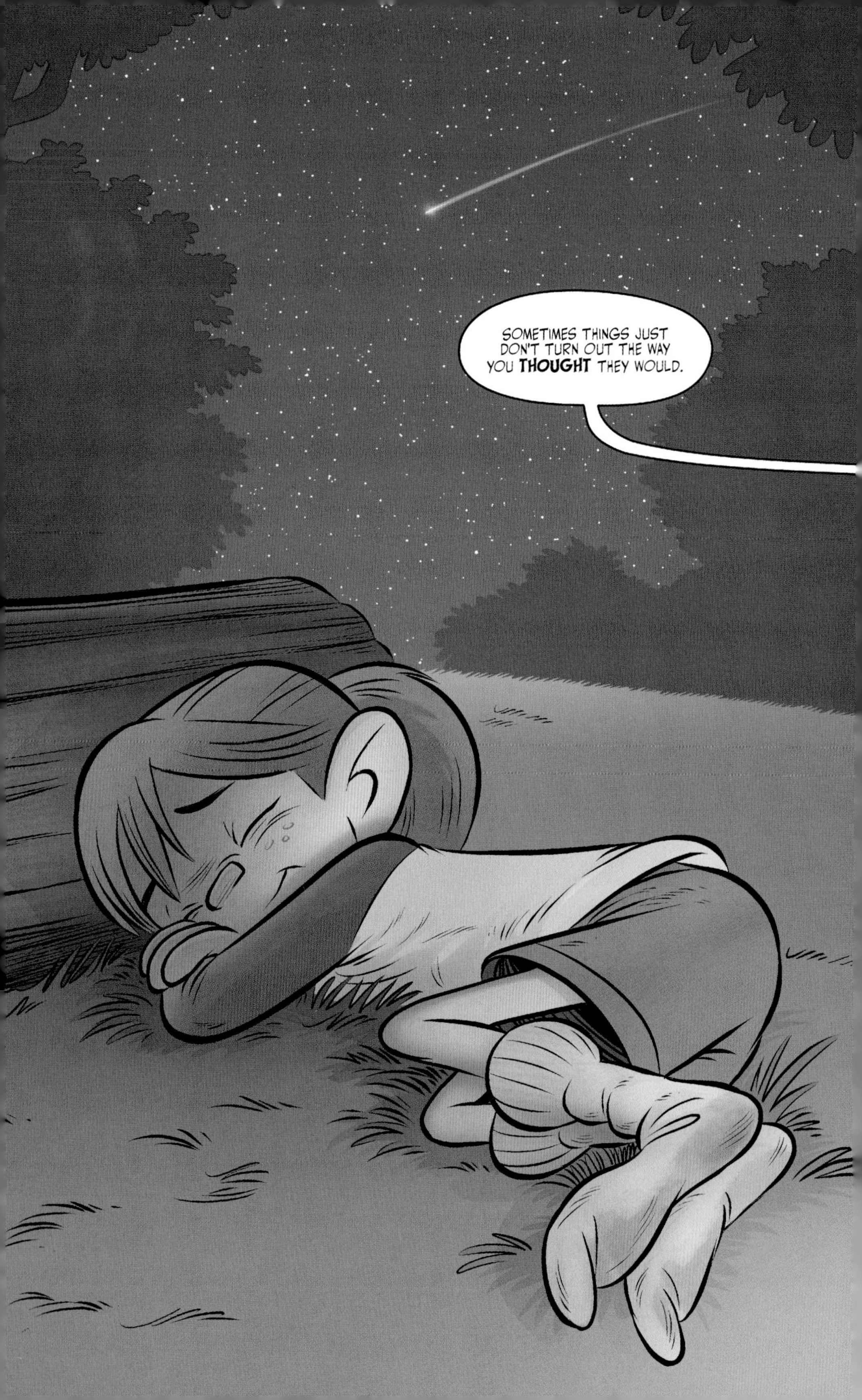
SOMETIMES THINGS JUST DON'T TURN OUT THE WAY YOU **THOUGHT** THEY WOULD.

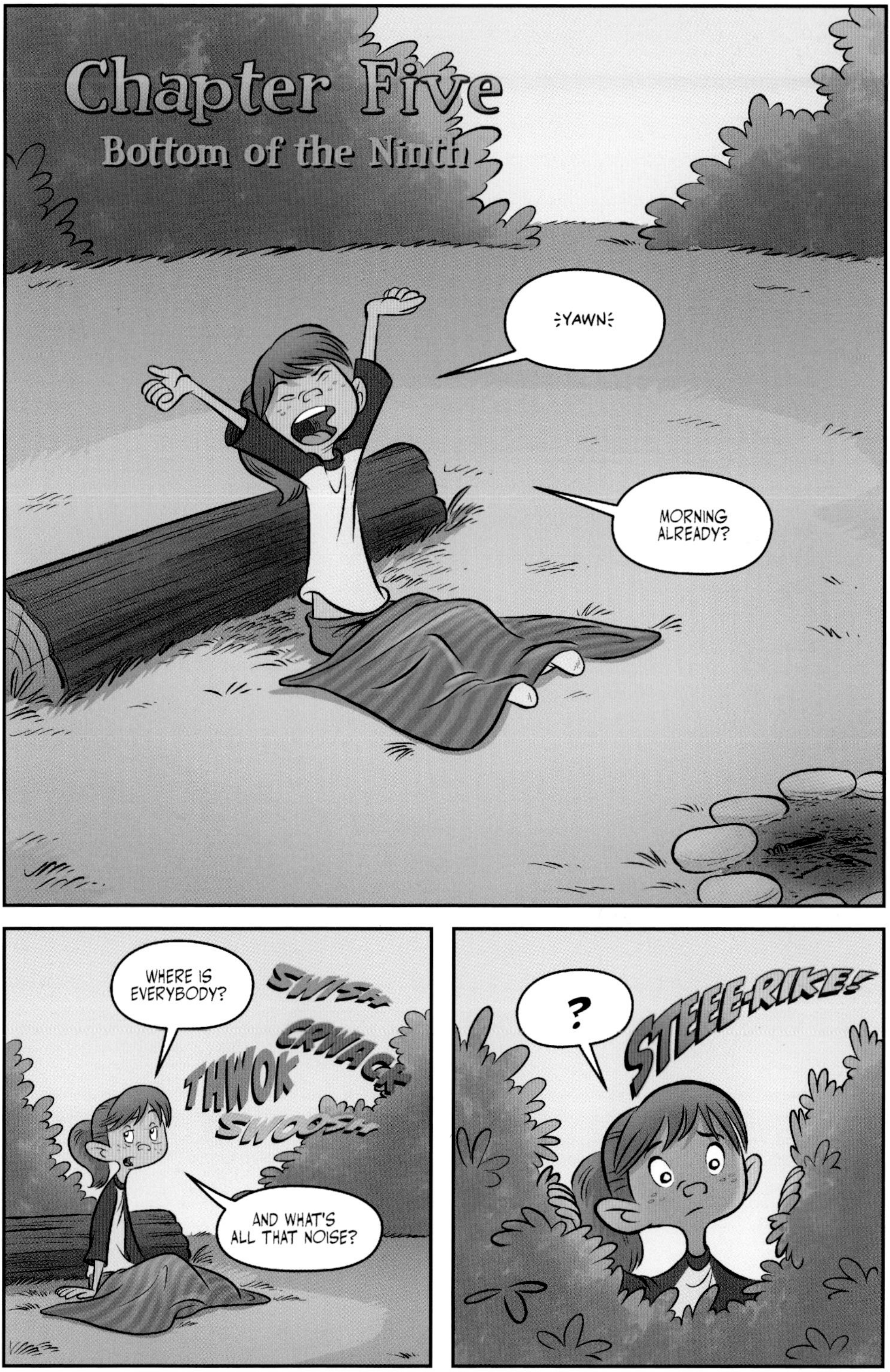
Chapter Five
Bottom of the Ninth
YAWN
MORNING ALREADY?
WHERE IS EVERYBODY?
SWISH
CRWACK
THWOK
SWOOSH
AND WHAT'S ALL THAT NOISE?
?
STEEE-RIKE!

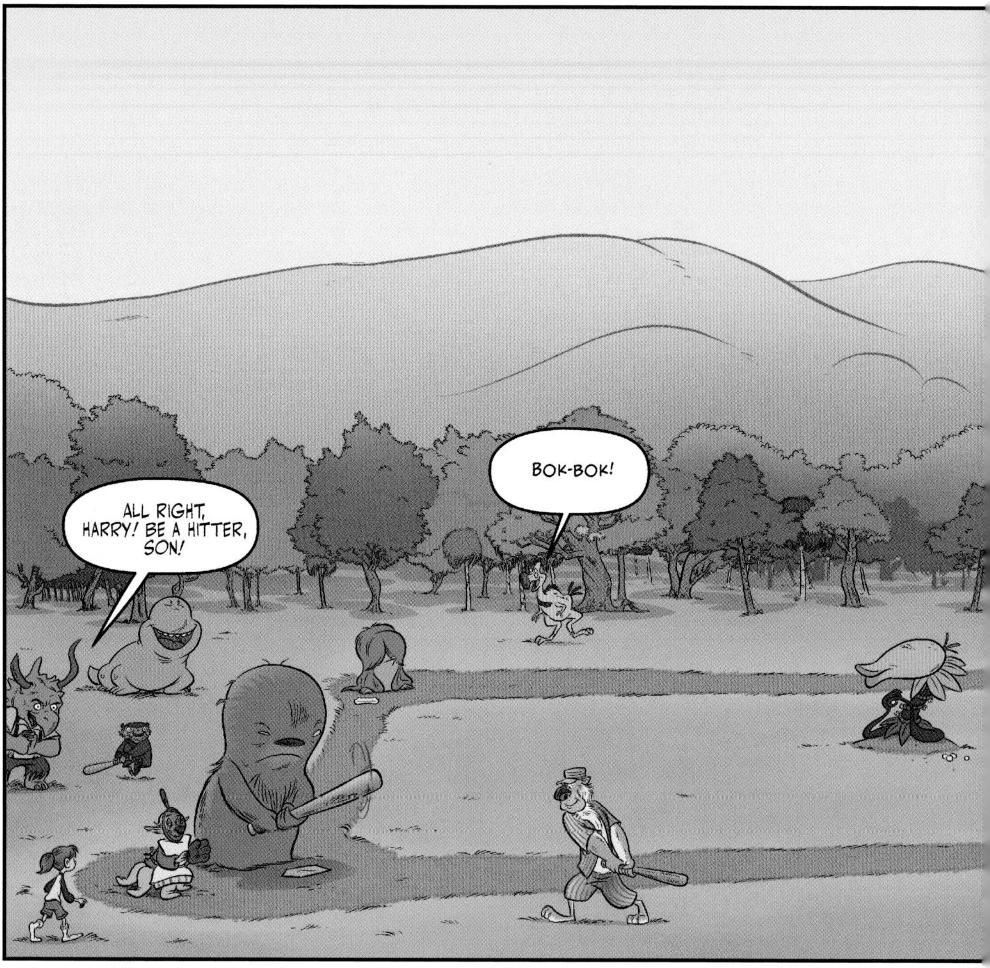
ALL RIGHT, HARRY! BE A HITTER, SON!
BOK-BOK!

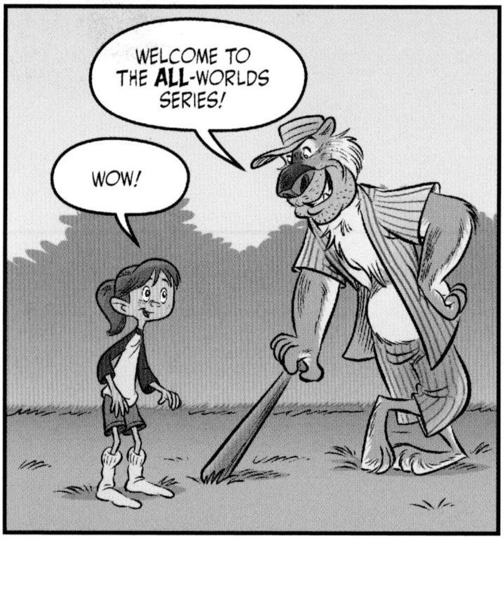
WELCOME TO THE **ALL**-WORLDS SERIES!
WOW!

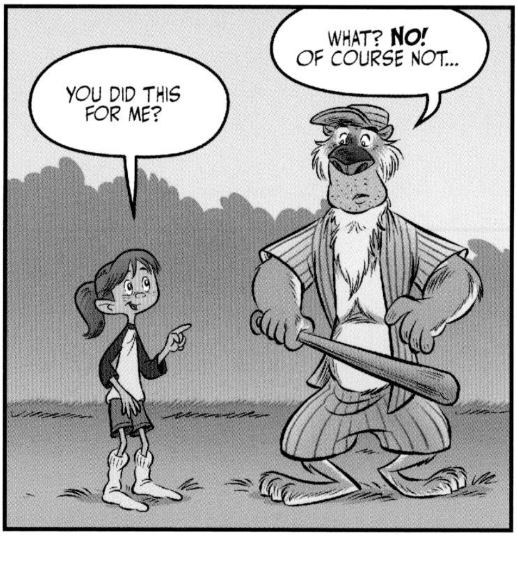
YOU DID THIS FOR ME?
WHAT? **NO!** OF COURSE NOT...

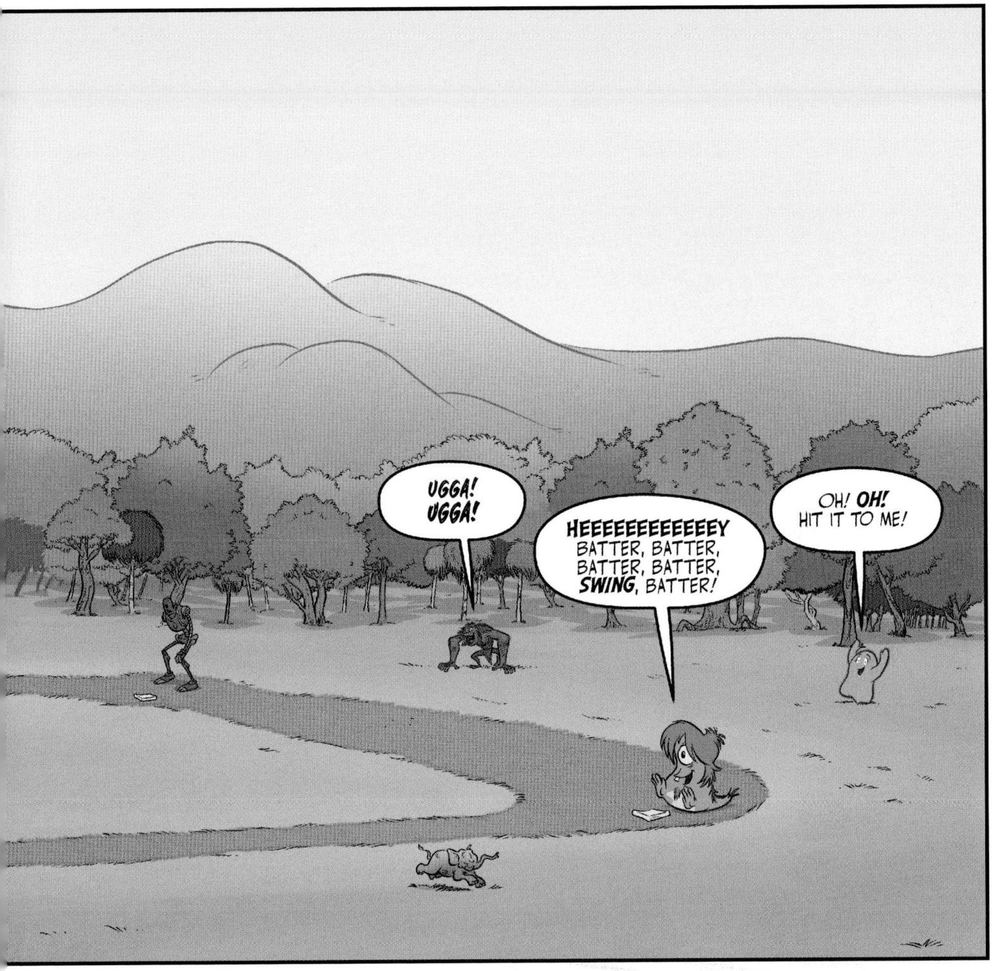
UGGA! UGGA!
HEEEEEEEEEEEEY BATTER, BATTER, BATTER, BATTER, SWING, BATTER!
OH! OH! HIT IT TO ME!

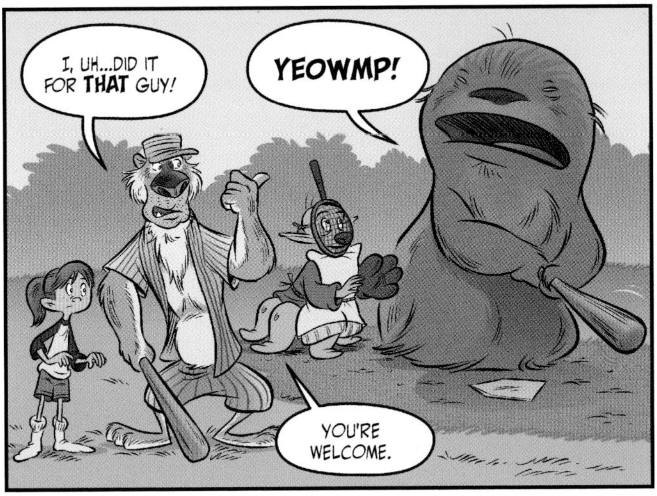
I, UH...DID IT FOR THAT GUY!
YEOWMP!
YOU'RE WELCOME.

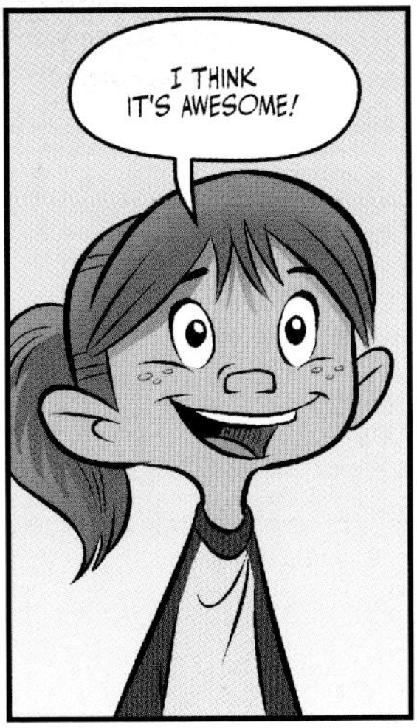
I THINK IT'S AWESOME!

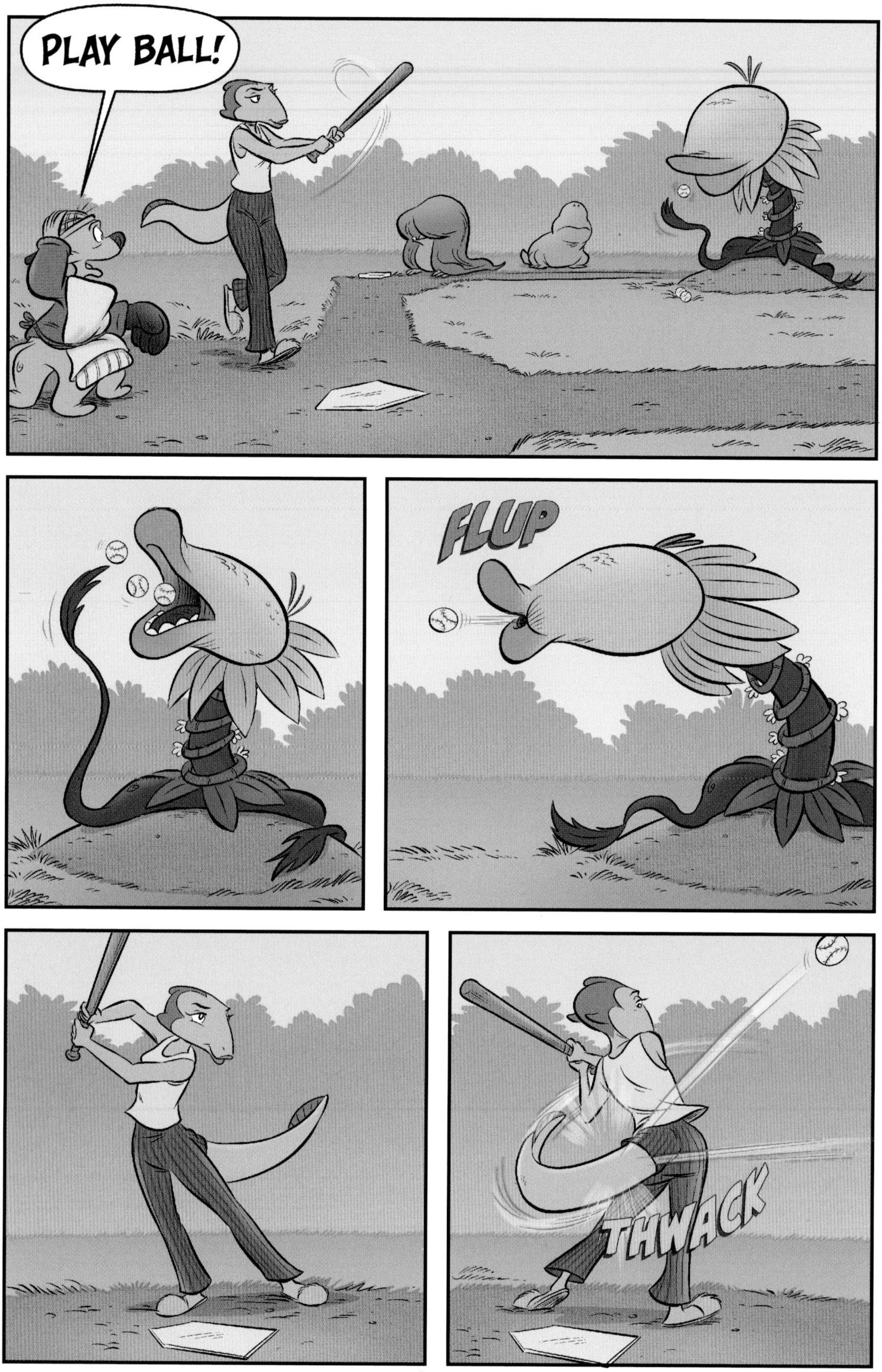
PLAY BALL!
FLUP
THWACK

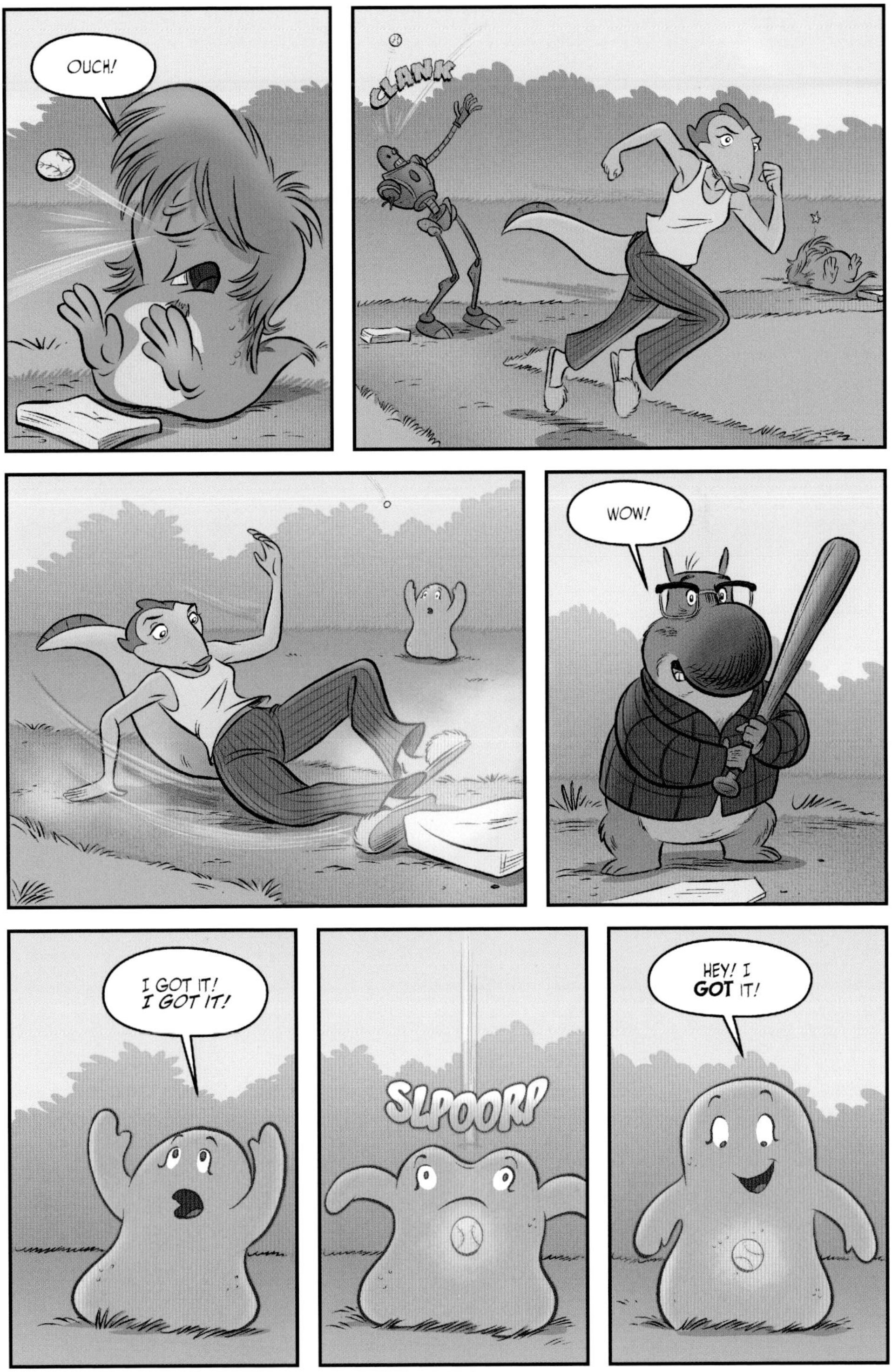
OUCH!
CLANK
WOW!
I GOT IT! I GOT IT!
SLPOORP
HEY! I **GOT** IT!

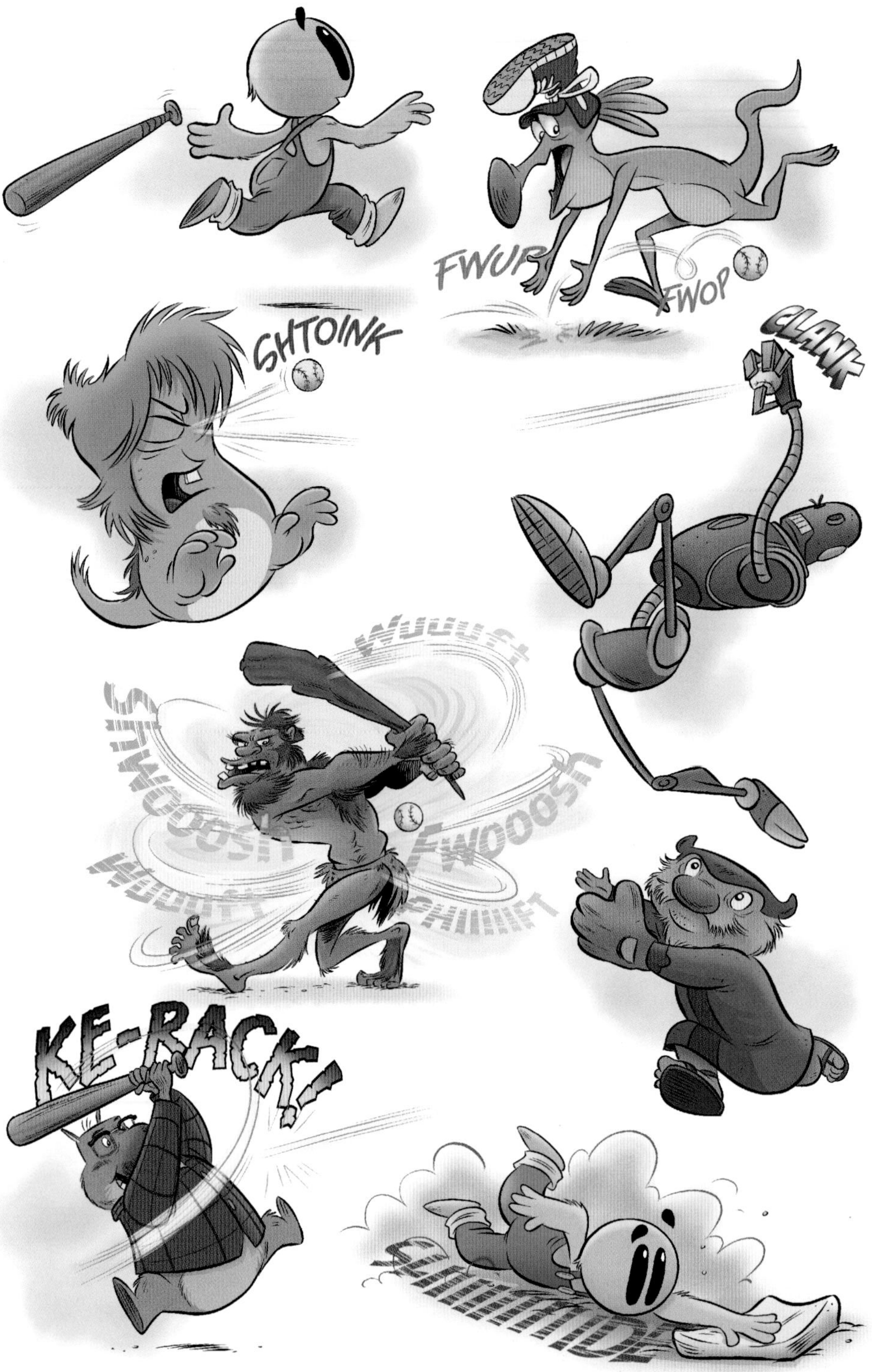
FWUP
FWOP
SHTOINK
CLANK
FWOOOSH
KE-RACK!

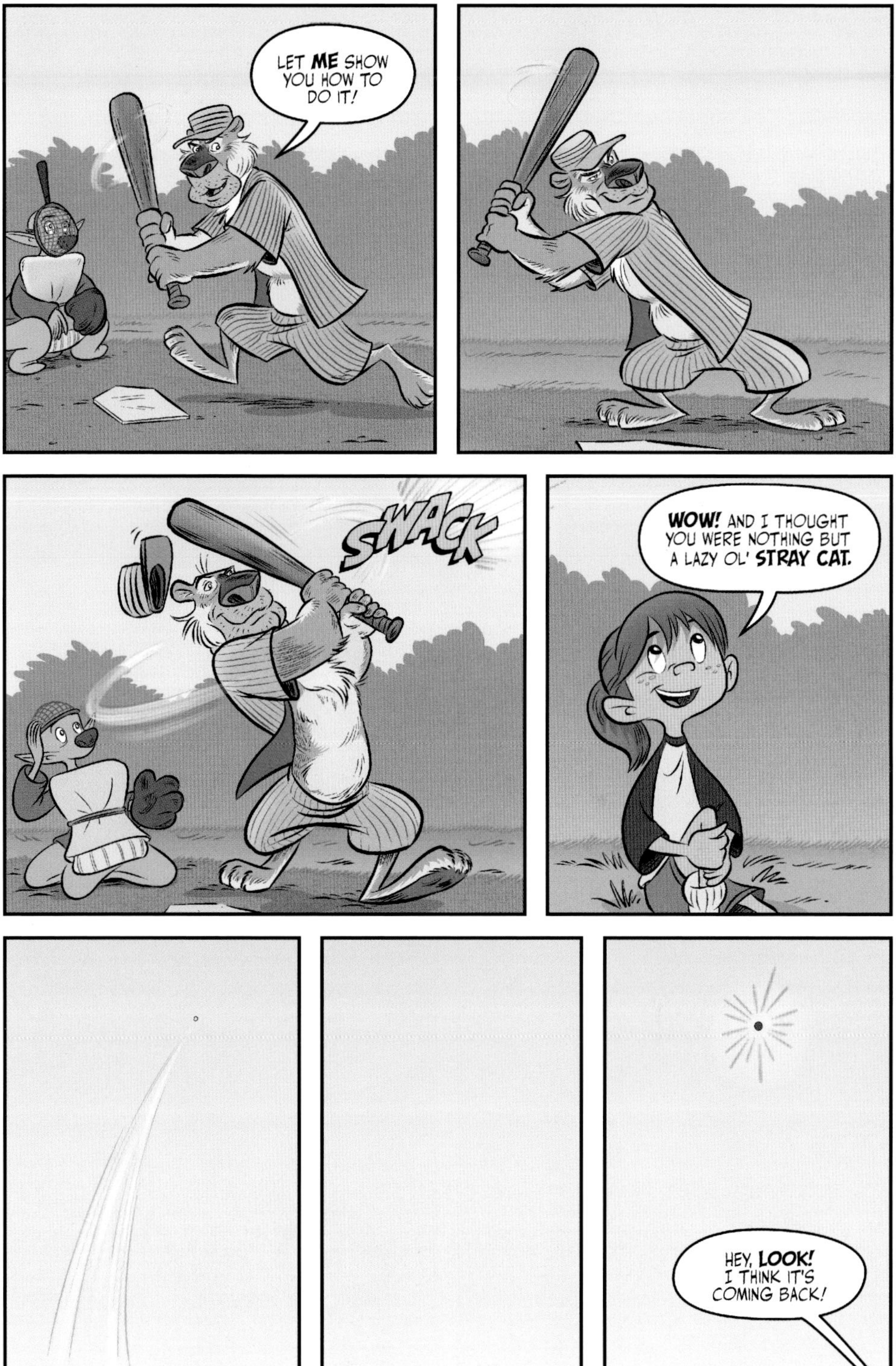
LET **ME** SHOW YOU HOW TO DO IT!
SWACK
WOW! AND I THOUGHT YOU WERE NOTHING BUT A LAZY OL' **STRAY CAT.**
HEY, **LOOK!** I THINK IT'S COMING BACK!

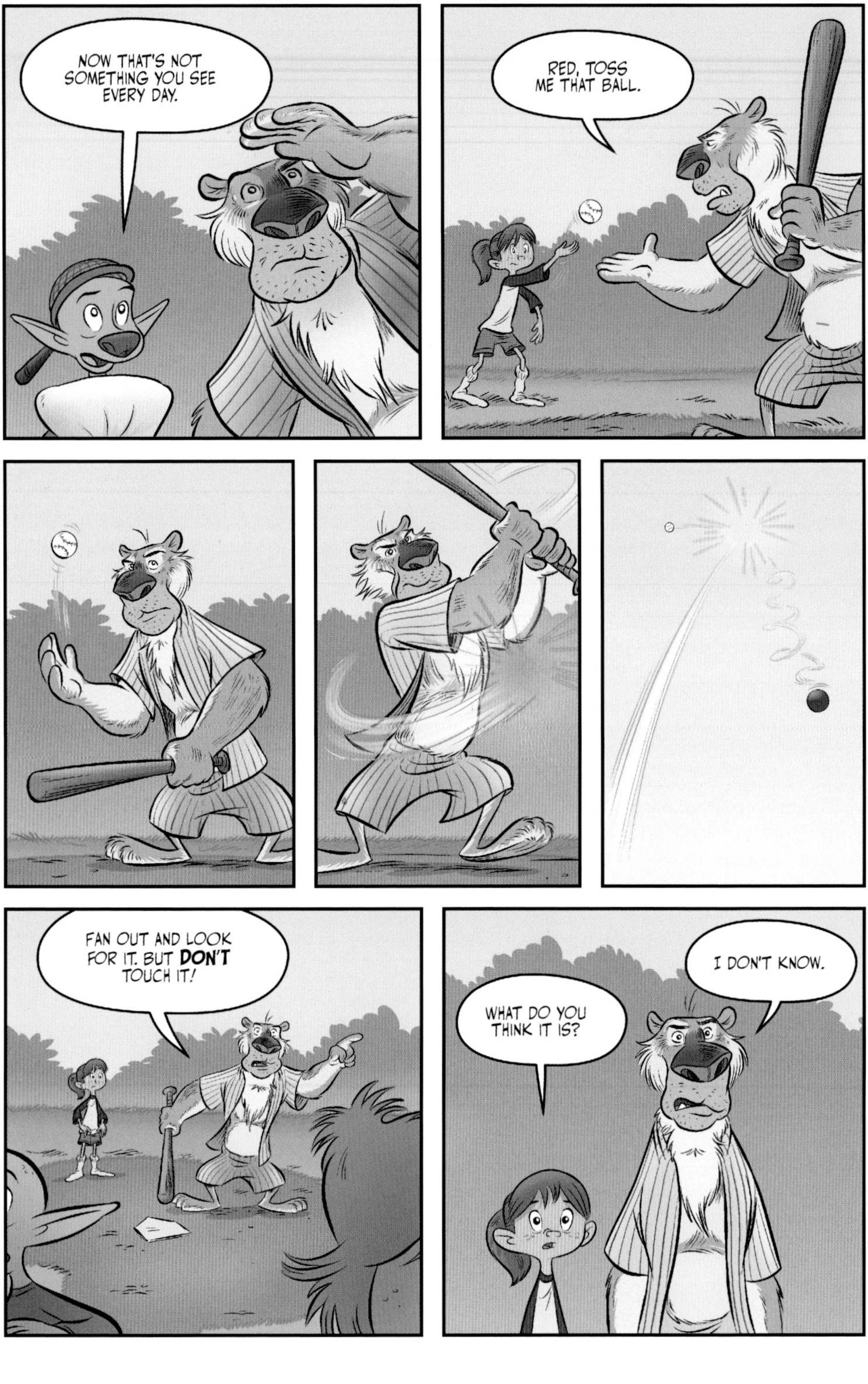
NOW THAT'S NOT SOMETHING YOU SEE EVERY DAY.
RED, TOSS ME THAT BALL.
FAN OUT AND LOOK FOR IT. BUT **DON'T** TOUCH IT!
WHAT DO YOU THINK IT IS?
I DON'T KNOW.

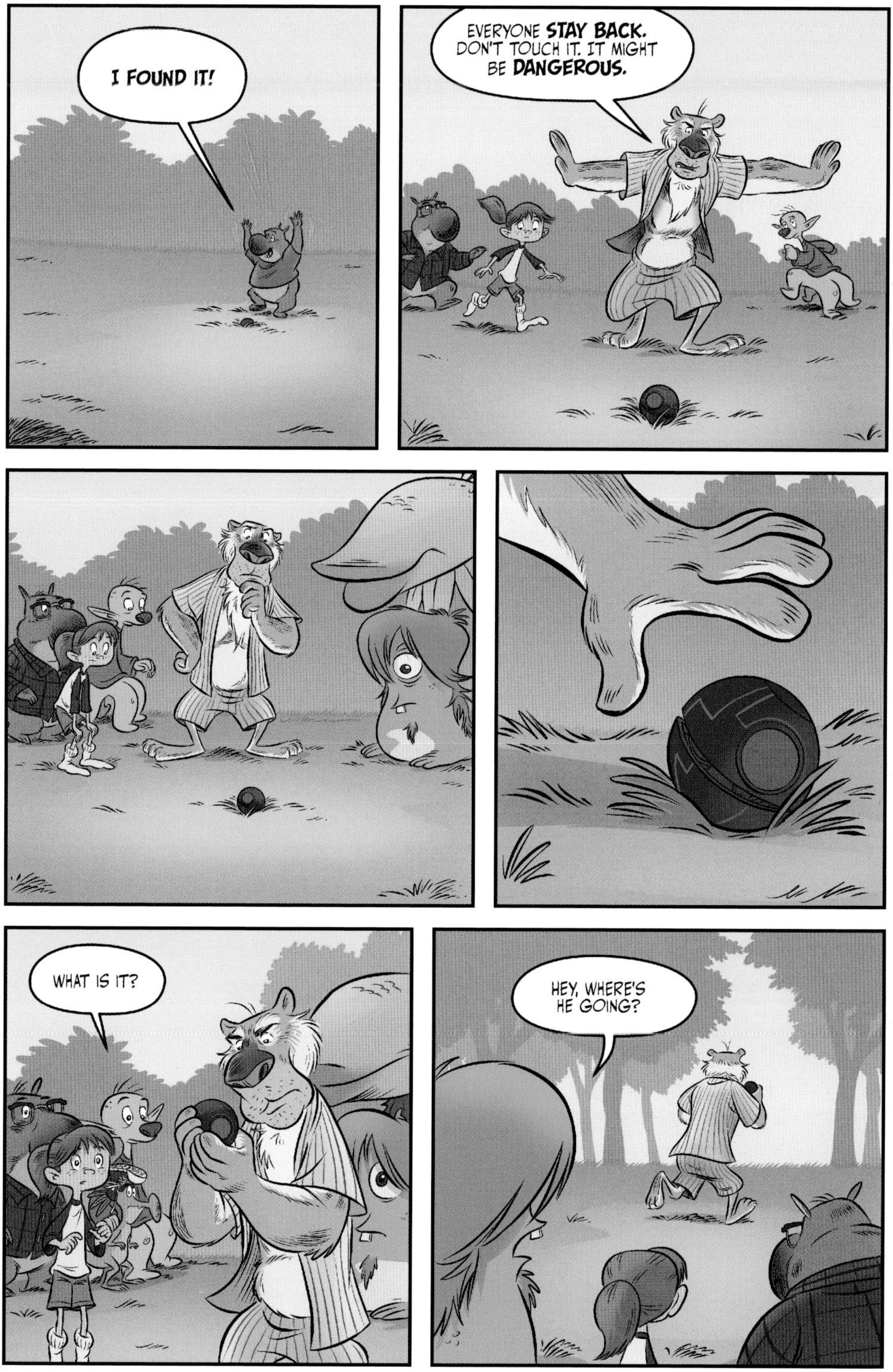
I FOUND IT!
EVERYONE STAY BACK. DON'T TOUCH IT. IT MIGHT BE DANGEROUS.
WHAT IS IT?
HEY, WHERE'S HE GOING?

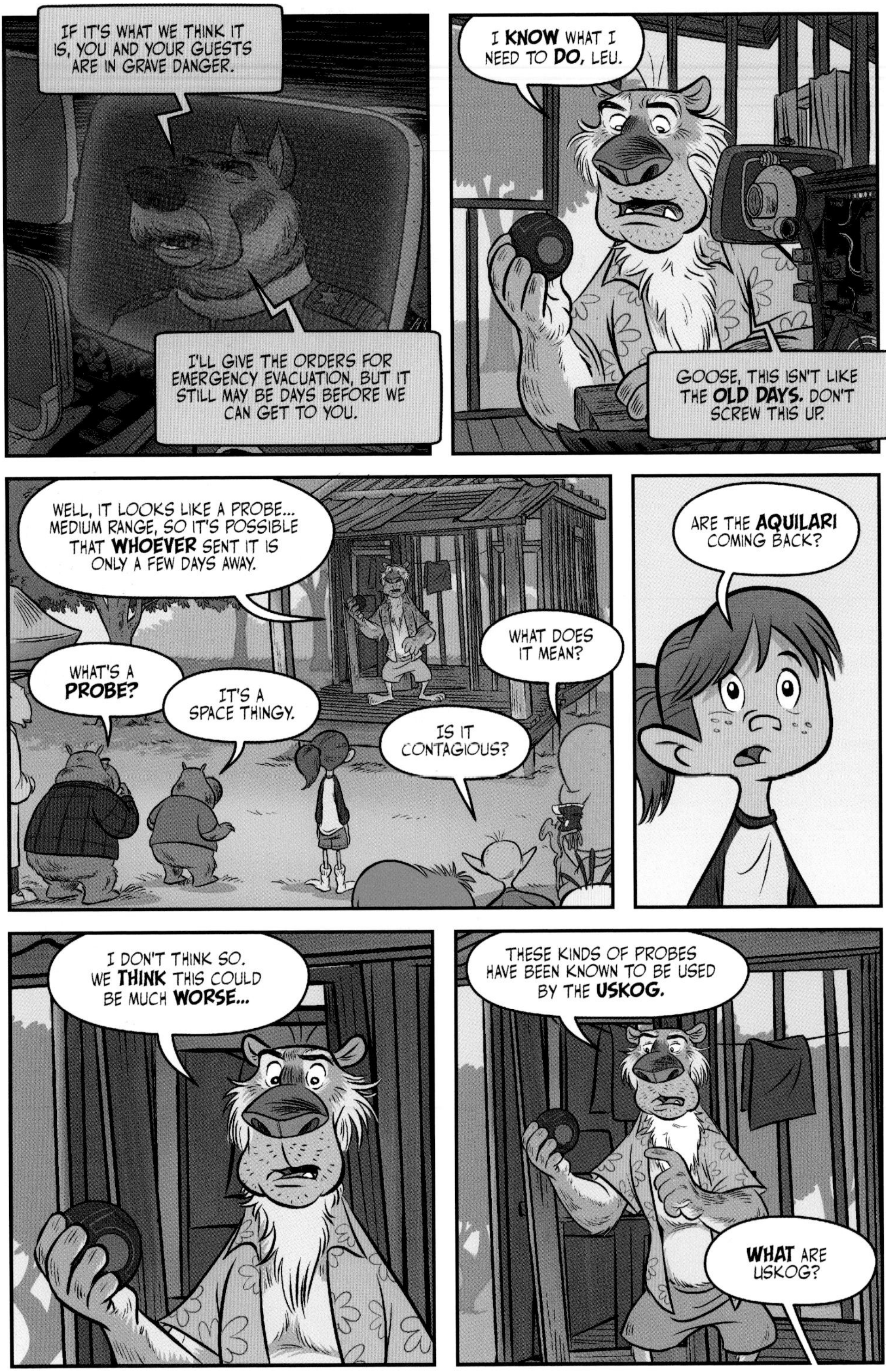
IF IT'S WHAT WE THINK IT IS, YOU AND YOUR GUESTS ARE IN GRAVE DANGER.
I'LL GIVE THE ORDERS FOR EMERGENCY EVACUATION, BUT IT STILL MAY BE DAYS BEFORE WE CAN GET TO YOU.
I KNOW WHAT I NEED TO DO, LEU.
GOOSE, THIS ISN'T LIKE THE OLD DAYS. DON'T SCREW THIS UP.
WELL, IT LOOKS LIKE A PROBE... MEDIUM RANGE, SO IT'S POSSIBLE THAT WHOEVER SENT IT IS ONLY A FEW DAYS AWAY.
WHAT'S A PROBE?
IT'S A SPACE THINGY.
WHAT DOES IT MEAN?
IS IT CONTAGIOUS?
ARE THE AQUILARI COMING BACK?
I DON'T THINK SO. WE THINK THIS COULD BE MUCH WORSE...
THESE KINDS OF PROBES HAVE BEEN KNOWN TO BE USED BY THE USKOG.
WHAT ARE USKOG?

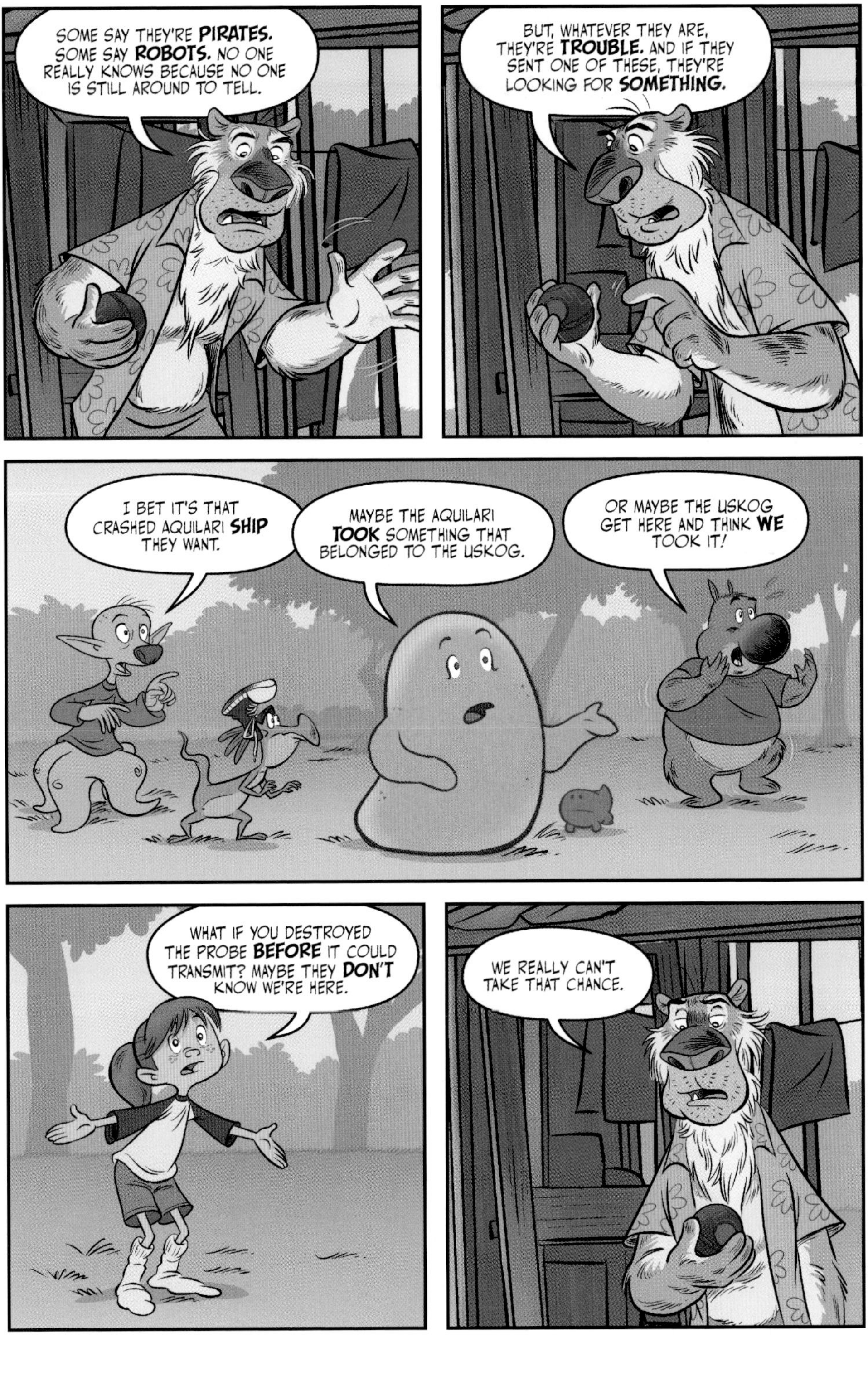
SOME SAY THEY'RE **PIRATES.** SOME SAY **ROBOTS.** NO ONE REALLY KNOWS BECAUSE NO ONE IS STILL AROUND TO TELL.
BUT, WHATEVER THEY ARE, THEY'RE **TROUBLE.** AND IF THEY SENT ONE OF THESE, THEY'RE LOOKING FOR **SOMETHING.**
I BET IT'S THAT CRASHED AQUILARI **SHIP** THEY WANT.
MAYBE THE AQUILARI **TOOK** SOMETHING THAT BELONGED TO THE USKOG.
OR MAYBE THE USKOG GET HERE AND THINK **WE** TOOK IT!
WHAT IF YOU DESTROYED THE PROBE **BEFORE** IT COULD TRANSMIT? MAYBE THEY **DON'T** KNOW WE'RE HERE.
WE REALLY CAN'T TAKE THAT CHANCE.

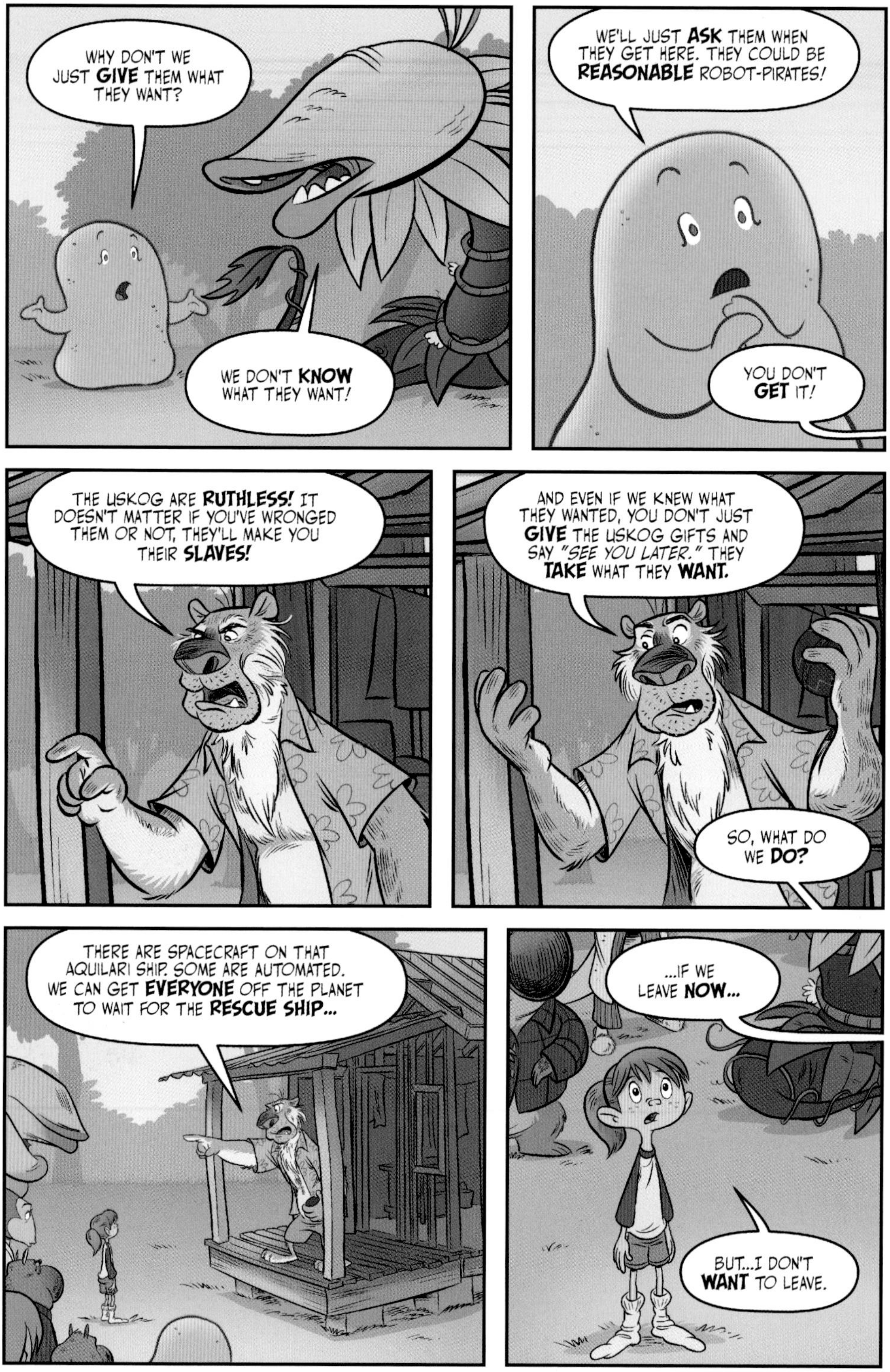

WHY DON'T WE JUST **GIVE** THEM WHAT THEY WANT?
WE DON'T **KNOW** WHAT THEY WANT!
WE'LL JUST **ASK** THEM WHEN THEY GET HERE. THEY COULD BE **REASONABLE** ROBOT-PIRATES!
YOU DON'T **GET** IT!
THE USKOG ARE **RUTHLESS!** IT DOESN'T MATTER IF YOU'VE WRONGED THEM OR NOT, THEY'LL MAKE YOU THEIR **SLAVES!**
AND EVEN IF WE KNEW WHAT THEY WANTED, YOU DON'T JUST **GIVE** THE USKOG GIFTS AND SAY *"SEE YOU LATER."* THEY **TAKE** WHAT THEY **WANT.**
SO, WHAT DO WE **DO?**
THERE ARE SPACECRAFT ON THAT AQUILARI SHIP. SOME ARE AUTOMATED. WE CAN GET **EVERYONE** OFF THE PLANET TO WAIT FOR THE **RESCUE SHIP...**
...IF WE LEAVE **NOW...**
BUT...I DON'T **WANT** TO LEAVE.

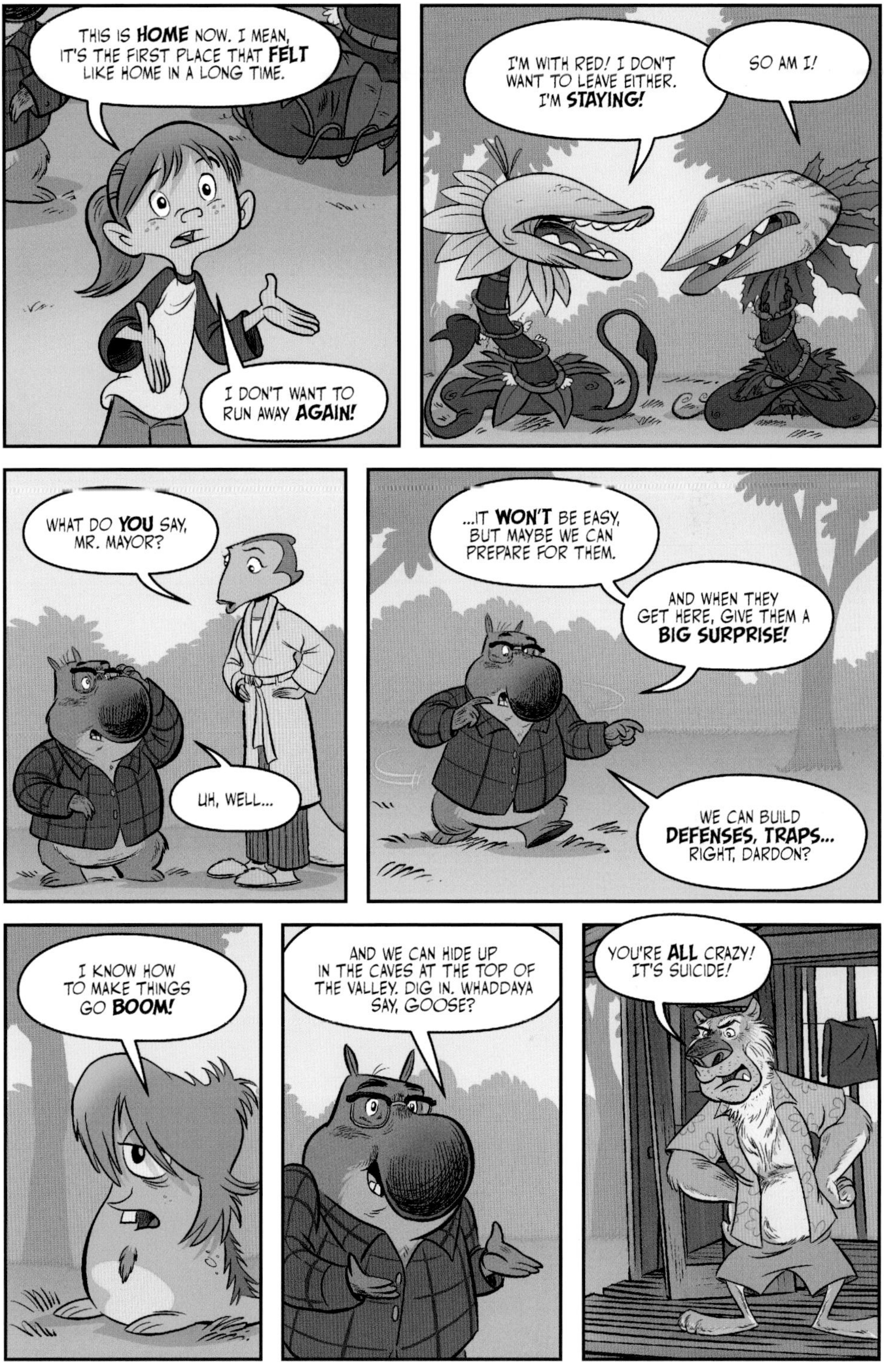

THIS IS HOME NOW. I MEAN, IT'S THE FIRST PLACE THAT FELT LIKE HOME IN A LONG TIME.
I DON'T WANT TO RUN AWAY AGAIN!
I'M WITH RED! I DON'T WANT TO LEAVE EITHER. I'M STAYING!
SO AM I!
WHAT DO YOU SAY, MR. MAYOR?
UH, WELL...
...IT WON'T BE EASY, BUT MAYBE WE CAN PREPARE FOR THEM.
AND WHEN THEY GET HERE, GIVE THEM A BIG SURPRISE!
WE CAN BUILD DEFENSES, TRAPS... RIGHT, DARDON?
I KNOW HOW TO MAKE THINGS GO BOOM!
AND WE CAN HIDE UP IN THE CAVES AT THE TOP OF THE VALLEY. DIG IN. WHADDAYA SAY, GOOSE?
YOU'RE ALL CRAZY! IT'S SUICIDE!

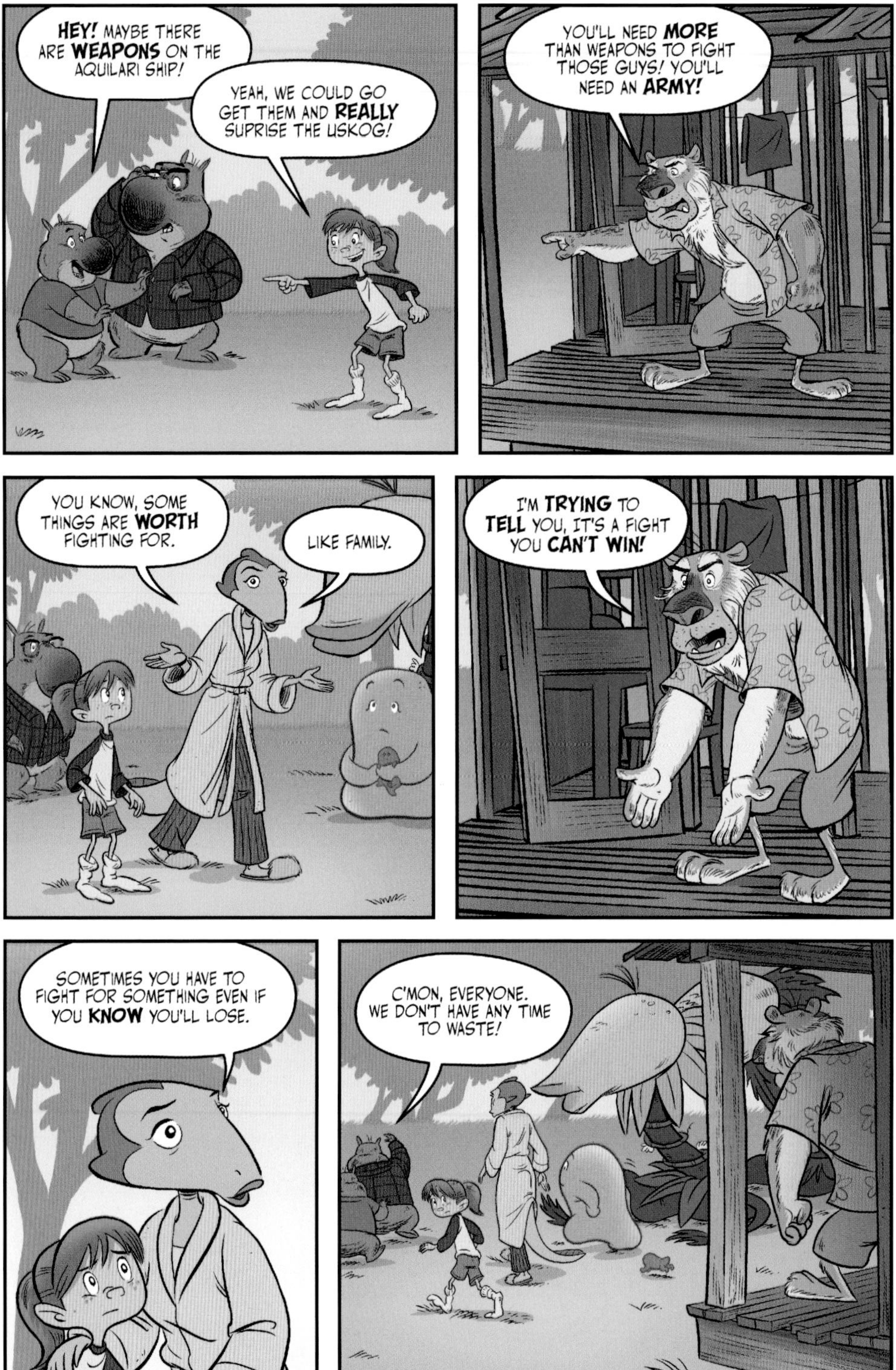
HEY! MAYBE THERE ARE WEAPONS ON THE AQUILARI SHIP!
YEAH, WE COULD GO GET THEM AND REALLY SUPRISE THE USKOG!
YOU'LL NEED MORE THAN WEAPONS TO FIGHT THOSE GUYS! YOU'LL NEED AN ARMY!
YOU KNOW, SOME THINGS ARE WORTH FIGHTING FOR.
LIKE FAMILY.
I'M TRYING TO TELL YOU, IT'S A FIGHT YOU CAN'T WIN!
SOMETIMES YOU HAVE TO FIGHT FOR SOMETHING EVEN IF YOU KNOW YOU'LL LOSE.
C'MON, EVERYONE. WE DON'T HAVE ANY TIME TO WASTE!

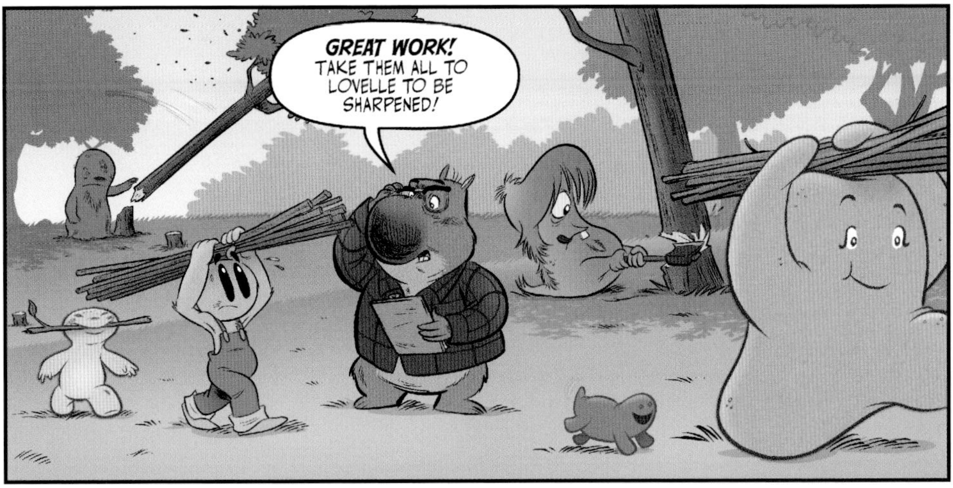
GREAT WORK! TAKE THEM ALL TO LOVELLE TO BE SHARPENED!

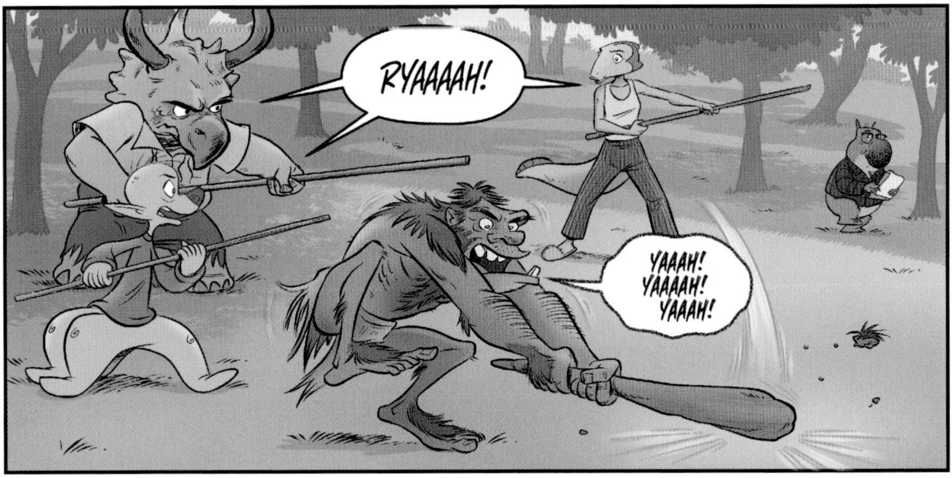
RYAAAAH!
YAAAH! YAAAAH! YAAAH!

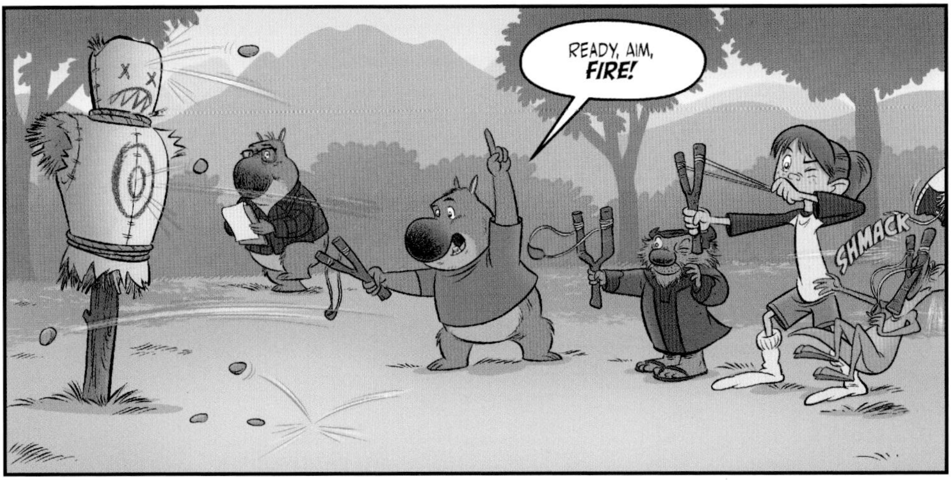
READY, AIM, FIRE!
SHMACK

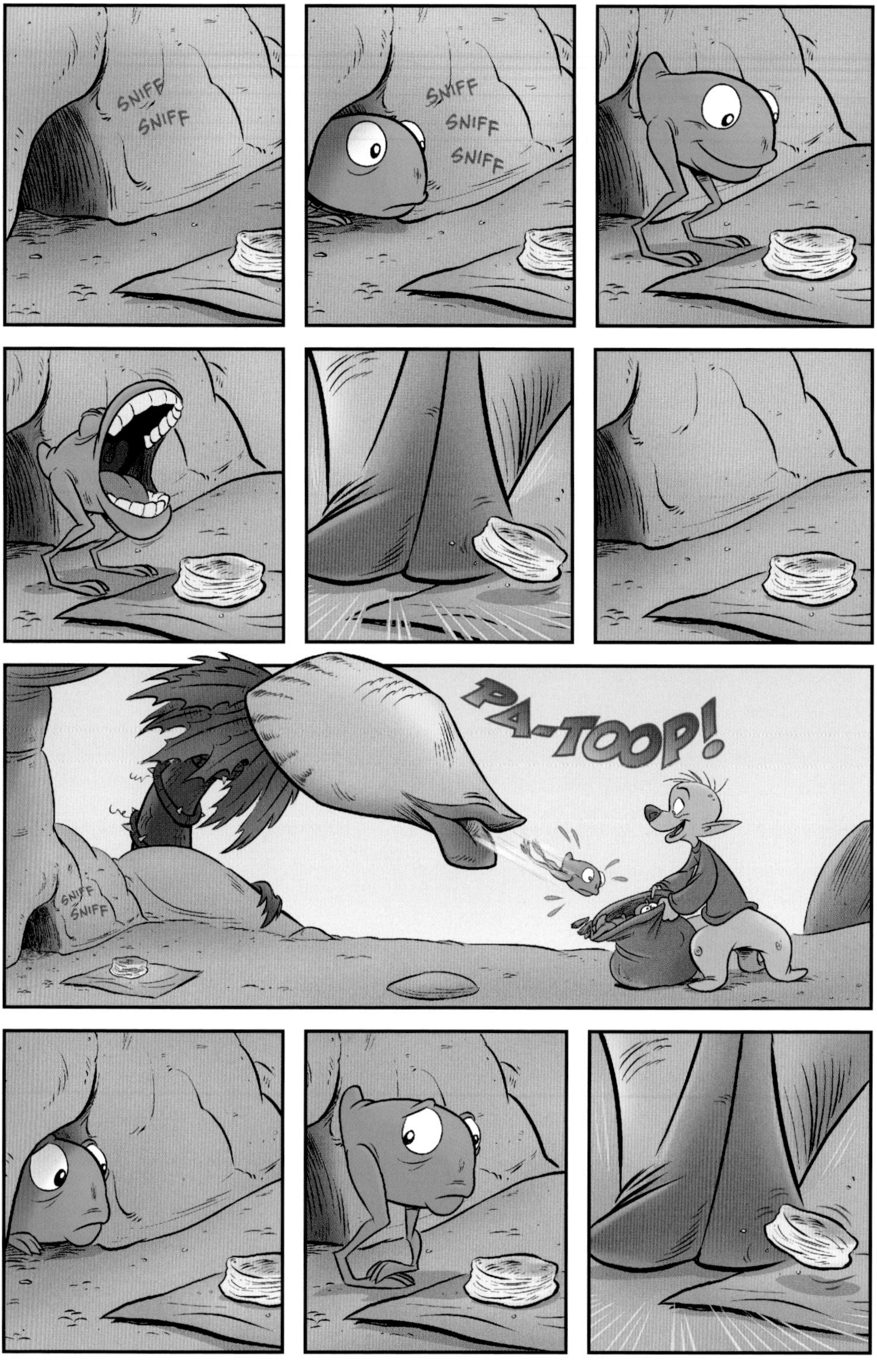
SNIFF
SNIFF
SNIFF
SNIFF
SNIFF
PA-TOOP!
SNIFF
SNIFF

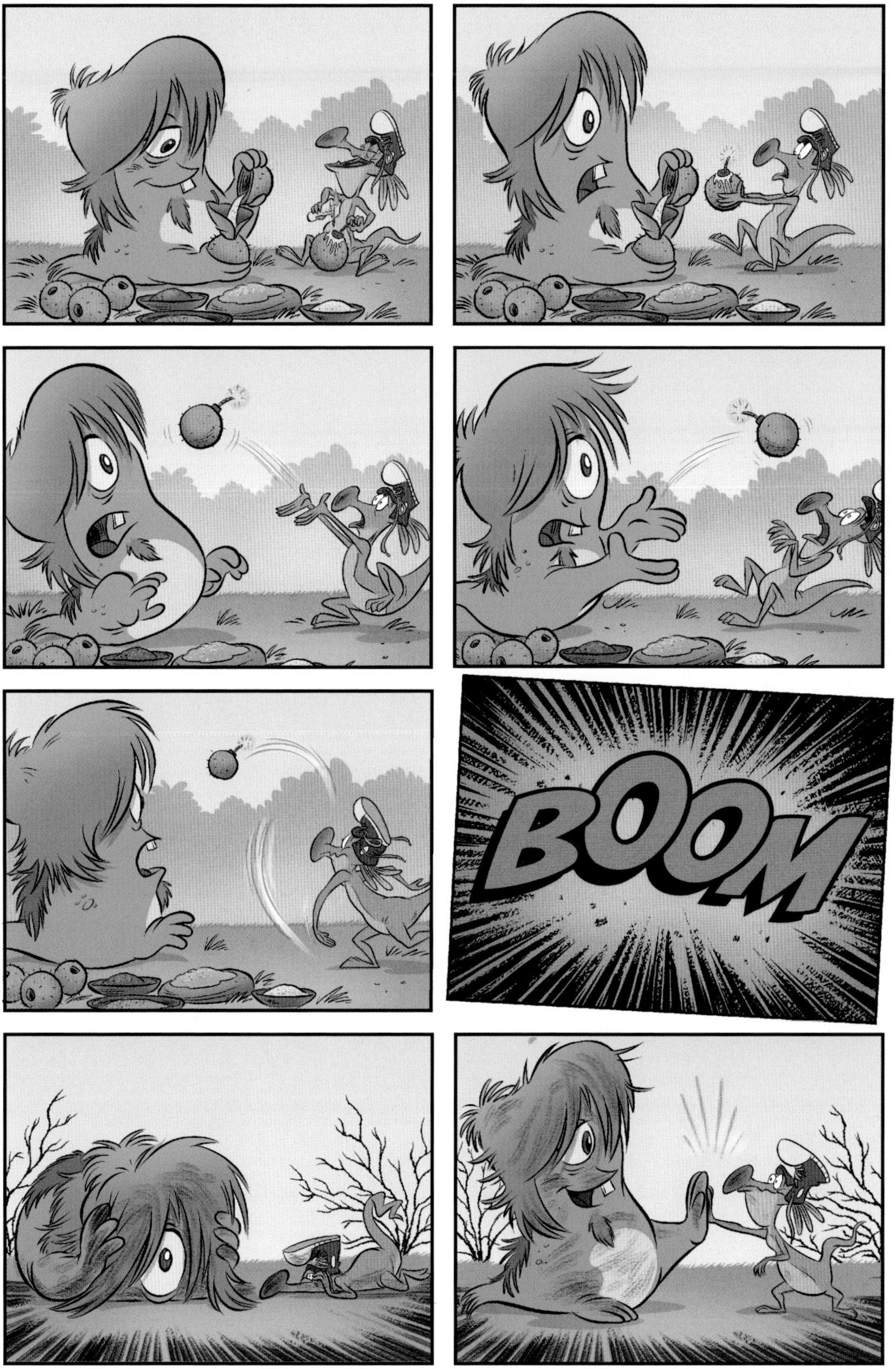
BOOM

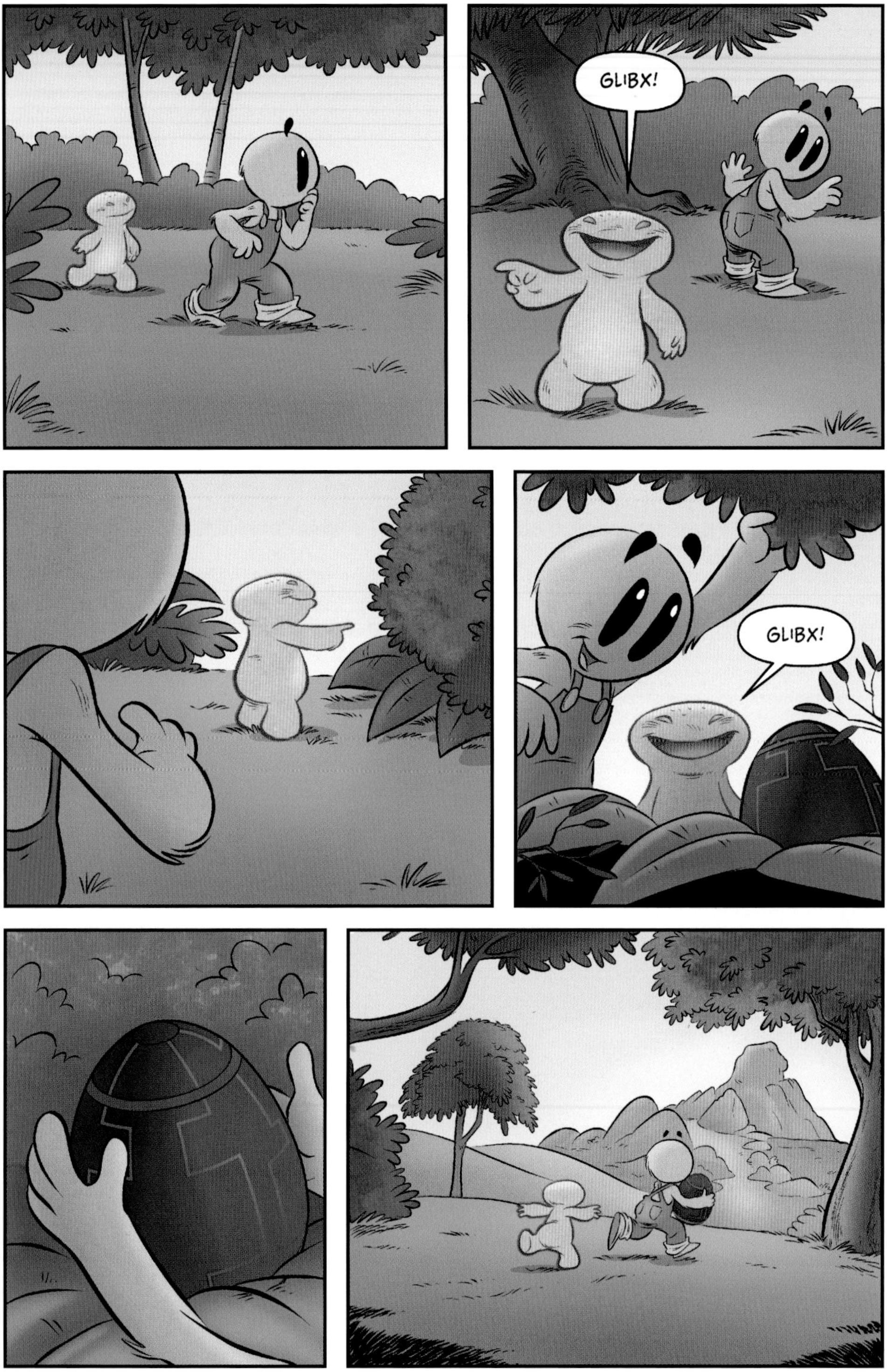
GLIBX!
GLIBX!

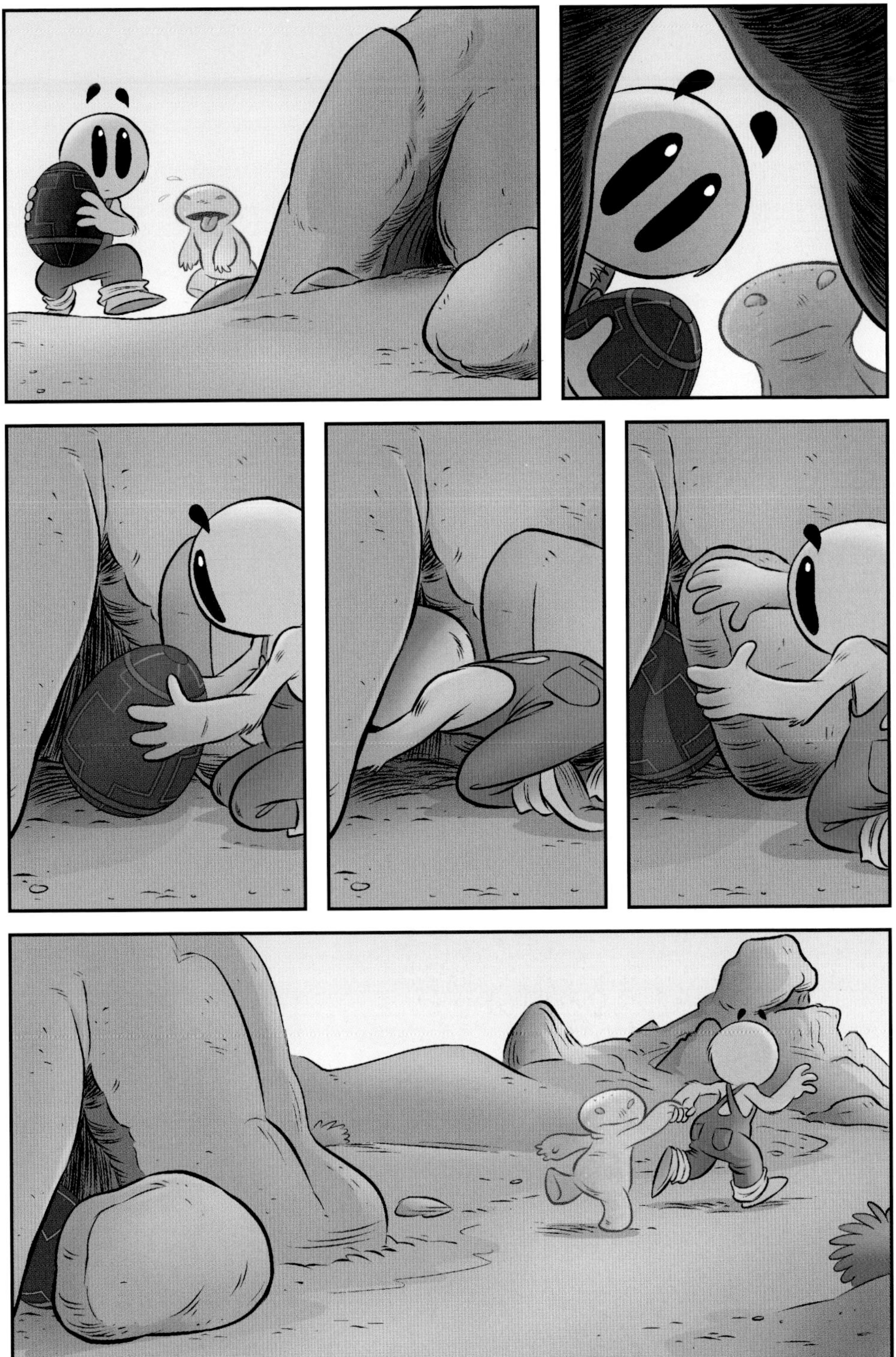

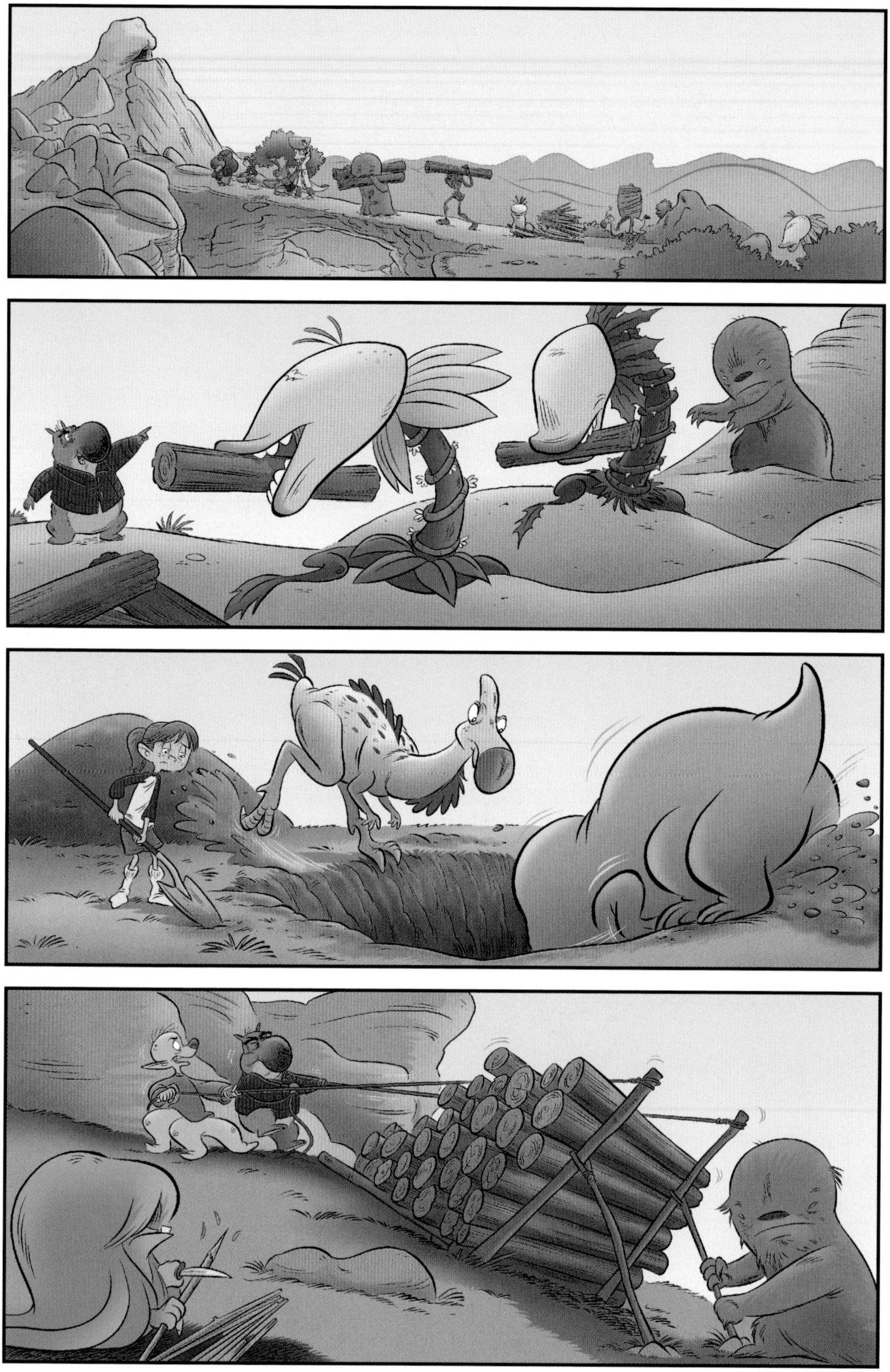

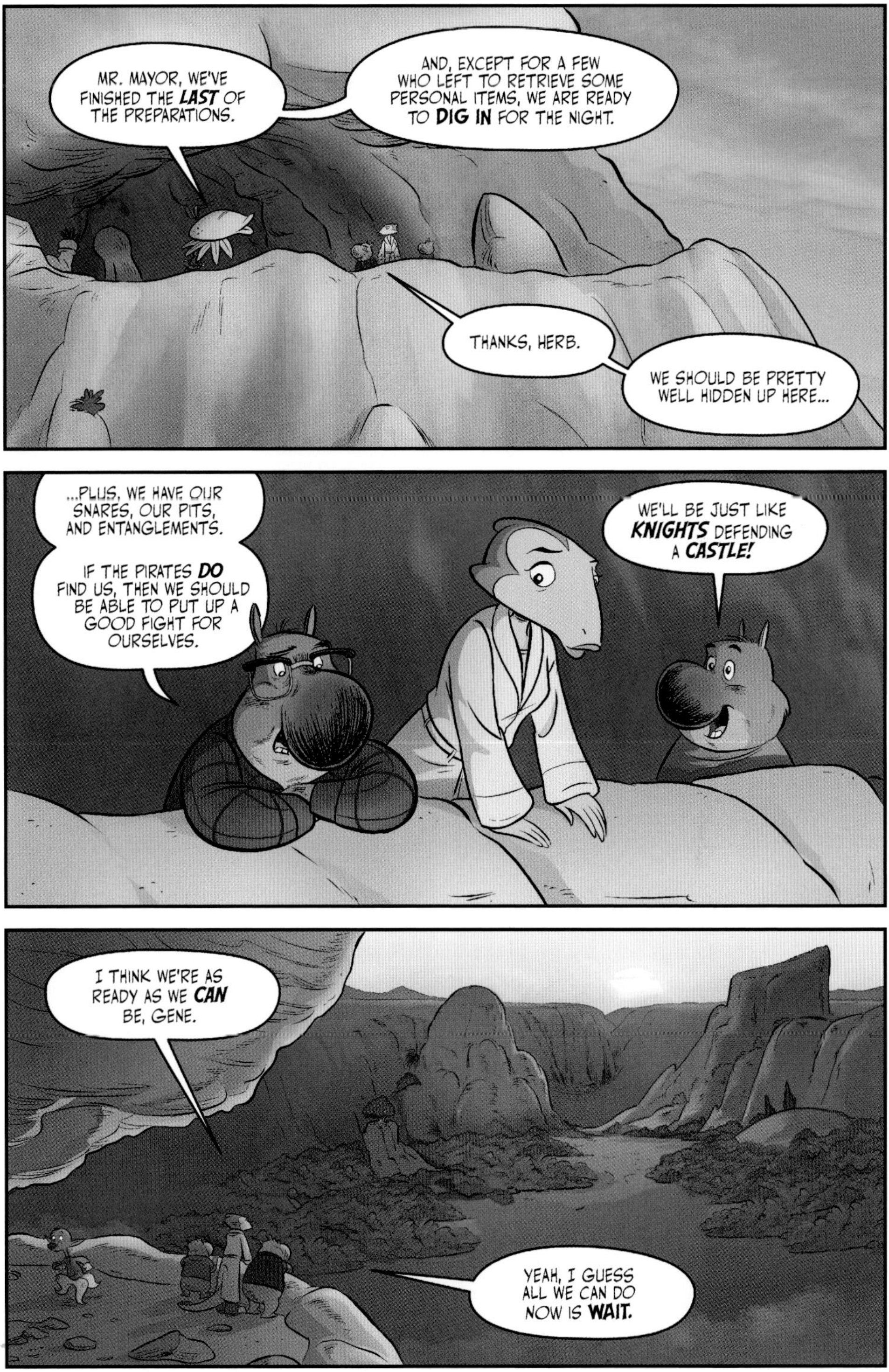
MR. MAYOR, WE'VE FINISHED THE LAST OF THE PREPARATIONS.
AND, EXCEPT FOR A FEW WHO LEFT TO RETRIEVE SOME PERSONAL ITEMS, WE ARE READY TO DIG IN FOR THE NIGHT.
THANKS, HERB.
WE SHOULD BE PRETTY WELL HIDDEN UP HERE...
...PLUS, WE HAVE OUR SNARES, OUR PITS, AND ENTANGLEMENTS.
IF THE PIRATES DO FIND US, THEN WE SHOULD BE ABLE TO PUT UP A GOOD FIGHT FOR OURSELVES.
WE'LL BE JUST LIKE KNIGHTS DEFENDING A CASTLE!
I THINK WE'RE AS READY AS WE CAN BE, GENE.
YEAH, I GUESS ALL WE CAN DO NOW IS WAIT.

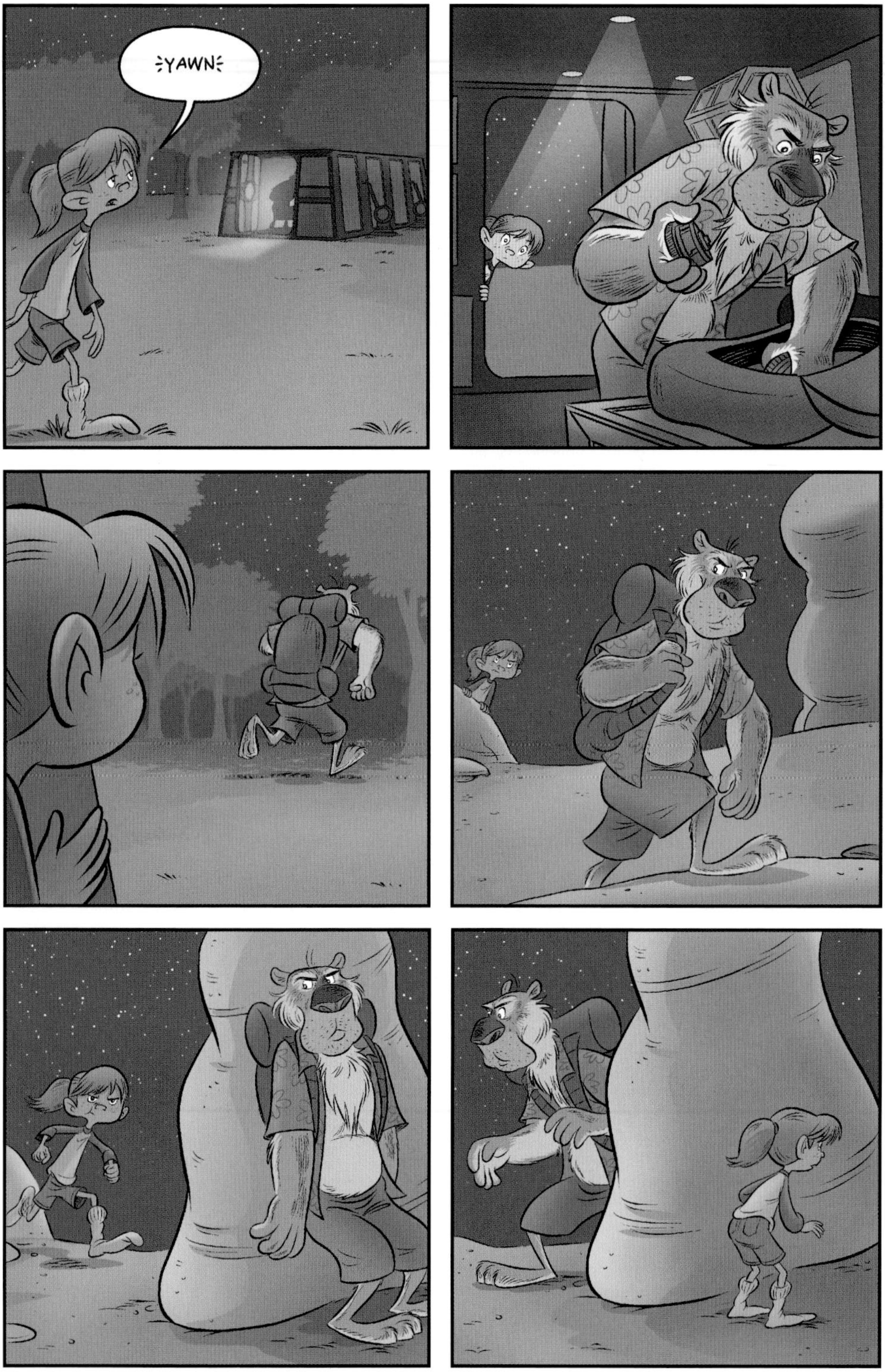
YAWN

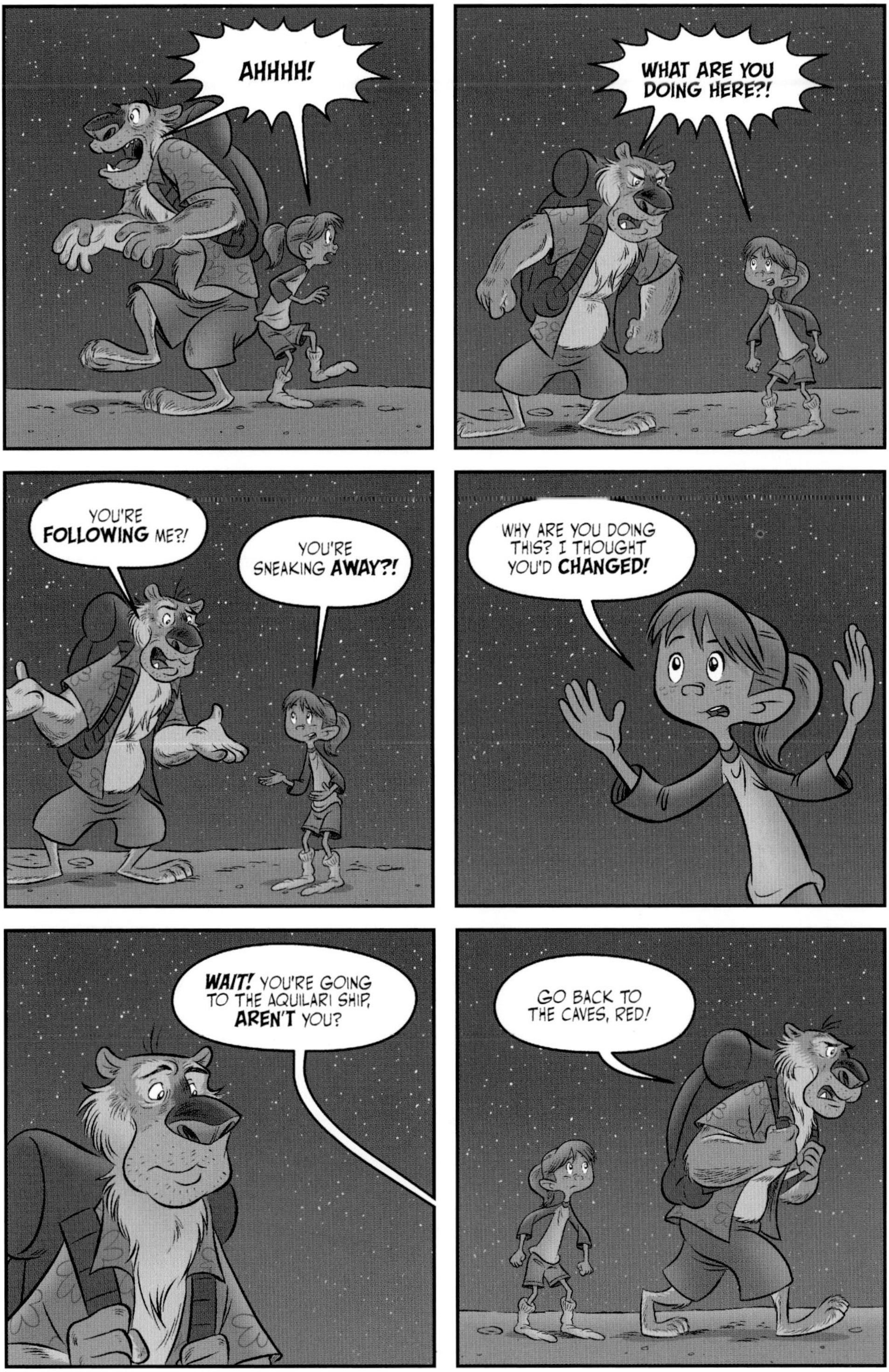
AHHHH!
WHAT ARE YOU DOING HERE?!
YOU'RE **FOLLOWING** ME?!
YOU'RE SNEAKING **AWAY?!**
WHY ARE YOU DOING THIS? I THOUGHT YOU'D **CHANGED!**
WAIT! YOU'RE GOING TO THE AQUILARI SHIP, **AREN'T** YOU?
GO BACK TO THE CAVES, RED!

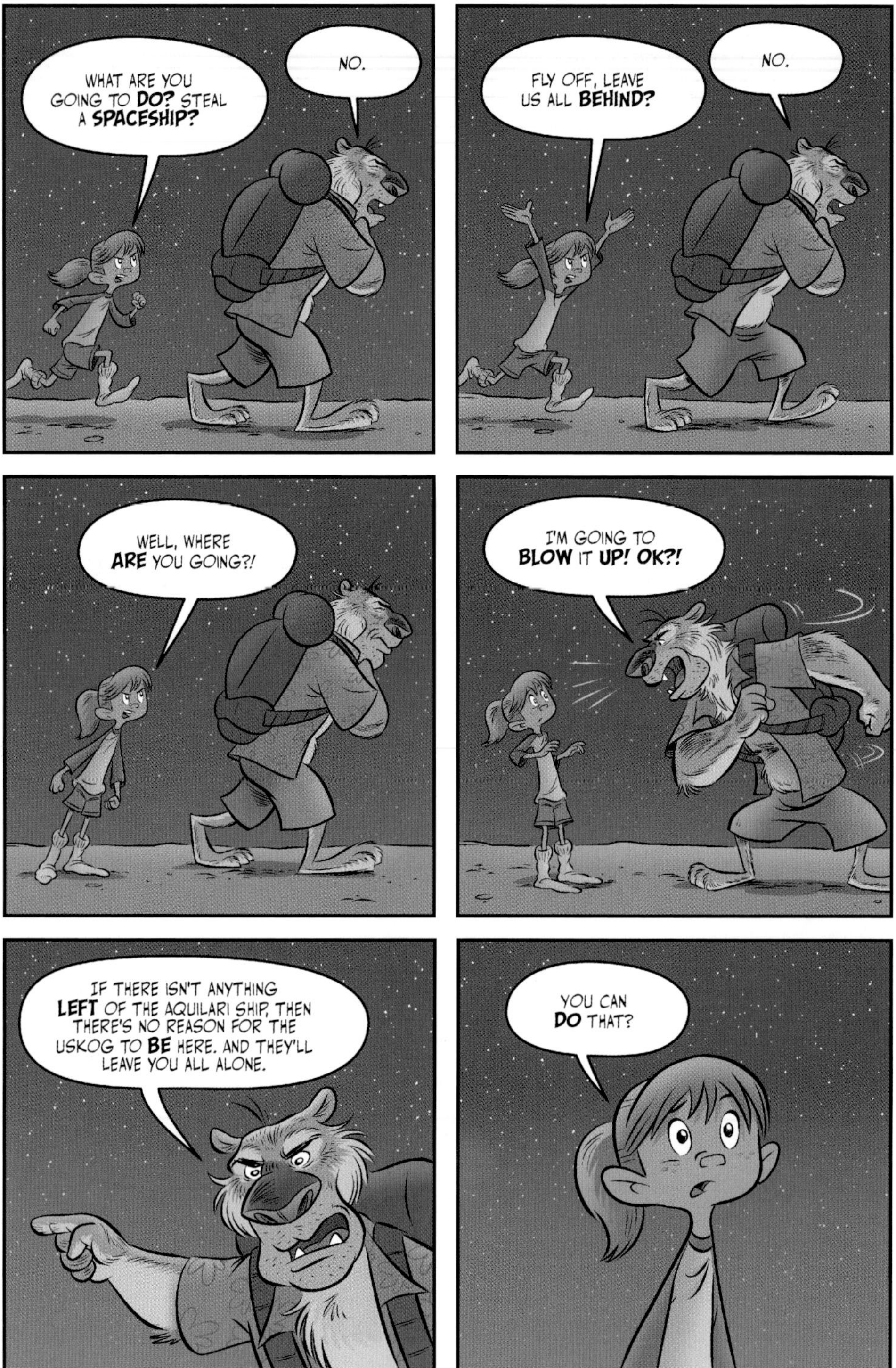
WHAT ARE YOU GOING TO **DO?** STEAL A **SPACESHIP?**
NO.
FLY OFF, LEAVE US ALL **BEHIND?**
NO.
WELL, WHERE **ARE** YOU GOING?!
I'M GOING TO **BLOW** IT **UP! OK?!**
IF THERE ISN'T ANYTHING **LEFT** OF THE AQUILARI SHIP, THEN THERE'S NO REASON FOR THE USKOG TO **BE** HERE. AND THEY'LL LEAVE YOU ALL ALONE.
YOU CAN **DO** THAT?

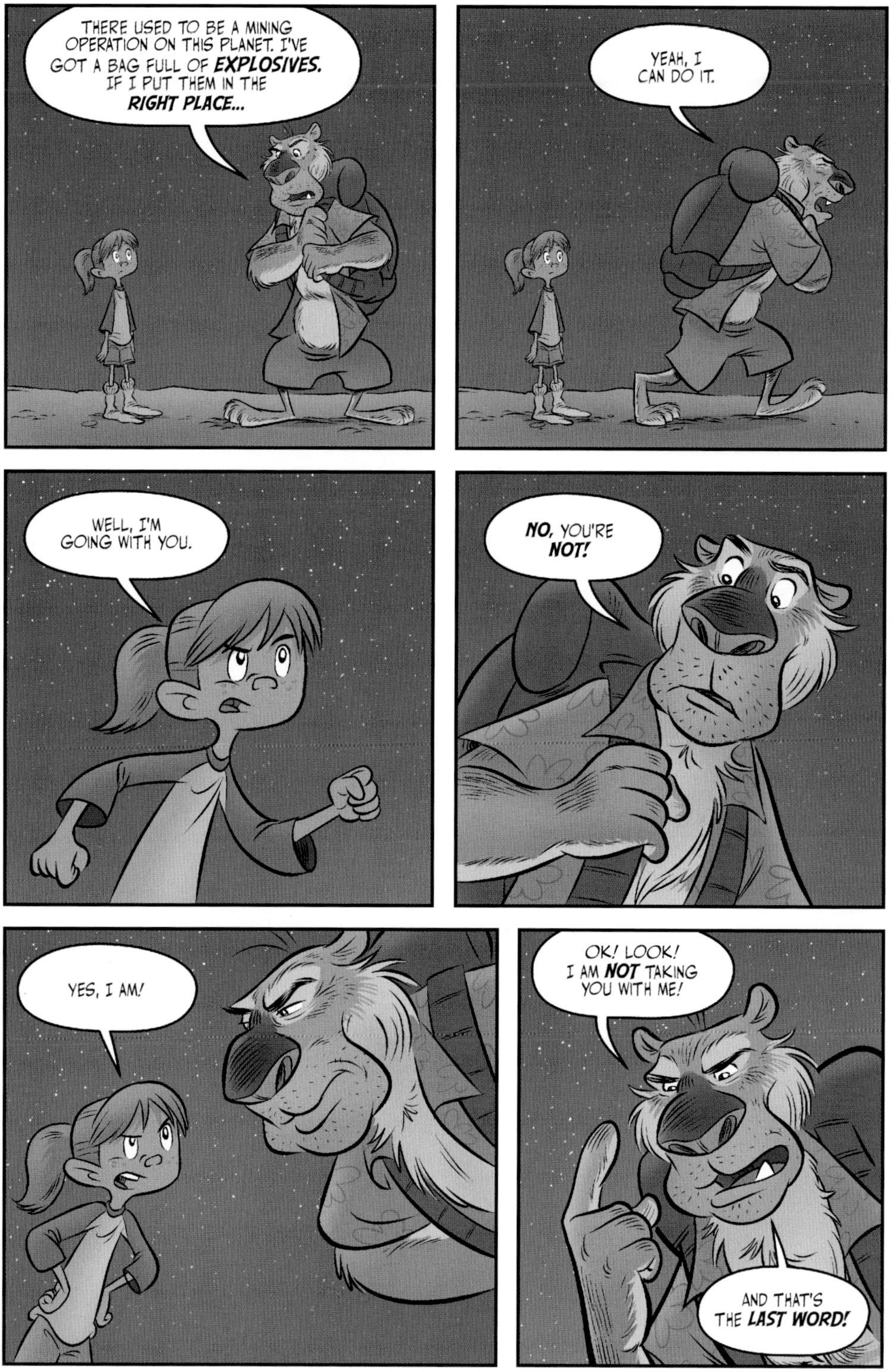
THERE USED TO BE A MINING OPERATION ON THIS PLANET. I'VE GOT A BAG FULL OF EXPLOSIVES. IF I PUT THEM IN THE RIGHT PLACE...
YEAH, I CAN DO IT.
WELL, I'M GOING WITH YOU.
NO, YOU'RE NOT!
YES, I AM!
OK! LOOK! I AM NOT TAKING YOU WITH ME!
AND THAT'S THE LAST WORD!

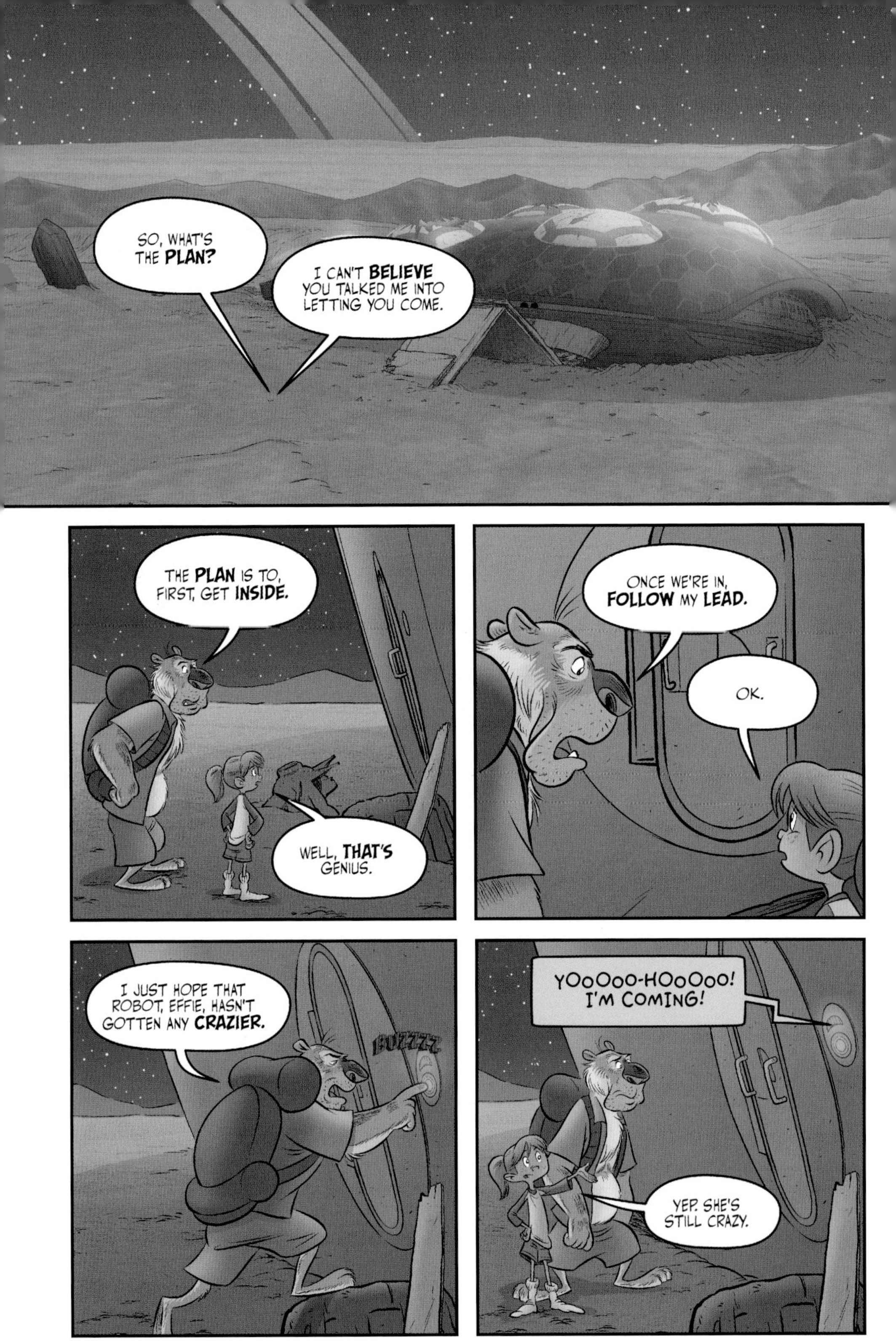
SO, WHAT'S THE PLAN?
I CAN'T BELIEVE YOU TALKED ME INTO LETTING YOU COME.
THE PLAN IS TO, FIRST, GET INSIDE.
WELL, THAT'S GENIUS.
ONCE WE'RE IN, FOLLOW MY LEAD.
OK.
I JUST HOPE THAT ROBOT, EFFIE, HASN'T GOTTEN ANY CRAZIER.
BUZZZZ
YOoOoo-HOoOoo! I'M COMING!
YEP. SHE'S STILL CRAZY.

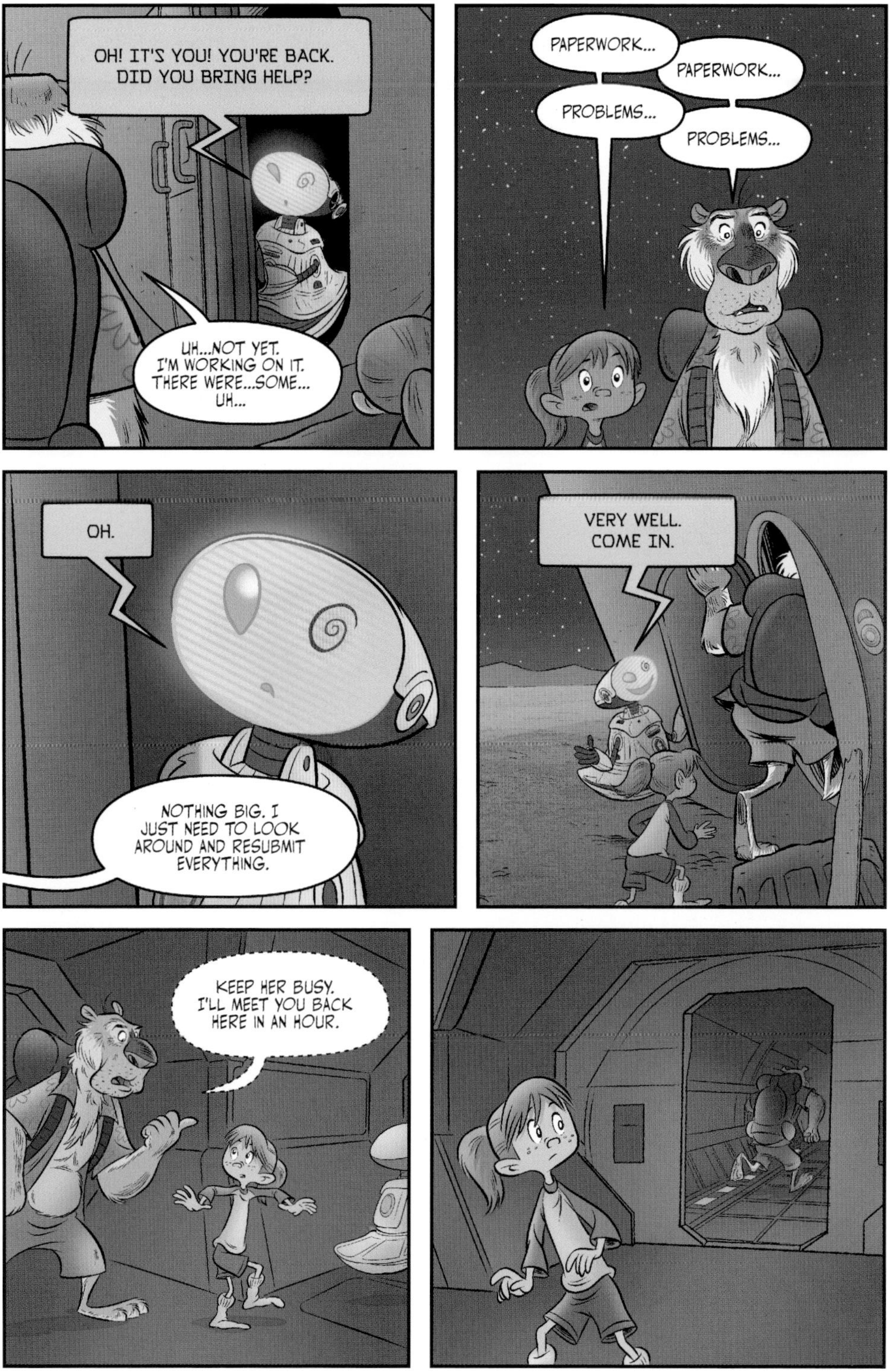
OH! IT'S YOU! YOU'RE BACK. DID YOU BRING HELP?
UH...NOT YET. I'M WORKING ON IT. THERE WERE...SOME... UH...
PAPERWORK...
PAPERWORK...
PROBLEMS...
PROBLEMS...
OH.
NOTHING BIG. I JUST NEED TO LOOK AROUND AND RESUBMIT EVERYTHING.
VERY WELL. COME IN.
KEEP HER BUSY. I'LL MEET YOU BACK HERE IN AN HOUR.

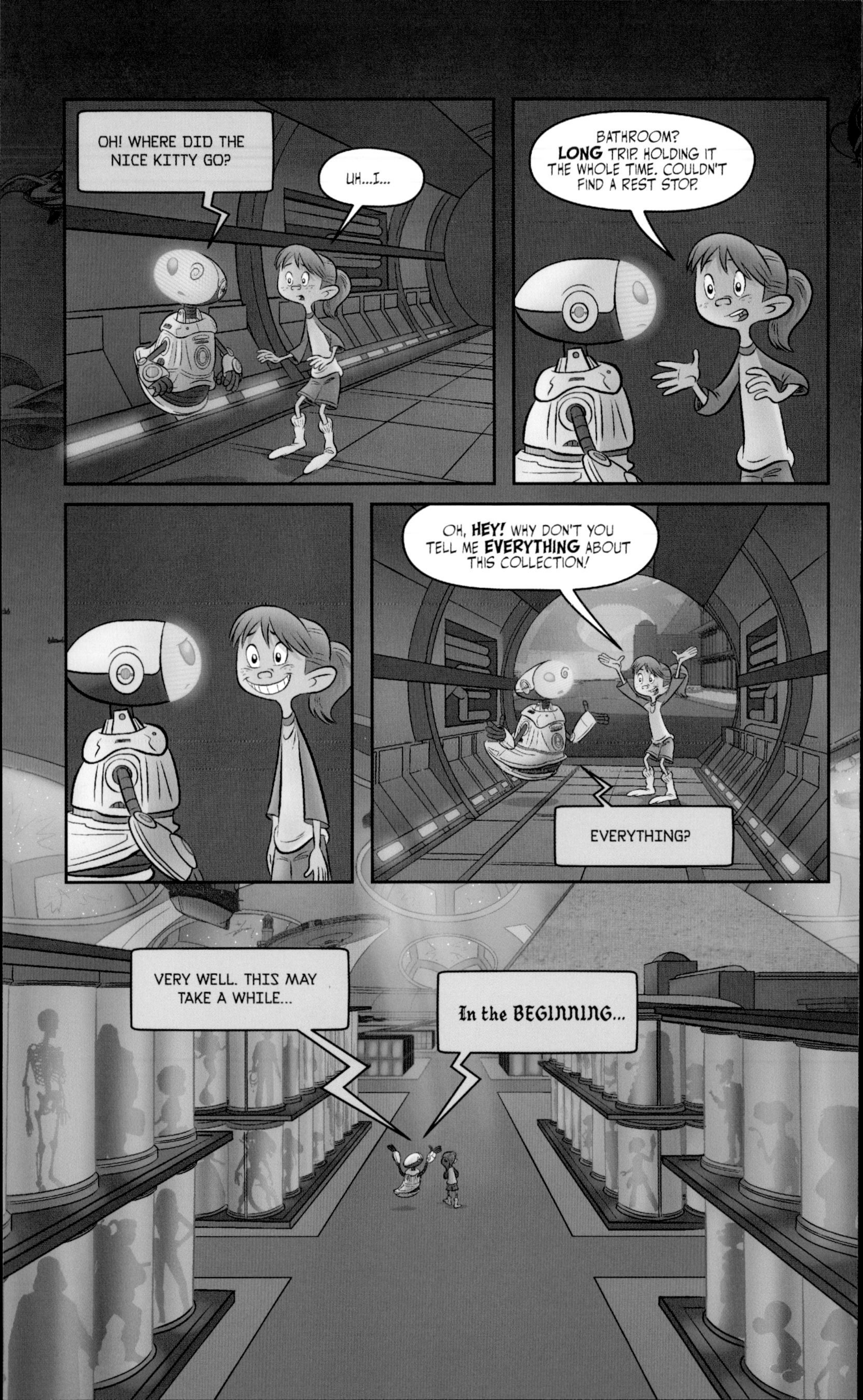
OH! WHERE DID THE NICE KITTY GO?
UH...I...
BATHROOM? LONG TRIP. HOLDING IT THE WHOLE TIME. COULDN'T FIND A REST STOP.
OH, HEY! WHY DON'T YOU TELL ME EVERYTHING ABOUT THIS COLLECTION!
EVERYTHING?
VERY WELL. THIS MAY TAKE A WHILE...
In the BEGINNING...

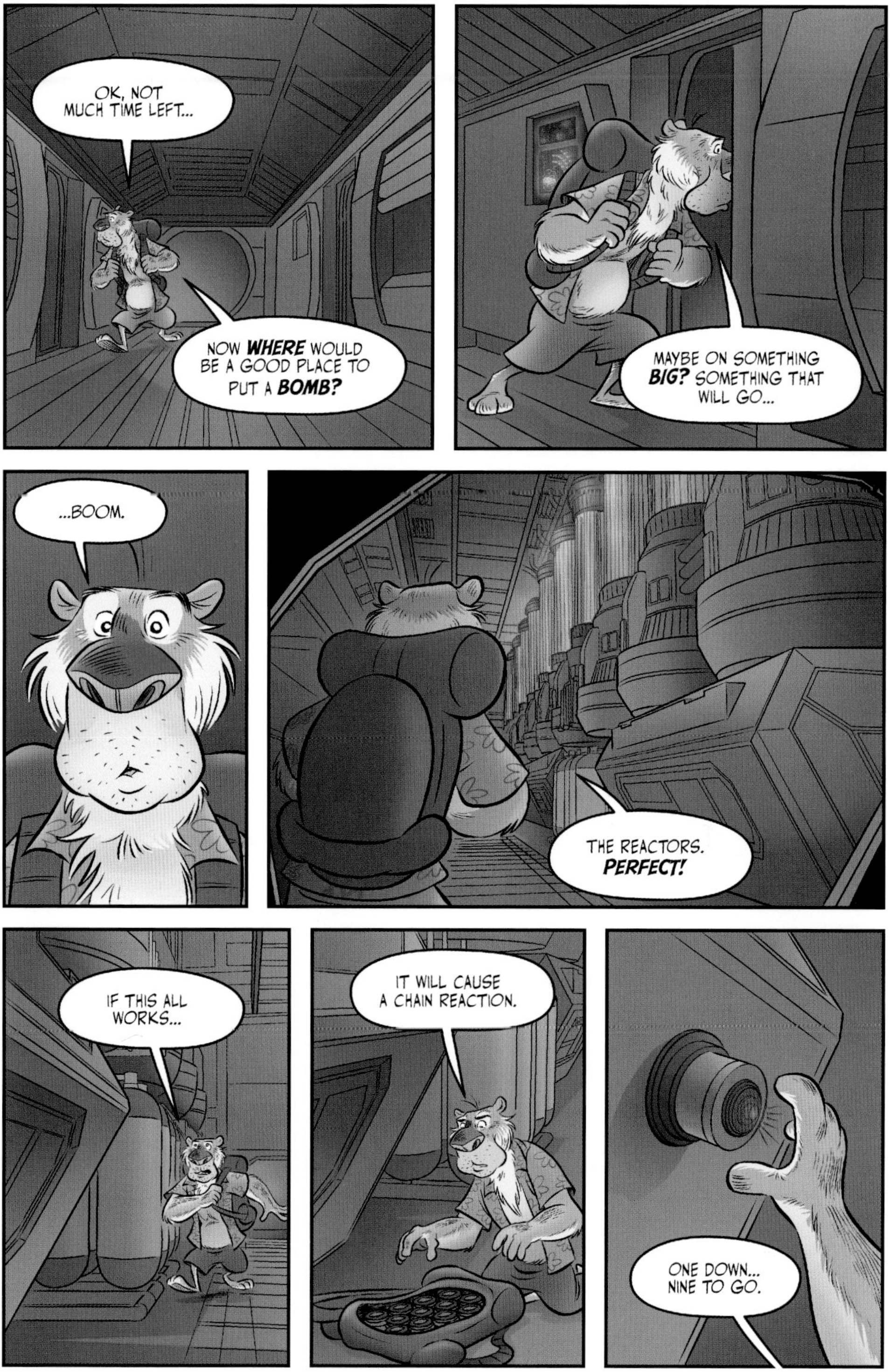
OK, NOT MUCH TIME LEFT...
NOW **WHERE** WOULD BE A GOOD PLACE TO PUT A **BOMB?**
MAYBE ON SOMETHING **BIG?** SOMETHING THAT WILL GO...
...BOOM.
THE REACTORS. **PERFECT!**
IF THIS ALL WORKS...
IT WILL CAUSE A CHAIN REACTION.
ONE DOWN... NINE TO GO.

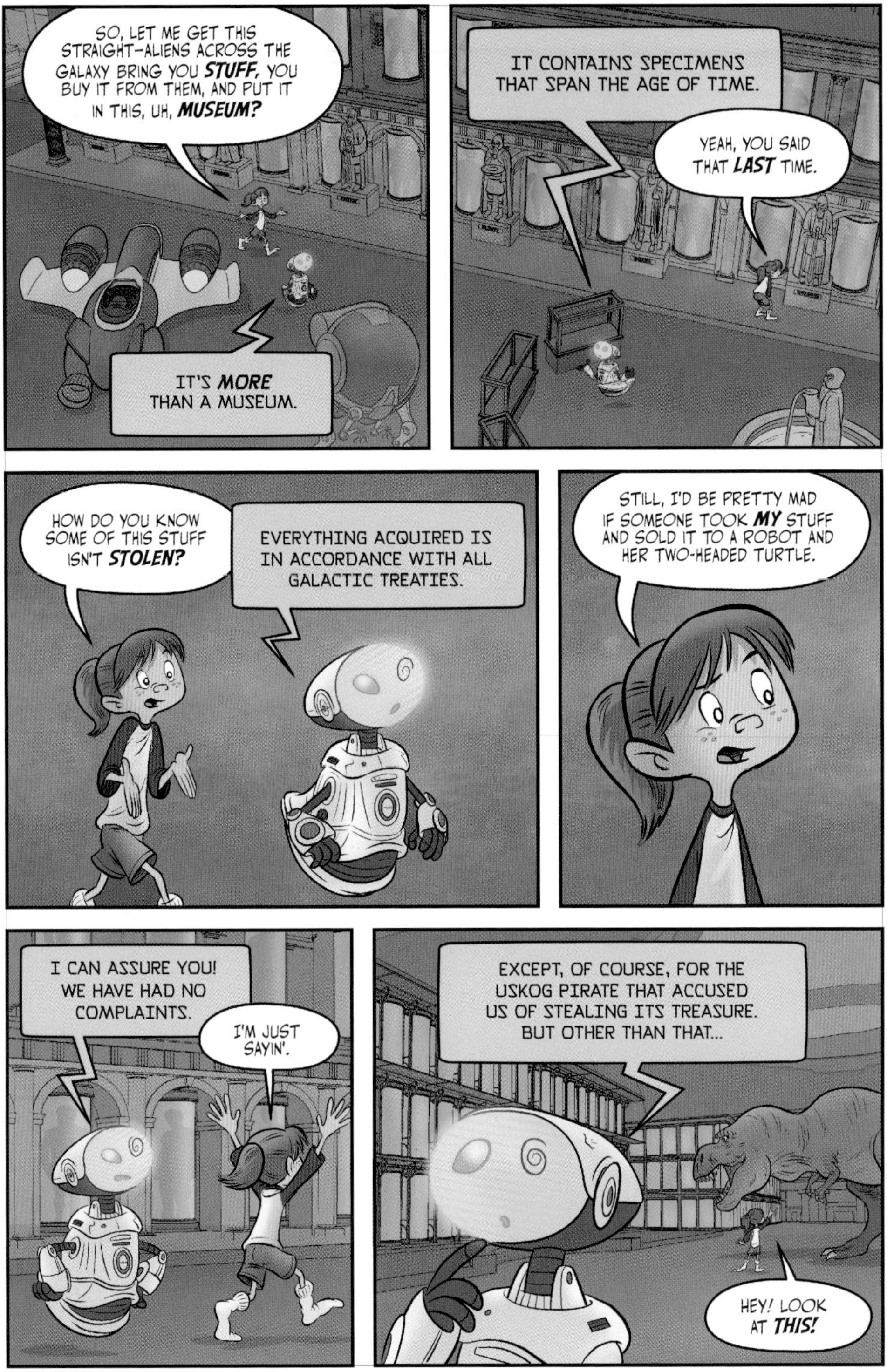
SO, LET ME GET THIS STRAIGHT—ALIENS ACROSS THE GALAXY BRING YOU **STUFF,** YOU BUY IT FROM THEM, AND PUT IT IN THIS, UH, **MUSEUM?**
IT'S **MORE** THAN A MUSEUM.
IT CONTAINS SPECIMENS THAT SPAN THE AGE OF TIME.
YEAH, YOU SAID THAT **LAST** TIME.
HOW DO YOU KNOW SOME OF THIS STUFF ISN'T **STOLEN?**
EVERYTHING ACQUIRED IS IN ACCORDANCE WITH ALL GALACTIC TREATIES.
STILL, I'D BE PRETTY MAD IF SOMEONE TOOK **MY** STUFF AND SOLD IT TO A ROBOT AND HER TWO-HEADED TURTLE.
I CAN ASSURE YOU! WE HAVE HAD NO COMPLAINTS.
I'M JUST SAYIN'.
EXCEPT, OF COURSE, FOR THE USKOG PIRATE THAT ACCUSED US OF STEALING ITS TREASURE. BUT OTHER THAN THAT...
HEY! LOOK AT **THIS!**

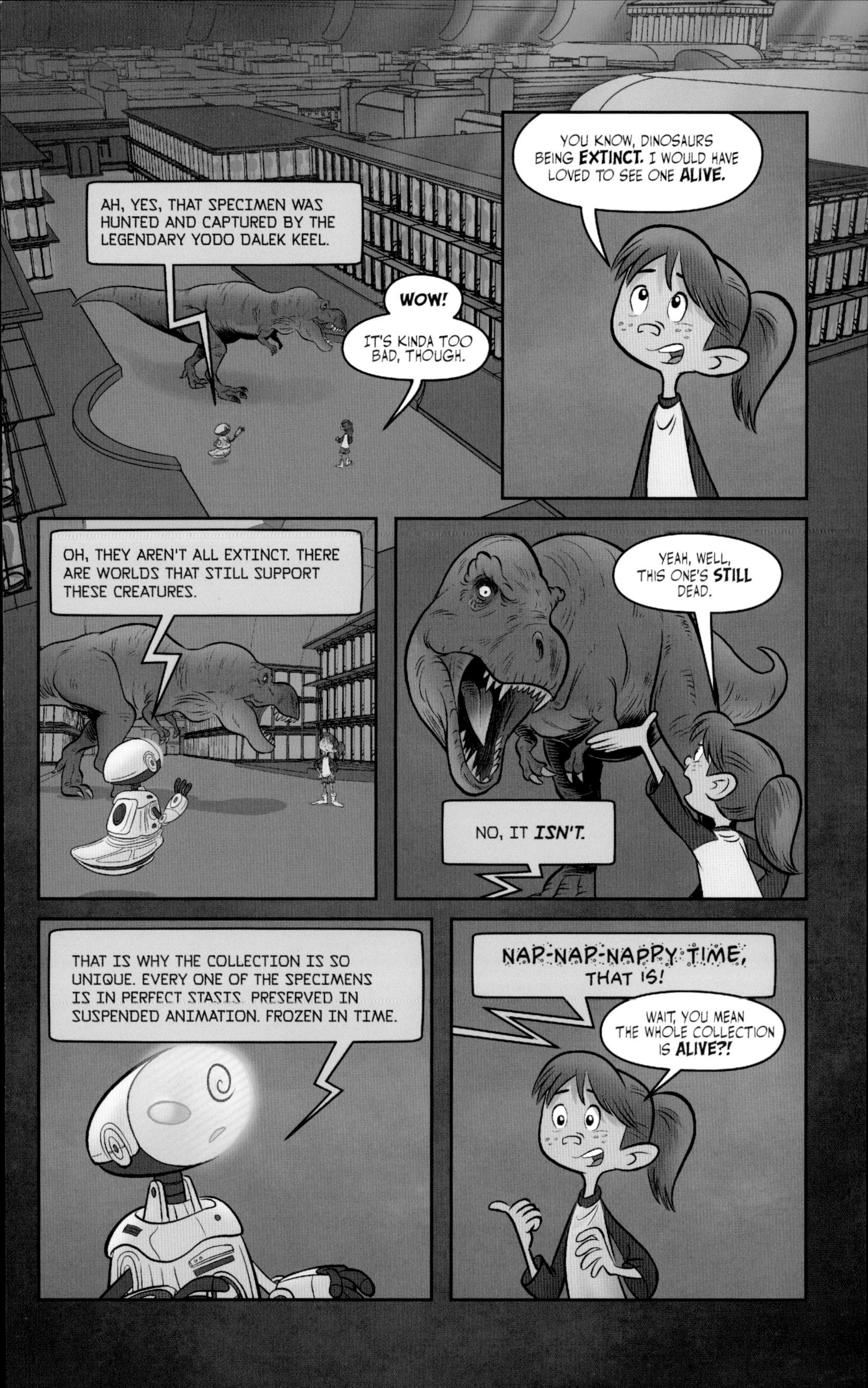
AH, YES, THAT SPECIMEN WAS HUNTED AND CAPTURED BY THE LEGENDARY YODO DALEK KEEL.
WOW!
IT'S KINDA TOO BAD, THOUGH.
YOU KNOW, DINOSAURS BEING EXTINCT. I WOULD HAVE LOVED TO SEE ONE ALIVE.
OH, THEY AREN'T ALL EXTINCT. THERE ARE WORLDS THAT STILL SUPPORT THESE CREATURES.
YEAH, WELL, THIS ONE'S STILL DEAD.
NO, IT ISN'T.
THAT IS WHY THE COLLECTION IS SO UNIQUE. EVERY ONE OF THE SPECIMENS IS IN PERFECT STASIS. PRESERVED IN SUSPENDED ANIMATION. FROZEN IN TIME.
NAP-NAP-NAPPY TIME, THAT IS!
WAIT, YOU MEAN THE WHOLE COLLECTION IS ALIVE?!

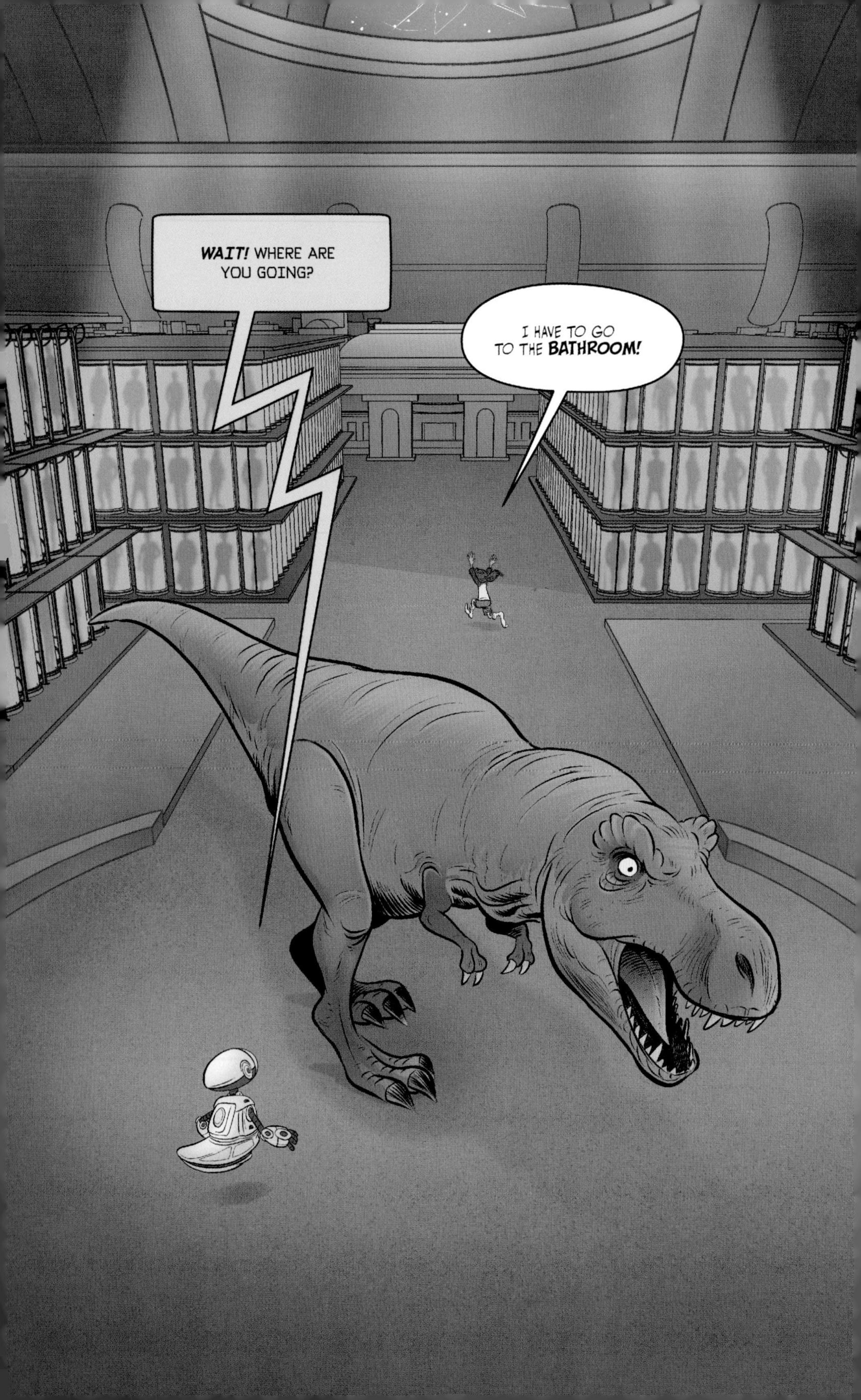
WAIT! WHERE ARE YOU GOING?
I HAVE TO GO TO THE BATHROOM!

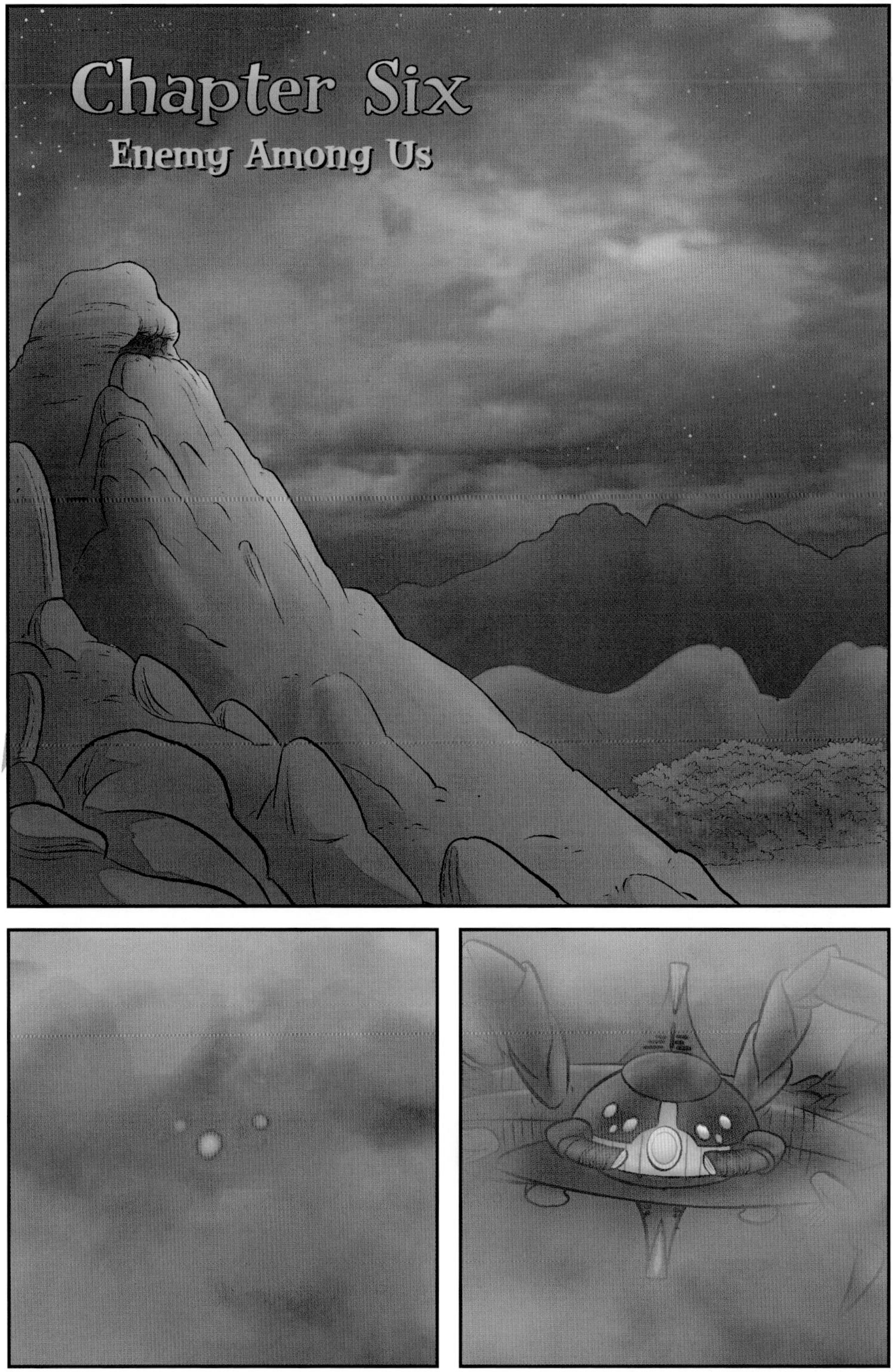
Chapter Six
Enemy Among Us

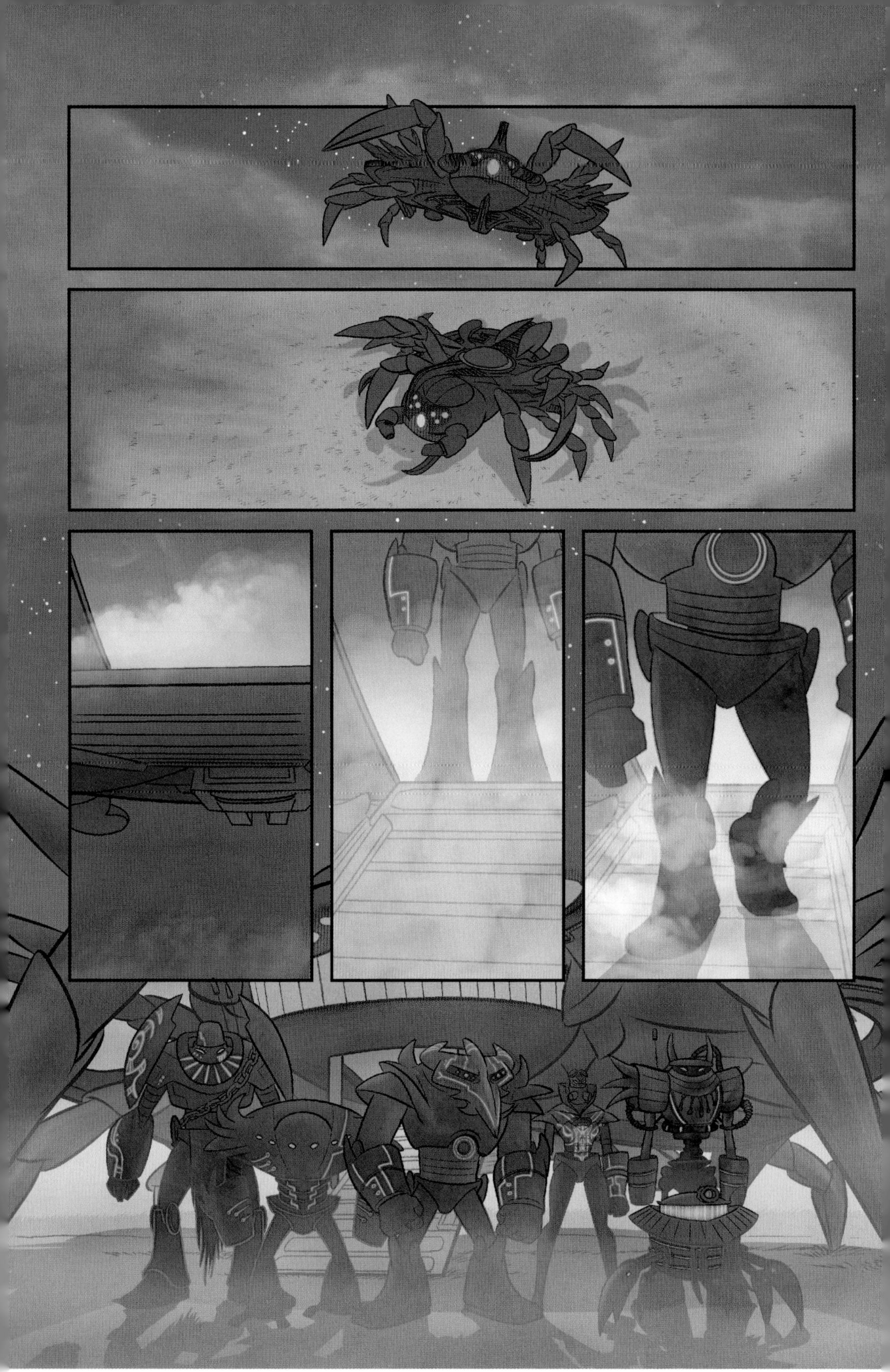

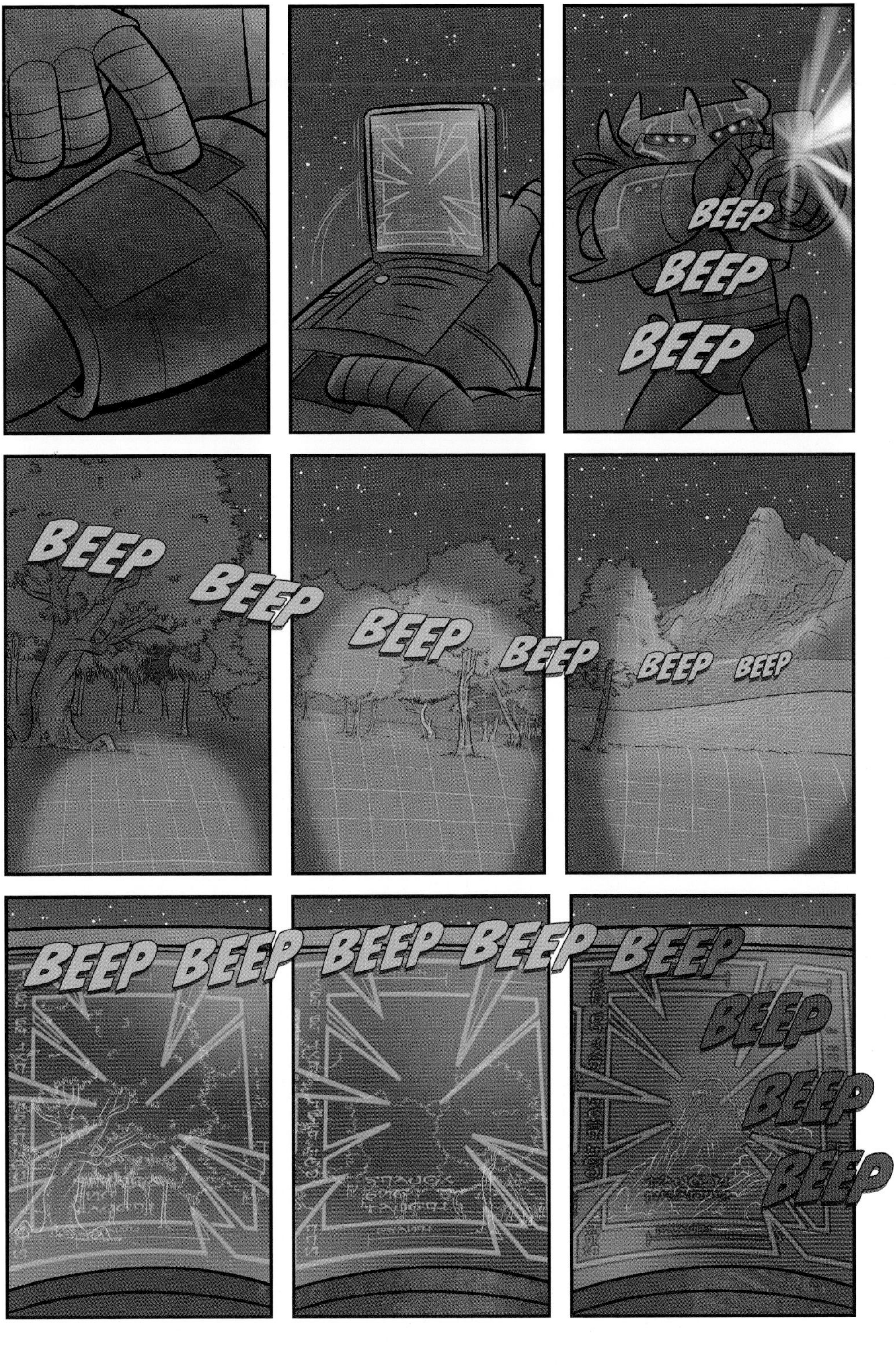
BEEP
BEEP
BEEP
BEEP
BEEP
BEEP
BEEP
BEEP
BEEP
BEEP
BEEP
BEEP
BEEP
BEEP
BEEP
BEEP
BEEP

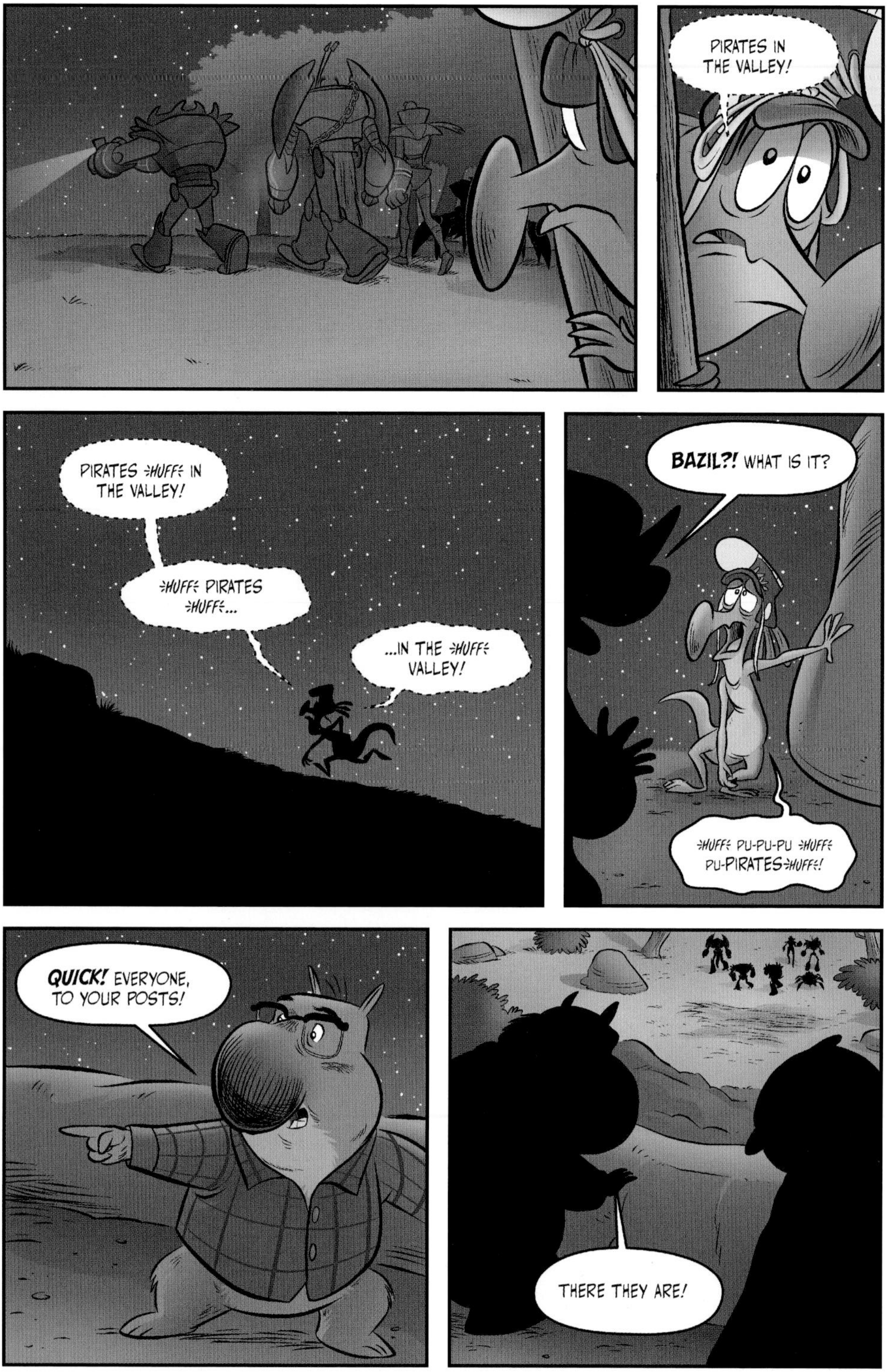
PIRATES IN THE VALLEY!
PIRATES ≈HUFF≈ IN THE VALLEY!
≈HUFF≈ PIRATES ≈HUFF≈...
...IN THE ≈HUFF≈ VALLEY!
BAZIL?! WHAT IS IT?
≈HUFF≈ PU-PU-PU ≈HUFF≈ PU-PIRATES≈HUFF≈!
QUICK! EVERYONE, TO YOUR POSTS!
THERE THEY ARE!

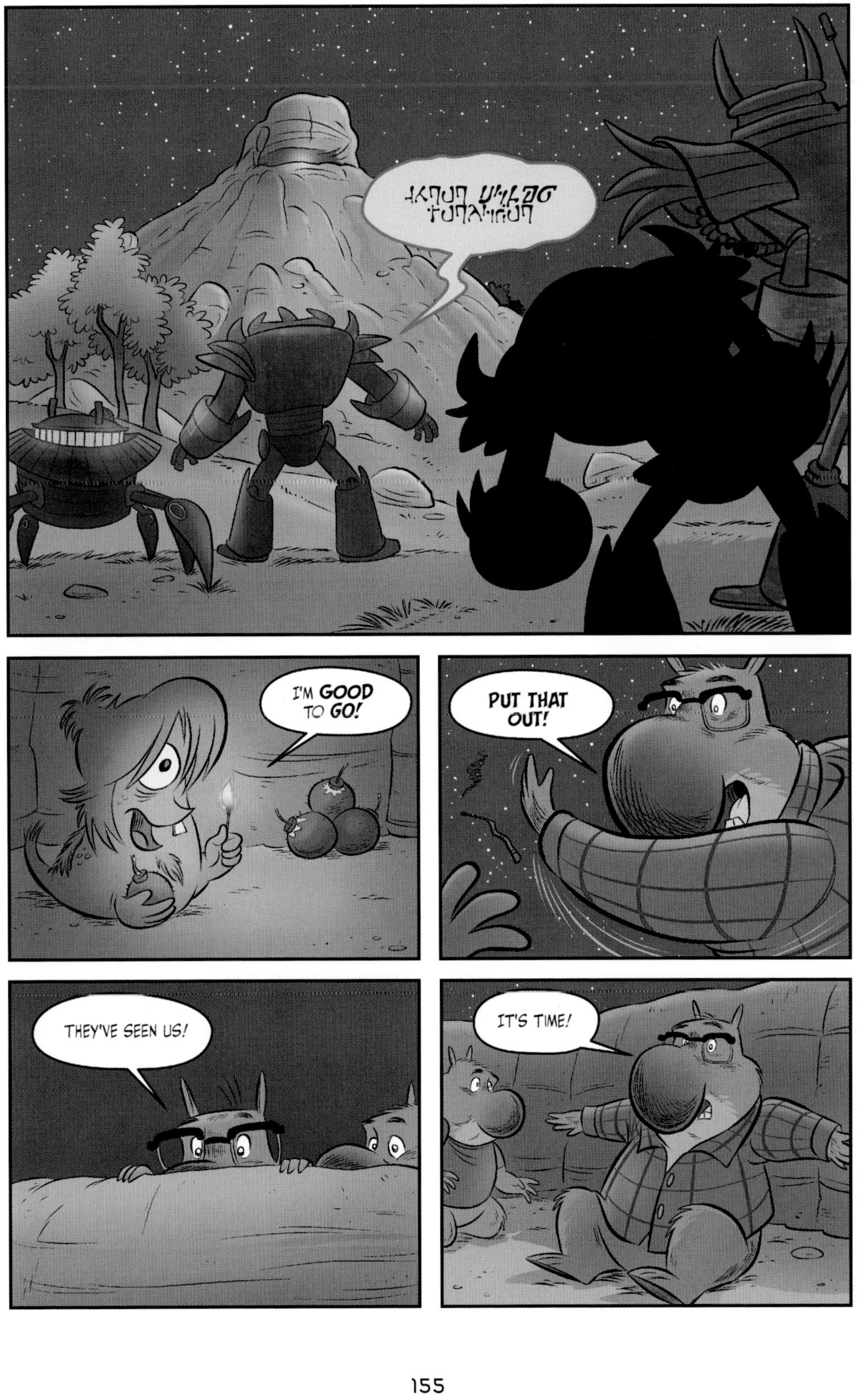
I'M GOOD TO GO!
PUT THAT OUT!
THEY'VE SEEN US!
IT'S TIME!

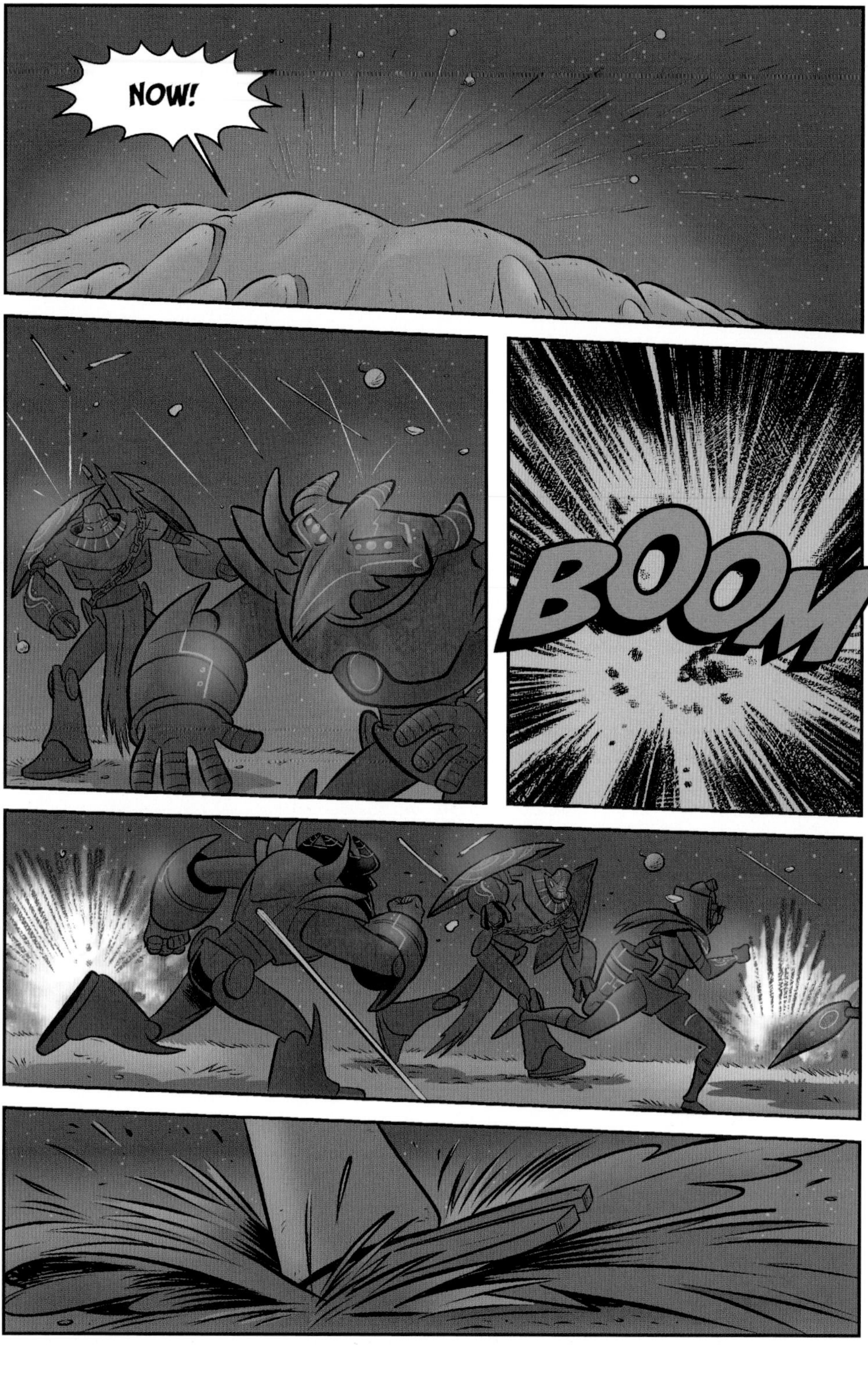
NOW!
BOOM

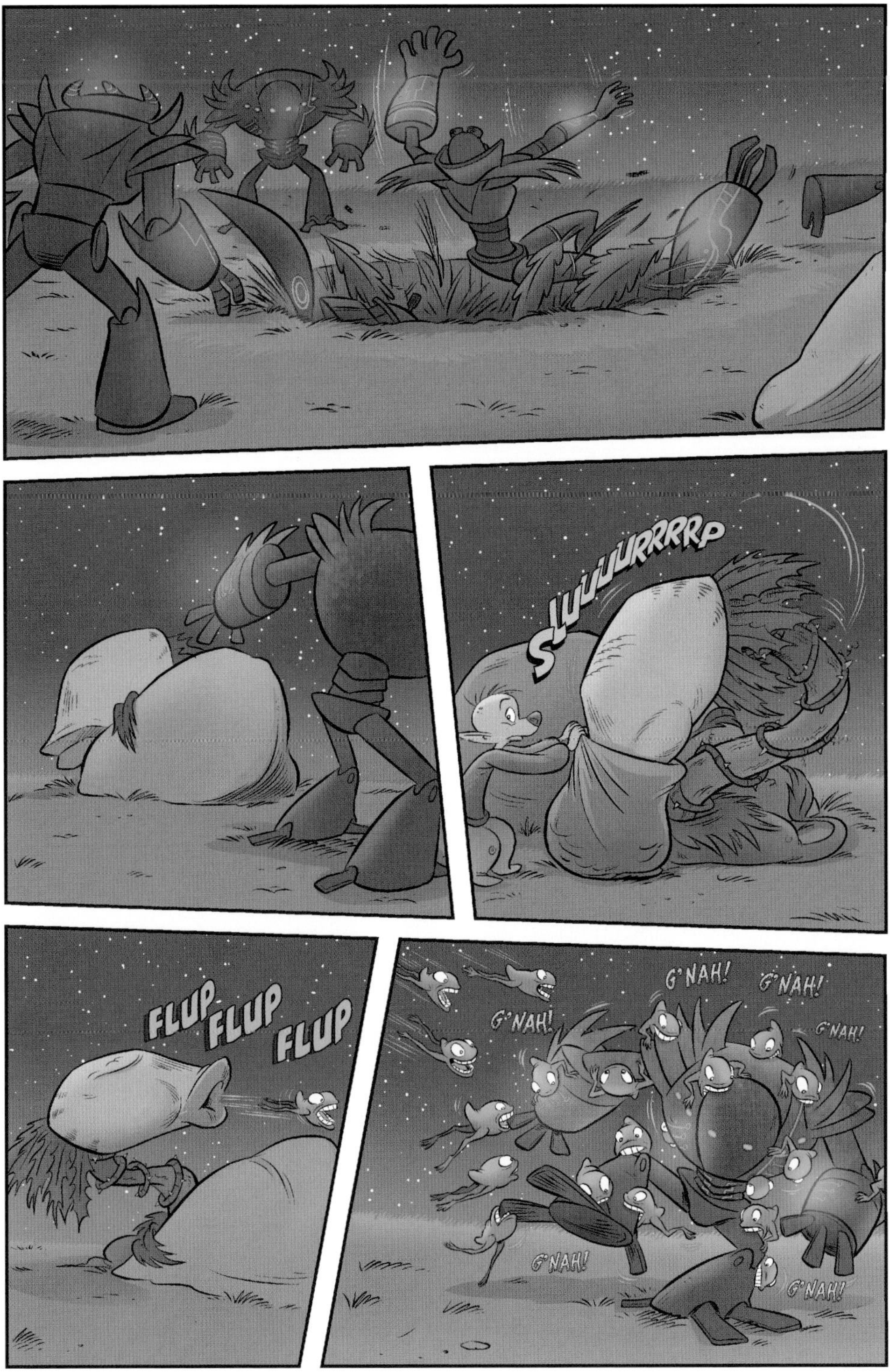
SLUUUURRRRP
FLUP
FLUP
FLUP
G'NAH!
G'NAH!
G'NAH!
G'NAH!
G'NAH!
G'NAH!

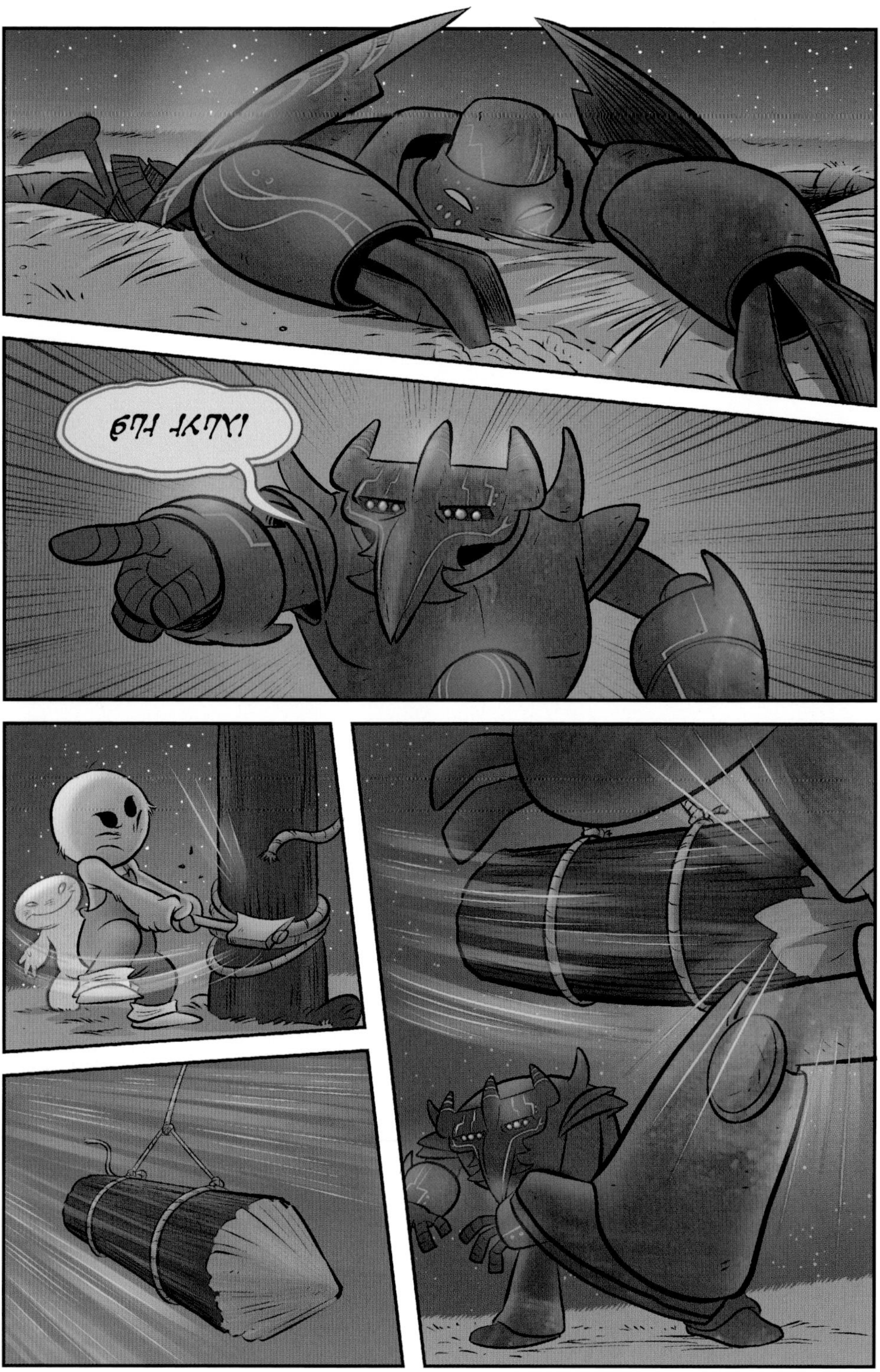

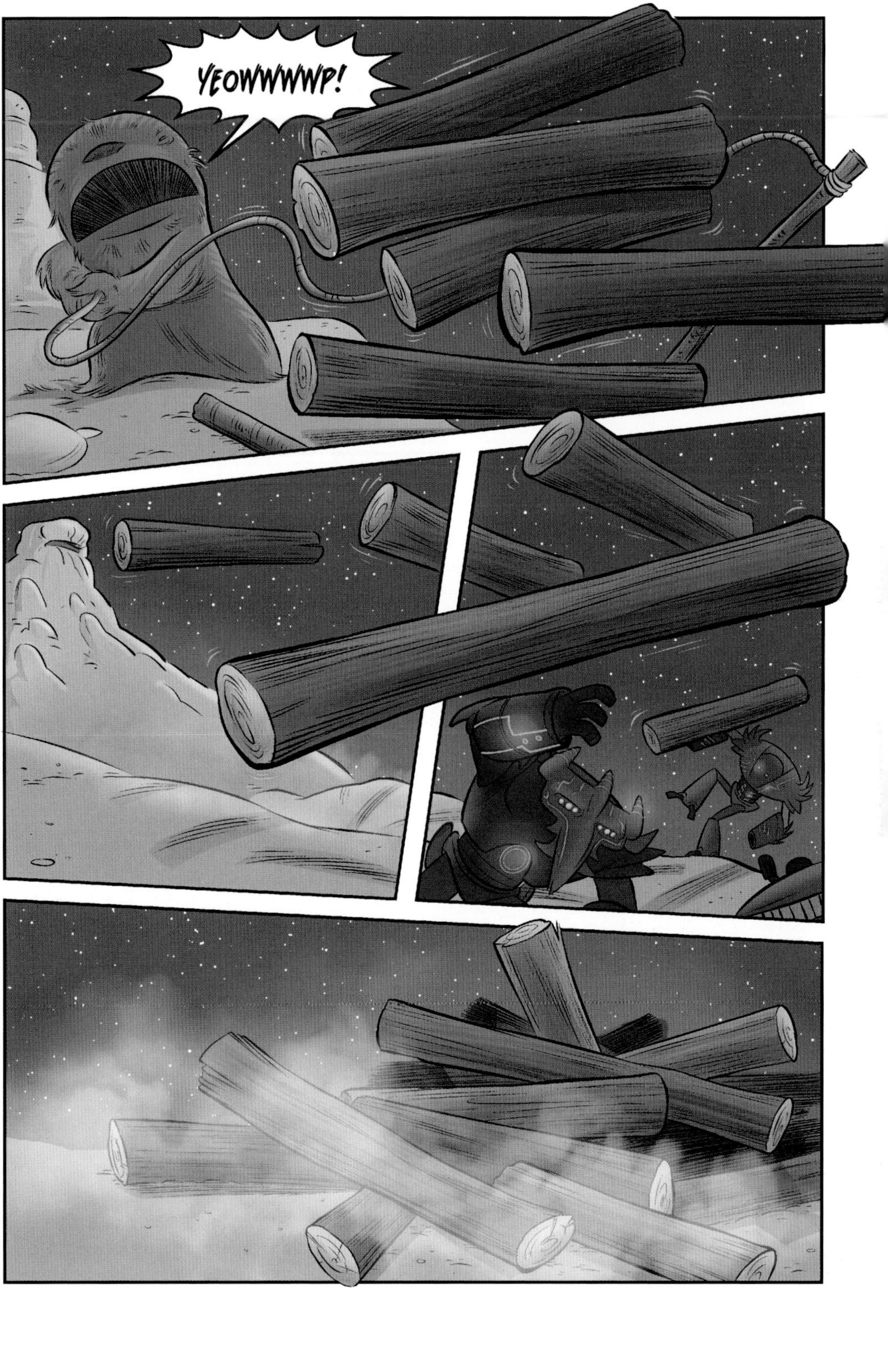
YEOWWWWP!

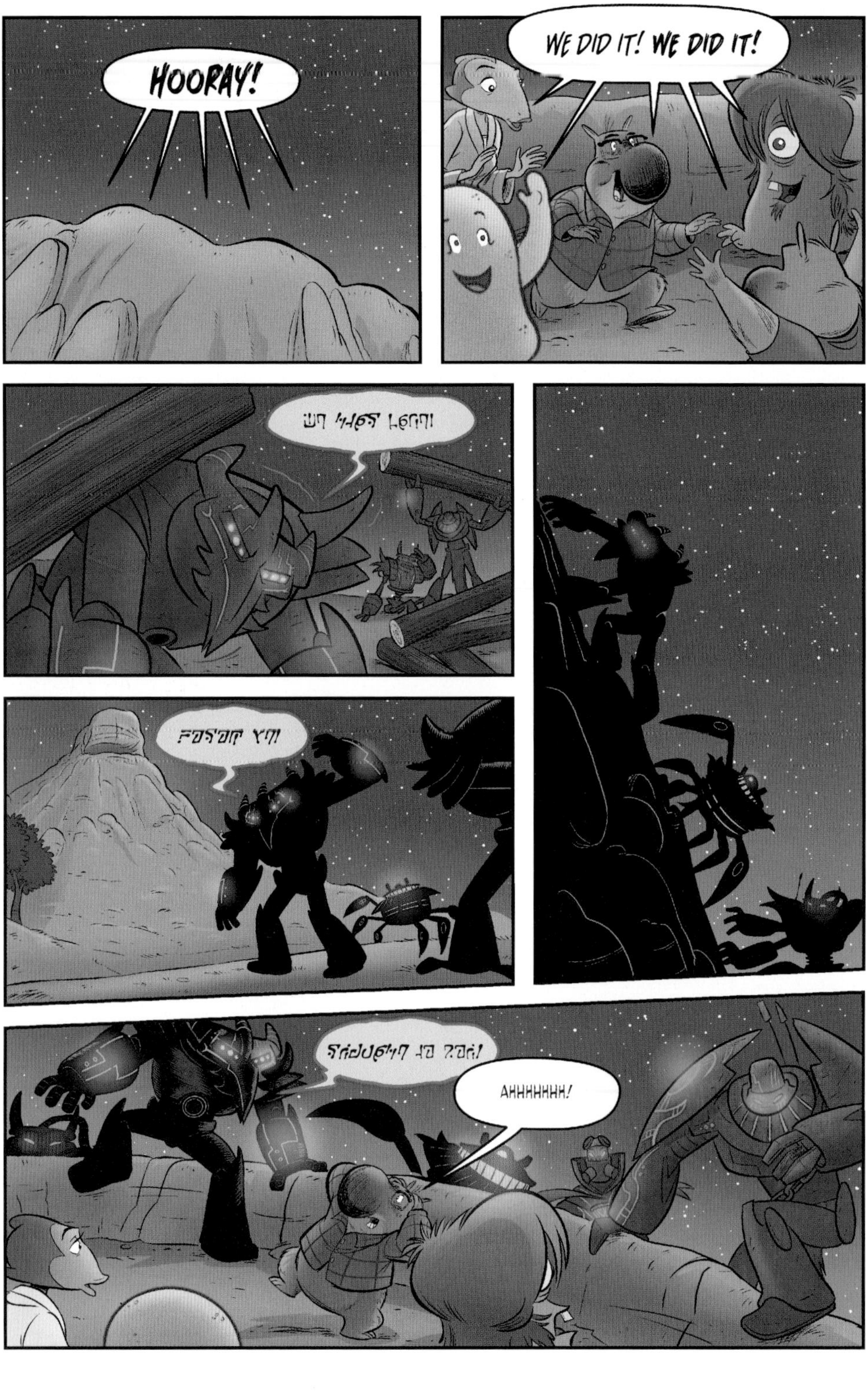
HOORAY!
WE DID IT! WE DID IT!
AHHHHHHH!

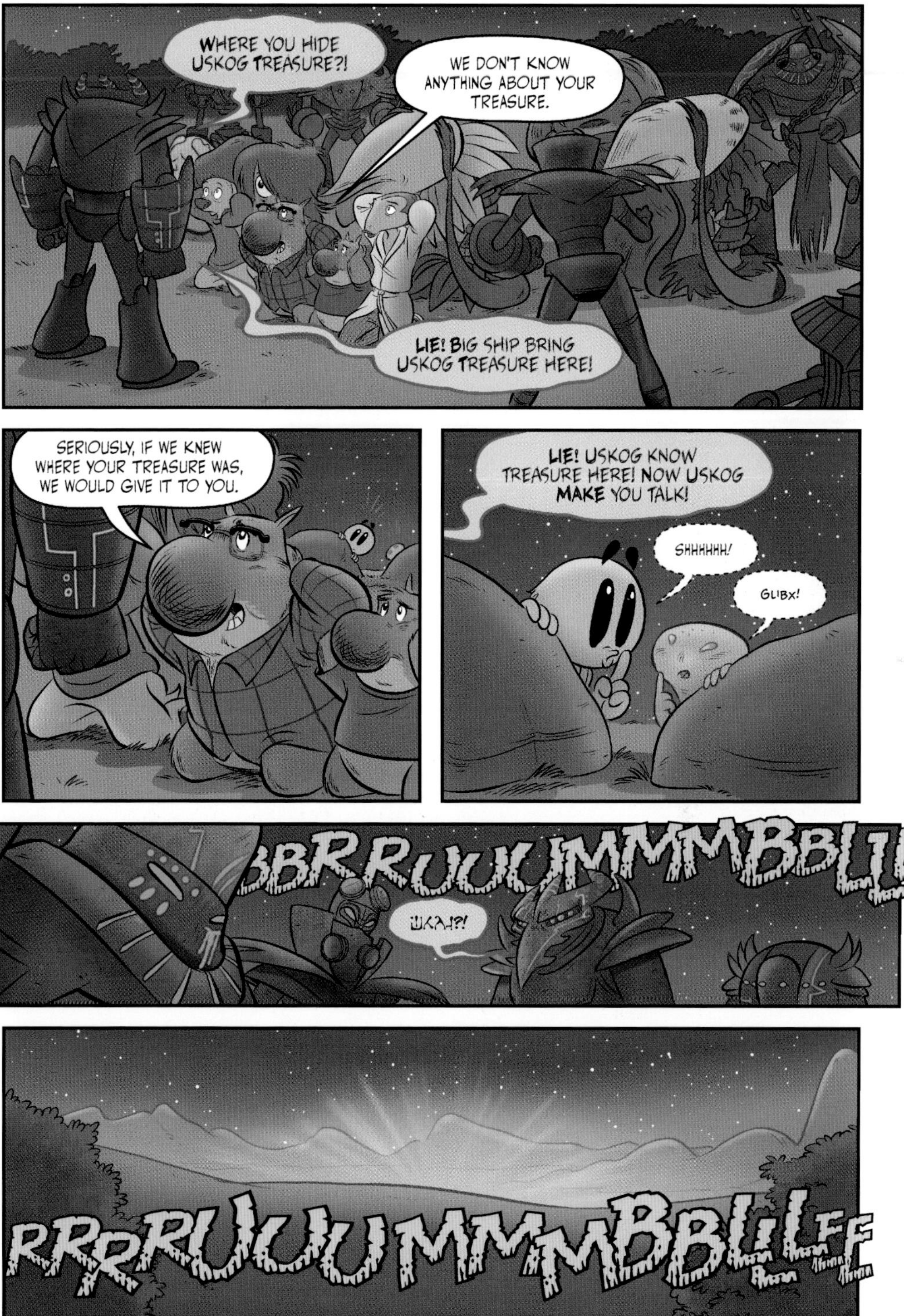
WHERE YOU HIDE USKOG TREASURE?!
WE DON'T KNOW ANYTHING ABOUT YOUR TREASURE.
LIE! BIG SHIP BRING USKOG TREASURE HERE!
SERIOUSLY, IF WE KNEW WHERE YOUR TREASURE WAS, WE WOULD GIVE IT TO YOU.
LIE! USKOG KNOW TREASURE HERE! NOW USKOG MAKE YOU TALK!
SHHHHHH!
GLIBX!
BBRRUUUMMMMBBLLL
RRRRUUUUMMMMBBLLLFF

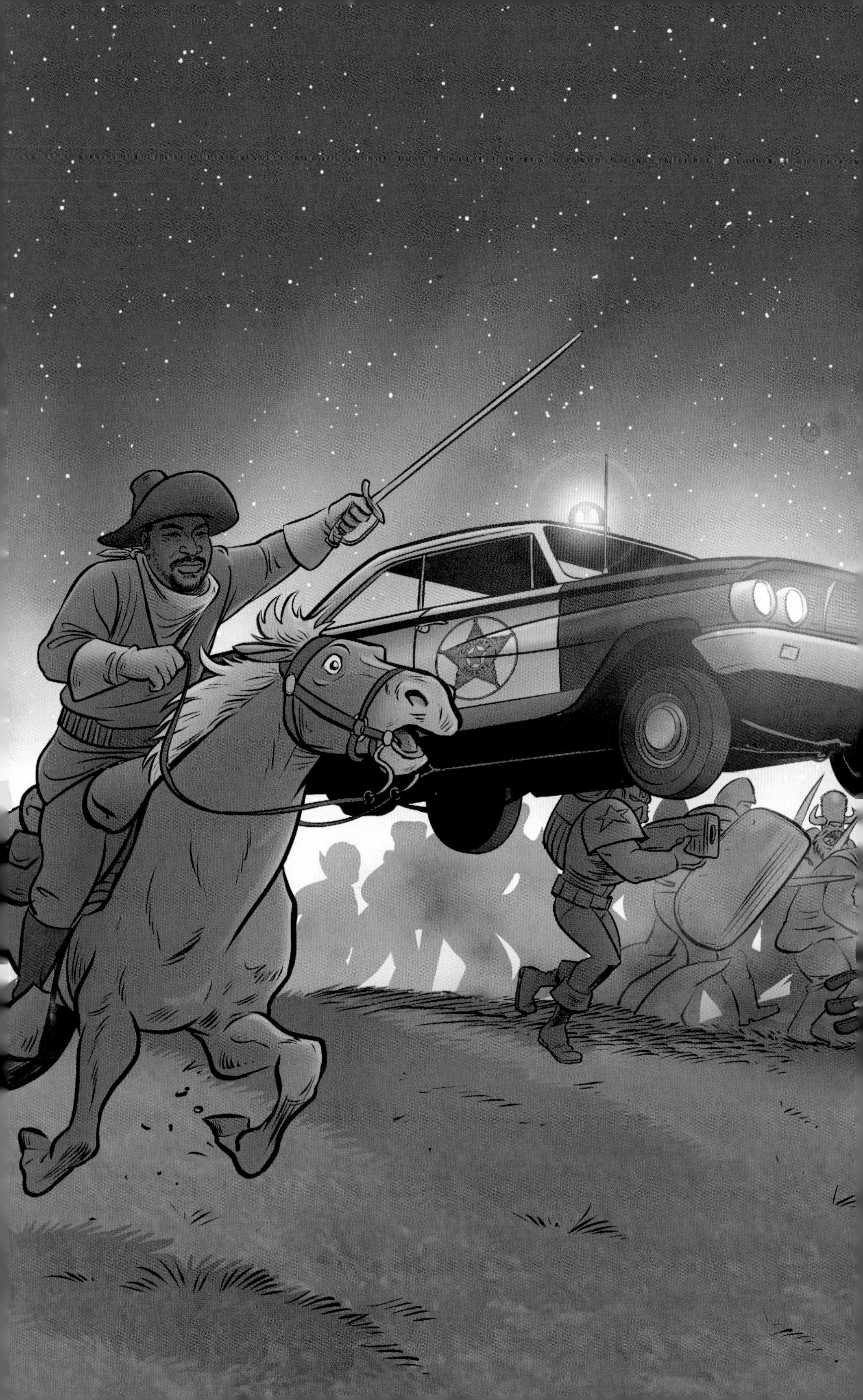
COUNTY
SHERIFF

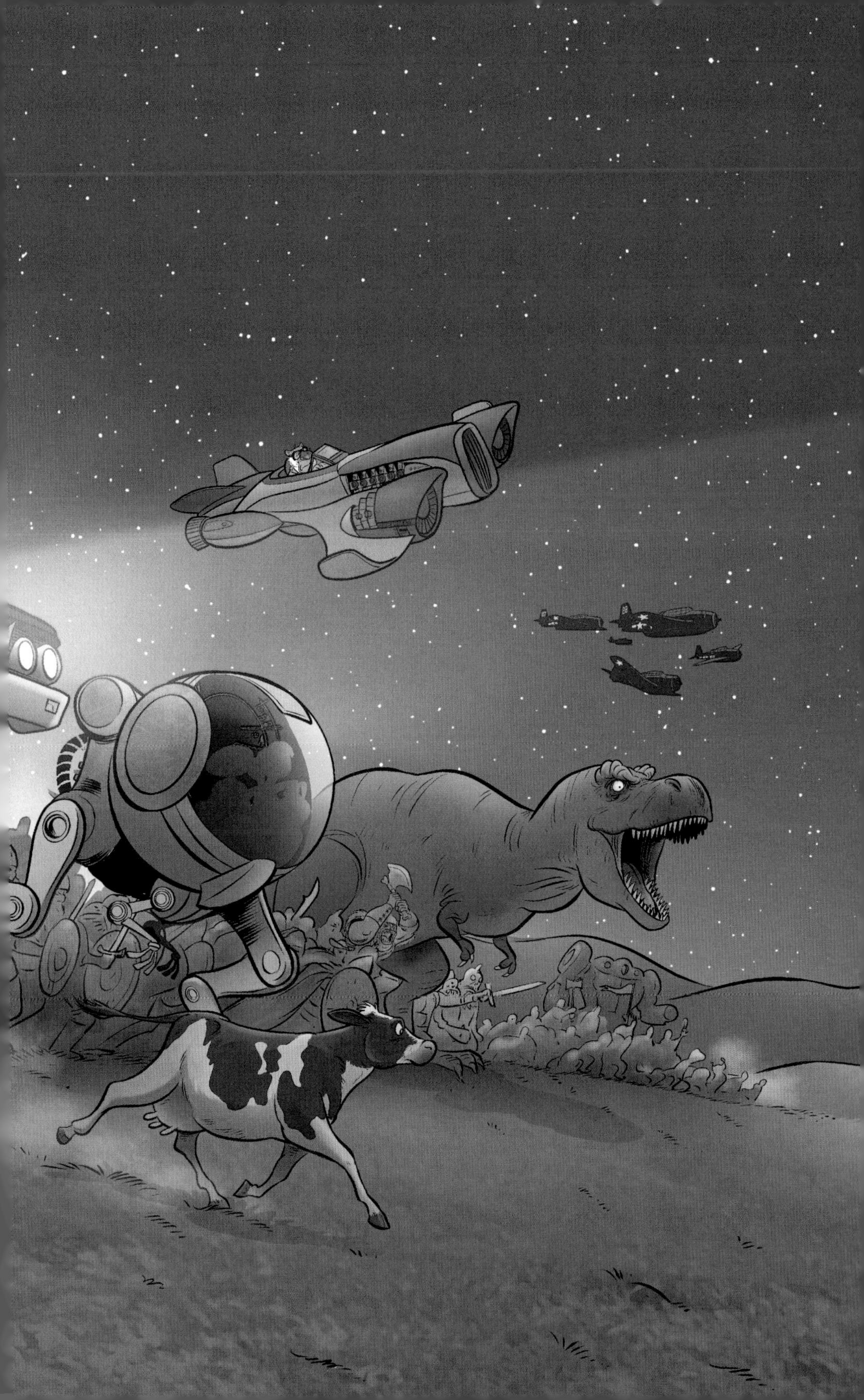

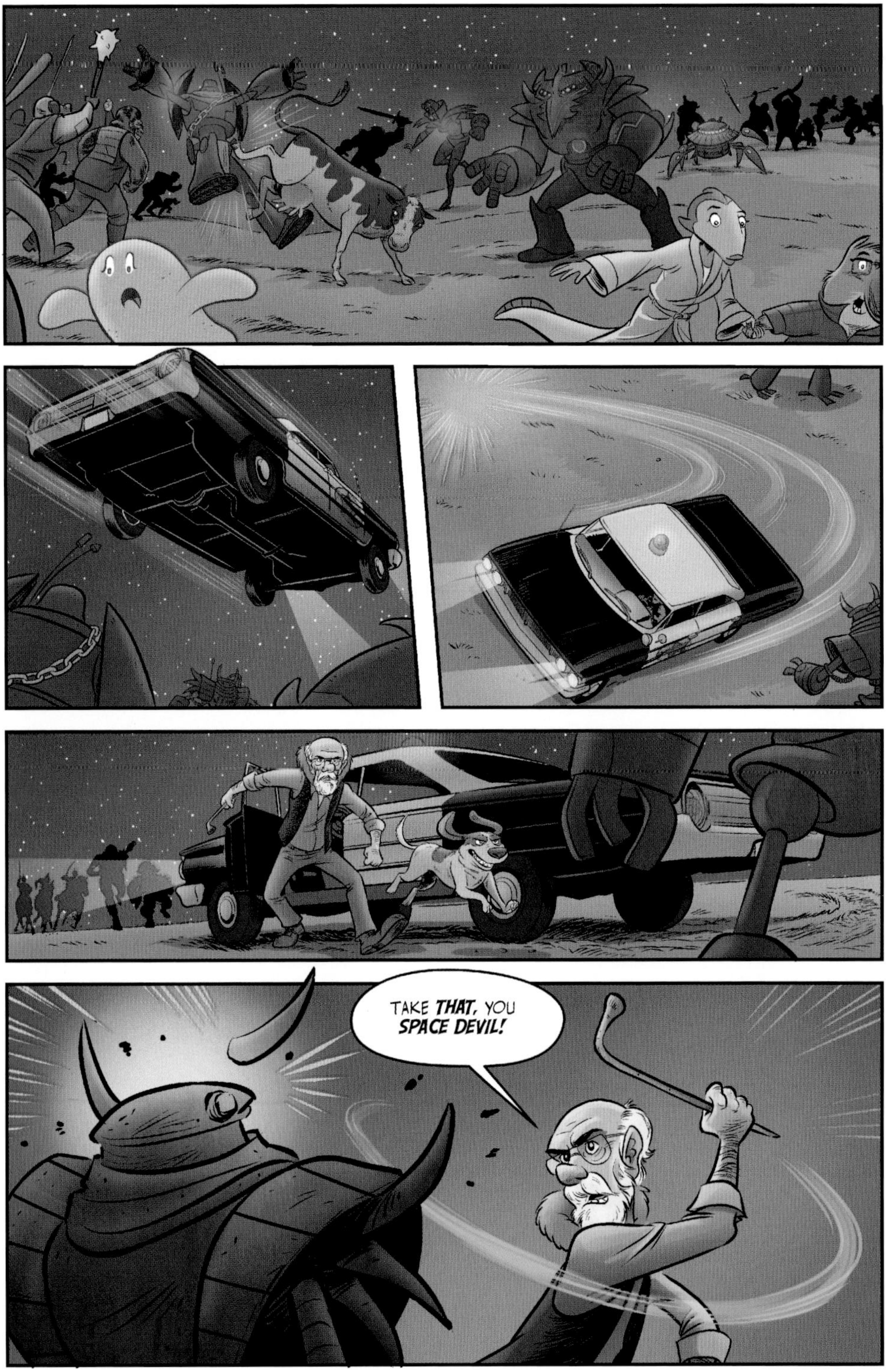
TAKE THAT, YOU
SPACE DEVIL!

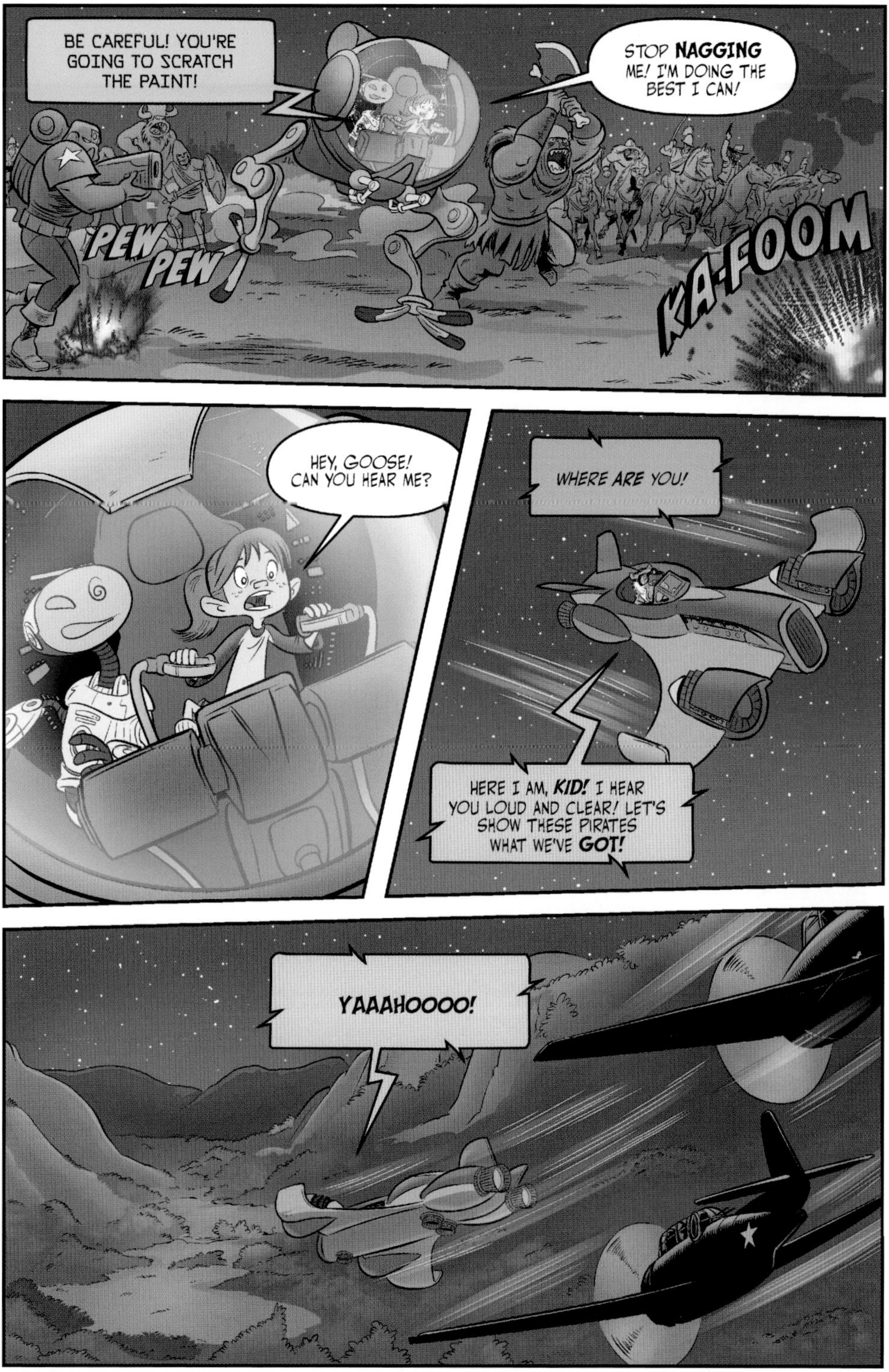
BE CAREFUL! YOU'RE GOING TO SCRATCH THE PAINT!
STOP **NAGGING** ME! I'M DOING THE BEST I CAN!
PEW PEW
KA-FOOM
HEY, GOOSE! CAN YOU HEAR ME?
WHERE *ARE* YOU!
HERE I AM, ***KID!*** I HEAR YOU LOUD AND CLEAR! LET'S SHOW THESE PIRATES WHAT WE'VE **GOT!**
YAAAHOOOO!

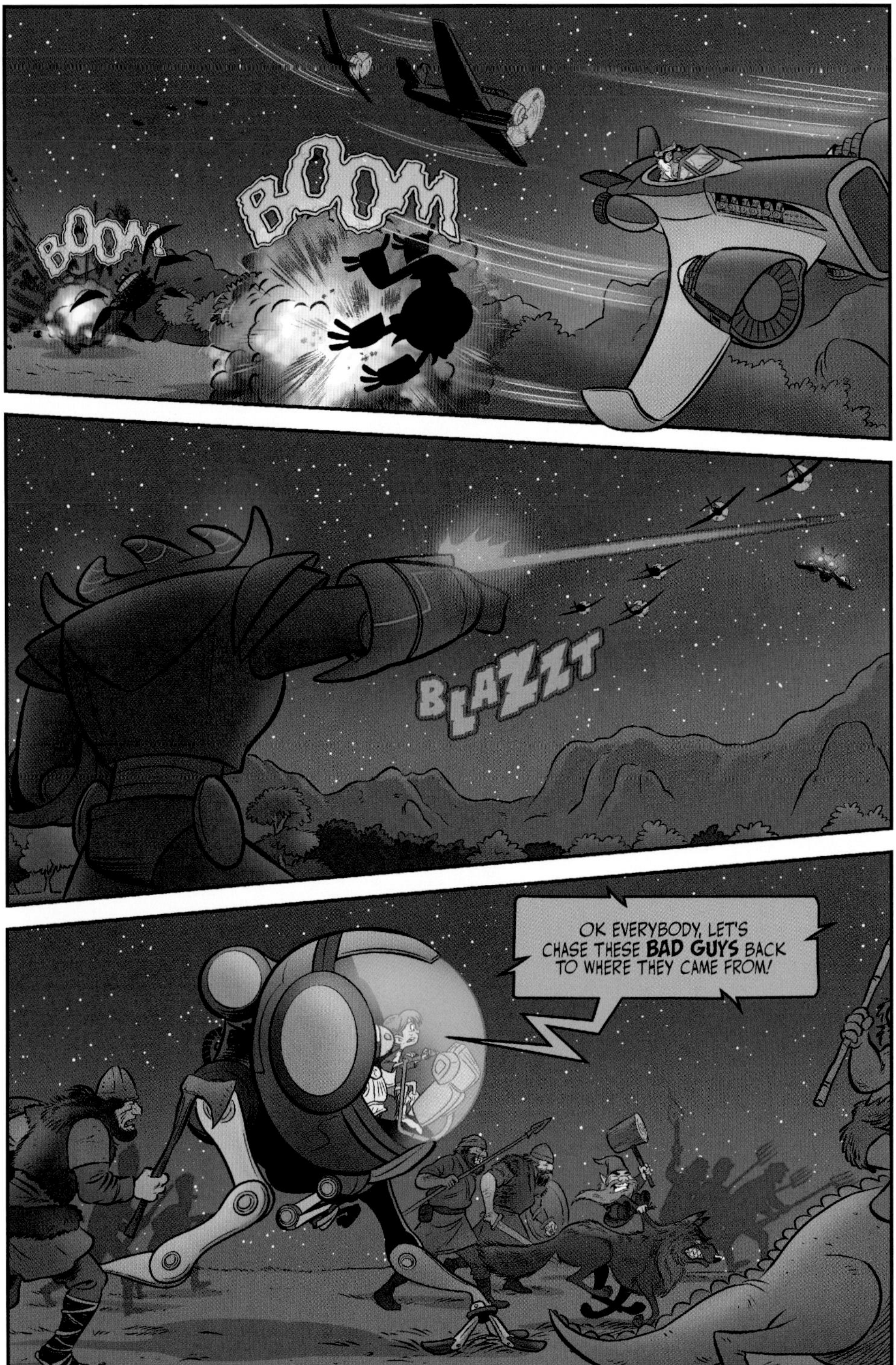
BOOM
BOOM
BLAZZZT
OK EVERYBODY, LET'S CHASE THESE **BAD GUYS** BACK TO WHERE THEY CAME FROM!

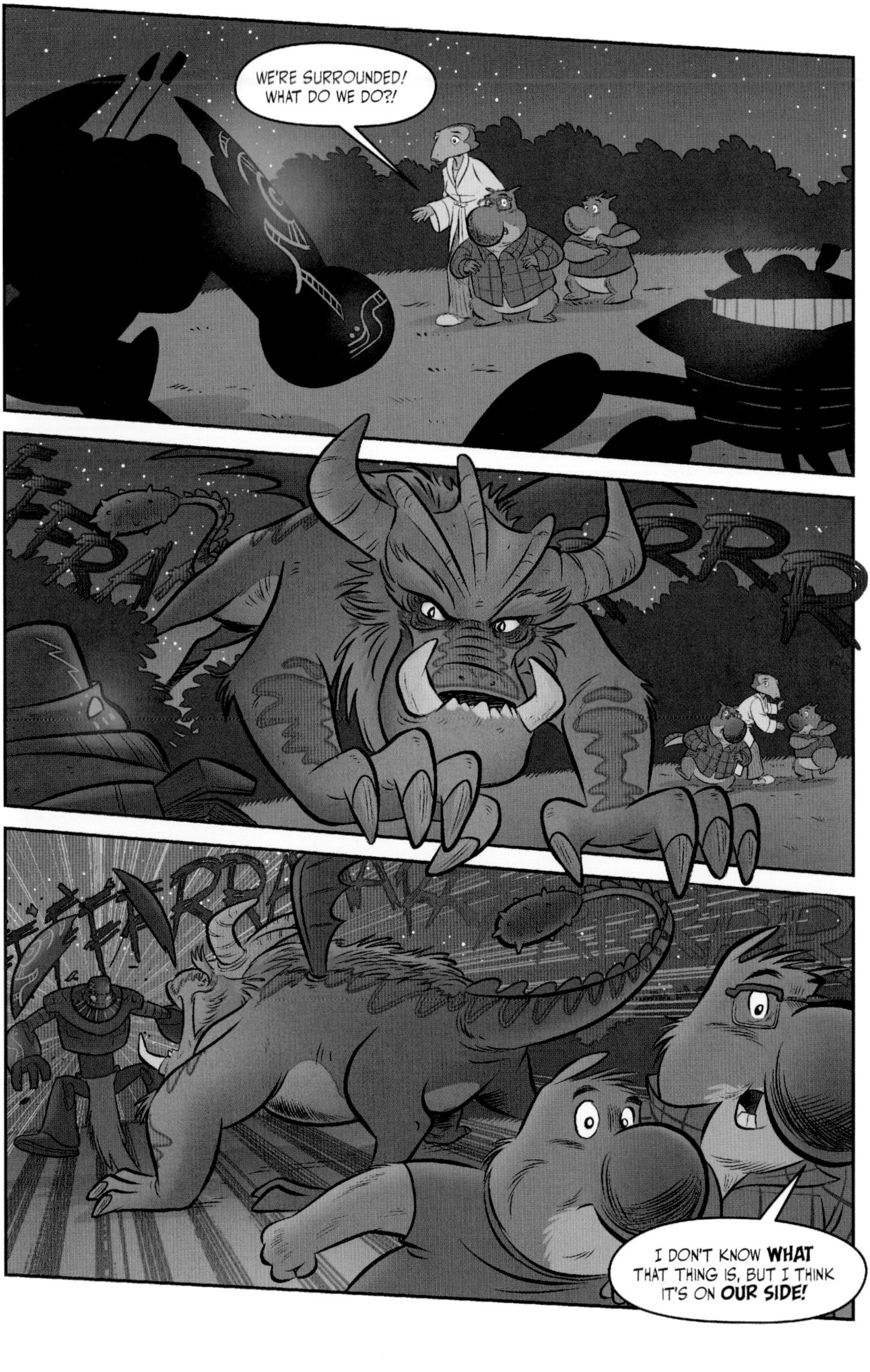
WE'RE SURROUNDED! WHAT DO WE DO?!
I DON'T KNOW **WHAT** THAT THING IS, BUT I THINK IT'S ON **OUR SIDE!**

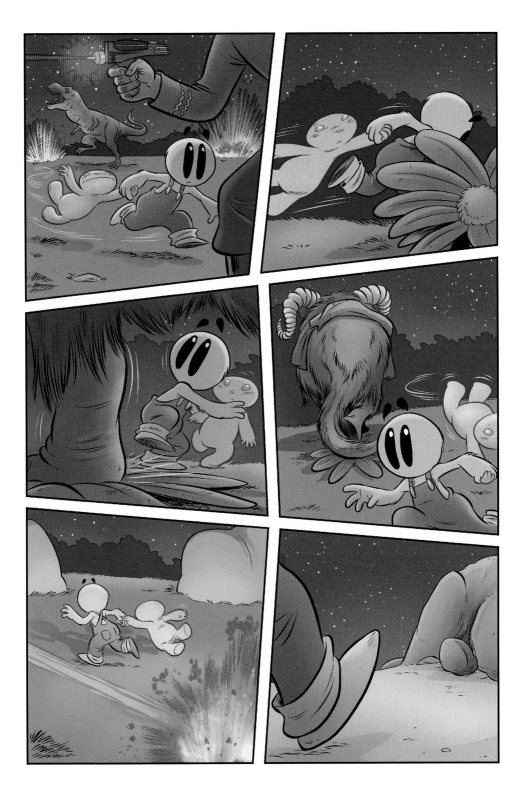

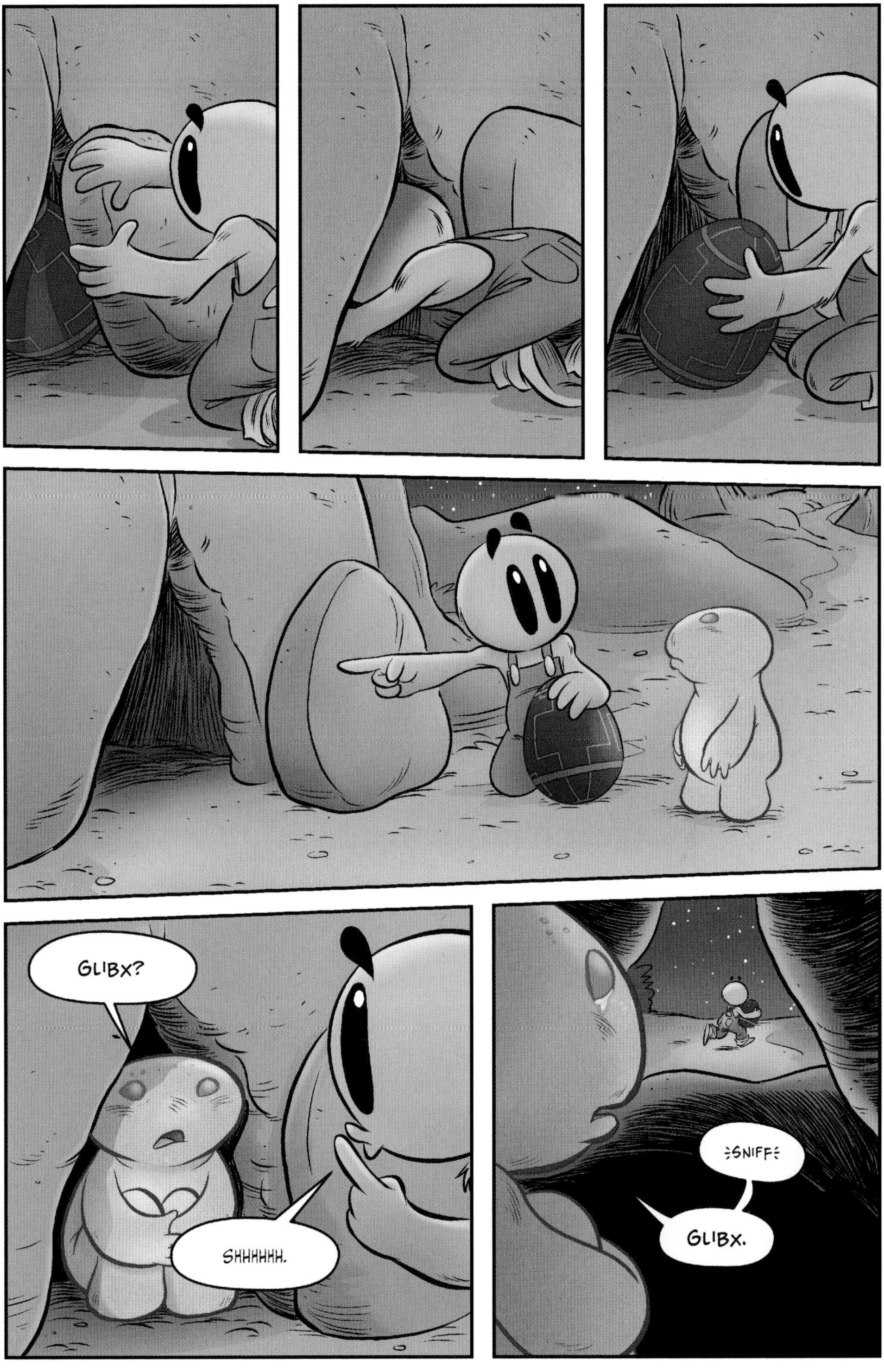
GLIBX?
SHHHHHH.
SNIFF
GLIBX.

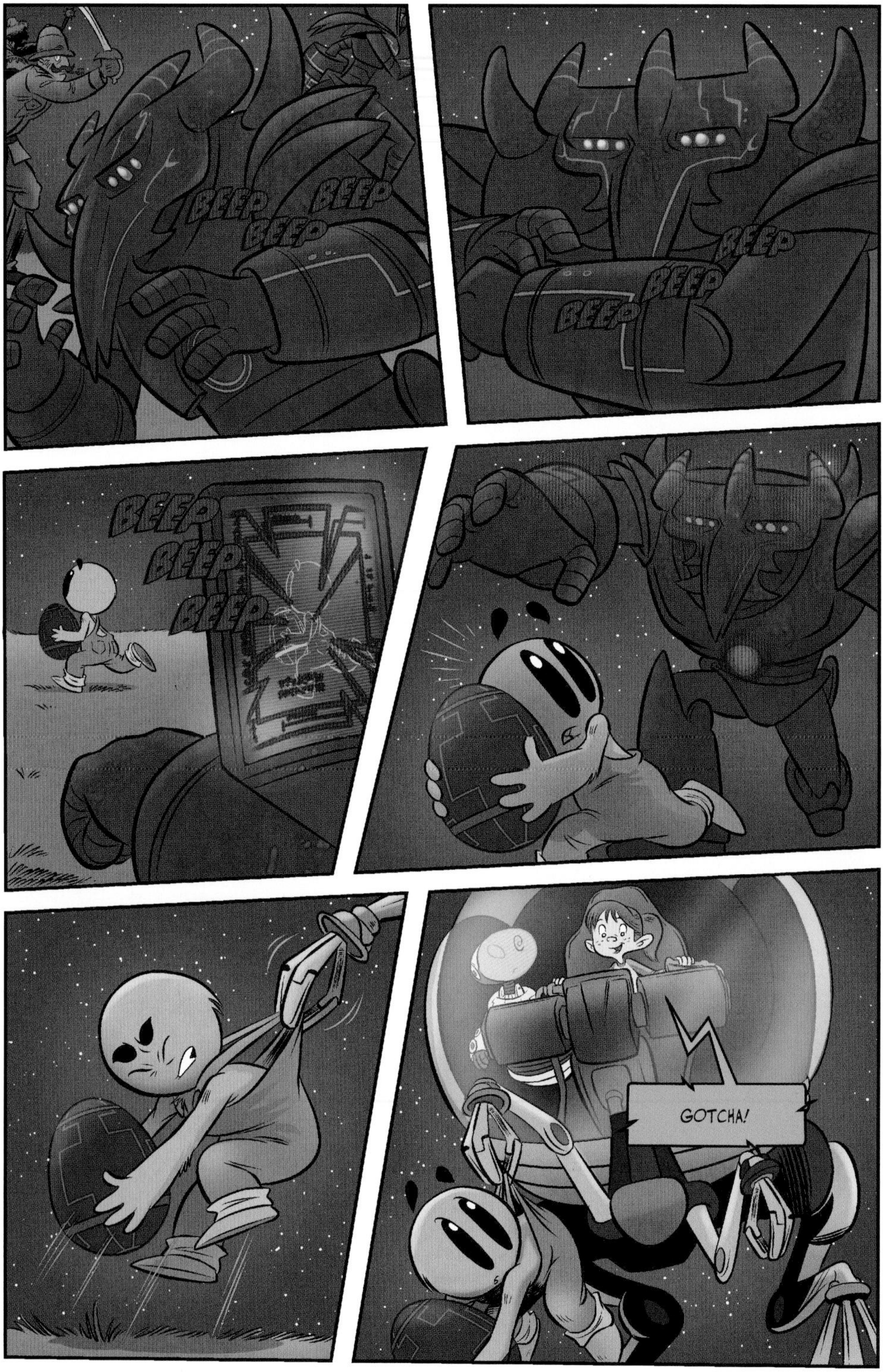
BEEP
BEEP
BEEP
BEEP
BEEP
BEEP
BEEP
BEEP
BEEP
GOTCHA!

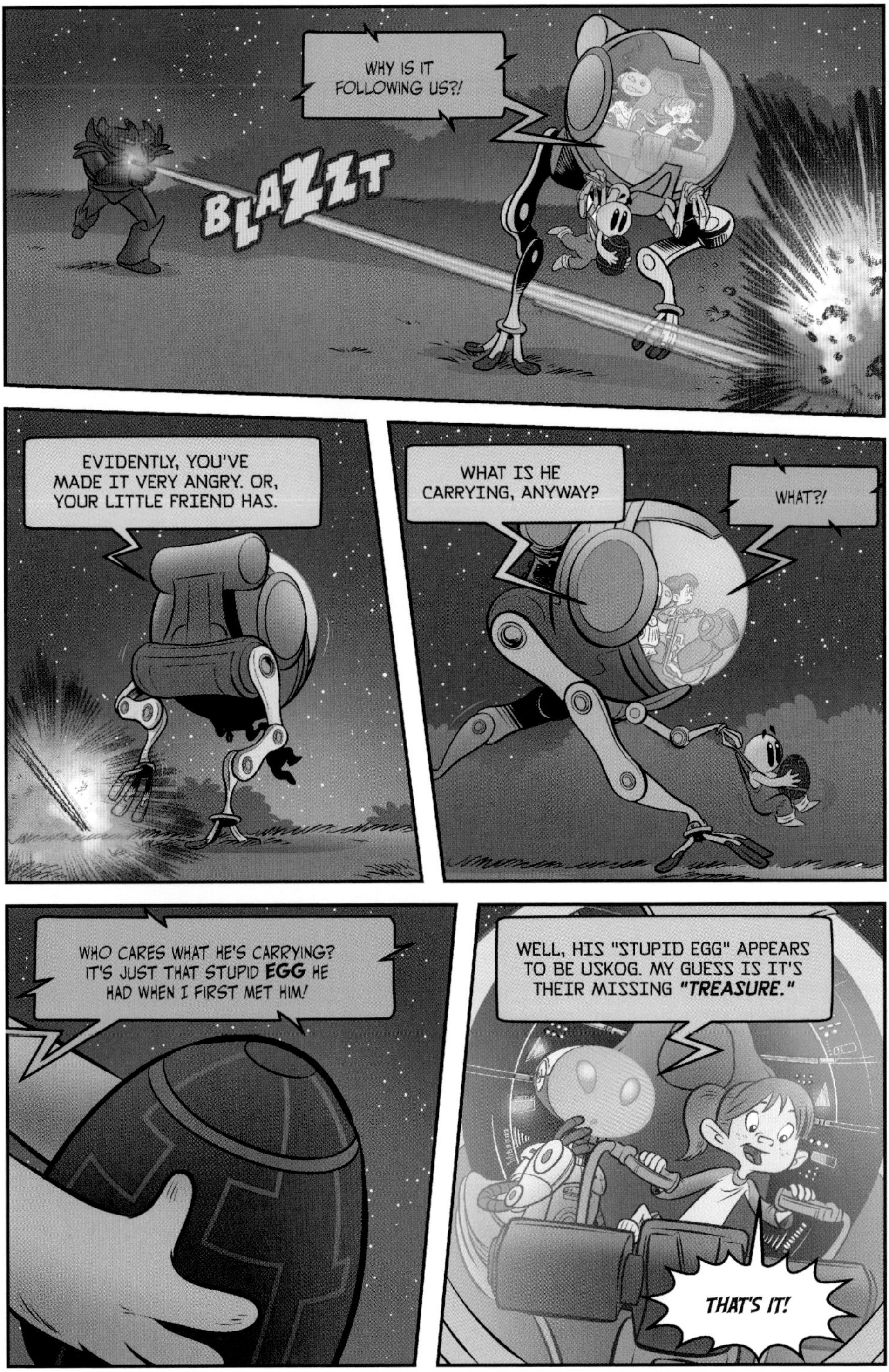
WHY IS IT FOLLOWING US?!
BLAZZZT
EVIDENTLY, YOU'VE MADE IT VERY ANGRY. OR, YOUR LITTLE FRIEND HAS.
WHAT IS HE CARRYING, ANYWAY?
WHAT?!
WHO CARES WHAT HE'S CARRYING? IT'S JUST THAT STUPID **EGG** HE HAD WHEN I FIRST MET HIM!
WELL, HIS "STUPID EGG" APPEARS TO BE USKOG. MY GUESS IS IT'S THEIR MISSING ***"TREASURE."***
THAT'S IT!

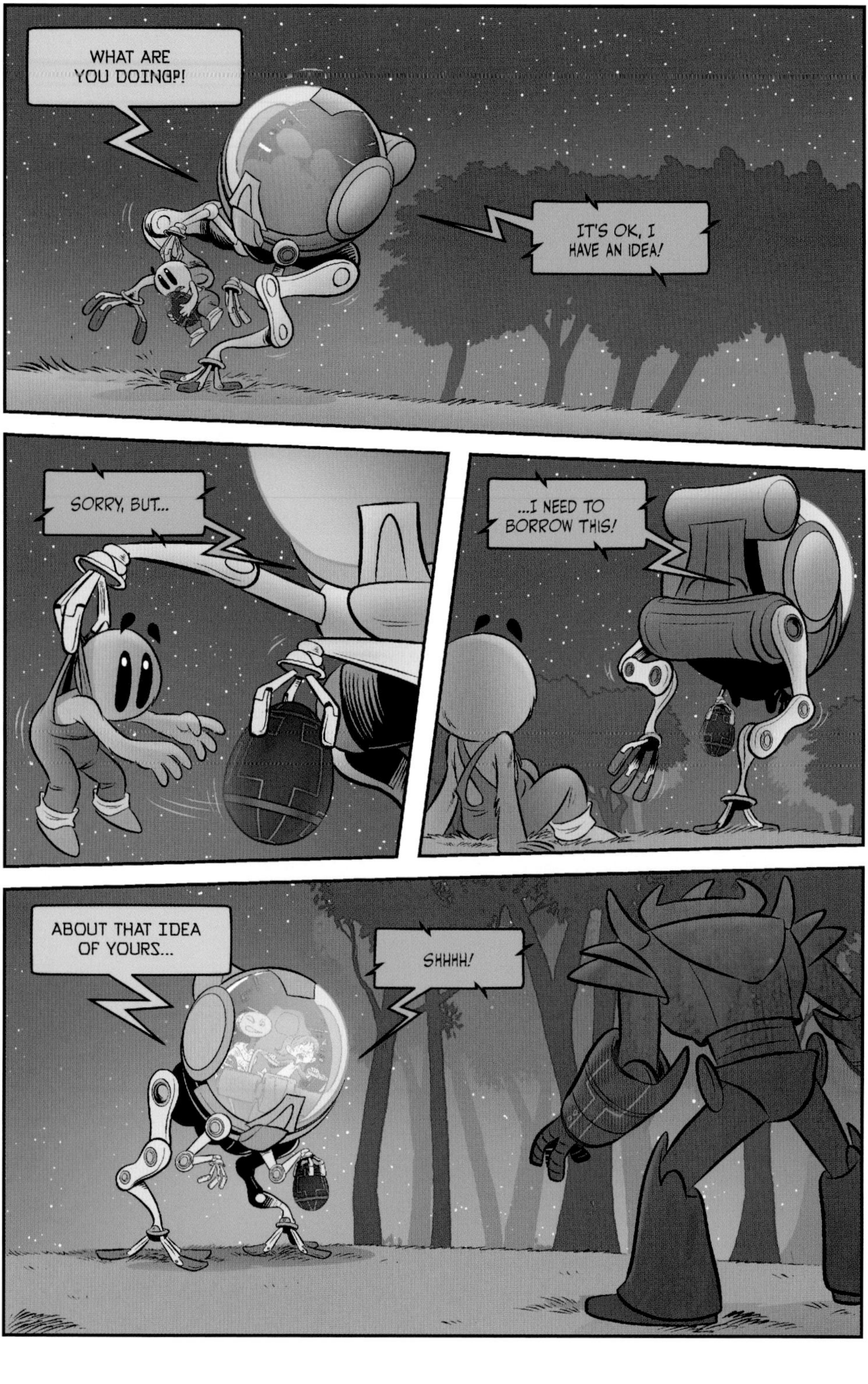
WHAT ARE YOU DOING?!
IT'S OK, I HAVE AN IDEA!
SORRY, BUT...
...I NEED TO BORROW THIS!
ABOUT THAT IDEA OF YOURS...
SHHHH!

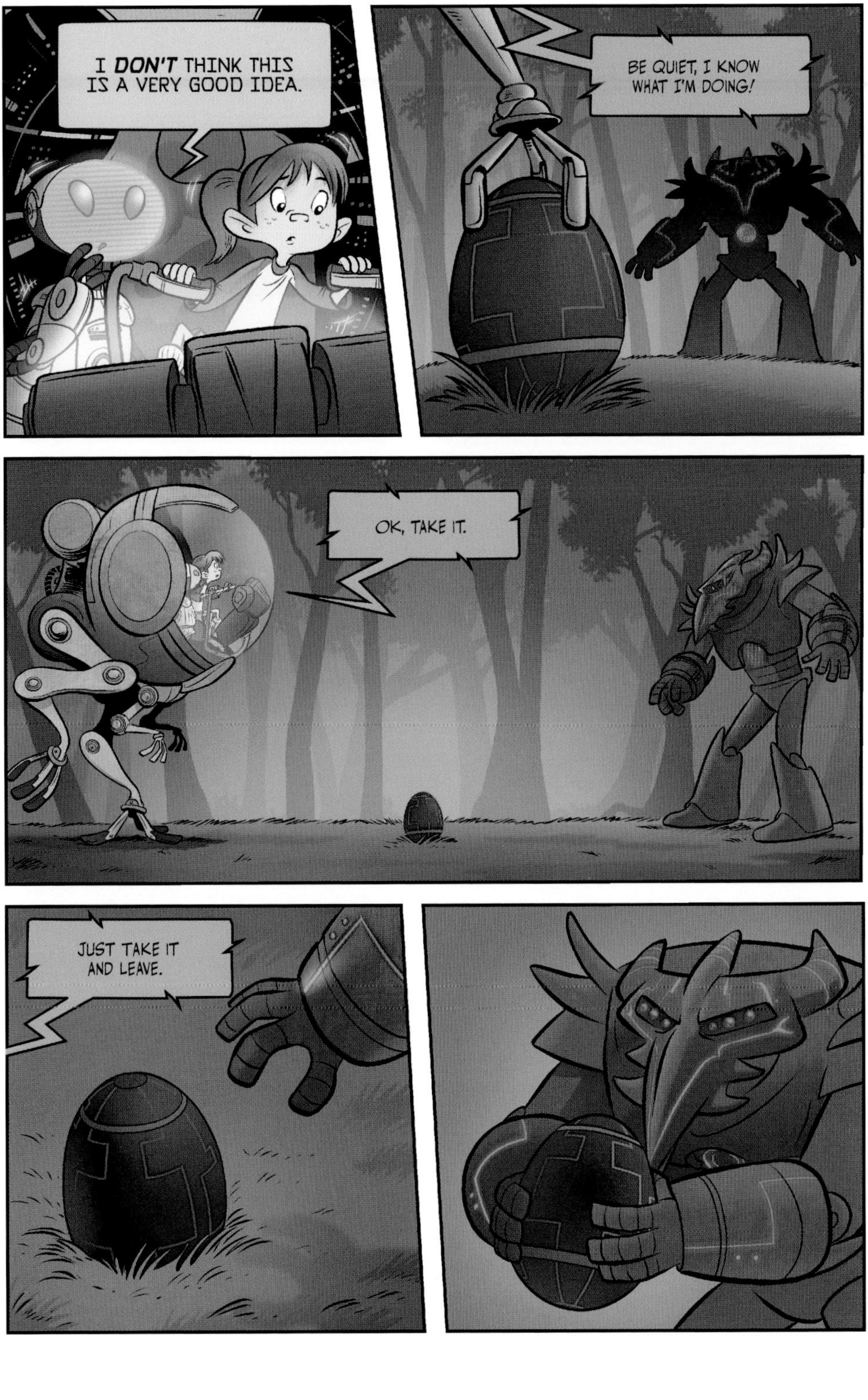
I **DON'T** THINK THIS IS A VERY GOOD IDEA.
BE QUIET, I KNOW WHAT I'M DOING!
OK, TAKE IT.
JUST TAKE IT AND LEAVE.

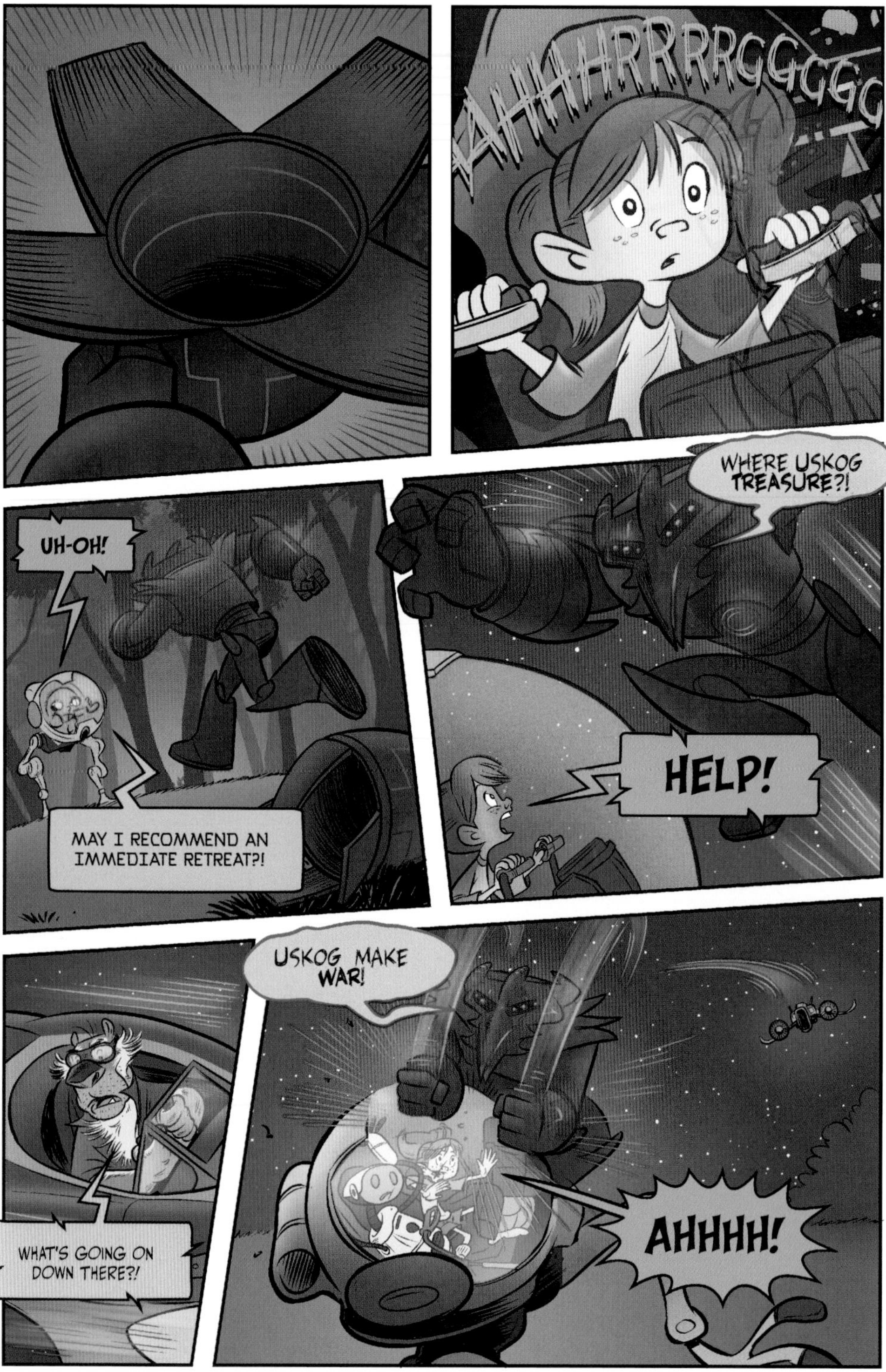

AHHHHRRRRGGGGG
UH-OH!
MAY I RECOMMEND AN IMMEDIATE RETREAT?!
WHERE USKOG TREASURE?!
HELP!
WHAT'S GOING ON DOWN THERE?!
USKOG MAKE WAR!
AHHHH!

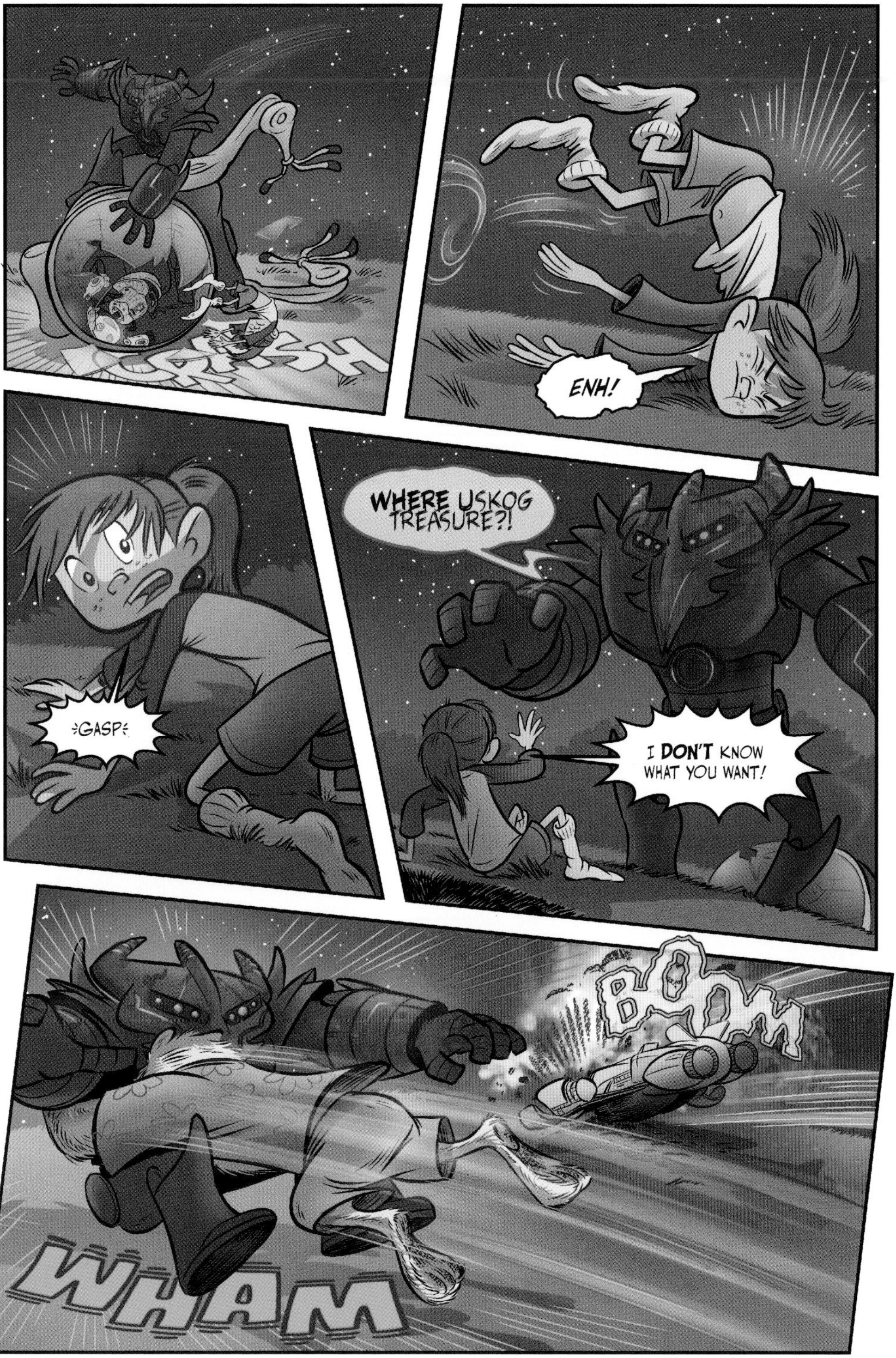
ENH!
WHERE USKOG TREASURE?!
GASP
I DON'T KNOW WHAT YOU WANT!
BOOM
WHAM

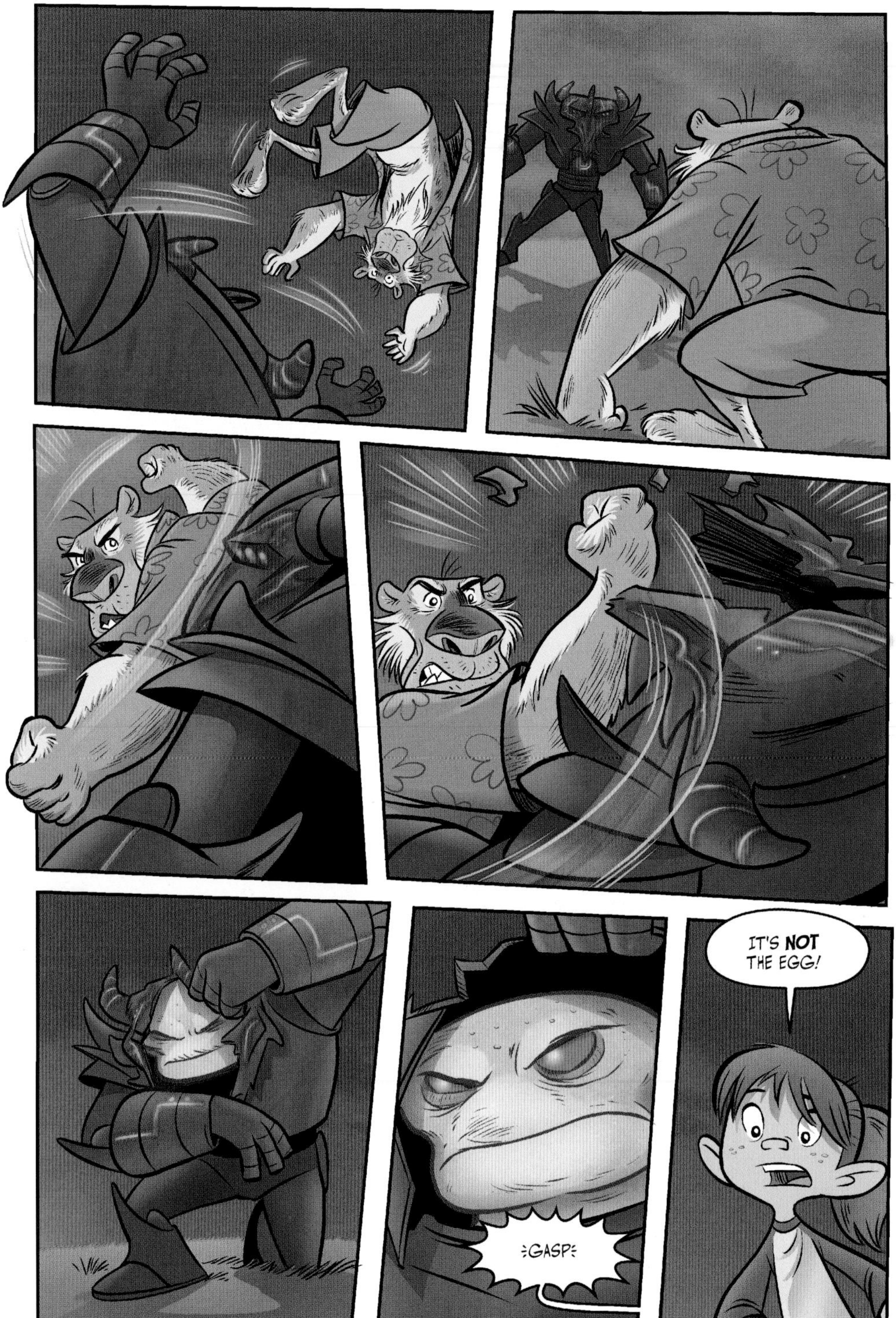
:GASP:
IT'S NOT THE EGG!

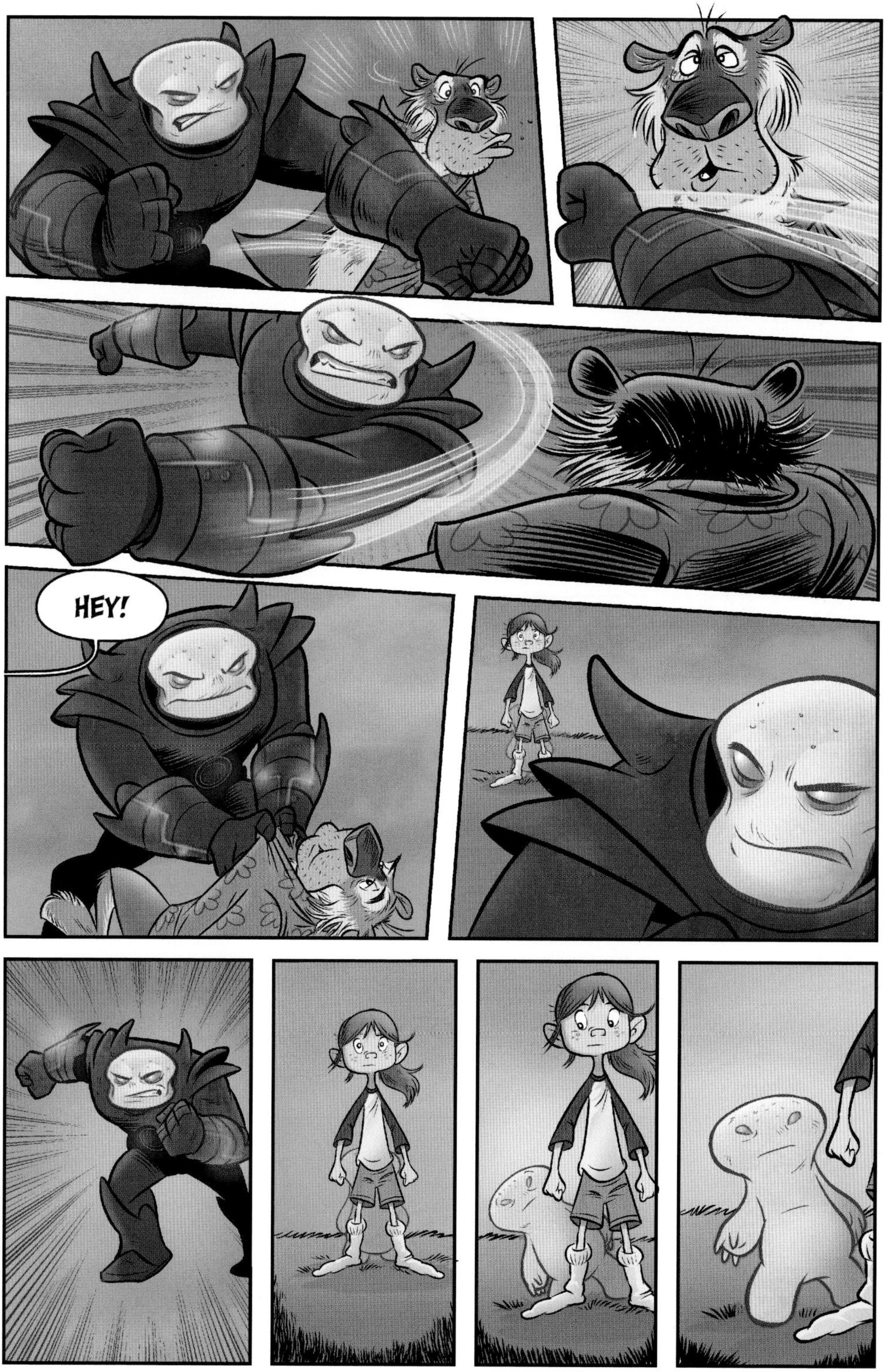
HEY!

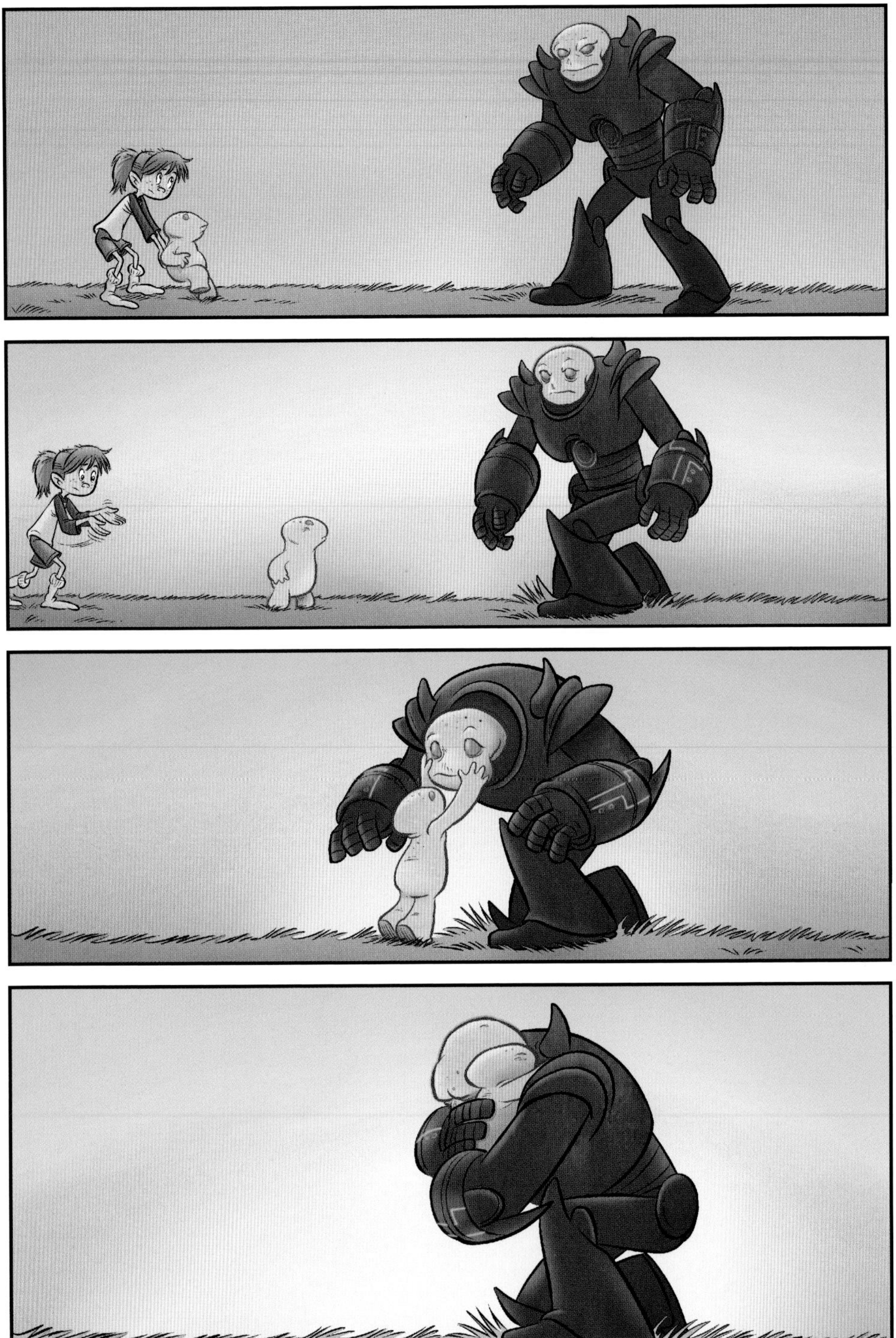

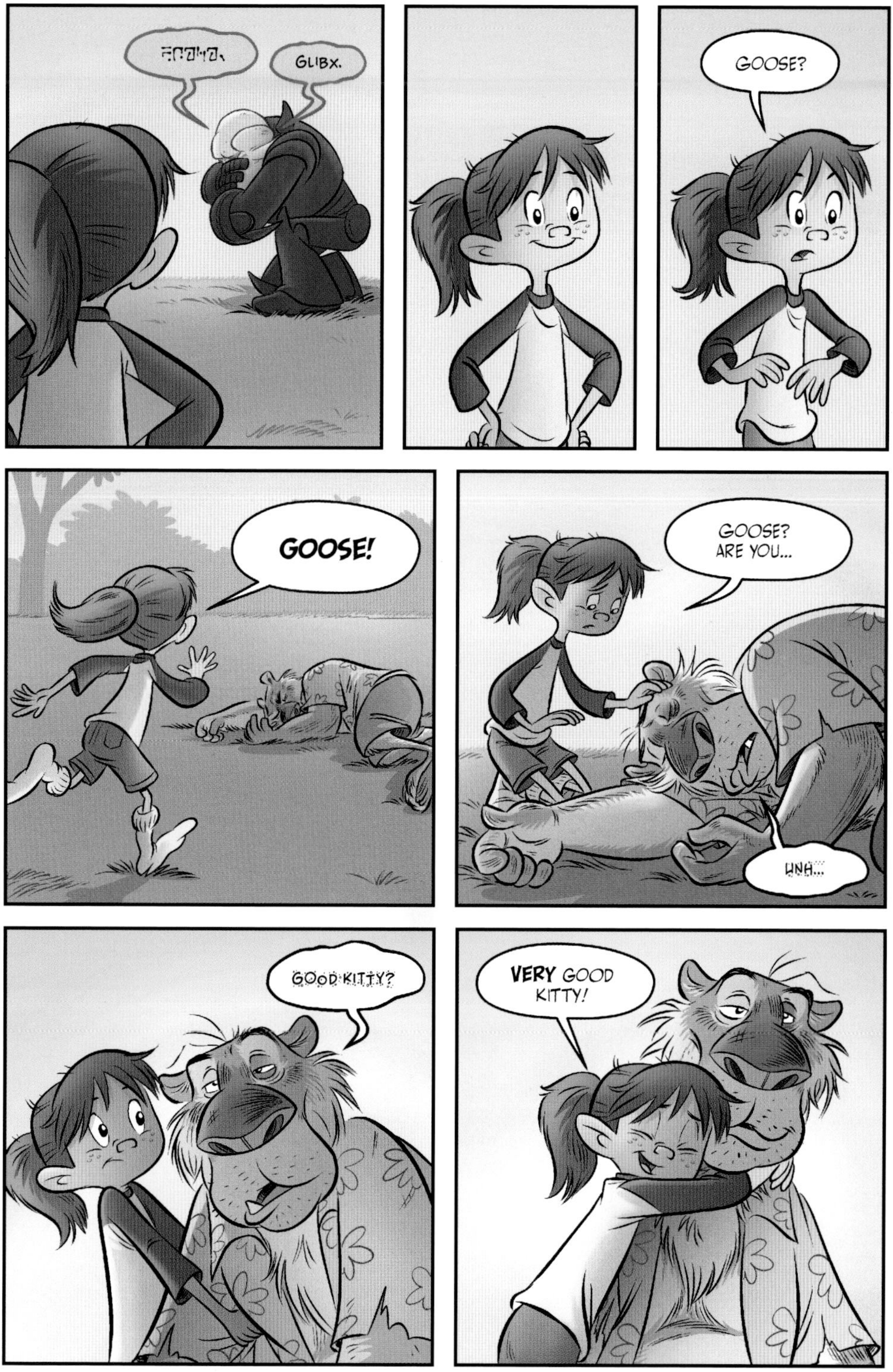
GLIBX.
GOOSE?
GOOSE!
GOOSE? ARE YOU...
UNA...
GOOD KITTY?
VERY GOOD KITTY!

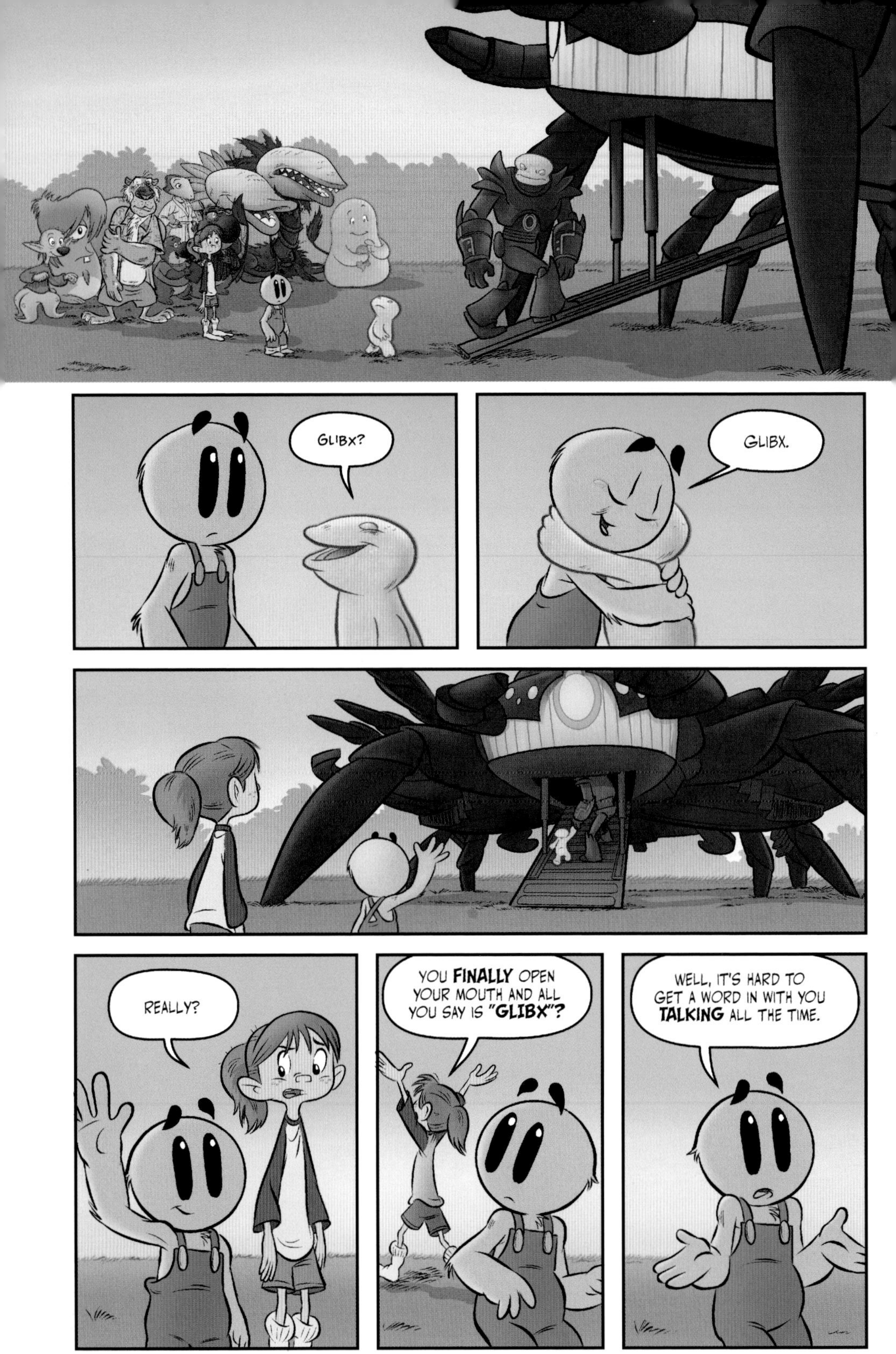
GLIBX?
GLIBX.
REALLY?
YOU **FINALLY** OPEN YOUR MOUTH AND ALL YOU SAY IS "**GLIBX**"?
WELL, IT'S HARD TO GET A WORD IN WITH YOU **TALKING** ALL THE TIME.

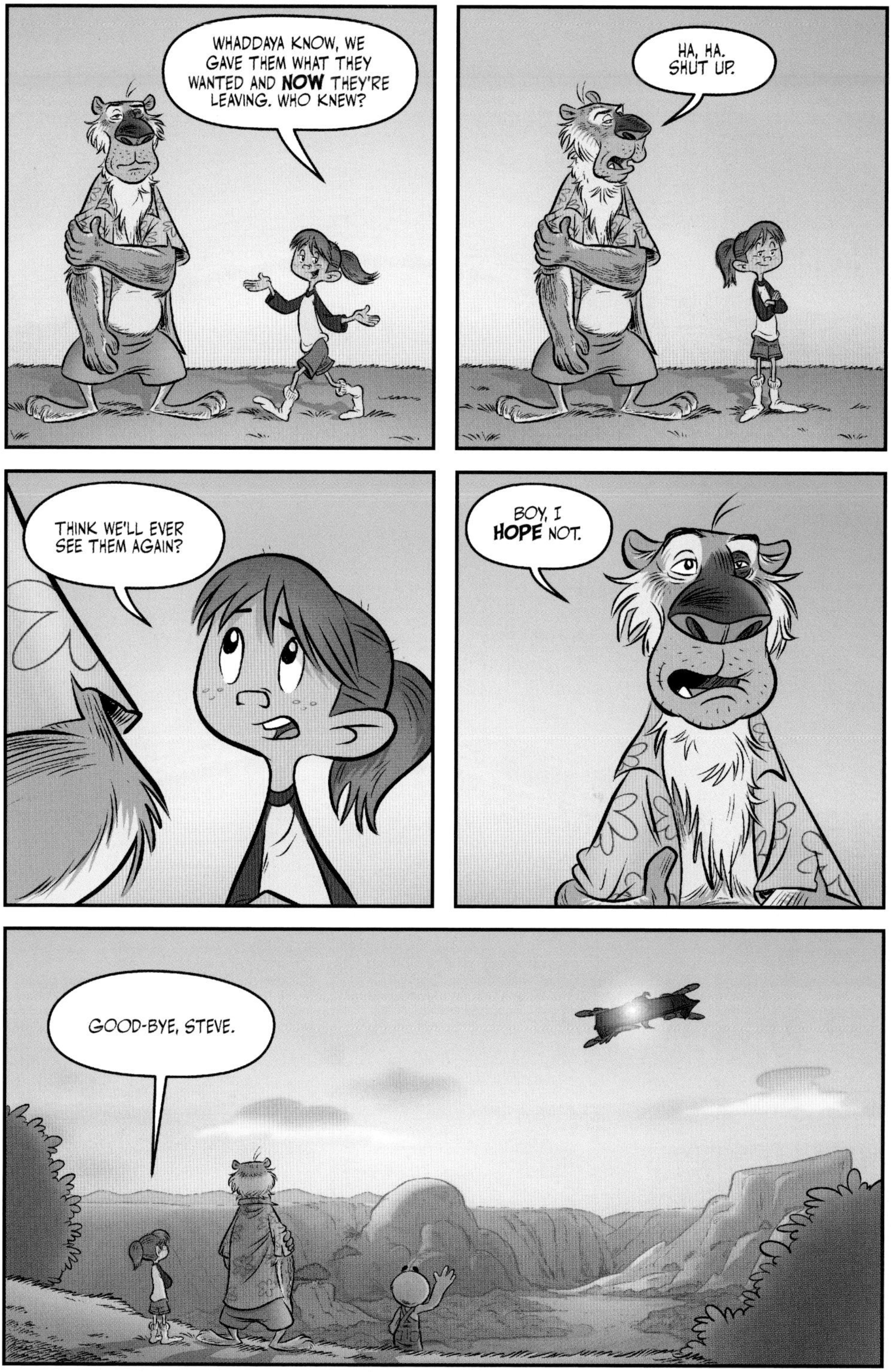
WHADDAYA KNOW, WE GAVE THEM WHAT THEY WANTED AND **NOW** THEY'RE LEAVING. WHO KNEW?
HA, HA. SHUT UP.
THINK WE'LL EVER SEE THEM AGAIN?
BOY, I **HOPE** NOT.
GOOD-BYE, STEVE.

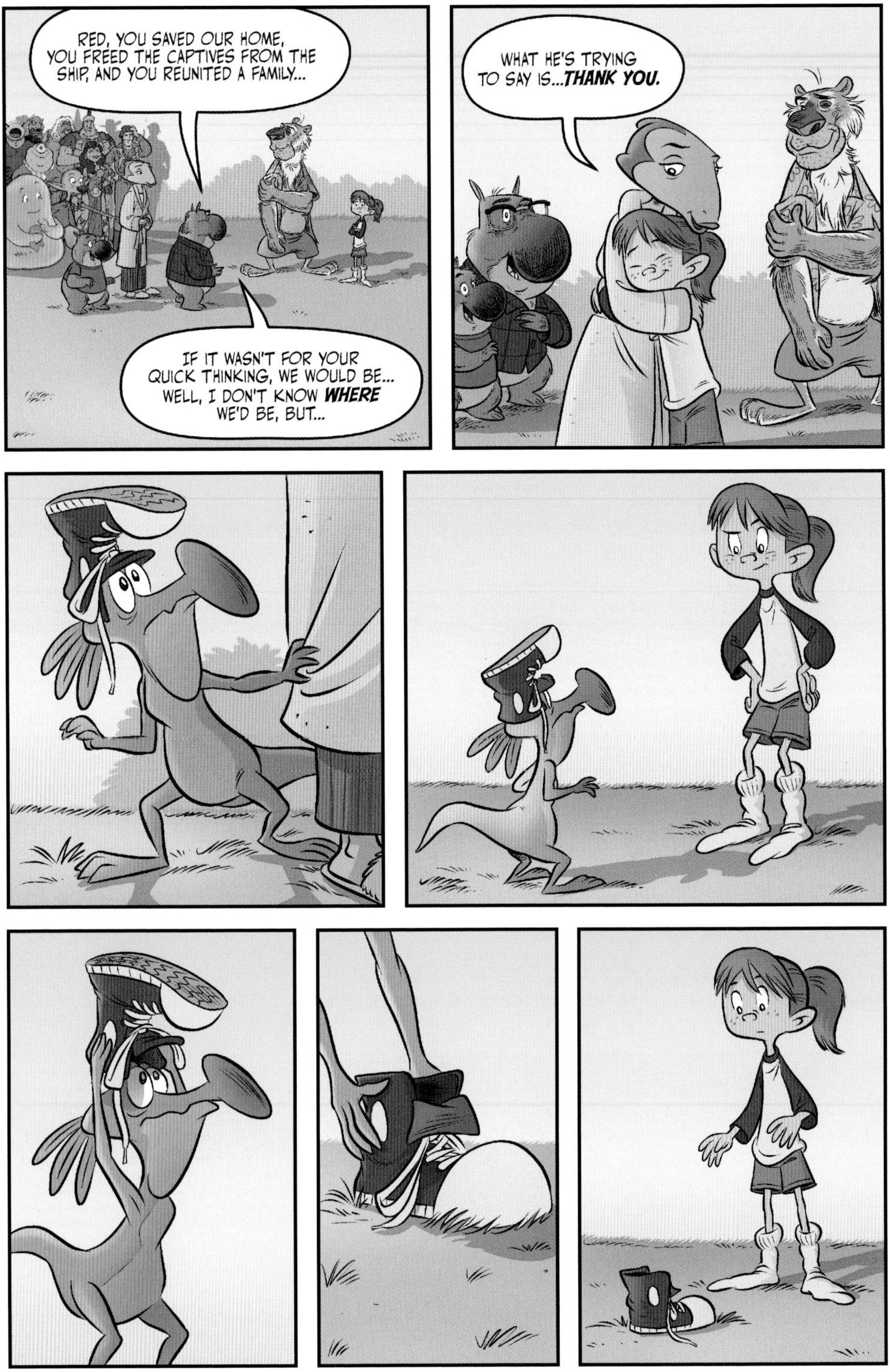
RED, YOU SAVED OUR HOME, YOU FREED THE CAPTIVES FROM THE SHIP, AND YOU REUNITED A FAMILY...
IF IT WASN'T FOR YOUR QUICK THINKING, WE WOULD BE... WELL, I DON'T KNOW ***WHERE*** WE'D BE, BUT...
WHAT HE'S TRYING TO SAY IS...***THANK YOU.***

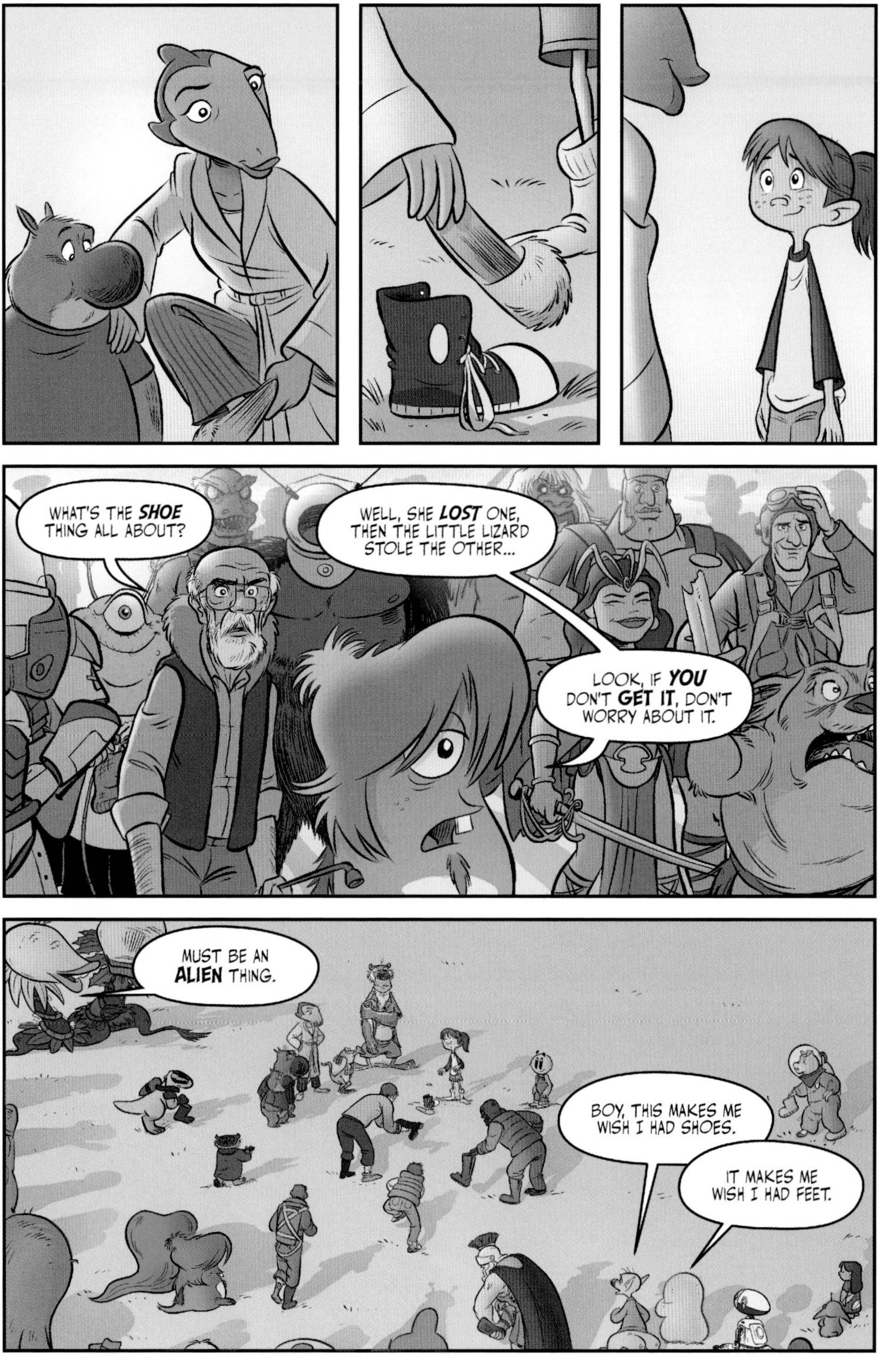
WHAT'S THE **SHOE** THING ALL ABOUT?
WELL, SHE **LOST** ONE, THEN THE LITTLE LIZARD STOLE THE OTHER...
LOOK, IF **YOU** DON'T **GET IT**, DON'T WORRY ABOUT IT.
MUST BE AN **ALIEN** THING.
BOY, THIS MAKES ME WISH I HAD SHOES.
IT MAKES ME WISH I HAD FEET.

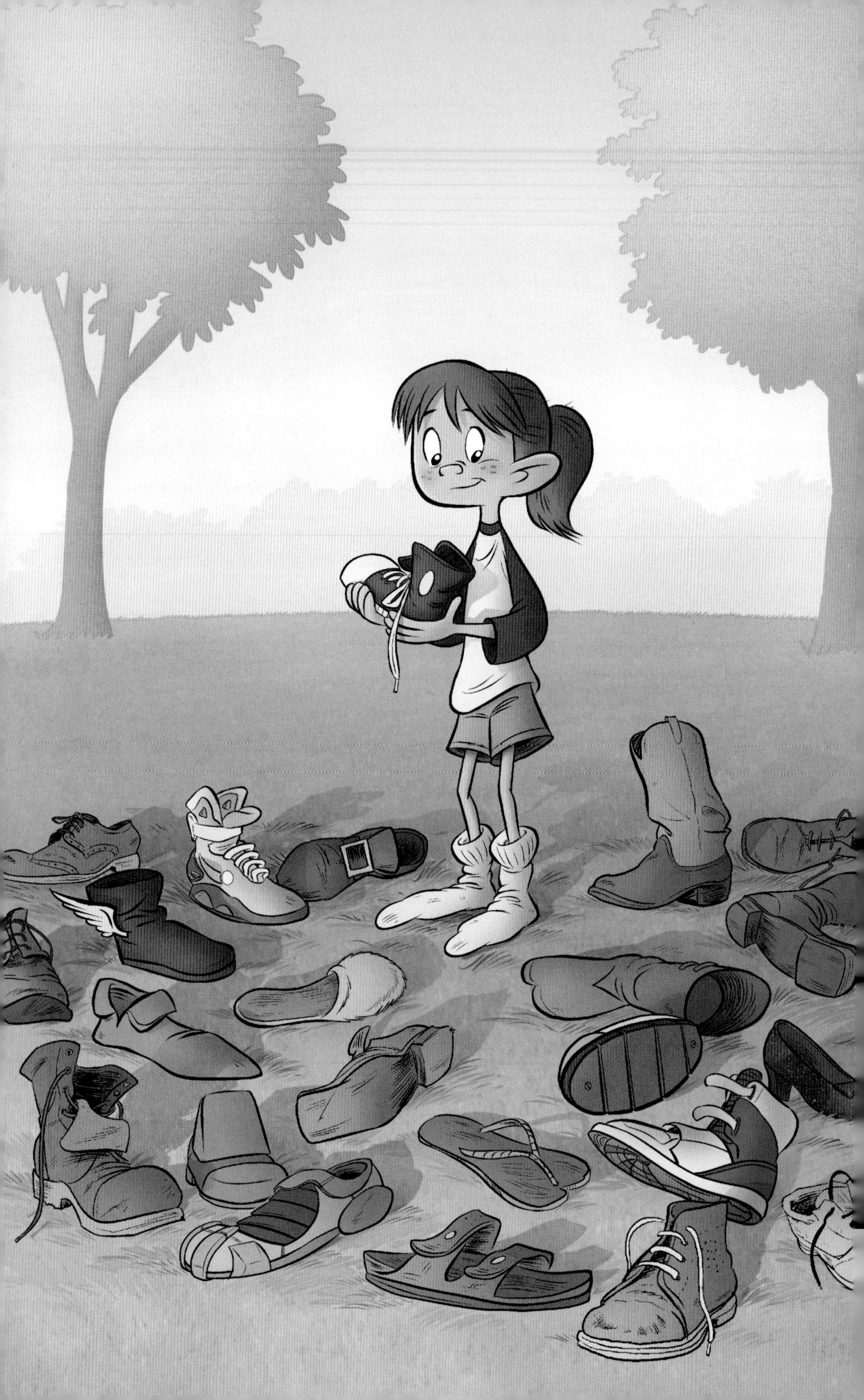

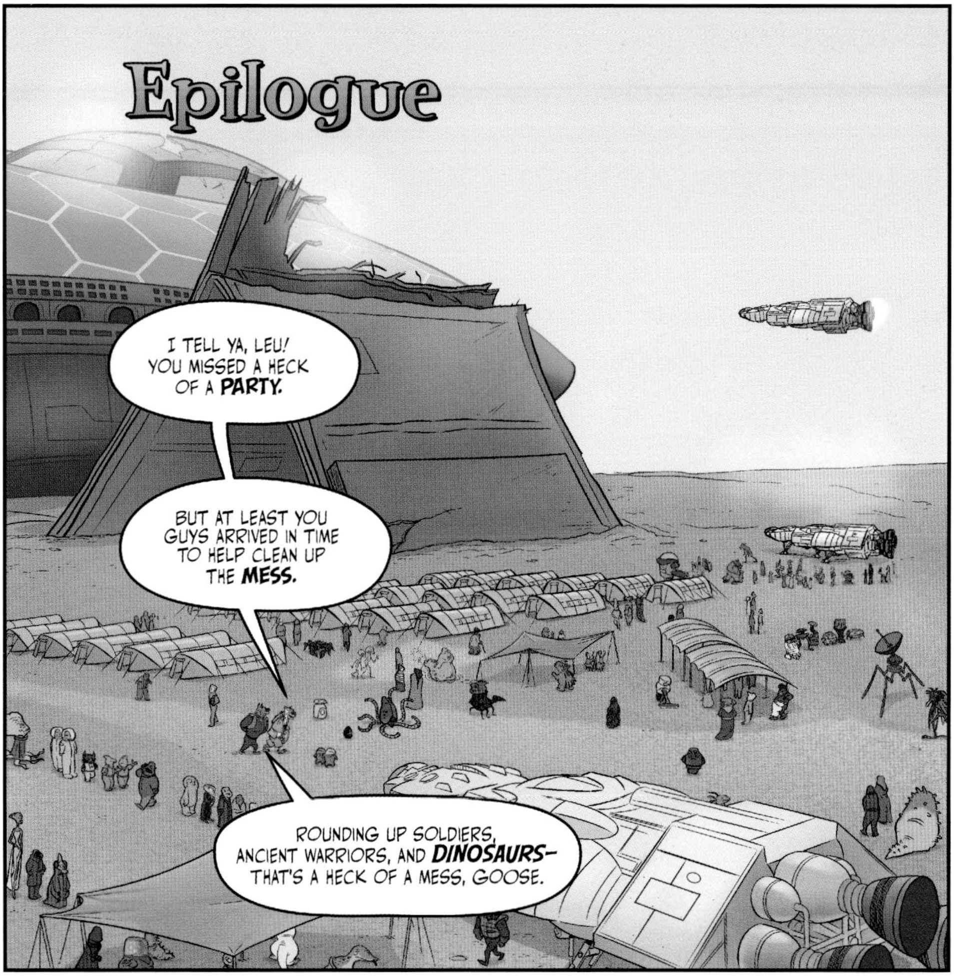
Epilogue
I TELL YA, LEU! YOU MISSED A HECK OF A PARTY.
BUT AT LEAST YOU GUYS ARRIVED IN TIME TO HELP CLEAN UP THE MESS.
ROUNDING UP SOLDIERS, ANCIENT WARRIORS, AND DINOSAURS– THAT'S A HECK OF A MESS, GOOSE.

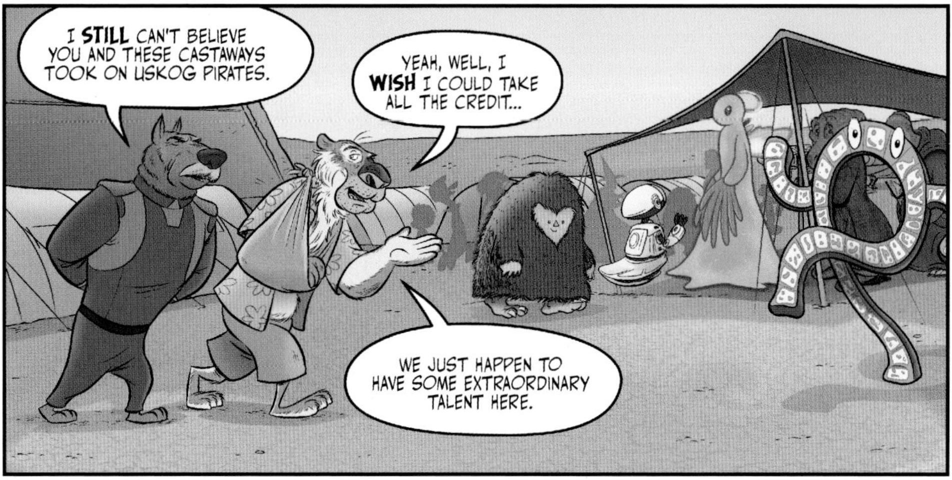
I STILL CAN'T BELIEVE YOU AND THESE CASTAWAYS TOOK ON USKOG PIRATES.
YEAH, WELL, I WISH I COULD TAKE ALL THE CREDIT...
WE JUST HAPPEN TO HAVE SOME EXTRAORDINARY TALENT HERE.

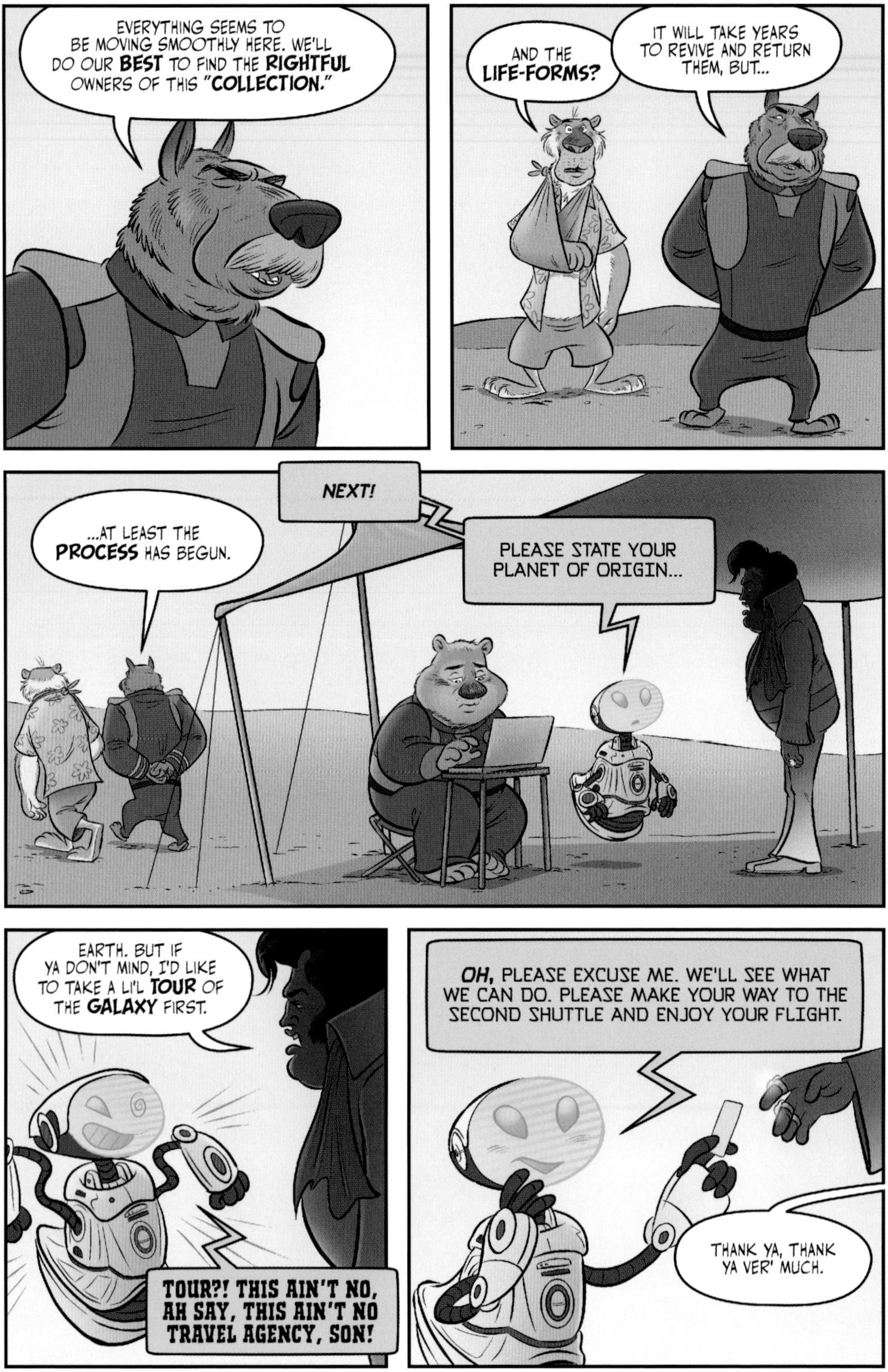
EVERYTHING SEEMS TO BE MOVING SMOOTHLY HERE. WE'LL DO OUR BEST TO FIND THE RIGHTFUL OWNERS OF THIS "COLLECTION."
AND THE LIFE-FORMS?
IT WILL TAKE YEARS TO REVIVE AND RETURN THEM, BUT...
...AT LEAST THE PROCESS HAS BEGUN.
NEXT!
PLEASE STATE YOUR PLANET OF ORIGIN...
EARTH. BUT IF YA DON'T MIND, I'D LIKE TO TAKE A LI'L TOUR OF THE GALAXY FIRST.
TOUR?! THIS AIN'T NO, AH SAY, THIS AIN'T NO TRAVEL AGENCY, SON!
OH, PLEASE EXCUSE ME. WE'LL SEE WHAT WE CAN DO. PLEASE MAKE YOUR WAY TO THE SECOND SHUTTLE AND ENJOY YOUR FLIGHT.
THANK YA, THANK YA VER' MUCH.

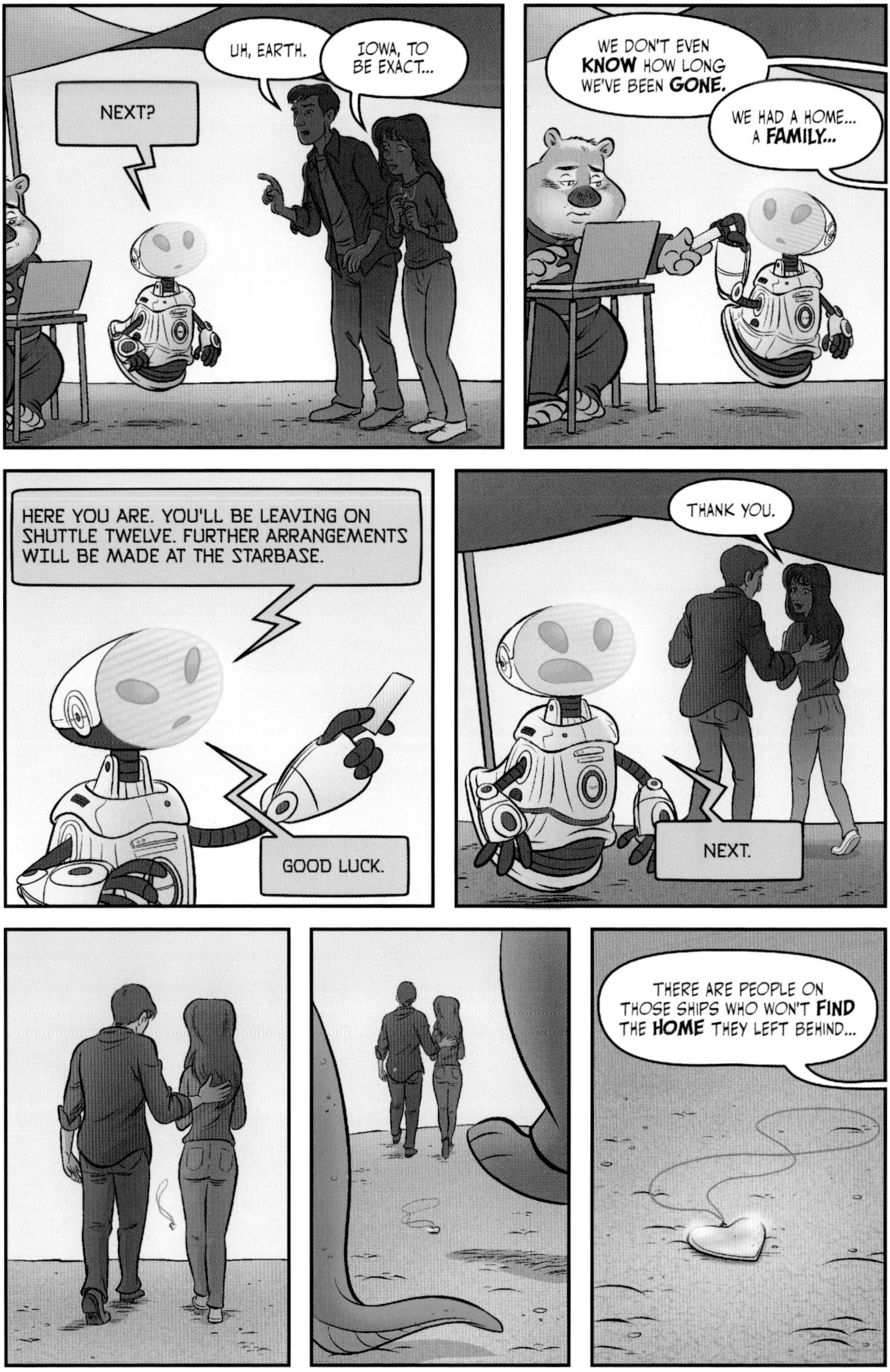
NEXT?
UH, EARTH.
IOWA, TO BE EXACT...
WE DON'T EVEN KNOW HOW LONG WE'VE BEEN GONE.
WE HAD A HOME... A FAMILY...
HERE YOU ARE. YOU'LL BE LEAVING ON SHUTTLE TWELVE. FURTHER ARRANGEMENTS WILL BE MADE AT THE STARBASE.
GOOD LUCK.
THANK YOU.
NEXT.
THERE ARE PEOPLE ON THOSE SHIPS WHO WON'T FIND THE HOME THEY LEFT BEHIND...

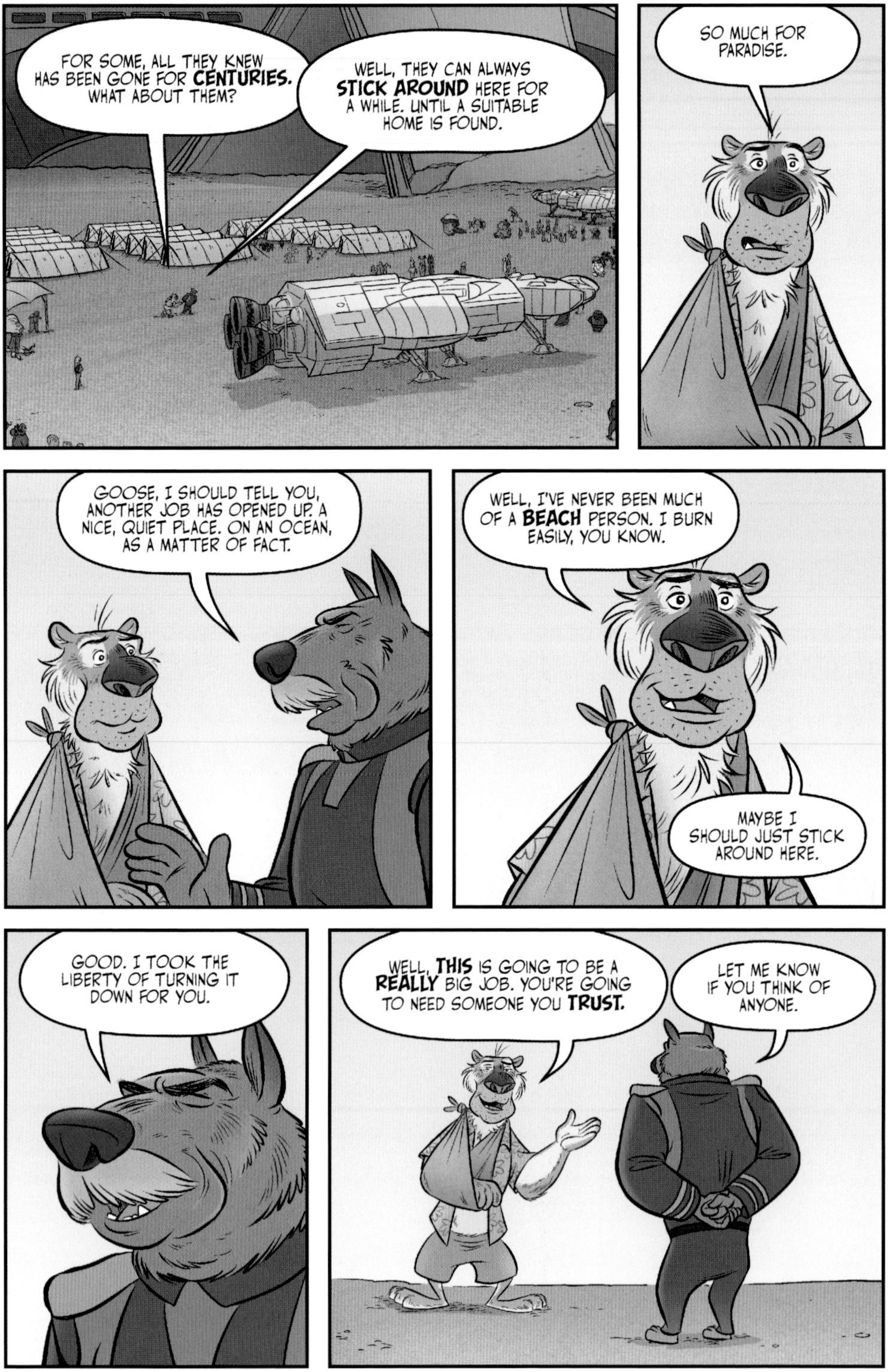
FOR SOME, ALL THEY KNEW HAS BEEN GONE FOR CENTURIES. WHAT ABOUT THEM?
WELL, THEY CAN ALWAYS STICK AROUND HERE FOR A WHILE. UNTIL A SUITABLE HOME IS FOUND.
SO MUCH FOR PARADISE.
GOOSE, I SHOULD TELL YOU, ANOTHER JOB HAS OPENED UP. A NICE, QUIET PLACE. ON AN OCEAN, AS A MATTER OF FACT.
WELL, I'VE NEVER BEEN MUCH OF A BEACH PERSON. I BURN EASILY, YOU KNOW.
MAYBE I SHOULD JUST STICK AROUND HERE.
GOOD. I TOOK THE LIBERTY OF TURNING IT DOWN FOR YOU.
WELL, THIS IS GOING TO BE A REALLY BIG JOB. YOU'RE GOING TO NEED SOMEONE YOU TRUST.
LET ME KNOW IF YOU THINK OF ANYONE.

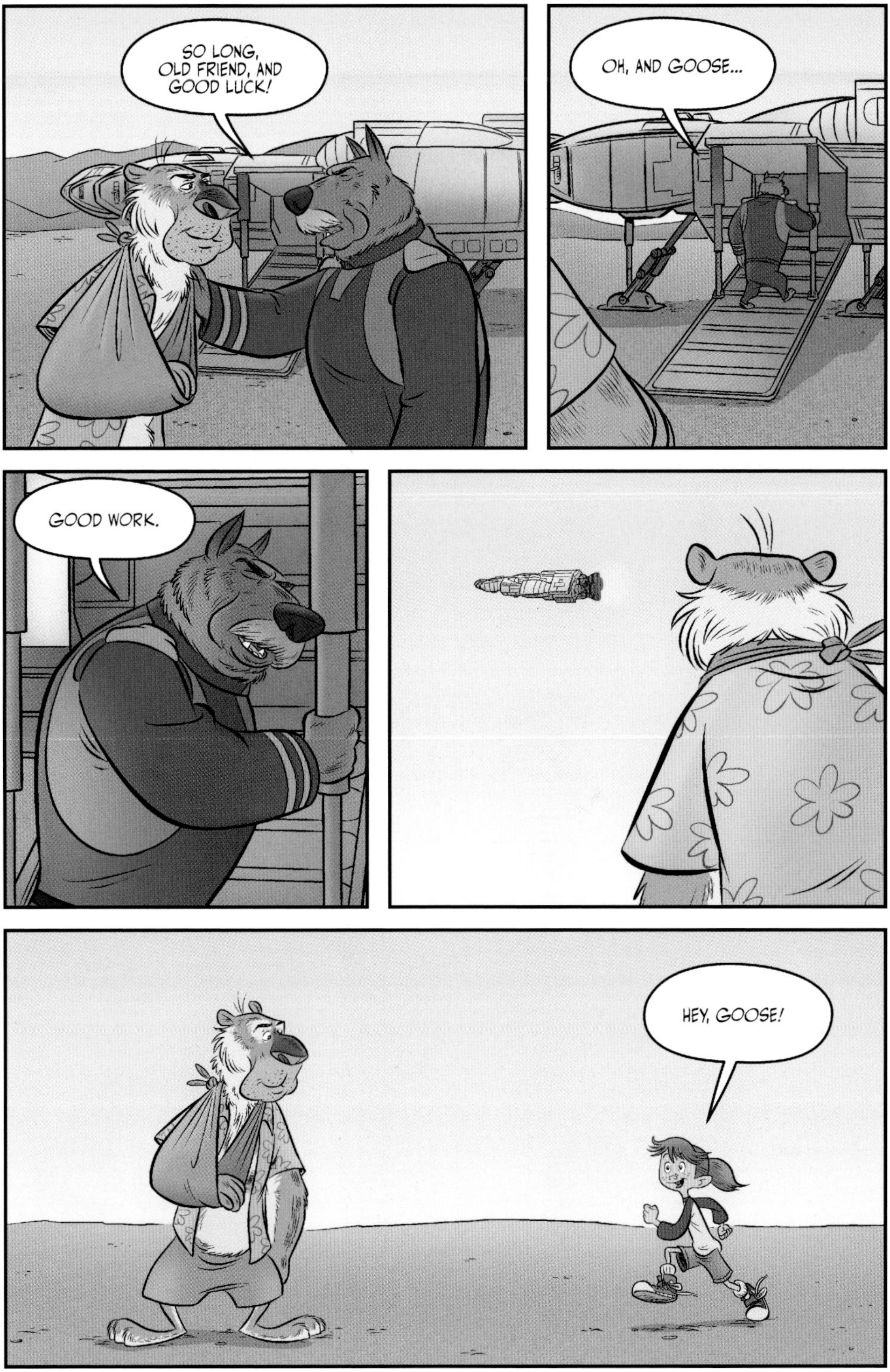
SO LONG, OLD FRIEND, AND GOOD LUCK!
OH, AND GOOSE...
GOOD WORK.
HEY, GOOSE!

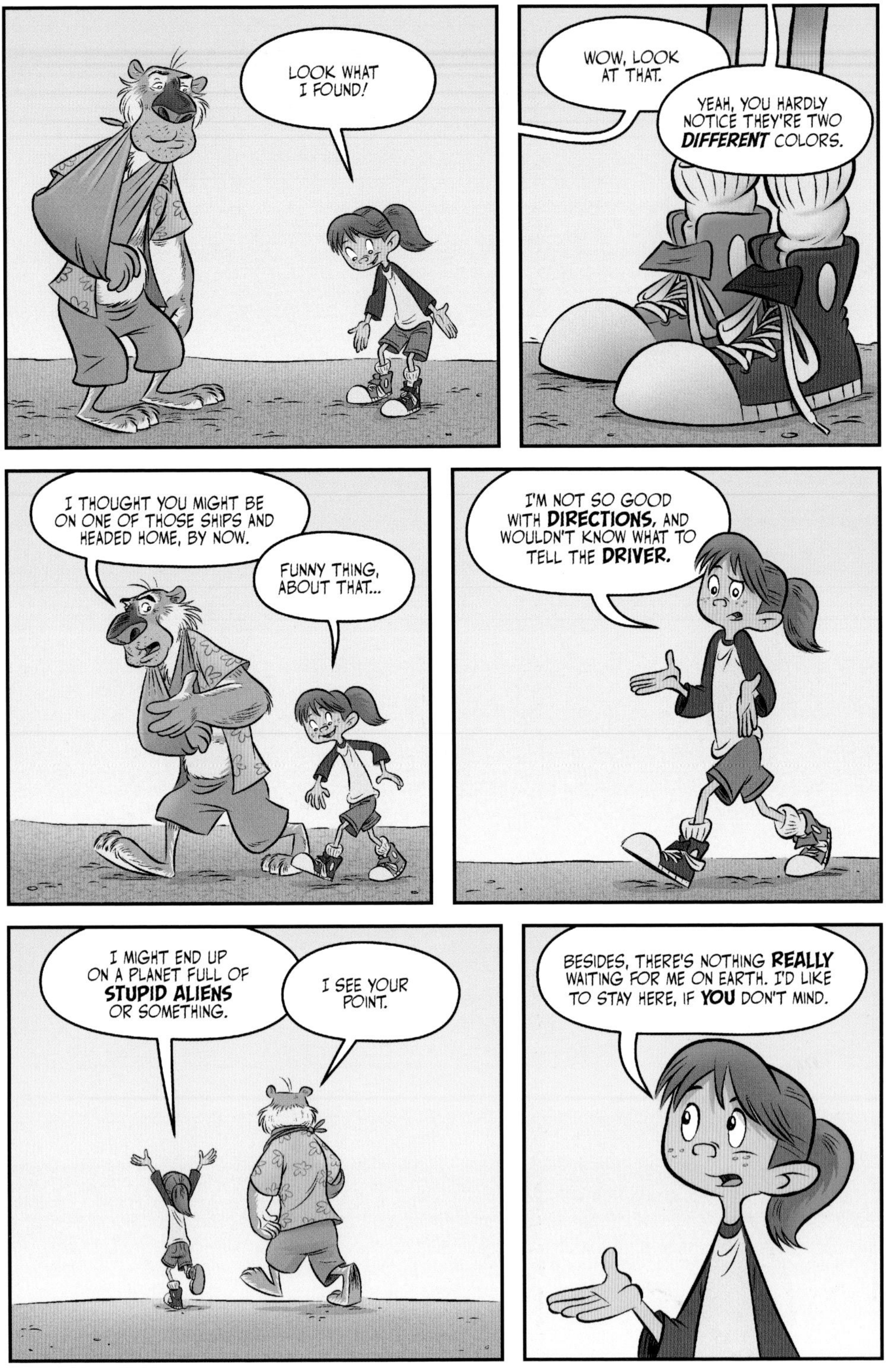
LOOK WHAT I FOUND!
WOW, LOOK AT THAT.
YEAH, YOU HARDLY NOTICE THEY'RE TWO DIFFERENT COLORS.
I THOUGHT YOU MIGHT BE ON ONE OF THOSE SHIPS AND HEADED HOME, BY NOW.
FUNNY THING, ABOUT THAT...
I'M NOT SO GOOD WITH DIRECTIONS, AND WOULDN'T KNOW WHAT TO TELL THE DRIVER.
I MIGHT END UP ON A PLANET FULL OF STUPID ALIENS OR SOMETHING.
I SEE YOUR POINT.
BESIDES, THERE'S NOTHING REALLY WAITING FOR ME ON EARTH. I'D LIKE TO STAY HERE, IF YOU DON'T MIND.

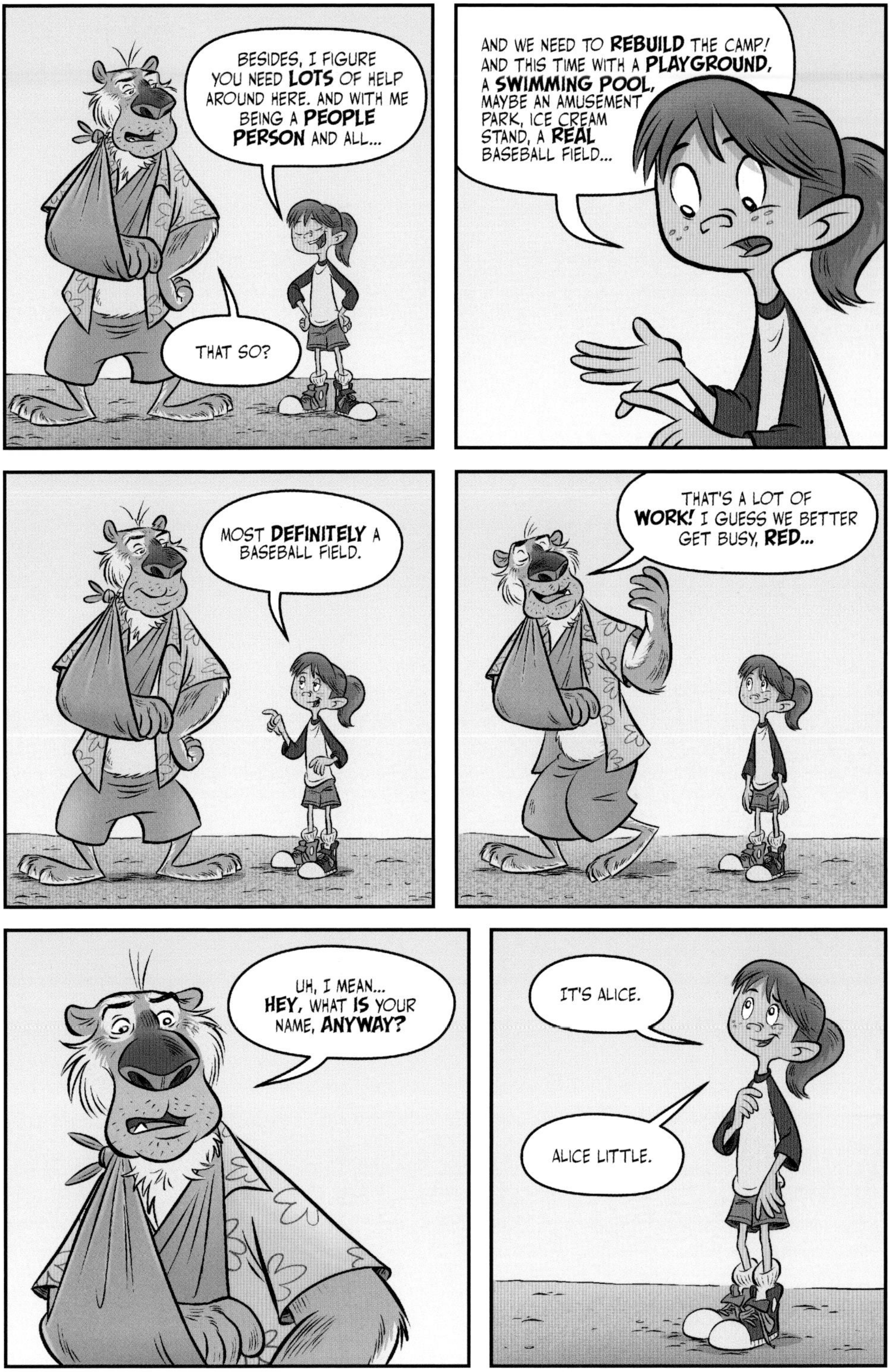
BESIDES, I FIGURE YOU NEED **LOTS** OF HELP AROUND HERE. AND WITH ME BEING A **PEOPLE PERSON** AND ALL...
THAT SO?
AND WE NEED TO **REBUILD** THE CAMP! AND THIS TIME WITH A **PLAYGROUND**, A **SWIMMING POOL**, MAYBE AN AMUSEMENT PARK, ICE CREAM STAND, A **REAL** BASEBALL FIELD...
MOST **DEFINITELY** A BASEBALL FIELD.
THAT'S A LOT OF **WORK!** I GUESS WE BETTER GET BUSY, **RED...**
UH, I MEAN... **HEY**, WHAT **IS** YOUR NAME, **ANYWAY?**
IT'S ALICE.
ALICE LITTLE.

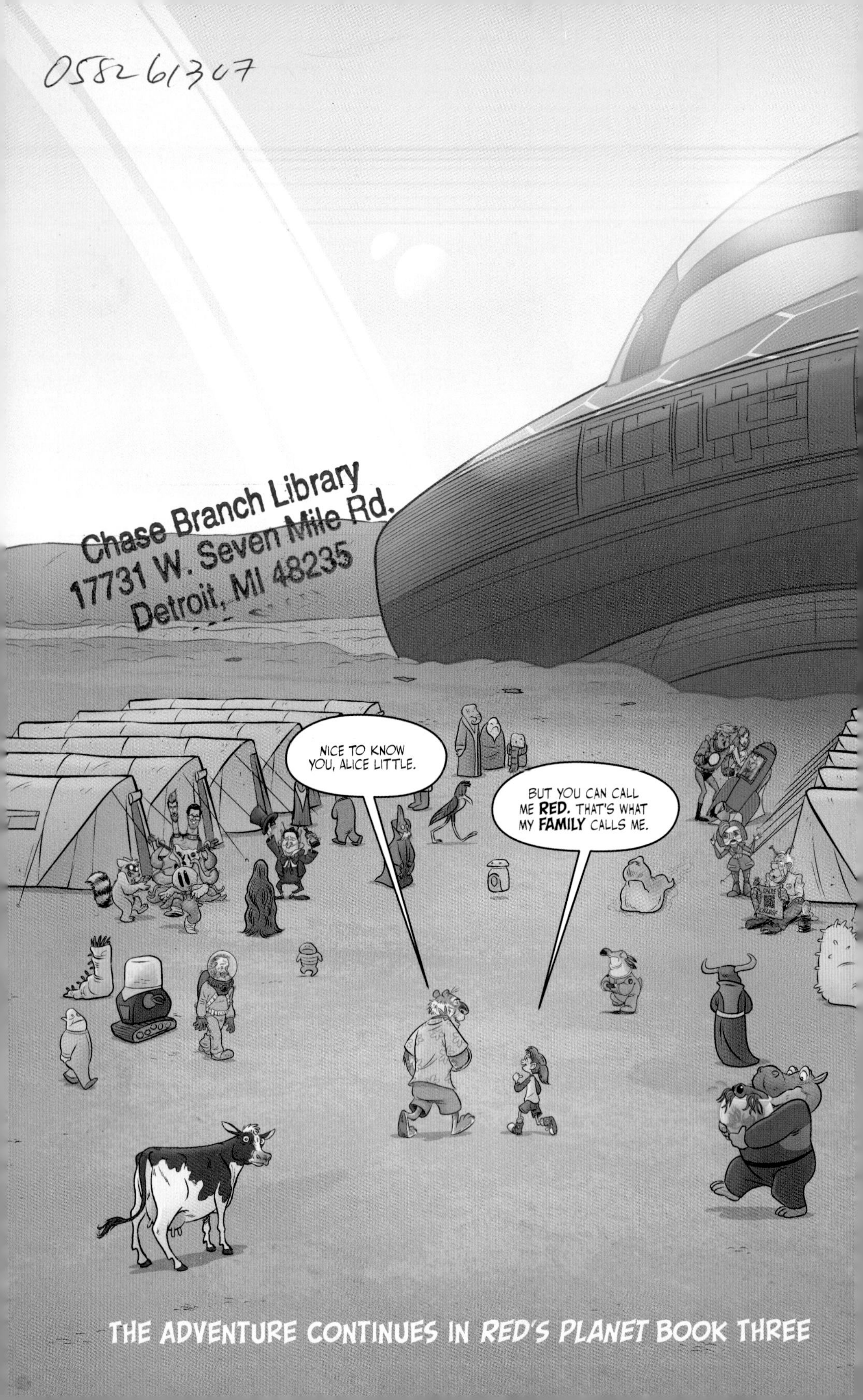
NICE TO KNOW YOU, ALICE LITTLE.
BUT YOU CAN CALL ME **RED.** THAT'S WHAT MY **FAMILY** CALLS ME.
THE ADVENTURE CONTINUES IN *RED'S PLANET* BOOK THREE